BIRTH AND DEATH
OF AN EAGLE

五边诗丛
中国当代诗歌名家系列

鹰的诞生和死亡

吉狄马加 著

中国文联出版社

图书在版编目（CIP）数据

鹰的诞生和死亡：汉英对照 / 吉狄马加著 . — 北京：中国文联出版社，2020.12
　ISBN 978-7-5190-4550-0

　Ⅰ . ①鹰… Ⅱ . ①吉… Ⅲ . ①诗集－中国－当代－汉、英②诗歌研究－文集－汉、英 Ⅳ . ① I227 ② I052-53

　中国版本图书馆 CIP 数据核字 (2021) 第 013850 号

著　　者	吉狄马加
责任编辑	郭　锋
责任校对	鹿　丹　田宝维
书籍设计	XXL Studio
出版发行	中国文联出版社有限公司
社　　址	北京农展馆南里 10 号　邮编：100125
电　　话	010-85923025（发行部）　010-85923091（总编室）
经　　销	全国新华书店等
印　　刷	湖北恒泰印务有限公司
开　　本	787 毫米 ×1092 毫米　1/16
印　　张	24
字　　数	195 千字
版　　次	2020 年 12 月第 1 版第 1 次印刷
定　　价	130.00 元

版权所有·侵权必究
如有印装质量问题，请与本社发行部联系调换

BRIEF BIOGRAPHY

简介

鹰的诞生和死亡

作者简介

吉狄马加,是中国当代最具代表性的诗人之一,同时也是一位具有广泛影响的国际性诗人,其诗歌已被翻译成近四十种文字,在世界几十个国家出版了九十多种版本的翻译诗集。现任中国作家协会副主席、书记处书记。

主要作品:诗集《初恋的歌》《鹰翅和太阳》《身份》《火焰与词语》《我,雪豹……》《从雪豹到马雅可夫斯基》《献给妈妈的二十首十四行诗》《吉狄马加的诗》《大河》(多语种长诗)等。

曾获中国第三届新诗(诗集)奖、郭沫若文学奖荣誉奖、庄重文文学奖、肖洛霍夫文学纪念奖、柔刚诗歌荣誉奖、国际华人诗人笔会中国诗魂奖、南非姆基瓦人道主义奖、欧洲诗歌与艺术荷马奖、罗马尼亚《当代人》杂志卓越诗歌奖、布加勒斯特城市诗歌奖、波兰雅尼茨基文学奖、英国剑桥大学国王学院银柳叶诗歌终身成就奖、波兰塔德乌什·米钦斯基表现主义凤凰奖、齐格蒙特·克拉辛斯基奖章、瓜亚基尔国际诗歌奖。

创办青海湖国际诗歌节、青海国际诗人帐篷圆桌会议、凉山西昌邛海国际诗歌周以及成都国际诗歌周。

CV of Jidi Majia

简

介

A Yi Chinese, one of the most representative poets in contemporary Chinese literature, Jidi Majia's literary career has spanned over thirty-five years and has won international acclaim by having 90 collections of poetry and prose translated into 40-odd languages. He at present serves in the capacity of vice-chairman of China Writers Association.

Major works include: *The Song of My First Love; Self-portrait and Other Poems; The Dream of a Yi Native; The Eagle's Wing and the Sun; Fire and Words; I, the Leopard…; From the Leopard to Mayakovski; 24 Sonnets Dedicated to My Mother; A Great River.*

Major literary honors conferred: Top prize for the 3rd Edition of New Poetry Contest; Guo Moro Literary Prize; Zhuang Zhongwen Literature Prize; Sholokhov Memorial Medal for literature; Rougang Literature Prize; Mkhiva Humanitarian Award; Gold Award for Master Soul of Chinese Poetry of International Chinese Poets PEN; Homer European Medal of Poetry and Art; Excellent Peotry Prize for Romania Contemporanal Magazine; Bucharest City Poetry Prize; Silver Willow Lifetime Achievement Award at Xu Zhimo Poetry Festival, King's College Cambridge; the Janicki Literary Prize; the Tadeusza Micińskiego Prize; the Medal of Zygmunta Krasińskiego; the Guayaquil International Poetry Prize.

Jidi Majia has initiated a number of high-profile international poetic events such as Qinghai Lake International Poetry Festival, Qinghai International Poets Tent Roundtable Forum, Liangshan & Qinghai Inrernational Poetry Week, Chengdu International Poetry Week, etc.

Translated by Huang Shaozheng

PREFACE 序言

鹰的诞生和死亡

吉狄马加：
世界多元文化的杰出产物

托马斯·温茨洛瓦

千百年来，中国文学一直以十分独特的方式发展，几乎完全隔绝于西方的传统，造成这种情况的原因既有空间上的隔绝（长城是这种隔绝的标志），也有独特的社会结构的原因，以及很可能是首要的原因：象形文字的独特之处。另一方面，中华文化对其他远东文化有重要影响，而且经常是决定性的影响。中国文学发展孕育出的美妙果实就是发源于古代典籍的古代抒情诗。中华民族引以为傲的诗人，如：屈原、陶渊明、李白和杜甫，在世界文化之中的地位可与荷马、贺拉斯、彼得拉克相提并论。18世纪以前，中国古典文学对于西方来说完全是陌生的。

在19世纪，尤其是20世纪，东西方都经历了大规模的对外开放：欧洲和美洲对中国兴趣浓厚，反之亦然。远东地区的诗歌开始影响世界现代文学，而西欧、美国、俄罗斯甚至波兰的诗歌新潮流也渗透进中国文化，尽管这一过程总会带有不小的延迟。扰乱这一进程的不仅是文化之间巨大的差异，还有中国所经历的和在新时代正在经历的极其复杂、艰难的发展道路。今天我们仍然荡舟于相互渗透的激流之中，吉狄马加的创作就证明了这一点。他是最著名的中国当代诗人之一，也是中国文化中辨识度最高的人物之一。

吉狄马加的诗与众不同，尽管它同时也是新时代世界文化的特色产物。他用中文创作，但却属于聚居在离越南和泰国不远的山区——人口八百万左右的彝族，或称诺苏人。这样一来，可以说，诗人又离我们的文化远了一层，但对欧洲读者来说他的诗却很容易理解。

彝族使用的语言属于藏缅语族，有着独立的文字系统。文化中保留着许多与万物有灵信仰有关的古老元素。直到现在彝族人都尊崇萨满（毕摩），他们负责主持出生、婚礼和葬礼等仪式。他们崇拜山神、树神和石神，以及四大元素之神，即火、水、土和气。在学校里教授彝族的语言和文字，但并非一直如此。

吉狄马加的导师是中国著名诗人艾青。他早年熟读中国古典和20世纪文学，还有西方文学。然而他始终心系自己民族——彝族的文化及其原始迷人的、对世界各大洲人民来说全新的世界观的传承。他深切同情每一个命途多舛的民族，这对于许多欧洲人来说非常亲切。他的诗极具表现力，自由奔放，充满比喻，时常夸张化处理，属于后现代浪潮的"寻根文学"。吉狄马加在对民间艺术的痴迷中接近魔幻现实主义。他在作品中经常涉及欧洲、美国和非洲诗歌。读者很容易就能注意到作者的修辞风格与诗人巴勃罗·聂鲁达、奥克塔维奥·帕斯，以及"黑人精神"学派的关联性。在那里我们还能找到与多位中东欧诗人，从切斯拉夫·米沃什到戴珊卡·马克西莫维奇的作品之间的互文关系。诗人将这些与中国和远东的传统联系在一起，尤其与彝族远古神话传说相结合，得到了奇妙和出人意料的效果。

想努力理解我们这个时代的读者，能够在吉狄马加的诗中找到许多值得思考，能引起共鸣的东西。

托马斯·温茨洛瓦（1937-），立陶宛诗人、学者和翻译家，美国耶鲁大学斯拉夫语言文学系教授，与米沃什、布罗茨基并列"东欧文学三杰"，被称为"欧洲最伟大的在世诗人之一"。

Jidi Majia:
An Outstanding Product of World Multiculturalism

Tomas Venclova

For hundreds and thousands of years, Chinese literature has developed in its own unique way, almost wholly isolated from Western tradition. The reasons for this include geographical isolation (of which the Great Wall is an emblem), a unique social structure and, perhaps most importantly, the unique features of its ideographic writing system. Viewed from another perspective, Chinese culture has exerted an often-decisive influence on other Far-Eastern cultures. Among the remarkable fruits that emerged from Chinese ancient literary canon was classical lyrical poetry. Chinese people take pride in such poets as Qu Yuan, Tao Yuanming, Li Bai and Du Fu, all of whom belong in the front rank of world poets such as Homer, Horace and Petrarch. Yet prior to the 18th century, classical Chinese literature was virtually unknown in the Western world.

In the 19th and especially in the 20th centuries, the Far East underwent large-scale opening to the West. People in America and Europe took a strong interest in the Far East, and the reverse was also true. Poetry from the Far East began influencing the world's modern literature. At the same time, currents from Europe, America, Russia and even Poland permeated Chinese culture, although this was sometimes delayed. What interfered with this process, aside from huge disparities between cultures, was the complex and difficult road of development which China traveled and continues to travel. Today we are still weathering the turbulent currents of interpenetration between East and West. We can find proof of this fact in Jidi Majia's creative works. He is one of the foremost Chinese contemporary poets, and he is one of the most renowned cultural figures in China today.

As a poet, Jidi Majia stands out from the crowd, even though his poems were forged by the widespread cultural currents of our new world era. He writes in Chinese, but he belongs to the eight-million-strong Yi ethnic group, otherwise known as the Nuosu, who live in mountain areas not far from Vietnam and Thailand. Thus we can say that there is an additional layer of distance between this poet and our culture. Even so, European readers can readily understand his poems.

The Yi People speak a language which belongs to the Tibeto-Burmese language family, and they have an independently developed writing system. Their culture preserves archaic elements related to animistic beliefs. Even now the Yi People put their trust in shamans (which they call Bimos). Bimos preside over weddings, cremations and ceremonies of childbirth. They make offerings to deities of mountains, trees, boulders and the four elements of earth, air, fire and water. The Yi language and writing system is now being taught in schools, but this has not always been the case.

Jidi Majia's mentor was China's eminent poet Ai Qing. In his youth Jidi Majia pored over works of China's classical and twentieth-century literature, as well as Western literature. Yet his heart has remained tied to his own ethnic group—to that primal world view handed down by the Yi Minority which, being unknown to the world's major populations, holds an appealing novelty. Jidi Majia earnestly sympathizes with every ethnic group whose fate is beset by difficulties. His poems are extremely expressive, free-wheeling and rich in metaphor. In his frequently hyperbolic language and his "roots-seeking" orientation, he has an affinity with post-modernist currents. Jidi Majia is strongly attached to use of folkloric elements, in a way that approaches magical realism. His writings are informed by the poetic practice of Africa, Europe and America. Readers will readily notice a strong stylistic connection to Pablo

Neruda, Octavio Paz and poets of the "Negritude" school. In his works we can also trace a literary connection with eastern European poets, from Czeslaw Milosz to Desanka Maksimović. He links up these Western sources with Chinese and Far Eastern tradition, especially with ageless myths and legends from the Yi People, to achieve wondrous and unexpected effects.

For readers who endeavor to understand the era we live in, Jidi Majia's poems offer food for thought which will surely strike a chord of shared feeling.

      Translated by Denis Mair

Tomas Venclova (1937-) is a Lithuanian poet, scholar and translator. He is a professor of Slavic Languages and Literature at Yale University and has been grouped with Czeslaw Milosz and Joseph Brodsky as one of the three "Masters from Eastern Europe". He is recognized as one of the Europe's greatest poets.

时光在碾碎时针
——向吉狄马加及其诗作致敬

[叙利亚] 阿多尼斯

1

忧伤的字母，这今日世界的身躯，
其中时光在碾碎时针
在告诉日子：
"我和一颗星辰掷着骰子
我预言：药剂是否将成为疾病的诱因？
太空的邮差身披空气的丝绸
往返穿梭，它在传递什么？"

2

我在为万物披上面纱吗？然而，
我遮盖自己脸庞的
是爱情的纱巾？
还是神主的纱巾？
道路并非我的道路，步伐并非我的步伐
我该向一张面孔发问？
还是向一面镜子发问？
面孔何其少，镜子何其多！

3

此地或彼处，东方或西方
生命是否已成为臆想的迷宫？
天堂是否已将大门紧闭？

4

根柢，根柢的伤口，在字母的怀抱里

在呼唤和期待
对所谓"永恒"的叛逆

5
在死者和死者之间
还有人正在死去,为什么
杀手们遗忘了他的姓名?

6
我们终日劳作的痛苦书写的书籍
其中没有符号,没有音节
词语
在词语中繁衍
在荒漠中飘散

7
此刻,我信马由缰地翻阅,
目之所及皆是伤口:
星球在流血,被天启欺骗

8
灰烬在祝贺废墟
灰烬
忠实于自己的约定

9
诗篇能否拥抱存在
能否再次描绘存在的面容和皱纹?
诗的玫瑰在哭悼童年的朋友,在吟唱:
我只会凭借芬芳作战

10

大地怎么变成了一个声音
它只会道出自己的死亡?
天空怎么变成了一道血迹
在每一张脸庞流淌?

2020年10月末于巴黎
薛庆国译

阿多尼斯(1930-),阿拉伯世界最重要的诗人、思想家、文学理论家,享誉当今世界诗坛的诗歌巨匠。评论家认为,阿多尼斯对阿拉伯诗歌的影响,可以同庞德或艾略特对于英语诗歌的影响相提并论。

الوقت يكسرُ عقاربَ ساعاته
تحيّة إلى جيدي ماجيا وشعره

1
أبجديةُ حزنٍ: جسدُ العالمِ، اليومَ،- وقتٌ
يَكسرُ الوقتُ فيه عقاربَ ساعاتِهِ،
ويقول لأيّامه:
ألعبُ النردَ مع نجمة
أتنبّأ- هل سيكون الدواءُ خميرةَ داءٍ؟
وماذا يقول بريدُ الفضاء
آتيا ذاهبا في حرير الهواء؟

2
أ تراني ألقي حجابا على كلّ شيءٍ؟ ولكن
هل سأحجب وجهي
بمنديل حبٍّ
أم بمنديل ربٍّ؟
وأنا، لا طريقي طريقي، ولا خطاي خطايا
هل أسائل وجهًا،
أم أسائل مرآته؟
ما أقلَّ الوجوهَ وما أكثرَ المرايا.

3
أتُراها الحياةُ هنا وهناك، شرقا وغرباً،
متاهاتُ ظنٍّ؟
أتراها الفراديسُ تُغلق أبوابَها؟

4
الجذورُ، جراحُ الجذور نداءٌ وشوقٌ
للتمرُّد في كنَف الأبجديّة،
ضدَّ ما سُمِّي الأبديّة.

5
بين ميْتٍ وميْتْ
ميِّتٌ آخرُ- لماذا

نسيَ القاتلون اسمَه؟

6

لا فواصلَ، لا حركات
في الكتابِ الذي كتبتْه تباريحُ أعمالنا وأيّامنا:
كلماتٌ
تتناسلُ في كلمات
تتناثرُ في مَهْمَهٍ.

7

شغفي يقرأ الآن ما يتيسّرُ: جرحٌ
نازفٌ كوكبيٌّ
خدعتْهُ نبوءاتُه.

8

الرمادُ احتفاءٌ بأنقاضه:
الرمادُ،
وفيٌّ لمواعيده.

9

أتُراها القصيدةُ تقدر أن تحضنَ الوُجودَ وأن تتهجَّى
من جديد تقاطيعَه وتجاعيدَه؟
هي ذي وردةُ الشعر تبكي أصدقاءَ طفولاتِها ـ تغنّي:
لن أقاتلَ إلا بعِطري.

10

كيف يحدثُ أن تصبح الأرضُ صوتا
لا يقول سوى موتِها؟
كيف يحدث أن تصبح السماءُ دمًا سائلا
على كلّ وجهٍ؟

أدونيس
باريس، أواخر أكتوبر، 2020

أدونيس، ولد عام 1930 في سورية. شاعر ومفكر وناقد أدبي كبير ذاع صيته في العالم العربي، ويعتبر أحد أهم الشعراء في عالمنا اليوم. يرى كثير من النقاد أن تأثيره في الشعر العربي المعاصر يشبه تأثير عزرا باوند وإليوت في أشعار اللغة الإنجليزية.

Time is Pulverizing the Clock Hands
—*In Honor of Jidi Majia and his poems*

1
Grief-laden letters, this body of today's world,
within which time is pulverizing the clock hands
and telling the days:
"I'm throwing dice with a star
I predict: will medicine become the cause of illness?
The postman in space is draped in silk air
shuttling back and forth; what is he transmitting?"

2
Am I putting on a veil for all living things? But,
am I covering my face
with love's scarf
or god's scarf?
The road really isn't my road, these steps really aren't my steps
Should I ask a face,
or ask a mirror?
How few faces are, how plentiful mirrors are!

3
In this place or that, East or West,
has life already become a subjective maze?
Has heaven already closed its gates?

4
The roots, the roots' wounds, are in the bosom of letters
shouting out and looking forward
to all so-called "eternal" rebellions

5
Between the dead and the dead
more people are dying; why

have their murderers forgotten their names?

6

The pain of our daily labor, the books we write
have no punctuation marks, have no syllables
Words multiply within words
and drift in barrenness

7

Now, I ride with lax reins,
flip through books
There are wounds wherever my eyes reach:
the planet is bleeding, deceived by the oracle

8

Ashes are congratulating ruins
Ashes
are faithful to their own promises

9

Can poems embrace existence;
can they once again describe the face and wrinkles of existence?
The roses of poems are crying for childhood friends, chanting:
We only rely on fragrance to fight

10

How has the earth become one voice
that only knows how to speak of its own death?
How has the sky become one bloodstain
that flows on every face?

October, 2020, Paris
Jami Proctor Xue
(translated from the Chinese translation)

Adonis (1930-), The most significant poet, ideologist, literary theorist in the Arab world. He is honoured as a great master in the world of poetry today. Critics say that Adonis' influence on Arabic poetry is comparable to that of Pound or Eliot on English poetry.

目 录

诗歌

3	我是如此困倦
4	I Am So Very Weary
5	我要去布加勒斯特
7	I Will Go to Bucharest
9	巨子 ——献给康斯坦丁·布朗库西
10	Titan —For Constantin Brancusi
11	选择 ——致作家欧根·乌里卡鲁
13	Choice —For the writer Eugen Uricaru
14	词语的工匠 ——写给翻译家鲁博安
15	Craftsman of Words —For the translator Constantin Lupeanu
16	双重意义
17	Double Meaning
18	写给我在海尔库拉内的雕像 ——致诗人伊利耶·柯里斯德斯库
19	For My Statue in Herculane —For Ilya Cristescu
20	在尼基塔·斯特内斯库的墓地
21	At the Gravesite of Nichita Stanescu
22	运河
23	Grand Canal
24	我始终热爱弱小的事物
26	I Will Always Feel Love for Meek Lives
28	口弦的力量
29	The Power of a Mouth Harp
30	马鞍的赞词
36	Praise Song for a Saddle
41	鹰的诞生和死亡
48	Birth and Death of an Eagle
54	人性的缺失
56	The Flaw in Human Nature
58	叫不出名字的人
60	Someone Whose Name I Can't Say
62	对我们而言……
63	To Our Way of Thinking…
64	一个人的克智
65	A Flyting Spoken to Oneself

鹰的诞生和死亡

66	致尼卡诺尔·帕拉
68	For Nicanor Parra
70	一个士兵与一块来自钓鱼城的石头
73	A Soldier and a Stone from Diaoyu Fortress
75	商丘，没有结束的
77	Shang Mound, There Is No Ending
78	但我的歌唱却只奉献给短暂的生命
79	Yet My Song Is Offered to Fleeting Lives
80	而我们……
81	As for Us...
82	诗歌的秘语……
83	The Secret Language of Poems...
84	暮年的诗人
85	A Poet in His Waning Years
86	致父辈们
88	For My Father's Generation
89	姐姐的披毡
90	My Sister's Woolen Cape
91	口弦大师 ——致俄狄日伙
92	Jaw Harp Master —*For Edi Rihuo*
93	印第安人 ——致西蒙·奥迪斯
95	Indian —*For Simon Ortiz*
97	尼子马列的废墟
98	The Ruins of Nizi Malie
99	我曾看见……
100	Once I Saw...
101	诗人
103	Poet
105	犹太人的墓地
106	Jewish Graveyards
107	何塞·马里亚·阿格达斯
109	José María Arguedas
111	悼胡安·赫尔曼
112	Juan Gelman
113	自由的另一种解释
114	An Alternate Explanation of Freedom
115	大河 ——献给黄河
123	Great River —*To the Yellow River*

130	火焰上的辩词
138	Disputation Over the Flames
145	死神与我们的速度谁更快
	——献给抗击2020新型冠状病毒的所有人
152	Who is Faster, Us or Death
	—To all who beat against COVID-19 in 2020
159	裂开的星球 ——献给全人类和所有生命
179	Split-Open Planet —For all of humankind and all living things
200	迟到的挽歌 ——献给我的父亲吉狄·佐卓·伍合略且
211	Late Elegy —For my father, Jidi Zuozhuo Wuhelüeqie

文学演讲和访谈

225	诗影光芒中的茅屋
	——在2017年第一届"国际诗酒文化大会"开幕式演讲
227	Du Fu's Thatched Cottage—Both A Reality and A Legend
	—Address at the Opening Ceremony of 2017 International Festival of Poetry & Liquor
230	个人身份·群体声音·人类意识
	——在剑桥大学国王学院"徐志摩诗歌艺术节论坛"上的演讲
235	Personal Identity · Group Voice · Human Awareness
	—Speech given at the Xu Zhimo Poetry and Art Festival, University of Cambridge
241	诗歌与光明涌现的城池
	——在2017年"成都国际诗歌周"开幕式上的演讲
245	A City Hemmed in with Radiant Beams of Poetry
	—Address at the Opening Ceremony of 2017 Chengdu International Poetry Week
251	光明与鹰翅的天石
	——在2017年第二届中国凉山"西昌邛海'丝绸之路'国际诗歌周"开幕式上的致辞
254	Heavenly Stones Made of Eagle Wings and Light
	—Remarks at the Opening Ceremony of the 2nd Liangshan, Xichang Silk Road Intl Poetry Week
258	诗人仍然是今天社会的道德引领者
	——答英国诗人格林厄姆·莫特

	265	Poets Are Still the Moral Leaders of the Civic Society Today ——*Written replies to Graham Mort*
	273	另一种创造：从胡安·鲁尔福到奥克塔维奥·帕斯 ——在北大"中墨建交45周年文学研讨会"上的演讲
	280	To Create Differently: From Juan Rulfo to Octavio Paz ——*A speech given at a seminar held in Peking University marking the 45th anniversary of Sino-Mexico diplomatic relations*
	290	词语的盐·光所构筑的另一个人类的殿堂——诗歌语言的透明与微暗 ——在2018年中国自贡"一带一路"诗歌之灯点亮世界国际诗歌周开幕式上的演讲
	293	Word as Salt · an Alternative Human Paradise Made of Light ——Transparence and Dimness of Poetic Diction ——*Address at the Opening Ceremony of 2018 Zigong "Belt and Road" International Poetry Week*
	298	诗歌的责任并非仅仅是自我的发现 ——在2018年塔德乌什·米钦斯基表现主义凤凰奖颁奖仪式上的致答词
	300	Narcissistic Self ——Seeking Is Not the Sole Responsibility of a Decent Poet ——*Acceptance Speech at the Awarding Ceremony of Tadeusza Micińskiego Prize*
	303	附体的精灵：诗歌中的神秘、隐蔽和燃烧的声音 ——在2019年第四届"西昌邛海·丝绸之路"国际诗歌周上的演讲
	306	Poets Empowered by a Mysterious, Dark and Burning Sound ——*Address at 2019 4th Xichang Qinghai Silk Road International Poetry Week*
	310	诗歌中未知的力量：传统与前沿的又一次对接 ——第六届"青海湖国际诗歌节"主题演讲
	313	Forces Hidden in Poetry: Let's Make a Rendezvous with Tradition! ——*Address at the 6th Qinghai Lake International Poetry Festival*
	318	诗歌：不仅是对爱的吟诵，也是反对一切暴力的武器 ——在中捷文化交流70周年暨捷克独立日"中捷文学圆桌会议"上的主题演讲
	323	Poetry, a Tribute to Love, an Arsenal Against All Violence ——*A keynote address delivered at the Sino-Czech Roundtable on Literature on the Commemoration of the 70th Anniversary of Sino-Czech Republic Cultural Exchange and the Independent Czechoslovak State Day*

329　　诗歌本身的意义、传播以及其内在的隐秘性
　　　　——在第三届泸州国际诗歌大会诗歌论坛上的演讲

331　　The Meaning, Dissemination and Inner Secrecy of Poetry
　　　　—Address at the seminar of 3rd International Poetry & Liquor Conference

334　　让诗歌为我们迈向明天和未来注入强大的力量
　　　　——在2020年印度克里提亚国际诗歌节上的致辞

337　　Let Poetry Empower Us Strongly for Marching Toward Tomorrow and Future
　　　　—An Address on 2020 Kritya Poetry Festival, India

340　　太阳还会在明天升起
　　　　——在第三十届麦德林国际诗歌节开幕式上的致辞

342　　The Sun Will Still Rise Tomorrow
　　　　—Speech for the Opening Ceremony of the Thirtieth Medellín International Poetry Festival

345　　向河流、高山和大海的致敬
　　　　——2020年瓜亚基尔国际诗歌奖致答词

348　　Paying Tribute to the Rivers, Mountains, and Oceans
　　　　—Acceptance speech for the 2020 Guayaquil International Poetry Award

351　　一只羊，一位农夫与诗人直视的眼睛
　　　　——2020年度"1573国际诗歌奖"颁奖词
　　　　　暨诗集《月照静夜》序言

354　　A Sheep, a Farmer and a Poet's Steady Gaze
　　　　—Presentation of the 2020 "1573 International Poetry Prize" and Preface of Lucina Schynning in Silence of the Nicht: A Selection of Poems by Eiléan Ní Chuilleanáin

诗 歌

鹰的诞生和死亡

我是如此困倦

此时——
我是如此困倦
只想睡眠！
但我听见了群山的召唤：
这是死亡的
不容更改的时间。
但我不能用诗歌去抵押，
并获得短暂而无意义的数字。
是的，我要告诉你们，
——因为在此刻，
我必须从容地走向群山，
最终让火焰为我加冕。

I Am So Very Weary

At this hour—
I am so very weary
I only wish to sleep!
But I hear the mountains summon me:
It is the inalterable hour
Of death, from which
My poems cannot ransom me
Or grant me brief, meaningless numbers
Yes, I want to let each of you know—
Because that moment is at hand—
I must walk collectedly towards the mountains
Where I will finally be crowned in flames

Translated by Denis Mair

我要去布加勒斯特

我已经决定要去布加勒斯特,
去看这座我想象过无数次的城市。
我要选择一个高地能极目远望,
最好能覆盖它完美无缺的全貌。
从黎明时划破空气的第一辆电车,
以及直到深夜还亮着灯光的小屋。
我知道,在令人着迷的布加勒斯特,
它天空的颜色,有一半接近于天堂,
而另一半却闪烁着奇异灿烂的光。
那些飞过屋顶的一群群灰色的鸽子,
翅膀拍击的声音惊醒了沉睡的钟楼。

这是我的现实和虚幻的布加勒斯特,
它是用想象构建的另一座石头的城堡。
我要去一个地方,但不知道它的名字,
只是在睡梦中与它真实地有过相遇。
可以肯定那是一座古老灰色的教堂,
教堂的外墙上有一块斑驳发亮的石头,
那块石头沉默而幽暗,它躲在一角
等待着我不容更改早已期许的光临。

我还要去那家灯光温暖而暗淡的酒吧,
它就在人流如织异常热闹的波多尔大街[1],
谁能告诉我,爱明内斯库是否真的到过?
选择窗边的那个座位谁都认为十分惬意,
从这里能看见这座城市沸腾喧嚣的生活。
独自发呆是生命中必须经历的美好时刻,
如果没有遗忘死亡的段落和静止的空白,

---

[1] 波多尔大街,意译为桥街,现名为胜利街,在布加勒斯特闹市区。

2016.12.20

人类用不同方式活下去的理由就不够充分。
此时，我不需要任何一个人坐在我的身边，
我只希望享受这永恒中片刻无意义的宁静。
布加勒斯特，我要在最深处潜入你的传统，
在你光明和黑暗的缝隙里直抵你的脊柱。

据说我的诗歌在这里获得了又一次生命，
今天它一定在某几个人的手里窃窃私语。
有一册在一个老人的书柜里呼吸睁着眼睛，
还有一本被一位黄头发的少女翻阅了多次。
这是词语的光荣，语言的玄妙被再次张扬，
只有诗歌能进入每一个没有围栏的心灵，
因为它拒绝血腥、杀戮和一切形式的暴力，
同情弱者，伸张正义，站在被压迫者一边。
布加勒斯特，你温暖的气息古老而又年轻，
对于一个诗人而言，当我的诗歌在这里游历，
我相信从那一刻起我就成为了它的某个部分。

我要到布加勒斯特去，去完成一个愿望，
当我真的穿过这座想象中无比奇妙的城市，
但愿我手中的那把钥匙能真的打开时间，
让我在瞬间看见它那张隐没于不朽中的脸。

I Will Go to Bucharest

I have decided to go to Bucharest
To see that city I've imagined countless times;
I'll gaze to the limit of vision, from a chosen spot,
Commanding a panorama of its pristine sights,
From the first trolley that parts the air at dawn
To room-lights that keep glowing late at night.
I know, in an enchanting place like Bucharest
The sky's color verges halfway unto heaven
And half amazes us with its eerie scintillations,
As flocks of gray doves flying over rooflines
Wake drowsy steeples with their whirring wings.

I have my real-life fantasies of Bucharest
As another walled city, built in imagination.
I'll search for that place, yet unknown by name
Which I definitely encountered in a dream.
One thing is sure: it is an ancient, gray church;
In its outer wall is found a mottled, gleaming stone,
A silent stone, subdued in color, hiding in a corner
Waiting for my inevitable, long-expected coming.

I want to visit a dim barroom with warm lamplight
On Bulevardul Unirii[1], with its stream of pedestrians.
Who can tell me if Mihai Eminescu ever set foot there?
I'll choose a window-side seat to spend a genial hour
Affording views of life in this bustling, teeming city!
Life can't do without moments of wonderful reverie;
Were it not for times of quiet blankness, forgetful of death,
Our means of staying alive might strike us as hollow.
At such times, I don't need anyone sitting beside me;
Just let me enjoy an empty, tranquil sliver of eternity.
Let me be submerged in your city's tradition, through a crack

---

[1] This thoroughfare in downtown Bucharest was formerly named Podor Boulevard (meaning bridge) and then Bulevardul Victoria Socialismului, before being given its current name of Union Boulevard.

Between light and darkness, straight to the backbone.

Some say that my poems have found new life among you;
Today they surely whisper confidences in someone's hands.
On an old man's shelf, one volume breathes and opens its eyes;
One is leafed through twice and thrice by a blonde girl
Honor is being paid to words, the marvel of language held high.
Poetry can grant sole entry to hearts that erect no barriers,
For it refuses gore and slaughter and all forms of violence;
It pities the weak, calls for justice, stands with the oppressed.
Bucharest, your gentle temperament is ancient yet young;
As a poet, knowing that my poetry roams there,
I believe that henceforth I will become part of it.

I will go to Bucharest, to make my wishes come true.
As I venture into that city, wondrous beyond compare,
May the key I hold prove capable of opening time,
So I may glimpse the hidden face of the undying.

Translated by Denis Mair

巨 子
——献给康斯坦丁·布朗库西[1]

那些粗糙的石头
近似于核心
抵达了真实的港口。
就是木质的肌肤
也闪动着宇宙的纹理
它是积木搭成的梯子。
白色的弧形铸成黄金
由方角堆砌的脊椎
时间变形成鸟的脖颈。
在光滑柔软的另一面
裸体坍塌睁大着瞳孔。
只有单一的颜色被礼赞,
形式的牙齿熠熠生辉。
所有呈现的一切都朴素如初
被掩埋的事实还在藏匿遁隐。
最终是板材构建的弯墙
宣告了铁锤与线条的胜利。
没有结束留下的缝隙
在两个对比的物体之间
唯有光证明了永恒的原始。

[1] 康斯坦丁·布朗库西（1876-1957），罗马尼亚籍，被公认为20世纪最具原创性的雕塑家，简约主义雕塑代表人物。

Titan
—*For Constantin Brancusi*[1]

Those coarse stones
That closely resemble the core
Reach harbors true to themselves.
Even sinewy wood-grain
Flexes in cosmic patterns,
Erecting ladders of building blocks,
Casting white arcs in gold metal,
Stacking corners to raise a spine,
Warping time into a bird's neck.
On the obverse of smooth softness,
Nakedness collapses with dilated pupils.
Only monochrome is praised;
Teeth of form pulsate brilliantly;
All is brought forth in original plainness;
Buried facts hang back at vision's edge.
Lastly come panels, hung to make a curved wall,
Claiming victory for hammered-out lines.
Along a crack left by no conclusion
Between two corresponding objects
Only light proves the eternal primordium.

Translated by Denis Mair

---

[1] Constantin Brancusi (1876-1957), of Romanian nationality, is considered to be one of the most original sculptors of the 20th century. He was a representative figure of the Minimalist School.

选 择
——致作家欧根·乌里卡鲁[1]

在我们这个喧嚣的时代,
每天的日出和日落都如同从前,
只是日落的辉煌,比日出的
绚丽更令人悲伤和叹息!
遥远的星群仍在向我们示意,
大海上的帆影失而复得。
在我们这个时代,一部分人说:
我们要甘地[2],不要格瓦拉[3],
而另一部分人却扬言:我们
只要格瓦拉,不要甘地。
不知道这是谁出的一道命题,
竟然让这么多人陷入了争论。
昨天是追随格瓦拉的人在集会,
今天又有甘地的非暴力者在游行。
如果说这两部分人,仅仅是在选择
两种不同的颜色,表达自己的主张,
这样的争论早就已经有了结果。
但是,但是,却没有一个人,
在争论中,回答了这样一个问题:
是谁造就了格瓦拉?又是谁
造就了甘地?而选择他们中的
任何一位,都是大家的权利。
然而这样的结果,并没有让争论的
双方以及我们得到明确的答案。
我知道这样的争论还会继续下去,
对他人的好恶和价值观的认同
常常把人分裂成不同的对抗群体。

[1] 欧根·乌里卡鲁,1946年出生于罗马尼亚东部摩尔多瓦地区的布胡希,罗马尼亚当代最具有代表性的小说家之一,曾担任罗马尼亚作协主席。

[2] 甘地,莫罕达斯·卡拉姆昌德·甘地(1869.10-1948.1),尊称圣雄甘地,是印度民族解放运动的领导人,其"非暴力"的哲学思想,影响了全世界的民族主义者和争取能以和平变革的国际运动。

[3] 格瓦拉,切·格瓦拉(1928.6-1967.10),阿根廷的马克思主义革命家、国际政治家及古巴革命的核心人物,是游击战争英雄和世界左翼运动的象征。

2017.1.21

但是尽管这样，我们却无法预测在下一个时间，会不会出现——另一个格瓦拉，另一个甘地。

2017.1.21

Choice
—*For the writer Eugen Uricaru*[1]

In this noisy era of ours
Sunset and sunrise are much like in the past
Except that the brilliance of sunset makes us sigh
More heavy-heartedly than does the splendor
    of sunrise.
Faraway stars still signal their messages to us;
Shapes of cruising ships come in and out of view.
In this era of ours, one portion of the people say
This is a time for Gandhi[2], not Che Guevara[3],
While another part of the people proclaim
It's a time for Guevara, but not for Gandhi.
Who on earth could devise such a conundrum
That embroils so many in a clash of views?
Today Guevara's followers are holding their assembly
Then non-violent Gandhians hold a march tomorrow.
If the disputing parties were merely making a choice
Of this color or that, to show what they stand for
There should have been an outcome by now,
And yet…and yet, in the middle of such a dispute
There has been nobody to answer this question:
What led to the making of a man like Guevara?
Or one like Gandhi? And as for which to go with,
The right to choose belongs to everyone.
Whatever outcome this dispute arrives at,
It brings no clear answer, to either side or to us.
I know such disputes will continue unfolding;
Our preferences and the values we embrace
Often split us into opposing groups;
Yet even so, we have no way to foresee,
In the next phase, whether there will appear
Another Gandhi or another Guevara.

    Translated by Denis Mair

---

1 Eugen Uricaru, born in 1946 in Buhusi (eastern Romania), is one of the most influential Romanian writers of the 20th century. He served for a time as Chairman of the Romanian Writers Union.
2 Mohands Karamchand Gandhi (1869-1948), Indian leader of national liberation movement, whose idea of "non-violence" influenced international movements of peaceful reformation.
3 Che Guevara (1928-1967), Argentinian Marxist revolutionist, international politionist and core figure in Cuban revolution, who was a symbol of world leftist movements and hero of guerilla wars.

词语的工匠
——写给翻译家鲁博安[1]

翻越的不是一座群山
但你却翻越了沟壑、悬崖、深渊
跨越的虽然不是海洋
但你却在另一个彼岸,升起了
令人为之激动的白帆
来自另一个国度的工匠,你的房梁
已经被送上了没有缝隙的屋顶
你挥舞着手臂,让每一扇窗户
刹那间涌入了金黄的蜂群
你穿过了看不见的墙,在铁砧上
睁大眼睛,选择淬过火的钉子
每当你在更遥远的地方,回望
你亲手创造过的空间和意义
所有的寂静便会发出叮当的声响
一头伟岸无比高声鸣叫的双舌羊
是你在两种神秘隐喻的脊柱上
用红色替换红色,让黑色接近于完整
是你在布满了蓝色星星的天空
搭建了一座另一种纬度的中国

[1] 鲁博安,罗马尼亚诗人、汉学家、翻译家。1941年8月出生在罗马尼亚多尔日县穆尔加什乡,曾用罗马尼亚文翻译10余部中国古典文学作品和现当代作家的作品。

Craftsman of Words
—*For the translator Constantin Lupeanu*[1]

The trek was not over ranged mountains,
But you have traversed ravines, cliffs and chasms.
The crossing was not over an ocean,
Yet your heart-stirring white sail
Was raised on a distant shore of another kind.
A craftsman from another nation, your ridgepole
Has been raised to build a roof without cracks.
Each window you fitted with arms awhirl
Lets honeybees swarm in at just the right time.
You passed through invisible walls, and your eyes
Peered from an anvil, to choose the well-tempered spike.
Each time, from a further place, as you looked back
Upon the space and meaning you'd created,
That still expanse rang with clanging sounds.
Such a stately two-tongued ram, with far-carrying voice;
On a spine bearing two kinds of mystic allusions, it was you
Who switched red for red, helping blackness to be coherent.
Across a sky spread with blue stars, it was you
Who fashioned China at another latitude.

Translated by Denis Mair

---

[1] Constantin Lupeanu, born in August 1941 in Romania's Murgași Township, Dolj County, is a poet, sinologist and translator. He is the translator into Romanian of over ten works of Chinese classical philosophy and modern literature.

双重意义

诗人尼基塔·斯特内斯库[1]
在他临终前,对抢救他的年轻医生说:
"请给我一点点你们的青春!"
无疑这是对生命的渴望和赞美,
是对逝去的时间以及岁月的褒奖。
作为肉体的现实,穿越乌有的马匹,
不论是夜晚,还是更长的白昼,
当那一天来临,穹顶上再没有
一颗悬挂睡眠和头颅的钉子。
或许这不是一次回眸,仅仅是
死亡的一种最常规的形式。
如果说物体和思想的存在
本身就是另一种并非想象的虚无。
难怪作为一个曾经活着的人,
跟不同的影子捉迷藏和游戏,
就足以消耗螺旋形的一生。
尽管生命的磁铁并不单调乏味,
但那仍然是生者赋予了它双重的意义。
也许正因为此,荒诞的生活连同
被抽象的词语,才能在光的
指引下,一次次拒绝黑暗和死亡。

[1] 尼基塔·斯特内斯库(1933-1983)罗马尼亚当代诗歌的代表人物。

Double Meaning

On his deathbed, the poet Nichita Stanescu[1]
Said to the doctor who tried to save him
"Please give me some of your youth!"
This was said in a spirit of praise and yearning for life,
Showing appreciation for bygone days he'd lived through.
As a fleshly reality, a horse will pass into nothingness:
Whether that time comes in the night, or in long hours
Of sunlight…the day will come when a nail no longer affixes
A skull and its slumber to the vault of sky.
Perhaps it will not be a lingering glance,
But only death in the most conventional form.
If we say that the existence of a thinking entity
Is itself a nothingness, yet by no means imaginary,
Then no wonder, for one who leads a human life,
To play hide-and-seek with other shadows
Is sufficient to exhaust a spiraling lifetime.
Though life's magnetic field is in no way bland and dull,
This proves to be a double meaning, imputed to it by the living.
Perhaps for this reason, only life's absurd engagements
Along with abstracted words, guided by light,
Can repeatedly meet darkness and death with refusal.

Translated by Denis Mair

[1] Nichita Stanescu (1933-1983) was a famous Romanian poet and representative figure of modernist literature.

写给我在海尔库拉内[1]的雕像
——致诗人伊利耶·柯里斯德斯库[2]

我的眼睛
在海尔库拉内。
我的眼睛,犹如
静止的大海,透明的球体,
山峦、河流、城市、圣殿……
我的眼睛,以万物的名义
将黑暗和光明的幕布打开。
或许这就是核心和边缘的合一。
我的眼睛,如果含满了泪水,
只能是,也只可能是海尔库拉内的
悲伤,让我情不自禁地哭泣。
我的眼睛里露出了微笑,
那是因为唯一。唯一的海尔库拉内,
被众多语言的诗歌在宴席上颂扬。
我的耳朵
在海尔库拉内。
一只昆虫的独语,消失在
思想的白色的内部。
我的耳朵,知晓石头整体的黑洞,
能听见砂砾的呐喊,子宫的沉默。
更像坠落高处的星辰,置于头顶的铁具。
而只有我的嘴巴,在海尔库拉内,
等待着,等待着……有一天,
我进入它的体内,发出心脏的声音。

2018.5.9

[1] 海尔库拉内:罗马尼亚的著名城镇,位于该国的东部。
[2] 伊利耶·柯里斯德斯库:当代罗马尼亚著名诗人,罗马尼亚西方大学教授。

For My Statue in Herculane[1]
—*For Ilya Cristescu*[2]

[1] Herculane is a walled town in eastern Romania.
[2] Ilya Cristescu is a well-known Romanian poet and a professor at Romania Western University.

Oh, Ilya Cristescu,
My eyes
Are in Herculane.
My eyes, calling up visions
Of a quiet ocean, transparent spheres
Hills and rivers, cities and shrines…
My eyes, in the name of ten-thousand things
Open the stage curtain of darkness and light;
Perhaps this is the unity of center and margin.
My eyes, if they are brimming with tears,
This must be…and can only be the sorrow
Of Herculane, making me weep in spite of myself.
My eyes show the hint of a smile
Because the one-and-only Herculane
Was praised at a banquet by poems in many languages.
My ears
Are in Herculane
Like the soliloquy of an insect that subsides
Into the white interior of thought;
My ears know the black hole of a stone's totality;
They hear the outcry of crushed rock, the womb of silence,
Like a star plunging from above, an iron band to crown one's head,
But only my mouth still waits, in Herculane
For the day I will enter its body
And serve as the voice for its heart.

Translated by Denis Mair

2018.5.9

在尼基塔·斯特内斯库的墓地

如果再晚一分钟,
你居住的墓园就要关闭
夜色降临前的门。
用一种姿势睡在泥土里,
时间的板斧终于成了盾牌。
此刻,手臂是骨头的笛子,
词语将被另一个影子吹响。
凝视的眼睛,穿过黑暗的石头,
思想的目光爬满永恒的脊柱。
一个过客,吞食语言的钢轨,
吞食饥渴的星球,吞食虚无的圆柱。
当死亡成为你的线条的时候,
当生命变成四轮马车发黑的时候,
当发硬的颅骨高过星辰的时候:
唯有你真实的诗歌犹如一只大鸟,
静静地漂浮在罗马尼亚的天空。

2018.5.16

At the Gravesite of Nichita Stanescu

Had it been one minute later
The gate of this cemetery where your body rests
Would have been closed under encroaching darkness.
Due to your sleeping posture under the mud
The axe of time has become your shield.
By this time, your arm is a flute of bone;
Words will become the piping of another shadow,
Staring eyes will pass through the stone of darkness,
Thought's gaze climbs vine-like around eternity's backbone,
A passing guest swallows up the steel rails of language;
He gulps down famished stars and the pillar of nothingness.
When life turns into a darkened carriage
When death defines your contour
And your unyielding skull overlooks the stars,
Only your truthful poems, like a great bird
Will drift quietly through the sky over Romania.

Translated by Denis Mair

运　河

并不是所有人类对自然的
改造，都是一种破坏，
虽然这已经有数千年的历史。
比如对运河的开凿，就是
一个伟大而完整的例证……
当叮当的金属划开大地的身躯，
自由的胸腔鼓动着桅杆的羽翼。
在水的幻影之上，历史已被改写。
疾驰的木船，头上是旋转的天体，
被劈开的石钟，桨叶发出动听的声音。
挖掘坚硬的水槽，直到硕大的生铁，
将线路固定，词语定位成高空的星座。
不是山峦的原因，更不是风的力量，
而是清澈柔软的水创造了奇迹：
君王的权杖。宫殿的圆柱。战争的粮草。
帝国的命脉。晃动的酒杯。移动的国库。
被水滋养的财富。用盐解除的威胁。
输入权力中心的血液。压倒政敌的秘籍。
流动的方言。女人真情或假意的啜泣。
并非对抗的交易。埋葬过阴谋的河床。
相对存在的虚拟。一直活着的死亡。

多么不幸，如果运河里再没有了水，
它所承载的一切，当然就只能成为
零碎的记忆和云中若隐若现的星星。

Grand Canal

Not all alterations wrought by mankind
Upon nature are acts of destruction
Though some have lasted thousands of years.
A great and multi-faceted example of this
Is the excavation of the Grand Canal...
When clinking metal opened the earth's body
And winged masts swelled with lungfuls of freedom
History was rewritten in wavery images on water,
Heavenly bodies revolved above a hastening boat;
Its oars sounded pleasantly along with a split stone bell.
A durable sluice was dug, until a mass of raw iron settled
Upon a route. Words were fixed in lofty positions of stars,
Not by height of mountains or strength of wind...
Pristine water is what made this miracle:
Scepter of rulers. Pillars for palaces. Grain-ears for war.
Life-pulse of empire. Tipped-over goblet. Mobile treasury.
Wealth nurtured by water. Threat dispelled by salt.
Blood transfused to power's center. Secret files of political foes.
Diffusing dialects. Women's sobs. Genuineness or contrivance.
Transacted appeasements. Riverbed that buried conspiracies.
Relative existence of nothingness. Death that goes on living.

How unlucky, if the Grand Canal has no more water
All the freight it carried will become fragmentary memories
And stars showing intermittently through clouds.

Translated by Denis Mair

我始终热爱弱小的事物

我始终热爱弱小的事物,
也许是我与生俱来的一种偏好。

在我们这个世界,
强大的事物已经足够显赫。
主宰旋转的星球以真理和正义的名义,
手持太阳光辉的利剑保护道德的法则。
可是古老野蛮的罪行却还在出现:
在利比亚和阿富汗,在今天的耶路撒冷,
从对抗的科索沃到血亲复仇的车臣,
在流血的伊拉克,也在哭泣的叙利亚。

还有直到今天仍陷入内战的索马里,
发生犯罪的现场绝不仅仅在这些地方,
被无辜杀害的人数还在快速增长。
诚然对灵魂的救赎一天也没有停止,
但当我们面对无辜的叫喊和呻吟,
却不能将他们拯救出人间的地狱。

我不知道大地与天空真实的距离,
但我却能辨别出魔鬼与天使的差异。
哦!这是谁的手在向空中抛掷骰子?
为什么总是弱小的一边遭到惩罚。

我始终热爱弱小的事物,
也许是我与生俱来的一种偏好。
这些弱小的事物就在那里,
遍及世界的每一个角落。

在黑暗的阴影里,像一滴凝固的泪,
一段母语哽咽的歌谣。
这些被所谓人权忽视的声音,
偏远。落后。微弱。永远不在
强势文明定义的中心。但我却
选择了与他们站在一起。

I Will Always Feel Love
for Meek Lives

I always feel love for the meekest lives
Perhaps my partiality toward them is inborn.

In our world, powerful things are imposing enough
Laying claim to rotations of stars in the name of truth and justice
Holding the sword of solar radiance to defend morality's rules,
Yet ancient barbaric crimes are still happening
In Libya and Afghanistan, in today's Jerusalem,
From the resistance of Kosovo to blood feuds of Chechnya
In bleeding Iraq and weeping Syria.

Also in Somalia, still mired in civil war today,
And the sites of criminality are not just in these places
Numbers of slaughtered innocents are still increasing.
Admittedly the salvation of souls has not stopped for a day
But when confronted by screams and moans of the blameless
We are unable to save them from the hell of the human realm.

I do not know the true distance between heaven and earth
But I can distinguish the demonic from the angelic.
Oh! Whose hand is this hurling dice into the air
Why does the meek side so often suffer punishment?

I always feel love for the meekest lives
Perhaps my partiality for them is inborn.
Those meek lives are right next to us
Distributed in every corner of the world,
In dark shade, like a congealed teardrop
Or a broken-voiced folksong in the mother tongue,
These sounds overlooked by so-called powerful people
Are remote, backward, weak. They are never

At the center defined by the dominant civilization. Yet I
Have chosen to stand by their side.

        Translated by Denis Mair

口弦的力量

细小的声音
从大地和宇宙的深处
刺入血的
叫喊
我的心脏
开始了
体外的跳动
就像一个
传统的勇士
还在阵地上
我曾有过
这样的战绩
用一把口弦
打退了
一个乐团的进攻

The Power of a Mouth Harp

Sound as fine as floss
From depths of the good earth and the cosmos,
A cry that penetrates
Right into the blood:
My heart
Has begun
Beating outside the body
Like a stalwart
Of our tradition
Still on the battle line
Such was my merit
Won in battle:
With a mouth harp
I once warded off
The attack of an orchestra.

Translated by Denis Mair

马鞍的赞词

沉默的时候,时间的车轮,
并没有停止

一 等待

回忆昔日的黄金,
唯独只有骑手醒来;

风吹过眼球;

吹过头颅黑色的目光。
鼓动的披风,自由的
手势,与空气消融。

鹰隼的儿子,
另一半隐形的翅膀,
呈现于光的物体。

飞翔于内在的
悬疑,原始的秘密,
熄灭在鸟翅之上。

至尊的荣誉,
在生命之上,死亡的光环
涌动在群山的怀抱。
骑手,还在颂词中睡眠,
但黎明的吹奏
却已经在火焰的掩护下

开始了行进。

二 符号的隐喻

骑手没有名字,
他们的名字排列成阶梯。
鞍座只记忆胜利者,
唯有光明的背影,永远
朝前的姿势融化于黑暗。

眼底的空洞透明晶莹,
风的手指紧紧地拽着后背。
马脊骨是一条直线,
动与静在相对中死去,
旋转的群山坠落入蓝色,
苍穹和大地脱离了时间。

耳朵转向存在的空白,
在迅疾的瞬间,进入了灭亡。
针孔。黑洞。无限。盲点。
声音弥散在巨大的宇宙,
周而复始的替换,没有目的,
喉咙里巫语凝固后消失。

哦,骑手!不论你的血统怎样,
是紫色,是黑色,还是白色,
马背上的较量只属于勇士。
没有缝隙,拒绝任何羞耻的呼吸,
比生命更高贵的是不朽的荣誉。
你看,多快的速度穿过了肋骨,
只有它能在天平上分出高低。

2018.5.24

三 马蹄铁的影子

永远不会衰竭……
每一次弯曲,都以绝对的
平衡告别空虚。
肢体的线条自由地起伏,
踏着大地盛开的花朵。
无数的幻影叠加飞行,
前倾的身体刺入了未来,
肩膀上只有摇曳的末端。

四肢的奔腾悬浮空中,
撒落的种子,
受孕于无形的胎心。
持续性的那一边,
没有燃烧的箭矢。
名字叫达里阿宗的坐骑,
被传颂在词语的虹膜,
不被意识的空格拉长,
但能目睹马蹄铁的坠落。
无须为不朽的勇士证明,
那些埋下了尸骸的故土,
只要低头凝视,就能找到
碎铁的一小片叶子。

四 三色的原始

黑色的重量透彻骨髓,
那是夜晚流动的秘密,
大地中心的颜色,
往返坐直的权杖。

在缄默的灵魂里，
没有，或者说，它的高贵
始终在黄金之上，
所有的天体守候身旁。

太阳的耳环，
光明涌入的思想，
哦，永恒的金属，
庞大溢满的杯子。

抓住万物的头发，
吹动裸露的胸膛，
唯恐逃离另一个穹顶，
词语的舌尖舔舐了铁。

血液暗红的色素，
来自于祭祀的牛羊。
红色的生命之躯，
渴望着石头的水。

只有含盐的血
拌入矿物质的疯狂，
那只手，才能伸向
成熟乳房的果实。

朝我们展开了
生殖力最强的部分，
没有别的颜料，
只有红黄黑
在诞生前及死亡后
成为了纯粹的记忆。

2018.5.24

五 静默的道具

能听见无声的嘶鸣,
但看不到那匹马。
当火焰,穿过岩石和星座,
是谁在呼喊骑手的名字?
否则,抬起的前蹄
不会踏碎虚无的存在。

那只手抓住了缰绳,
在马背之上如弧形的弓,
等待奔向黑暗的瞬间。
是骨骼对风的渴望,
还是马鞍自由的意志,
让虚幻的骑手,在轻唤
月色中隐形的骏马?

三色原始的板块,
呈现出宁静的光芒,
原始的底色,潜藏着
断裂后的秘密。
哦,伟大的冲刺才属于你,
拒绝进入那永恒的睡眠。

总有一天,那个时刻,
要降临到词语的中心,
你会突然间醒来,
在垂直的天空下飞翔,
没有头部,没有眼睛,也没有
迎风飘扬的尾巴。
你的四蹄被分成影子,

虽然已经脱离了躯体，
但那马蹄铁哒哒的回声
却响彻回荡在天际。
是的，你已经将胜利的
消息，提前告诉了我们。

2018.5.24

Praise Song for a Saddle

During silence, the wheel of time does not stop.

One: Waiting

Recalling the gold of past times
Only the horseman is awake;

Wind blows past the eyeball;

It blows past a skull's black stare,
A bellied-out cape, gesturing motions
Of freedom that merge into an aura…

Son of the eagle
Invisible other half of wings
Manifested in entities of light…

Soaring inwardly through
What is unresolved, secret of origin
Extinguished on a bird's wing…

Honor exalted
Above life…a halo of death
Shimmers in the lap of ranged mountains
A horseman still sleeps in a verse of praise
But the flute-notes of dawn
Defended by flames
Have begun their advance.

Two: The Implicit Sense of a Symbol

The horseman has no name
His names line up as rungs on a ladder.

The saddle's seat only recalls victors,
Only a receding shape, a backlit posture
Forever heading forward, melting into darkness.

Hollowness behind eyes suffused with light,
Fingers of wind tightly clasp at the back…
The horse's backbone is a straight line;
Movement and stillness die in relation to each other;
Revolving mountains fall into the blue;
Sky-vault and broad land slip away from time.

Ears incline toward the blankness of existence
Which enters extinction in a flitting instant.
Eye of needle. Black hole. Infinity. Blind spot.
A sound pervades and reaches of the cosmos
In cyclic succession, without a goal…
Incantations congeal in the throat, then fade away.

Oh horseman, whatever your bloodline
Be it violet or black or white
Contention on horseback favors the valiant.
He has no crevice, refuses to draw a shameful breath;
Undying honor is more noble than life.
Look, what a great speed, passing through a ribcage!
Only on such scales can the high and low be distinguished.

Three: **Shadow of a shod hoof**

Forever unflagging…
At every curve, its absolute balance
Bids farewell to nothingness.
Contours of limbs undulate freely
Treading the land's flowers in full bloom;
An overlapping flight of countless phantoms,
A forward-tilting body stabbing into the future,
Nothing above its shoulders but swaying tips.

Its galloping limbs are suspended in mid-air,
Seeds are strewn, that were fertilized
At the core of an invisible womb.
On the far side of that continuance
There is no burning arrow.
Praises of the steed named Daliyazong
Have been handed down in the iris of words,
Not stretched in blank spaces of consciousness,
Yet it witnesses a horseshoe plunging downward.
For stalwarts whose valor is undying, there is no need
To prove where remains are buried on native ground;
You need only gaze with lowered head to find
A leaf-like flake of fragmentary iron.

Four: **The Three-Color Primordium**

Weight of blackness goes straight to the marrow:
That is the secret of late evening's fluidity,
Color of the broad land's heart,
A scepter's comings and goings, firmly upright…

In the meditative silence of a soul,
There is none of that, or I should say, its nobility
Is forever above that of gold
Watched over by near celestial bodies…

Earrings of the sun
Cogitation with an influx of light
Oh, eternal metal
Massive cup brimming.

Grab the hair of the ten-thousand things
Blow air out of a bared chest,
Liable to flee from another celestial vault
With its tongue-tip of words that licked iron.

Crimson coloration of flowing blood

From the ox or sheep offered for slaughter,
Red vessel of life
Water thirsting for stone.

Only by blood that contains salt
Admixed with the frenzy of minerals
Can that hand reach out for
The fruit of a ripe breast.

It has opened out to us,
The most powerful part of electricity,
Having no other colors
Only red and yellow and black
From before birth and after death
They are memory in the purest form.

Five: **Silent Stage Prop**

One can hear the soundless neigh
But the horse cannot be seen
Flames pass through rock walls and star clusters.
Who calls out the horseman's name?
If not for him, those raised front hooves
Wouldn't smash the existence of nothingness.

That hand grasps the reins
Like a bow's arc on the horse's back
Waiting for the moment to gallop into darkness:
Is it a skeleton's thirst for wind…
Or is it a saddle's wish to be free
That causes the phantom horseman to call
Under moonlight, to that invisible steed?

Blocs of the three-color primordium
Manifest a tranquil light,
Those underlying colors of origin holding
The secret of what was split apart.

Oh, the great charge forward belongs to you alone
Who refuses to enter eternity's slumber.

The time will come, that certain moment
Will descend into the heart of words,
You will suddenly awaken
To soar under the vertical sky,
Without head, without eyes, not even
A tail that streams on the wind.
Your four hooves have been divided into shadows;
Though parted from their fleshly frame
The echo of clopping horseshoes
Still reverberates where sky meets earth.
Indeed, you have brought tidings of victory;
You have notified us ahead of time.

Translated by Denis Mair

鹰的诞生和死亡

你的诞生和死亡
都同样伟大

一 孵的标志

在最高的地方,
那是悬崖迎接曙色
唯一国度,
什么也看不见,
只是一个蛋,不会旋转
那无数针孔的门。
没有从前,都是开始,
悬浮的空气和记忆
在转世前已经遗忘。

一块圆滑的石头,
柔软的水的核心,
这是真正胎腹的混沌,
那里是另一个大海
时间涌动着渴望的水,
直到那四肢成形,
心脏的拳头敲击着
未来虔诚的胸膛。

哦,是的,那是你的宇宙,
它的外面是宇宙的宇宙。
穹顶飘落鹅黄色的光,
无法用嘴说出一种意义。

能看见无色无味的瀑布,
尽管没有声音,自上而下
弥漫在思想的周围。

你的呼吸不在内部,
是太阳的光纤
进入了蓝色的静脉。
抽象的一,或者七[1],
那才是你伟大的父亲,
因为最终孕育的脐带,
都被它们始终握住。

二 天空之心

向太阳致敬,
向天空和无限的
牵引之力致敬……
是你用金属的嘴角,
以诞生和反抗的名义,
用光的铁锤,敲打着
倒立在顶部的砧板。
当你的天体破裂的时刻,
光明见证了你的诞生:
没有风暴的迹象,但白昼的
雷电却在天际隐约地闪现。

你没有出现的时候,
父子连名的古老传统,
就已经为你的到来命名。
当你瞩望浩瀚的星空,
陨石的坠落,就像梦境里

---

[1] 诺苏人《始源书》中叙述的人类起源神话:诺苏人的女性祖先坐在门口织布时,看见一只鹰在头顶上飞。数滴鹰血落在她裙子上,她由此受孕,生下文化英雄吉格·阿鲁。在这部史诗的另一版本中,名叫普莫·尼依的女人被数只不同颜色的鹰造访。数字从一到七,说法不一。神鹰代表太阳的血统。

嬉戏的星星那样无常。
或许你还并不了解
生命虚无的全部意义,
但你的出现,却给天空的
心脏,装上了轮子和羽翼。
因为你,天空的高度
才成为其中一种高度,
否则,没有那个黑色的句号,
一分为三的白色只是白色。

时刻与万物保持着
隐秘的对话和情感,
站立在黎明的巢中,
对于你清澈反光的镜子,
那些影像和柔软的思绪,
已经从第三方听到了
你的心跳黑洞的节奏。
对于草原和群山而言,你或许是
一匹马,一种速度,一段久唱不衰的
民歌,然而对于天空
你的存在要大于数字的总合。

三 退隐时间

伟大的高度,才会有
绝对的孤寂,迎着观念的
空无,语言被思想杀死。
有一百种姿势供你选择,
但只有一种姿势是你
盘旋在粒子之上的威仪:
那就是浮动于暂停的时间,

没有前没有后，没有左和右，
没有上没有下，失去了存在。

没有重量循环的影子，
仅仅是飞翔的一种形式。
涡流的气体，划过内部的
薄片，巨大无形的力量
比受益的睡眠还轻。
翅膀上羽毛的镀铜闪亮，
承载着落日血红的余晖。
不能再高，往上是球体的空白，
往下巡视，比线还细的江河
冒着虚拟水晶的白烟。
绿色的森林，不是混合色块，
除了居住在星球外的果实，
你的目光都能捕捉到踪迹。

一片叶子，一只昆虫，
迁徙的蚂蚁，被另类抚摸过的石头，
瞳孔里的映像，被放大了千倍。

目睹过生物间的杀戮，
那是自然法则又非法则，
所有的生命都参与其中，
唯有人类的罪孽尤为深重。

在人迹罕至的崖顶，
每一次出发和归来，
哦，流动的谜一样的灵物，
只留下了空无的气息。

四 守护圆圈

如同守护疆域，
没有丢失过一次阵地，
作为一个物种，
捍卫了自由和生命的
权利……

尽管思想的长矛
被插入了椎骨的肚脐，
但词语构筑的星星和月亮，
仍然站立在肩头。
祖先留下的那副盾牌，
迎击了一次次风暴。

承接过宇宙的巨石，
吮吸传统的谚语，将受伤的
木碗，运往安全的地方。
那是秘密的护身符，
它将从魔鬼和天使的中间
从容不迫地滑翔而过。

将大地和天空的语言，
抒写在果实内脏的部位，
如果失去另一半自我，
无疑就已经临近死亡。
紧紧握住磁铁的一端，
否则，将会在失血时倾倒。

从颅骨到坚硬的脚趾，
神枝插满了未知的天幕，

没有名字的星座,部族的祭司
在梦里预言了你最后的死期。

五 葬礼

知道那个时辰已经来临,
它比咒语的速度更要迅捷。
你的眼睛,蓄满黑色之盐,
祖先的绳结套住了脊柱。

这是一件献给不朽未来的
最后的礼物,也是一次
向生命的致敬和道歉。
无须将活着的意义告诫万物,
它们知道的或许还要更多。

哦,天空的道路,已经
呈现出白色的路线,
那是通往死亡的圣殿。
送魂的经文将被重复吟诵,
死亡的仪式在今天
已经超过了诞生的隆重,
而这一切都将独自完成。

朝着落日的位置瞩望,
那里的风速正在改变着
永恒的方向,在更高的地方,
紫色的云朵静止如玻璃。

哦,快看!是你正朝着太阳的位置
迅速地拔高,像一道耀眼的光芒,

羽毛发出咝咝的声音，划破的
空气溅射出疼痛无色的血浆。

你还在拔高，像失控箭矢，
耗尽最后的力量，力争达到
那个毁灭与虚无的顶点。
是的，你达到了：一声沉闷的爆炸，
在刺眼的光环中，完成了你的
祖辈们都完成过的一件事情。
此时，辽阔的天空一片沉寂，
只有零碎的羽毛还在飘落。[1]

---

[1] 与秃鹫不同，鹰的死尸很少在荒野发现。这是动物学的一个谜：鹰死的时候，隐形匿迹，只留下飘落的羽毛。为什么?

2018.5.25

Birth and Death of an Eagle

Your birth and death are equal in greatness.

One: Signs of Hatching in Progress

Up in the highest place
The only domain
Where a cliff greets daybreak
There is nothing to be seen
Only an egg, unable to spin,
Gate of countless needles' eyes.
There is no "formerly"; all is a beginning,
Air and memory are suspended,
Forgotten before the next incarnation.

A smooth-rubbed stone,
Core of mild, soft water,
This placental chaos;
Another ocean lies therein;
Time churns its yearning waters,
Until those four limbs take shape,
The fist of a beating heart,
Future chest swelling with devotion.

Oh, yes, that is your cosmos; outside of it,
Is the macrocosm; down from the sky-vault
Sifts light of gosling yellow,
With no meaning the mouth can utter.
A colorless, odorless waterfall can be perceived,
Albeit with no sound, from above to below
It pervades the periphery of thought.

Your breath is not internal;
It is in fibers suffused with sunlight;

It enters a blue, pulsing vein,
An abstraction of one, or of seven[1]—
None else but they could be your father,
Because the umbilical cord of final generation
Is always gripped by them.

Two: **Heart of the Heavens**

Hail to the sun
And the boundless force that draws things
    along.
It was you, with your mouth-corners of metal
In the name of birth and resistance
With a sledge-hammer of light that struck
The crown of an upended anvil.
The moment your celestial body splits,
Light bears witness to your birth.
There is no sign of a storm, but daytime
    lightning
Flickers faintly at the horizon.

When you had not yet appeared
The ancient tradition of patronymics
Had already prepared a name for your
    coming…
As you view the oceanic sweep of starry space
The plunging of a meteor is as ephemeral
As the frolicking of stars in a dream.
Perhaps you do not understand
The entire meaning of life's nothingness
But by grace of your emergence
The sky's heart was fitted with wheels and
    wings.
Only because of you, the sky's height
Could be one among other heights,
Elsewise there'd be no black period to end a sentence,

---

1 An origin myth of the Nuosu people is presented in *Hnewo Tepyy* (The Book of Origins): The female progenitor of the Nuosu people sits weaving in front of her doorway as she watches an eagle fly overhead. After drops of the sacred eagle's blood fall upon her skirt, she becomes pregnant and gives birth to the culture hero Zhyge Alu. In a variant of this epic, the woman Pumo Hniyy is visited by several eagles of different hues. The difference in numbers of eagles—from one to seven—is not important: what matters is the solar lineage of the sacred eagle/eagles. See the version of *Hnewo Tepyy* translated by Mark Bender and Aku Wuwu, in which several eagles are mentioned. (Mark Bender, "Tribes of Snow" in *Asian Ethnology* Volume 67, Number 1 • 2008, 5-42). The version translated by Qubi Shimei in 1978 mentions only one eagle. (Liangshan yiwenzi liaoxuanyi, Leeteyi [Selected Translation of Liang Mountain Yi-Language Materials, Vol. 1, *Hnewo Tepyy*], Southwest Minzu Institute Printing House, Chengdu, 1978)—Tr.

And tripartite whiteness would be mere whiteness.

Moment by moment, with ten thousand beings maintaining
A hidden dialogue and tie of feeling,
Sitting in a nest of dawn
The limpid mirror that reflects your image
Projecting you and your wispy trains of thought
Has already heard, by way of a third party
The black-hole rhythm of your heartbeat.
For the plains and mountains, perhaps you are
A horse, a velocity, a time-honored folk song
That keeps its freshness, and for the sky
Your existence is greater than a numerical total.

Three: **Reclusive Interval**

Only the greatest height can be
Absolutely solitary; in the face of emptiness
Of ideas, language falls prey to thought.
You have 100 postures to choose from
But only one shows the lordly bearing
That turns in a gyre over particles,
An act of floating over a pause in time;
There is no ahead, no behind, no right or left
No above or below, their existence is gone.

No shadow of weight goes through cyclical changes,
It is only a form of soaring,
Turbulence in a gas, a thin edge streaking through
Inwardness, a gigantic invisible force
Lighter than restful slumber,
Bronze gleam on a wing's feathers
Bearing blood-redness of sunset's lingering rays.
There is no going higher, upward is spherical blankness;
A downward look shows rivers thinner than threads
Emitting white mist which appears like white quartz;
Forests are green color blocs unmixed with other hues.

Aside from the fruits that abide off-planet
Your gaze captures traces of everything.

The sliver of a leaf, an ant traversing the ground,
An insect, a rock receiving an alternate kind of caress,
Image projected in a pupil, magnified a thousand times…

Having viewed slaughter between living things
That is the law of nature—to be lawless;
All beings take part in it,
But human sins are especially heavy.

Around a precipice seldom reached by human traces
Such an enigmatic conscious creature
In its flowing movements of departure and return
Leaving only a breath of nullity.

Four: **Watching over a Circle**

As if watching over rangeland
Never losing sight of any battlefront,
As an organism it defended freedom
And its right to live.

Though the spine's omphalos
Has been riven by the lance of thought,
Even so the stars and moon of words
Still stand at its shoulder;
The shield bequeathed by ancestors
Confronts the buffetings of each storm.

Bearing up under the megalith of a cosmos,
It sucks on old proverbs, and it transports
A wounded wooden bowl to a place of safety.
By strength of that secret talisman
In will soon glide nonchalantly
Between a devil and an angel.

It will inscribe the language of earth and sky
On the entrails of fruition,
If the self's other half be lost
Death by then had surely drawn near.
Hold firm to one pole of the magnet
Or else topple from loss of too much blood.

From skull to tenacious toes, all are divine branches
Bedecking the celestial canopy of the unknown,
And nameless constellations. The hierophant of a tribe
In a dream foretells your final hour of death.

Five: **Funeral**

Once the hour of death's coming is known
Its speed is more rapid than a curse.
Your eyes are stocked full of black salt;
The cords of ancestors harness your spine.

This is a gift, made in offering
To an enduring future, and it is
An apology and salute to life.
Don't admonish creatures with life's meaning;
What they know may encompass even more.

Oh, the skyward road has revealed
Its route into whiteness
Which leads toward the palace of death.
The Soul-Sending Scripture will be chanted repeatedly.
In these times, the rituals of death
Have surpassed those of birth in grandeur,
All of which comes about by itself.

As one's gaze is directed toward the setting sun
The wind speed thereabouts is changing
The direction of eternity, while in a higher place
Violet clouds are still like glass.

Oh look! It is you heading towards the sun's
    position,
Gaining altitude quickly, streaking like a beam
    of light,
Your feathers emit a whizzing sound, flinging
    pain
Like colorless blood into the parted air.

Still you gain altitude, like an arrow out of
    control,
Exhausting your last strength, straining to
    arrive
At the apex of destruction and nothingness.
Yes, you have reached it—a peal of thunder booms,
Amid a dazzling aura you complete the act
That all your ancestors have completed.
This moment, the vast sky subsides to stillness,
Only a few stray feathers are drifting down.[1]

    Translated by Denis Mair

---

[1] Unlike vultures, corpses of dead eagles are seldom found in the wilderness. This is a mystery of zoology: when eagles die, they apparently disappear, leaving only a few stray feathers. Why?

人性的缺失

我在达基沙洛的祖屋里读书,
火塘里的火正在渐渐地熄灭。

这是谁书写的一部历史?
远处的群山似乎也在聆听。

从1781年瓦特先生的发明开始,
他们就挥动着旗帜开着蒸汽机,
带来了巨人般的新世界的动力。
在荒原,在海上,在人类渴望的地方,
当火车高声鸣笛冒出乳白色的气体,
轮船以从未有过的马力破浪前行。
那时,世纪的婴儿发出第一声啼哭,
莱特兄弟的飞机,让多少人的梦想
穿越了无法想象的白色的高度。
哦,人类!为什么不为我们自己取得的
成就而倍感自豪又欣喜若狂呢?
钢铁的速度抵达了人迹罕至的部落,
在送去所谓文明的时候也送去了梅毒,
任何一个被定义为野蛮人生活的区域,
都能听到原始的乐器发出啜泣的声音。

无论是古代希腊,还是我们的时代,
这个星球的历史并非在简单重复,
当我们瞩望浩瀚无垠神秘的星空,
总会在一个瞬间遗忘生命遭遇的不幸,
但酷刑和杀戮却每时每刻都还在发生。
爱迪生的灯光,在圣诞时多么明亮,

那一双双眼睛充满了对新年的期待。
但纳粹的焚尸炉，却用电将还活着的人
连同他们的绝望和恐惧都烧成了灰烬。
其实今日的现实就如同逝去的昨天，
叙利亚儿童在炮火和废墟上的哭声，
并没有让屠杀者放下了手中的武器。
这一个多世纪以来人类又拥有了：
原子能，计算机，纳米，超材料，机器人，
基因工程，克隆技术，云计算，互联网，
数字货币，足以毁灭所有生物的武器。

但是面对生命，只是他们具备了杀死对方
更快捷更精准的办法。而人类潜藏的丑恶
却没有因为时间的洗礼而发生任何改变。

我在达基沙洛的祖屋里读书，
火塘里的火正在渐渐地熄灭。

2018.6.12

The Flaw In Human Nature

2018.6.12

I was in my ancestral home at Dajyshalo
The hearth-fire was gradually dying down.

Whose hand had written this work of history?
Distant mountains also seemed to listen intently.

Beginning with James Watt's invention in 1781
They waved the banner of steam power to bring
A huge driving force into a world made new.
In wastelands, on oceans, in places humans had yearned to go
When steam whistles of trains released their white vapor
And ships with unheard-of horsepower ploughed through waves.
When the infant of a century was sounding its first wails,
The Wright brothers' plane allowed the dreams of men
To pass through the whiteness of unimaginable heights.
Oh humanity! How could such an achievement
Not fill our hearts with pride and jubilation?
Velocity of steel reached seldom-visited tribes;
While bringing so-called civilization it also brought syphilis.
In any region where people were defined as barbarians
One could hear the sobs of primitive musical instruments.

Whether in ancient Greece or in our own period
This planet's history has not been simple repetition.
As we gaze into vast reaches of starry space
At times we can forget the misfortunes life has undergone,
But torture and slaughter still happen, every hour of the day.
How brightly Edison's light bulbs shine at Christmas;
So many pairs of eyes fill with expectation of New Year,
But Nazi incinerators used electricity to turn living people,
Along with their fear and despair, into ashes.
In fact, today's reality is much like the vanished past:
Wails of Syrian children coming from shell-scarred ruins

Have not moved the killers to put down their weapons.
In the past century, humankind has also gained possession
Of atomic energy, computers, nanotech, metamaterial, robots,
Genetic engineering, cloning, cloud computing, the internet, digital currency
And weapons sufficient to destroy all living things.

As ways of treating life, they are often only methods
To kill foes more quickly and precisely. As for latent evil
It has not yet been altered by the baptism of time.

I was reading in my ancestral home at Dajyshalo,
The hearth-fire was gradually dying down.

Translated by Denis Mair

叫不出名字的人

2018.6.13

什么是人民？就是每天在大街上行色
匆匆而面部各异的男人和女人，就是
一个人在广场散步，因为风湿痛颤栗着走路
需要扶着手杖，走出十米也比登天还难的老人。
就是迎风而行，正赶去学堂翩跹而舞的少年，
当然，也是你在任何一个地方，能遇见的
叫不出名字的人，因为你不可能一一认识他们。
人民是一个特殊用语？还是一个抽象的称谓？
我理解如果没有个体的存在，就不可能有我们
经常挂在嘴边和文章中提到的这个词。
因为人民也许是更宏达的一种政治的表述，
我们说大海的时候，就很像我们在说着人民。
有人说一滴水并不是大海，就如同说他对面那个
人不是人民，这样的逻辑是否真的能够成立？
也许你会说没有一粒粒的沙，怎么可能形成
浩瀚无边的沙漠？但仍然会有一种观点一直坚持
他们的说法：沙和沙漠就是吹动的风和风中的影子。
对于一滴水，我们也许忽视过它的存在，当成千上万
滴水汇聚成大海的时候，我们才会在恍然间发现
它的价值。对于人民？我没有更高深复杂的理解，
很多时候它就是那些走出地铁通道为生活奔波
而极度疲乏的人。就是那些爬上脚手架劳累了
一天的人。还有那些不断看着时间赶去幼儿园
接孩子的人。这些人的苦恼和梦想虽然千差万别，
但他们却有着一个共同的特点：都是最普通的人。
这些人穿过城市，穿过乡村，穿过不同的幸福和悲伤，
他们有时甚至是茫然的，因为生存的压力追赶着他们，
但作为一个人就像大海中的一滴水，当隐没于蓝色，

我们就很难从那汹涌澎湃的波涛中找寻到它的踪迹。

正因为此,我才相信一个个鲜活的生命。

2018.6.13

Someone Whose Name
I Can't Say

Who are "the people"? They are men and women rushing past
On an avenue; no two of them have the same facial features.
They are an old man walking on a plaza, his rheumatic legs trembling,
To walk fifty feet, using a cane, seems as hard as climbing to the sky,
Or a youth with a bounce in his step, walking to his academy.
Of course they may be someone you could meet anywhere
Whom you can't call by name, because you never got acquainted.
Is "the people" an idiomatic usage or an abstract term?
As I see it, without the presence of individuals, we would not have
This word that often appears in our speech and texts.
Perhaps "the people" conveys an expansive view of politics,
So when we speak of the sea, it relates somehow to "the people".
Some say that a droplet isn't a sea, just as the person across from us
Is not the people, but is such logic valid?
You could say if it weren't for grains of sand, how could a vast desert
Ever take shape? Yet some would persist in their conception, saying
Sand is to a desert as the wind's movement is to a shadow in the wind.
As for a drop of water, perhaps we ignore its existence;
Only when drops converge into an ocean do we discover
Their value. As for "the people", I have no deep or lofty understanding.
Often it is someone emerging from a subway exit, tired out
By her hectic life, or one who climbs on a scaffold, working hard
All day; it could be one who checks her watch and hurries to pick up
A kindergartner. Although their worries and dreams vary widely
They have one point in common: they are ordinary people.
They pass through cities and villages, through gladness and sadness;
At times they lose focus, due to survival pressures dogging their foot-
    steps,
But as persons they are drops in an ocean: once they disappear into
    blueness
It is hard to seek their traces amid crashing waves.

That is why I believe in the vibrant life of each conscious being.

    Translated by Denis Mair

对我们而言……

对我们而言,祖国不仅仅是
天空、河流、森林和父亲般的土地,
它还是我们的语言、文字、被吟诵过的
千万遍的史诗。
对我们而言,祖国也不仅仅是
群山、太阳、蜂巢、火塘这样一些名词,
它还是母亲手上的襁褓、节日的盛装、
用口弦传递的秘密、每个男人
都能熟练背诵的家谱。
难怪我的母亲在离开这个世界的时候
对我说:"我还有最后一个请求,一定
要把我的骨灰送回到我出生的那个地方。"
对我们而言,祖国不仅仅是
一个地理学上的概念,它似乎更像是
一种味觉、一种气息、一种声音、一种
别的地方所不具有的灵魂里的东西。
对于置身于这个世界不同角落的游子,
如果用母语吟唱一支旁人不懂的歌谣,
或许就是回到了另一个看不见的祖国。

To Our Way of Thinking…

To our way of thinking, the Motherland is not only sky;
It is more than rivers and forest and the fatherly land
It is also our language, our words and epics down through time.
To our way of thinking, the Motherland is not just a lexicon
Of terms like "ranged mountains", "sun", "beehive" and "hearth"
It is mother's hands that swaddled us and put on holiday finery;
It lies in a mouth harp's secrets…in the family tree each householder
    can recite
No wonder my mother said to me, before she left this world:
"I have one last request. Please make sure
To send my remains back to where I was born."
To our way of thinking, the Motherland is more
Than a geographical idea: it calls to mind
A taste, a scent, a voice, something in the soil
That is not present anywhere else.
When wandering sons find themselves in far corners of the world
Just singing a verse in their own tongue, that many may not know
They return to an alternate, unseen land—the one that mothered
    them.

       Translated by Denis Mair

一个人的克智[1]

当词语的巨石穿过针孔的时候,
针孔的脊柱会发出光的声音。

针孔的肋骨覆盖词语的巨石,
没有声音,但会引来永恒的睡眠。

鹰翅上洒下黄金的雨滴,
是天空孵化的蛋吗?

不是,那是苍穹的虚无,
但蛋却预言了宇宙的诞生。

[1] 克智(类似苏格兰语的"flyting"),是彝族人节日聚会时表演的一种言语比赛或文字游戏。

2019.6.20

A Flyting[1] Spoken to Oneself

When a rock passes through the eye of a needle,
The needle's backbone gives off a sound of light.

The needle's eye have ribs that enfold rocks of words,
Without sound, yet lulling to eternal slumber.

That golden raindrop flung from an eagle's wing—
Is it an egg the sky has been hatching?

No it is emptiness from the celestial vault,
But an egg did foretell the birth of a universe.

<blockquote>Translated by Denis Mair</blockquote>

[1] A "*kne-re*" (similar to the Scots word "flyting") is a performance of wordplay or verbal dueling heard on festive occasions among the Yi people.

致尼卡诺尔·帕拉[1]

他活着的时候"反诗歌",
他反对他理应反对的那些诗歌。
反它们与人类的现实毫无关系,
反它们仅仅是抽空了
血液的没有表情的词语,
反它们高高在上凌驾万物
以所谓精神的高度自居,
反空洞无物矫情的抒情,
当然也反那些人为制造的纲领。
他常常在智利的海岸漫步,
脚迹在沙滩上留下一串串问号。
他对着天空吐出质疑的舌头
是想告诉我们雨水发锈的味道。
他一直在"反诗歌",那是因为
诗歌已经离开了我们的灵魂,
离开了不同颜色的人类的悲伤,
这样的状况已经有好长的时间。
他"反诗歌"是因为诗歌的
大脑已经濒临漫长的死亡,
词语的乳房没有了芬芳的乳汁,
枯萎的子宫再不能接纳生命的种子。
他的存在,就是反讽一切荒诞,
即便对黑色的死亡也是如此。
对生活总是报以幽默和玩笑,
他甚至嘲弄身边移动的棺材,
给一件崭新的衬衣打上补丁。
我在新闻上看见有关他葬礼的消息,
在他的棺材上覆盖着一面

[1] 尼卡诺尔·帕拉(1914-1976)是智利最著名的诗人之一,"反诗歌"诗人的领军人物,也是当代拉美乃至整个西班牙语世界最具影响力的诗人之一。

2019.7.15

还在他的童年时母亲为他缝制的
一床小花格被子，
不是所有的人，都能明白
这其中隐含的用意，
实际上他是在向我们宣告：
从这一刻起，他"反死亡"的
另一场游戏已经轰然开始。

For Nicanor Parra[1]

[1] Nicanor Parra (1914-1976) was one of Chile's most famous poets and a leader of the "anti-poetry" movement. His influence as a poet was felt in Latin America and worldwide.

In his lifetime he practiced "anti-poetry".
He opposed poems that ought to be opposed.
He was against their irrelevance to human reality,
Against them for being drained of blood,
And thus no more than faceless words,
For being aloof and setting themselves above things,
For presuming that they occupy the heights of spirit,
For lyric flights that are hollow and contrived. Of course…
He opposed the manifestoes they thought up.
He often strolled along the beaches of Chile;
His feet left a string of question marks in the sand;
He protruded a questioning tongue at the sky
So he could tell us about the rain's rusty flavor
He was always anti-poetry, because
So much of poetry has strayed away from the soul,
Away from sorrow of men with different skin colors.
Such a departure has been going on for a long time.
He is "anti-poetry", because the brain of poetry
Has been lingering at the edge of death;
The breasts of words have no fragrant milk,
Their withered womb cannot receive seeds of life.
His existence was a retort to all inanities,
It even hurled mockery at death's blackness,
And it always responded to life with a jest,
Even jeering as his coffin was moved into place,
And sewing a patch on a brand-new shirt.
Now I see news of his funeral in the papers:
Over his coffin was draped
A gaily-patterned quilt
Sewn by his mother in his childhood.
Not everyone can understand
What the message behind this could be.

In fact, he was saying to us:
"This moment marks the grand beginning
Of another game: this time 'anti-death' ".

    Translated by Denis Mair

一个士兵与一块来自
钓鱼城的石头

2019.8.12

一座孤城被围得水泄不通
尽管每隔一段间隙就会发起一次攻击
呐喊声,厮杀声,军鼓的喧哗震耳欲聋
伤亡一次比一次惨重,破城的
希望却变得越来越渺茫

这样相持的昼夜已经有一段时间
攻防双方似乎已渐渐习惯了在这
生与死的游戏中被未知凝固的日子

城内的旗幡还在飘扬,高昂的
斗志并没有减弱的迹象
据说他们的水源在城中的最高处
不用害怕被对方找到切断投毒
更不用担心粮食和柴禾,已有的储备
完全能让这些守城者支撑数年

城外的围困还在不断地加剧
更新的一次进攻也正在组织预谋

这是黄金家族的威力最鼎盛时期
在里海附近刚刚活捉了钦察首领八赤蛮
挥师南下的劲旅已经征服了西南的大理国
长途奔袭的骑手穿越了中亚西亚的丘陵和草原
所向披靡的消息已经抵达遥远的地中海
他们即将与埃及的马木留克王朝
进行落幕前的一场可预见的交战

但在这里所有的进攻都停滞不前
所谓克敌制胜的计划已经变得遥遥无期
两边的士兵都疲劳不堪,战事陷入胶着

就在这样的时候,有一天上午
(如果是下午呢?或者是黄昏的时候呢?)
蒙哥汗[1]又登上了高处的瞭望台
开始观望城里的敌军有何新的情况

同样是那个时辰,在炮台的旁边
有一个士兵远远地看见了在对面的高台上
有一位临风而立的瞭望人正在观望
(如果这个士兵没有接下来的反应,
更没有往下付诸他的行动,是不是
会出现另一个完全不同的结果?)

同样在接下来的时间里,这个士兵
如果没有和别的几个士兵将那块石头
从抛石机上准确无误地抛向那个目标
(如果更近了一点?更远了一点?更左了
一点?更右了一点?又会发生什么呢?)

这是一个偶然?还是纯属一个意外?
并不是所有的偶然以及意外的出现
都能改写扑朔迷离的历史和命运的规律

那个最早发现瞭望台站着一个人的士兵
他当然不会知道对面那个人究竟是谁
而他永远更不会知道,他和那块普通的炮石
在人类的宿命中扮演了什么样的角色

---

[1] 孛儿只斤·蒙哥(1209-1259),大蒙古国第四任大汗,史称"蒙哥汗",元太祖成吉思汗之孙,1259年在围攻钓鱼城时中炮受伤致死。

因为从这里发出的有关大汗死亡的消息
让各路凶悍的首领开始返回久别的故土

我们从正史上只能看到这样的记载：
1259年一代战神蒙哥汗受伤致死于钓鱼城
上帝之鞭——在这里发生了折断！

A Soldier and a Stone from Diaoyu Fortress

The lone fortress was under siege, hemmed in on all sides;
Although attacks were mounted at intervals, making the air ring
With whoops and clangs and drumbeats
Leading to more and more casualties each time, yet
Hopes of breaching the fort grew ever slimmer.

Those days of deadlock dragged on and on;
Both sides grew accustomed to this grim game
Joining life and death in an unresolved knot.

Banners over the fortress were a sign:
The will to fight still ran high in their veins.
Folks say their wellhead was at the fort's highest point—
No fear that their water would be cut off or poisoned.
Food and fuel gave them no cause for worry,
What they had in storage would last for years.

The siege was intensifying day by day;
Plans for a renewed assault were underway…

Fortunes of the Borigin clan were at their height
Having just captured the Kipchak chief near the Caspian Sea
A crack detachment had taken Dali Kingdom in the Southwest;
Their cavalry had crossed the hills and plains of Central Asia;
News of their blitz of victories reached the Mediterranean.
They were poised to clash with the Mamluk Sultanate of Egypt
In a battle to crown the outcome of their westward push,
But here their attack force could not move forward;
Their plan for decisive victory had hit a quagmire.
Both sides were bone-tired, the fight was in deadlock.

Around this time, during the morning hours,

(Had it been afternoon or dusk, what then?)
Mongke Khan[1] once again climbed a lookout tower
To see what the fort's defenders were up to.

At the very same hour, on a catapult platform
A soldier gazing across the wall at the enemy line
Saw someone viewing the fort from that tower.
(If that soldier hadn't reacted in a certain way,
and if he hadn't taken the following actions,
would things have turned out quite differently?)

Likewise, in the ensuing minute, if that soldier
Had not loaded the catapult, with his squad's help,
And if they hadn't loosed a stone with perfect aim.
(If that stone had fallen a bit short or a bit far,
Or a bit to one side, what would have happened?)

Was this a random event? Was it purely a fluke?
Not every fluke or random event, just by happening,
Can rewrite the obscure causes of history or fate.

The soldier who noticed a man standing on the tower
Had no way of knowing who that man was; still less
Could he have known that the round stone he used
Would play a huge role in steering the fates of men,
Because news of the Khan's death, sent forth that day,
Caused the Khanate's far-flung chieftains to turn homeward.

In official histories, we only see this record:
"1259— The great warrior Mongke Khan died at Diaoyu Fortress."
The scourge of God was broken there!

Translated by Denis Mair

---

[1] Borigin Mongke (1209-1259), the fourth Khan of Mongolia, was the grandson of Genghis Khan (founder of China's Yuan Dynasty). In 1259 Mongke Khan was fatally injured by a catapult projectile while laying siege to Diaoyu Cheng (Fisherman's Fortress in what is now Hechuan District, Chongqing City.)

商丘,没有结束的

商丘是一个被他者命名的名字
是一个被风和传说充盈的肚脐
在它被命名之前,商人就在这里
青铜的唇齿爬满了未知的天际
商队还在行走,他们从未消失
只是在时间的另一面,他们正在
走向我们称之为过去的现在
生与死只是两种不同的存在形式

只有声音能穿越不同的空间
只有光能渗透那坚硬的物质
不是轮回和循环在发号施令
是消亡和诞生在永无止境地
循环往复——毁灭替代了永恒
没有更高的地方,帝王的墓室
就在每一个登高者的脚下
墓室的门已经被无数次地打开
青苔早已覆盖每一面坚硬的石壁
因为金银、财富和欲望的诱惑
帝王的尸骨当然也不可能完整

没有更高的地方,因为在更低处
有人看见过,不同王朝的消失
就好像一颗流星划破蓝色的穹顶
丘,或许就是一个更高的存在
难怪后来的人都要登上所谓的高台
目睹宁静的水和光返回原始之地
穿越词语的麦芒开始极目望远

2019.8.29

看见那座斑驳砖石构筑的沧桑古城
在这一望无际的原野的波浪上
没有过去,没有现在,没有未来
时隐时现成为时间深处的点点帆影

2019.8.29

Shang Mound, There Is No Ending

"Shang Mound" is a name given this place by others.
It is an omphalos engorged by wind and legends.
Before it was named, the people of Shang were here,
Teeth of bronze defended the skyline from the unknown.
Caravans still traverse it, they have never disappeared,
They are just on the other side of time; they are trekking
Into an alternate present that we call the past;
Life and death are merely two forms of experience.

Only sound can pass through different spaces;
Only light can suffuse solid objects.
Reincarnation is not what calls the tune;
Dying and birth occur in endless alternation,
Visions of eternity give way to destruction.
There is no higher place, the tombs of supreme kings
Are under the feet of holiday climbers;
The tombs have been raided countless times,
Moss has coated the walls of stone.
Due to the lure of imagined riches
No one thought to leave king's bones intact.

There is no higher place, because in lower places
People watched their passing—one king after another
Like comets streaking across the firmament.
This mound may be a higher form of being,
No wonder the living are drawn to climb its height
To watch quiet, sunlit water, returning to its source
Across wheatfields of words, as we gaze afar,
Seeing mottled stone blocks of a weathered city wall
In these barrens that undulate to the edge of vision.
There is no past, present or future…just specks of sails,
Now in now out of view, on the depths of time.

                Translated by Denis Mair

2019.8.29

但我的歌唱却只奉献给短暂的生命

2019.10.11

宝刀，鹰爪的酒杯，坠耳的玛瑙
那是每一个男人与生俱来的喜爱
骏马，缀上贝壳的佩带，白色的披毡
从来都是英雄和勇士绝佳的配饰
重塑生命，不惧死亡，珍惜名誉
并不是所有的家族都有此传承
似乎这一切我都已经具备
然而我是一个诗人，我更需要
自由的风，被火焰洗礼过的词语
黎明时的露水，蓝色无垠的星空
慈母摇篮曲的低吟，恋人甜蜜的呓语
或许，我还应该拥有几种乐器
古老的竖笛、月琴、三叶片的口弦
我的使命就是为这个世界吟唱
诚然，死亡与生命是同样的古老
但我的歌唱却只奉献给短暂的生命

Yet My Song Is Offered to Fleeting Lives

Precious sword, eagle-talon goblet, agate earrings—
For such things each man has an inborn liking.
A stallion, a cowrie-studded sash, a white wool cape—
Are known as the manliest accoutrements of heroes.
To shape a new life and cherish honor with no fear of death…
Such is the legacy passed down by every clan.
It seems that all of this was made ready for me,
But I am a poet, what I need even more
Is wind of freedom and words abluted by fire,
Dewdrops at dawn, starry sky of boundless indigo,
Muted notes of cradle songs, a lover's sweet nothings…
Along with those, I should possess musical instruments
An old recorder, a moon guitar, a three-reed jaw harp.
To recite verses for such a world is my mission.
From time immemorial, death has shadowed the living,
Yet my song is offered to fleeting lives.

Translated by Denis Mair

而我们……

2019.10.20

诗歌,或许就是最古老的艺术,
伴随人类的时光已经十分久远。
哦,诗人,并不是一个职业,
因为他不能在生命与火焰之间,
依靠出卖语言的珍珠糊口。
在这个智能技术正在开始
并逐渐支配人类生活的时代,
据说机器人的诗歌在不久
将会替代今天所有的诗人。
不,我不这样看!这似乎太武断,
诗人之所以还能存活到现在,
那是因为他的诗来自灵魂,
每一句都是生命呼吸的搏动,
更不是通过程序伪造的情感,
就是诅咒也充满了切肤的疼痛。

然而,诗人,我并不惧怕机器人,
但是我担心,真的有那么一天
当我们面对暴力、邪恶和不公平,
却只能报以沉默,没有发出声音,
对那些遭遇战争、灾难、不幸的人们,
没有应有的同情并伸出宝贵的援手,
再也不能将正义和爱情的诗句,
从我们灵魂的最深处呼之欲出。

而我们,都成了机器人……

As for Us...

Poetry…perhaps it is the most ancient art,
It has kept humans company for a long time.
Ah, to be a poet is not a profession, because
One cannot fill his belly selling pearls of language
Which were snatched out of the flames of life.
In this era of relentless change,
As info-tech dominates human lives,
Some say that robotic poetry is on the verge
Of replacing all the poets of today.
I think not: that would be too arbitrary.
The reason that poets still survive today
Is that their poems come from the soul.
Each line throbs with life, breathes with feelings
Which aren't something a program could cook up.
Even curses are filled with deep-cut hurts.

And so, poets, I have no fear of robots,
But I worry that the day may really come
When we face violence, evil and injustice,
But can only stay silent, lacking words to speak
For victims of war and hardship and disaster,
And failing to lend a precious helping hand.
Lacking sympathy, we may fail to summon up
Words of justice and love from deep in our souls,

And by then, we will have turned into robots…

        Translated by Denis Mair

诗歌的秘语……

2019.10.20

彝人为了洁净自己的房子，
总会把烧红的鹅卵石
放在水里去祛除污秽之物，
那雾状的水汽弥漫于空间。
谁能告诉我？是卵石内核的呐喊？
还是火焰自身的力量？或许是
另一种意志在覆盖黑暗的山岩。
我相信神奇的事物，并非是一种迷信，
因为我曾看见过，我们部族的祭司
用牙咬着山羊的脖子甩上了屋顶。

罪行，每天都在发生，遍布
这个世界每一个有人的角落。
那些令人心碎的故事告诉我们，
人类积累的道德和高尚的善行，
并不随婴儿的第一声啼哭到来。
然而，当妈妈开始吟唱摇篮曲，
我们才会恍然觉悟，在朦胧中
最早接受的就是诗歌的秘语。
哦，是的，罪行还会发生，
因为诗人的执着和奉献，
荒诞的生活才有了意义，
而触手可摸的真实，
却让我们通往虚无。

The Secret Language of Poems…

When the Yi people want to purify their house
They dunk red-hot stones into herb-infused water
Letting steamy vapors permeate the interior
To rid the place of impure entities.
Who can say if the hiss of stones does this
Or is it by the power of flame itself? Or does
Another will overcome the boulders of darkness?
I believe in marvels, but not out of superstition,
Because I have seen a priest of my tribe
Clamp teeth on a goat's neck and fling it onto a roof.

Sinful acts are happening every day
In all corners of the globe where people live.
Many heart-wrenching stories tell us
That human morality and noble deeds
Don't arrive with an infant's first wails,
Yet when the mother starts to chant a lullaby
We realize that in her child's unknowing state
The secret language of poetry is being imparted.
Ah yes, those sinful deeds will still be committed,
Yet because of what poets feel driven to offer
This absurd life begins to take on meaning.
As for palpable actuality, it may lead us
Down the road to nothingness.

Translated by Denis Mair

暮年的诗人

2019.10.21

请原谅他,就是刻骨铭心,
也不能说出她们全部的名字。
那是山林消失的鸟影,
云雾中再找不到踪迹。
那是时间铸成的大海,
远去的帆影隐约不见。
那是一首首深情的恋歌,
然而今天,只有回忆用独语
去沟通岁月死亡一般沉默。
当然还有那些闪光的细节,
直到现在也会让他,心跳加速
双眼含满无法抑制的泪水。

粗黑油亮长过臀部的两条辫子。
比蜂蜜更令人醉心销魂的呼吸。
没有一丝杂质灵动如水的眼睛。
被诗歌吮吸过的粉红色的双唇。
哦,这一切,似乎都遗落于深渊,
多少容颜悄悄融化在失眠的风里。

哦,我们的诗人,他为诗奉献了
爱情,而诗却为他奉献了诗。

请原谅他,他把那些往事
都埋在了心底……

A Poet in His Waning Years

Please forgive him, despite what is etched in his bones
He can no longer utter all their names;
Those bird-shapes vanishing over highland groves,
Their traces gone in gathering mist.
That is an ocean given scope by time;
Sails that dotted it have slipped from sight.
That is a serenade of love songs,
But today only memory, in the form of soliloquy,
Communes with the deathly silence of years.
Of course, certain details still give off flashes
Even now his heartbeat quickens at them;
There is no holding back his brimming tears.

Two lacquer-black braids growing past the rump
And honeyed breath of heart-melting sweetness,
Crystalline eyes like animated pools,
Pink lips on which poetry has suckled,
Ah, all seems to have dropped into an abyss,
Lovely features swept off by an insomniac wind.

Ah, such is our poet, he had love to offer
For poetry's sake, and then poetry offered itself to him.

Please forgive him, he took time to bury bygone things
At the bottom of his heart…

Translated by Denis Mair

致父辈们

他们那一代人,承受
过暴风骤雨的考验。
在一个时代的巨变中,
有新生,当然也有的沉沦。
他们都是部族的精英,
能存活下来的,也只是
其中幸运的一部分人。

他们是传统的骄子,能听懂
山的语言,知晓祖先的智慧。
他们熟悉词根本身的含义,
在婚庆与葬礼不同的场所,
能将精妙的说唱奉献他人。
他们还在中年的时候,
就为自己做好了丧衣,
热爱生活,却不惧怕死亡。
他们是节日和聚会的主角,
坐骑的美名被传颂到远方。
他们守护尊严,珍惜荣誉,
有的人……就是为了……证明
存在的价值,而结束了生命。

与他们相比,我们去过
这个世界更多的地方。
然而,当我们面对故土,
开始歌唱,我们便会发现,
他们比我们更有力量。

2019.10.22

我们丢失了自我,梦里的
群山也已经死亡……

2019.10.22

For My Father's Generation

People of that era were put through trials
Of raging wind and pelting rain.
In that era's massive transformations
There were new chances and, of course, downfalls.
They were the elite of our tribe,
And those who managed to survive
Were only the lucky portion.

They were favored sons of tradition, well-versed
In mountain language and ancestral wisdom.
They knew the intrinsic meaning of word roots,
Which they served up in rhymes and sayings
On festive and mournful occasions.
While still in middle age they made ready
Their own coffin and burial clothes.
They had passion for life, without fear of death.
They were lead figures at holidays and parties;
The reputations of their mounts were known afar.
They defended dignity and cherished honor.
Some of them, to prove the value of living
Did not shrink from giving up their lives.

Compared to them, we have visited
Many more places in the world,
But when we attempt to sing
Of native ground, then we realize
They were more powerful than we are.
We have lost ourselves, and in our dreams
The ranged mountains live no more…

Translated by Denis Mair

姐姐的披毡

如果是黑色遭遇了爱情。
最纯粹的过渡，飘浮于藏蓝
幽深的夜空。哦，姐姐，那是你的梦？
还是你梦中的我？我不明白，
是谁创造了这比幻想更远的现实？
那还是在童年的时候，奇迹就已出现，
仿佛今天又重现了这个瞬间。

原谅我，已想不起过去的事情，
纵然又看见姐姐披着那件披毡，
但那只是幻影，不再属于我，
它是另一个人，遗忘的永恒。

2019.10.22

My Sister's Woolen Cape

If blackness were to encounter love
Most pure in its excess, adrift in the night sky
Of fathomless indigo, ah, sister, could that be your dream
Or myself as you've dreamt me? I don't know who created
This reality more distant than fantasy.
Could it be a miracle that came to pass in childhood,
Reappearing as an echo in this moment?

Forgive me, I can't call the incident to mind
Yet I see you wearing that woolen cape,
But it's just a figment, no longer mine
Seen by someone else, in an eternity of forgetting.

Translated by Denis Mair

口弦大师
——致俄狄日伙[1]

是恋爱中的情人,才能
听懂你传递的密语?还是
你的弹奏,捕获了相思者的心?
哦,你听!他彻底揭示了
男人和女人最普遍的真理。
每拨弹完一曲,咧嘴一笑,
两颗金牙的光闪耀着满足。
无论是在仲夏的夜晚,或是
围坐于漫长冬日的火塘,
口弦向这个世界发出的呼号,
收到了一个又一个的回应。

俄狄日伙说,每一次
弹奏,就是一次恋爱,
但当爱情真的来临,却只有
一个人能破译他的心声……

---

[1] 俄狄日伙,凉山彝族聚居区布拖一位民间音乐传承人。

2019.10.23

Jaw Harp Master
—*For Edi Rihuo* [1]

Is your secret code only to be understood
By the lover you pine for?
Does your twanging reed capture a lovestruck
    heart?
Ah, listen! You have fully revealed
The most universal truth of the two sexes.
As the piece ends, your mouth grins widely
Flashing satisfaction from two gold teeth,
Whether on a midsummer evening
Or around a hearth on a long wintry day
The jaw harp calls out to this world
And gathers in each and every response.

Each time Edi Rihuo strikes up a tune
It is like a love affair,
But when love truly comes, only one person
Will know the code of his heart's voice.

    Translated by Denis Mair

---

[1] Edi Rihuo is an heir to the Yi Minority's musical heritage. He lives in Butuo, deep in the Liang Mountain heartland.

印第安人
——致西蒙·奥迪斯[1]

西蒙·奥迪斯对我说:"他们称呼
我们是印第安人,但我告诉他们,
我们不是……是阿科马族人。"

是的,在他们所谓发现你们之前,
你们祖祖辈辈就已经生活在那里。

那时候,天空的鹰眼闪烁着光,
大地涌动生殖的根。
太阳滚过苍穹古铜的脊梁,
时间的巨臂,伸向地平线的尽头。

那时候,诸神已经预言,
苍鹭的返回将带回喜讯。
而在黎明无限苍茫的曙色里,
祭司的颂词复活了死灭的星辰。

把双耳紧贴大地的胸膛,
能听见,野牛群由远及近的轰鸣,
震颤着地球渴望血液的子宫。

在那群山护卫的山顶,
酋长面对
太阳,
繁星,
河流
和岩石,

---

[1] 西蒙·奥迪斯,生于1941年,美国当今健在的最著名的印第安诗人,被称为印第安文艺复兴运动中的旗手,曾获得原住民作家社团颁发的终身成就奖。

2019.10.23

用火焰洗礼过的
诗句,告诉过子孙——
"这是我们的土地"。

西蒙·奥迪斯,不要再去申明
你们不是印第安人。
据说土地的记忆
要远远超过人类的历史。
地球还在旋转,被篡改的一切
都会被土地的记忆恢复,
神圣的太阳,公正的法官
将在时间的法庭上作出裁决。

谁是这个世界的中心?任何时候
都不要相信他们给出的结论。

Indian
—For Simon Ortiz [1]

Simon Ortiz said to me: "To them,
We are Indians, but I tell them
We are Acoma…"

Indeed, before they supposedly "discovered" you
You had dwelled in your ancestral place for ages.

All that time, light flashed in the sky's eagle eye;
The root of fertility surged in the earth;
The sun in the firmament passed over a bronze backbone,
Time stretched huge arms towards the horizon's end…

Back then, gods had made a prophecy,
An eagle's return would bring good tidings,
And a chant in the dense pre-dawn gloom
Would revive an extinguished star.

An ear pressed to the earth's chest
Would hear a bison herds thunder approaching,
Making the earth's womb tremble with thirst for blood.

Atop a bluff defended by ranged mountains
A chief would meet face-to-face
With sun
With moon
With the starry sky
With rivers
With boulders
Words made poetic through fiery ablution
Would tell his descendants,
That this land is theirs.

---

[1] Simon Ortiz, born in 1941, is one of the foremost living Native American poets. He has been termed a leading figure in the Indian cultural renaissance, and has received a Lifetime Achievement Award from the Indigenous Writers Association.

2019.10.23

Simon Ortiz, no need to proclaim
That your people are not Indians.
I have heard that the land's memory
Goes far beyond human history.
The globe still spins, and all distorted truths
Will be restored by the land's memory;
The sacred sun—that impartial judge
Will render a verdict in the courtroom of time.

Who can claim to be at the world's center?
We must never believe the conclusion they have drawn.

Translated by Denis Mair

尼子马列[1]的废墟

已看不出这里曾经有过的繁华，
正在抽穗的玉米地也寂静无声。
山梁对面的小路早被杂草覆盖，
我们的到来，并非要惊醒长眠的祖先。
那是因为彝人对自己的祖居地，
时常怀有刻骨铭心的思念和热爱。
在我们的史诗记载迁徙的描述中，
关于命运的无常，随处都能读到，
难怪在先人生活过的每一个地方，
都会油然而生一种英雄崇拜的情感。
哦，沉默的落日，你伟大的叹息
甚至超过了刺向祭祀之牛脖颈流出的血，
物质的毁灭，我们知道，谁能抗拒？
那自然的法则，就守候在生和死的隘口。

因此我才相信，生命有时候要比
死亡的严肃更要可笑，至于死亡
也许就是一个假设，我们熟谙的
某种仪式，完全属于另一个世界。

千万不要告诉那些
缺少幽默感的人，
因为我们在死亡的簿册上，
找到了一个与他相同的名字。

[1] 尼子马列，诗人母亲故乡—彝语地名。

2019.10.24

The Ruins of Nizi Malie [1]

No sign is seen that this was once a thriving place;
Hardly a rustle is heard from the cornstalks in ear;
The lane across from the ridge is choked with weeds.
We have not come to rouse our long-sleeping ancestors,
But because we are drawn to our native ground;
Our longing and love for it are etched in our bones.
In accounts of migration, as told in ancestral epics
Many passages give a sense of fate's impermanence.
No wonder, when we set foot where they dwelt
A feeling of hero worship often comes over us.
Ah, sunset silence—the grand sigh you heave surpasses
Blood from the stabbed neck of an offered bull.
We know that none can resist material destruction;
Laws of nature guard the defile where life meets death;

Thus I find something laughable in life, when compared
To death's seriousness, and what we know of death
May be our supposition, while certain rituals—
The ones we are versed in—belong wholly to another world.

By no means should you say this
To one who lacks a sense of humor,
Because there is a legend of death
In which we can find a name like his.

Translated by Denis Mair

[1] Nizi Malie is the name of a historical site in the native district of the poet's mother.

我曾看见……

我曾看见,在那群山腹地,
彝人祭司完成的一次法事。
他的声音,虽然低沉浑厚,
却能穿透万物,弥漫天地。
这样的景象总会浮现于脑海。
为了祈福,而不是诅咒,
火光和青烟告诉了所有的神灵。
牛皮的幻影飘浮于天空,
唯有颂词徐徐沉落于无限。

暴力,不在别处,它跟随人
去过许多地方,就在昨天
还在叙利亚争抢儿童的血。
所谓道义和人权,或许只是
他们宣言中用烂了的几个词。
然而,对于不同的祈福,
我们都应报以足够的尊重,
他们让我们在那个片刻
忘记了暴力和世界的苦难。

2019.10.24

Once I Saw…

Once I saw, in the heartland of ranged mountains
A Nuosu priest brought a ritual to completion.
Though his voice was a gravelly baritone,
It could penetrate all things, pervade sky and earth.
Such a picture is ever-present in my mind's eye:
It is a prayer for blessings, not a curse;
Firelight and blue smoke take a message to all deities;
Phantoms from a drumskin float across the sky;
Chanted tones sink slowly into the infinite.

Violence is not elsewhere—it follows humans
Into so many places; just yesterday
It snatched the blood of a child in Syria.
So-called "justice" and "rights" may just be words
To which people pay lip-service in manifestoes.
Yet when prayers for blessings are said in various ways
We should accord them fitting esteem:
In that moment they allow us
To look beyond the sufferings of this world.

Translated by Denis Mair

诗 人

诗人不是商业明星,也不是
电视和别的媒体上的红人。
无须收买他人去制造绯闻,
在网络空间树立虚假的对手,
以拙劣的手段提高知名度。
诗人在今天存在的理由,
是他写出的文字,无法用
金钱换算,因为每一个字
都超过了物质确定的价值。
诗人不是娱乐界的超人,
不能丢失心灵之门的钥匙。
他游走于城市和乡村,
是最后一个部落的酋长。
他用语言的稀有金属,
敲响了古老城市的钟楼。
诗人是一匹孤独的野马,
不在任何一个牧人的马群,
却始终伫立在不远的地方。
合唱队没有诗人适合的角色,
他更喜欢一个人的时候独唱。
诗人是群体中的极少数,
却选择与弱者站在一边,
纵使遭受厄运无端的击打,
也不会交出灵魂的护身符。
诗人是鸟类中的占卜者,
是最早预言春天的布谷。
他站在自己建造的山顶,
将思想的风暴吹向宇宙。

2019.10.25

有人说诗人是一个阶级,
生活在地球不同的地方
上苍,让他们存活下去吧,
因为他们,没有败坏语言,
更没有糟蹋过生命。

2019.10.25

Poet

A poet is not a magnate of commerce, nor is he
A hyped-up figure on TV or other media.
He need not pay hacks to cook up lurid stories
Or clash with fake opponents on the Web,
Or resort to ruses to generate a buzz.
The reason poets exist in the present day
Is that words they write are not exchangeable
For money, because every word
Transcends the value of material things.
He is not a superman of the entertainment world;
He cannot throw away the key to his heart;
He wanders between city and countryside;
He is a chief of the last tribe; he uses
Rare metals of language to toll the bells
That hang in the tower of an ancient city.
The poet is a lone mustang; he does not run
With horses kept by any herdsman,
Yet he always stands in their vicinity.
A poet is not suited to a role in a choral troupe:
He would rather sing in solitude.
Amid the crowd, the poet is a tiny minority,
Yet he chooses to stand on the side of the weak.
Although he suffers the blows of malign fate
He will never give up his spirit-protecting talisman.
Among birds, the poet is of the omen-bringing kind;
He is the earliest cuckoo foretelling spring.
He stands on a peak he himself erected,
Releasing his storm of thought into the cosmos.
Some say that poets themselves are a social class
Scattered in various corners of the globe.
O azure vault above, let them survive

For they would never ruin language;
Still less would they despoil life.

Translated by Denis Mair

犹太人的墓地

那是犹太人的墓地,我在华沙、
布加勒斯特、布达佩斯和布拉格
都看见过。说来也真是奇怪,
它们给我留下了极为深刻的印象。
是墓园的布局吗?当然不是。
还是环境的不同?肯定也不对,
因为欧洲的墓园大同小异。
后来在不经意中我才发现,虽然
别的地方也有失修的墓室,待清的杂草,
但却没有犹太人的墓地那样荒芜。
到处是倾斜的碑石,塌陷的地基,
发黑的苔藓覆盖了通往深处的路径。
我以为死亡对人类而言,时刻都会发生,
而后人对逝者的追忆,寄托哀思,
到墓地去倾诉,或许是最好的选择。

我在东欧看见过许多
犹太人的墓地,它们荒芜而寂寥。
这是何种原因,我问陪同的导游,
在陷入片刻的沉默后,才低声说:
"他们的亲人,都去了奥斯威辛[1],
单程车票,最终没有一个回来。"

我在东欧看见过许多
犹太人的墓地。我终于知道,
天堂或许只是我们的想象,
而地狱却与我们如影相随。

---

[1] 奥斯威辛,是纳粹德国时期建立在波兰小城奥斯威辛的集中营,大约有110万人在这一集中营被杀害,其中绝大部分是犹太人。

Jewish Graveyards

There are Jewish graveyards: I have seen them
In Warsaw and Bucharest and Prague
And in Budapest. For a strange reason
They made a huge impression on me.
Were their the layouts? Not exactly
Were the different setting? That wasn't it either,
For Europe's graveyards don't have major differences.
Later, without much thought, it dawned on me
That other places were unkept, with weeds to be cleared,
But they were not as bleak as that Jewish graveyard.
Around me were leaning plaques and sunken graves;
Blackened moss covered a lane leading to its recesses.
I feel that death will happen to humans at any time.
It is good for survivors to find an outlet for grief,
To visit the grave and call up memories of the dead.

In Eastern Europe I saw many of them—
Those Jewish graveyards so bleak and deserted.
"Why is that?" I asked the guide who was with me.
After a short silence, he said in low tones:
"Their relatives all went to Auschwitz [1]
By one-way ticket, none came back."

In Eastern Europe, there are Jewish graveyards:
I saw quite a few, and only then did I know
Heaven may only be in our imagination,
But Hell trails our steps like a shadow.

Translated by Denis Mair

---

[1] Auschwitz: A death camp built in the polish town Auschwitz during the Nazi German regime, on which about 1.1 million people were killed, among whom most were Jews.

何塞·马里亚·阿格达斯[1]

我的血液来自那些巨石,
它让我的肋骨支撑着旋转的天体。
太阳的影子
以长矛的迅疾,
降落节日的花朵。

我,何塞·马里亚·阿格达斯,
秘鲁克丘亚人,一个典型的土著。
我的思想、意识和行为方式,
与他们格格不入。
因为我相信,我们的方式
不是唯一的方式,
只有差异
才能通向包容和理解。
所以,我才要捍卫
这种方式,
就是用生命
也在所不惜。

我的身躯被驼羊的绒毛覆盖,
在安第斯山蜜蜂嗡鸣的牧场。
当雄鹰静止于
时间,
风,
吹拂着
无形的
生命的排箫。
那是我们的声音

[1] 何塞·马里亚·阿格达斯,生于1911年,秘鲁当代著名印第安人小说家、人类学家,原住民文化的捍卫者,1969年自杀身亡。

2019.10.28

穿越了无数的世纪，
见证过
血，
诞生和
毁灭。
那是我们河流的回声，
它的深沉和自由
才铸造了
人之子的灵魂。
也因为此，我们才
选择了：
在这片土地上生，
在这片土地上死。

哦，未来的朋友
这不是我的遗言。
我不是那只山上的狐狸，
它的奔跑犹如燃烧的火焰。
也不是那只山下的狐狸，
它的鸣叫固然令人悲伤。

但我要告诉大家的是：
我，何塞·马里亚·阿格达斯，
并非死于贫穷
而是自杀。
没有别的原因，
只是我不愿意看到，
我的传统——
在我活着时候
就已经死亡。没有别的原因，
这并不复杂。

José María Arguedas [1]

My blood came from huge boulders; by
    their strength
My ribs support the revolving bodies of
    heaven;
But with a lance's swiftness
The shadow of the sun
Descends upon holiday flowers.

I am José María Arguedas,
A Quechua of Peru, a typical native.
My modes of thinking and acting
Do not fit in with those of others,
Because I believe that our way
Is not the only way.
Only through differences we can find
A way to tolerance and understanding,
And so I intend to defend it:
This way of ours,
Even at the cost of my life,
I will have no regrets.

My frame was clad in llama wool,
In Andean pastures abuzz with bees
As the male eagle paused
In the silence of time
And wind
Blowing upon
The invisible pan-pipes
Of our life-force. That is our voice
Which has passed
Through uncounted centuries.
It has borne witness
To blood,

---

[1] José María Arguedas, born in 1911, was a Peruvian Indian novelist, anthropologist and defender of Indigenous rights. He committed suicide in 1969.

2019.10.28

To birth
And destruction.
That is the sound of our river,
Its profundity and freedom
Were what forged the souls
Of the sons of the People.
Because of this…
We have chosen:
To live on this piece of land,
To die on this piece of land.

Ah, friends of the future
This is not my testament,
I am not that fox on the hill—
While running it looks like flame;
I am not that fox below the hill—
Its yelps strike sorrow into human hearts.

I want to tell people this:
I, José María Arguedas
Did not die of poverty
But of suicide,
For no other reason
Than my unwillingness to see
The death of my tradition
In my own lifetime.
It was for no other reason…
Not a complicated matter.

Translated by Denis Mair

悼胡安·赫尔曼[1]

你在诗中说我
将话语抛向火,是为
在赤裸的语言之家里,
让火继续燃烧。
而你却将死亡,一次次
抛向生命,抛向火。
你知道邪恶的缘由,
最重要的是,你的声音
动摇过它的世界。
没有诅咒过生活本身,
却承受了所有的厄运。
你走的那一天,据说在
墨西哥城,有一片天堂的叶子
终于落在了你虚空的肩上。

---

[1] 胡安·赫尔曼(1930-2014)当代阿根廷著名诗人,同时也是拉美洲最伟大诗人之一,2007年塞万提斯文学奖获得者。

2019.10.28

Juan Gelman[1]

In a poem you spoke of me
Throwing words into a fire
So that fire will keep blazing
In the house of naked language.
As for you, you kept throwing your death
Into life and into fire.
You know about the causes of evil;
Most importantly, your voice
Shook up the world of death.
You would never have cursed life itself,
You took fate's malignity on yourself.
On the day you departed, it is said
In Mexico City, a leaf from heaven
Finally fell onto your empty shoulder.

Translated by Denis Mair

[1] Juan Gelman (1930-2014) was a contemporary Argentinian poet and one of the foremost figures of Latin American poetry. He was recipient of the 2007 Cervantes Literary Award.

自由的另一种解释

让我们庆祝人类的又一次解放,
在意志的天空上更大胆地飞翔。
从机器抽象后的数据,你将阅读我,
而我对你而言,只是移动的位置。
我的甜言蜜语,不再属于一个人,
如果需要,全人类都能分享。
今天这个世界发生了什么,
我们都能在第一时间知晓。
而我,在地球的任何一个地方,
亲爱的,谢天谢地,你都
尽管可以把我放心地丢失,
再玩一次猫捉老鼠的游戏。

2019.10.28

An Alternate Explanation of Freedom

2
0
1
9
.
1
0
.
2
8

Let us celebrate yet another liberation of mankind,
As it soars boldly across the open sky of will.
Using machine-extracted data you will read me,
And to you I am no more than a moving location.
My sweet words no longer belong to one person,
If needed, all of mankind can enjoy them.
Whatever happens in the world today,
All of us can find out right away,
And I could be anyplace on the globe.
Dear ones, thank heavens, please feel at ease:
You can be done with me anytime you want,
Then go on to play the next cat and mouse game.

Translated by Denis Mair

大 河
——献给黄河[1]

[1] 黄河:发源于青藏高原,中国第二大河,世界第五大河,全长约5464公里,在山东东营境内流入大海。

在更高的地方,雪的反光
沉落于时间的深处,那是诸神的
圣殿,肃穆而整齐的合唱
回响在黄金一般隐匿的额骨
在这里被命名之前,没有内在的意义
只有诞生是唯一的死亡
只有死亡是无数的诞生

那时候,光明的使臣伫立在大地的中央
没有选择,纯洁的目光化为风的灰烬
当它被正式命名的时候,万物的节日
在众神的旷野之上,吹动着持续的元素
打开黎明之晨,一望无际的赭色疆域
鹰的翅膀闪闪发光,影子投向了大地
所有的先知都蹲在原初的那个入口
等待着加冕,在太阳和火焰的引领下
白色的河床,像一幅立体的图画
天空的祭坛升高,神祇的银河显现

那时候,声音循环于隐晦的哑然
惊醒了这片死去了但仍然活着的大海
无须俯身匍匐也能隐约地听见
来自遥远并非空洞的永不疲倦的喧嚣
这是诸神先于创造的神圣的剧场
威名显赫的雪族十二子就出生在这里
它们的灵肉彼此相依,没有敌对杀戮

对生命的救赎不是从这里开始
当大地和雪山的影子覆盖头顶
哦大河,在你出现之前,都是空白
只有词语,才是绝对唯一的真理
在我们,他们,还有那些未知者的手中
盛开着渴望的铁才转向静止的花束
寒冷的虚空,白色的睡眠,倾斜的深渊
石头的鸟儿,另一张脸,无法平息的白昼

此时没有君王,只有吹拂的风,消失的火
还有宽阔,无限,荒凉,巨大的存在
谁是这里真正的主宰?那创造了一切的幻影
哦光,无处不在的光,才是至高无上的君王
是它将形而上的空气燃烧成了沙子
光是天空的脊柱,光是宇宙的长矛
哦光,光是光的心脏,光的巨石轻如羽毛
光倾泻在拱顶的上空,像一层失重的瀑布
当光出现的时候,太阳,星星,纯粹之物
都见证了一个伟大的仪式,哦光,因为你
在明净抽象的凝块上我第一次看见了水

从这里出发。巴颜喀拉[1]创造了你
想象吧,一滴水,循环往复的镜子
琥珀色的光明,进入了转瞬即逝的存在
远处凝固的冰,如同纯洁的处子
想象吧,是哪一滴水最先预言了结局?
并且最早敲响了那蓝色国度的水之门
幽暗的孕育,成熟的汁液,生殖的热力
当图腾的徽记,照亮了传说和鹰巢的空门
大地的胎盘,在吮吸,在颤栗,在聚拢
扎曲之水,卡日曲之水,约古宗列曲之水[2]

1 巴颜喀拉:巴颜喀拉是黄河源头当地民族语一地名,意思是富饶的山之口。
2 扎曲、卡日曲、约古宗列曲:均为黄河源头三条最初源流的名字。

还有那些星罗棋布，蓝宝石一样的海子

这片白色的领地没有此岸和彼岸
只有水的思想——和花冠——爬上栅栏
每一次诞生，都是一次壮丽的分娩
如同一种启示，它能听见那遥远的回声
在这里只有石头，是没有形式的意志
它的内核散发着黑暗的密语和隐喻
哦只要有了高度，每一滴水都让我惊奇
千百条静脉畅饮着未知无色的甘露
羚羊的独语，雪豹的弧线，牛角的鸣响
在风暴的顶端，唤醒了沉睡的信使

哦大河，没有谁能为你命名
是因为你的颜色，说出了你的名字
你的手臂之上，生长着金黄的麦子
浮动的星群吹动着植物的气息
黄色的泥土，被揉捏成炫目的身体
舞蹈的男人和女人隐没于子夜
他们却又在彩陶上获得了永生
是水让他们的双手能触摸梦境
还是水让祭祀者抓住冰的火焰
在最初的曙光里，孩子，牲畜，炊烟
每一次睁开眼睛，神的面具都会显现

哦大河，在你的词语成为词语之前
你从没有把你的前世告诉我们
在你的词语成为词语之后
你也没有呈现出铜镜的反面
你的倾诉和呢喃，感动灵性的动物
渴望的嘴唇上缀满了杉树和蕨草

你是原始的母亲，曾经也是婴儿
群山护卫的摇篮见证了你的成长
神授的史诗，手持法器的钥匙
当你的秀发被黎明的风梳理
少女的身姿，牵引着众神的双目
那炫目的光芒让瞩望者失明
那是你的蓝色时代，无与伦比的美
宣告了真理就是另一种虚幻的存在
如果真的不知道你的少女时代
我们，他们，那些尊称你为母亲的人
就不配获得作为你后代子孙的资格
作为母亲的形象，你一直就站在那里
如同一块巨石，谁也不可以撼动

我们把你称为母亲，那黝黑的乳头
在无数的黄昏时分发出吱吱的声音
在那大地裸露的身躯之上，我们的节奏
就是波浪的节奏，就是水流的节奏
我们和种子在春天许下的亮晶晶的心愿
终会在秋天纯净的高空看见果实的图案
就在夜色来临之前，无边的倦意正在扩散
像回到栏圈的羊群，牛粪的火塘发出红光
这是自由的小路，从帐房到黄泥小屋
石头一样的梦，爬上了高高的瞭望台
那些孩子在皮袍下熟睡，树梢上的秋叶
吹动着月亮和星星在风中悬挂的灯盏
这是大陆高地梦境里超现实的延伸
万物的律动和呼吸，摇响了千万条琴弦

哦大河，在你沿岸的黄土深处
埋葬过英雄和智者，沉默的骨头

举起过正义的旗帜，掀起过愤怒的风暴
没有这一切，豪放、悲凉、忧伤的歌谣
就不会把生和死的誓言掷入暗火
那些皮肤一样的土墙倒塌了，新的土墙
又被另外的手垒起，祖先的精神不朽
穿过了千年还赶着牲口的旅人
见证了古老的死亡和并不新鲜的重生
在这片土地上，那些沉默寡言的人们
当暴风雨突然来临，正以从未有过的残酷
击打他们的头颅和家园，最悲壮的时候
他们在这里成功地阻挡了凶恶的敌人
在传之后世并不久远的故事里，讲述者
就像在述说家传的闪着微光温暖的器皿

哦大河，你的语言胜过了黄金和宝石
你在诗人的舌尖上被神秘的力量触及
隐秘的文字，加速了赤裸的张力
在同样事物的背后，生成在本质之间
面对他们，那些将会不朽的吟诵者
无论是在千年之前还是在千年之后
那沉甸甸丰硕的果实都明亮如火
是你改变了自己存在于现实的形式
世上没有哪一条被诗神击中的河流
能像你一样成为了一部诗歌的正典
你用词语搭建的城池，至今也没有对手

当我们俯身于你，接纳你的盐和沙漏
看不见的手，穿过了微光闪现的针孔
是你重新发现并确立了最初的水
唯有母语的不确定能抵达清澈之地
或许，这就是东方文明至高点的冠冕

作为罗盘和磁铁最中心的红色部分
凭借包容异质的力量,打开铁的褶皱
在离你最近的地方,那些不同的族群
认同共生,对抗分离,守护传统
他们用不同的语言描述过你落日的辉煌
在那更远的地方,在更高的群山之巅
当自由的风从宇宙的最深处吹来
你将独自掀开自己金黄神圣的面具
好让自由的色彩编织未来的天幕
好让已经熄灭的灯盏被太阳点燃
好让受孕的子宫绽放出月桂的香气
好让一千个新的碾子和古旧的石磨
在那堆满麦子的广场发出隆隆的响声
好让那炉灶里的柴火越烧越旺
火光能长时间地映红农妇的脸庞

哦大河,你的两岸除了生长庄稼
还养育了一代又一代名不虚传的歌手
他们用不同的声调,唱出了这个世界
不用翻译,只要用心去聆听
就会被感动一千次一万次的歌谣
你让歌手遗忘了身份,也遗忘了自己
在这个星球上,你是东方的肚脐
你的血管里流淌着不同的血
但他们都是红色的,这个颜色只属于你
你不是一个人的记忆,你如果是——
也只能是成千上万个人的记忆
对!那是集体的记忆,一个民族的记忆

当你还是一滴水的时候,还是
胚胎中一粒微小的生命的时候

当你还是一种看不见的存在
不足以让我们发现你的时候
当你还只是一个词,仅仅是一个开头
并没有成为一部完整史诗的时候
哦大河,你听见过大海的呼唤吗?
同样,大海!你浩瀚,宽广,无边无际
自由的元素,就是你高贵的灵魂
作为正义的化身,捍卫生命和人的权利
我们的诗人才用不同的母语
毫不吝啬地用诗歌赞颂你的光荣
但是,大海,我也要在这里问你
当你涌动着永不停息的波浪,当宇宙的
黑洞,把暗物质的光束投向你的时候
当倦意随着潮水,巨大的黑暗和寂静
占据着多维度的时间与空间的时候
当白色的桅杆如一面面旗帜,就像
成千上万的海鸥在正午翻飞舞蹈的时候
哦大海!在这样的时刻,多么重要!
你是不是也呼唤过那最初的一滴水
是不是也听见了那天籁之乐的第一个音符
是不是也知道了创世者说出的第一个词!

这一切都有可能,因为这条河流
已经把它的全部隐秘和故事告诉了我们
它是现实的,就如同它滋养的这片大地
我们在它的岸边劳作歌唱,生生不息
一代又一代,迎接了诞生,平静地死亡
它恩赐予我们的幸福,安宁,快乐和达观
已经远远超过了它带给我们的悲伤和不幸
可以肯定,这条河流以它的坚韧,朴实和善良
给一个东方辉煌而又苦难深重的民族

传授了最独特的智慧以及作为人的尊严和道义
它是精神的,因为它岁岁年年
都会浮现在我们的梦境里,时时刻刻
都会潜入在我们的意识中,分分秒秒
都与我们的呼吸、心跳和生命在一起
哦大河!请允许我怀着最大的敬意
——把你早已闻名遐迩的名字
再一次深情地告诉这个世界:黄河!

Great River
—To the Yellow River [1]

[1] The Yellow River, China's second largest river and fifth largest in the world, originates on the Qinghai-Tibet Plateau. With a total length of 5464 kilometers, it enters the ocean within the borders of Dongying, Shandong Province.

Up in a higher place, where light reflected from snow
Subsides into depths of time, that is a tabernacle
Of the gods, where a solemn, even-toned chorus
Resounds upon a brow sequestered like gold ore
As yet unnamed, no fixed meaning inheres there
Its sole death is none other than birth
Its countless births none other than death

Meantime, light the envoy takes a stance at the land's center
With a pure gaze that cannot but change into embers of wind
Once the name is given, a carnival of all beings, on the plain of gods
Pipes a tune that animates an ever-unfolding ground-stuff
As dawn's veil parts over rangeland of boundless ochre
Light flashes on an eagle's wings, casts their shadow on the earth
All prophets stoop at the entranceway of origination
Waiting to be crowned, ushered by sunbeams and flames
And in a white riverbed, like a voluminous tableau
The sky's altar ascends, the milky way of gods manifests

Meantime, sound circulating in obscure muteness
Rouses a great sea, deathly and yet alive
No need to crouch down, the heedful ear discerns
An untiring clamor, remote of source but not vacuous
From the sacred theater of gods, prior to creation
The legendary Twelve Tribes of Snow take birth
Their spirit and flesh cohering, never opposed and warring

The salvation of life begins far from here and now
When heads are shaded by shadows of snowy peaks
O Great River, before you appeared, all was blank
And the Word alone was sole truth, only thenceforth

Could iron abloom with longing, held by us
    and all our relations,
Change to garlands of equipoise, down to
    future generations
Frigid emptiness, slumber in whiteness, abyss
    being toppled
Bird of stone, another kind of face, ever-
    unsettled daylight

That time had no rulers, only stirring wind
    and passing fire
In company with Being—vast and limitless,
    desolate and immense
Who was true sovereign here? The figment
    that created everything
O Light, omnipresent light, which alone is the supreme ruler
By light alone could ethereal air be enkindled to dust specks
Light is the backbone of heaven, it is the lance of the cosmos
O Light…light is a heart pumping itself, a boulder as buoyant as
    feathers
Pouring through airspace of the sky-vault…like a cataract in free-fall
Upon light's appearance, sun and stars, such pure entities
Bear witness to a grand ceremony, O Light, because of you
In an abstract yet luminous consolidation I first saw water

From there you issued forth. Bayankela[1] created you
Just imagine, one drop of water, a mirror in cyclic circulation
Radiance mottled like agate, going into entities that vanish in a trice
Or distant concretions of ice, maiden-like in their purity
Just imagine, which single drop first foretold such outcomes
And first pounded the door of water's blue kingdom?
Gestation in seclusion, sap of maturation, heat of fertility
As the eagle's nest and gateway of legend light up totemic emblems
The placenta of earth is sucking and quivering and conglomerating
Water of Zhaqu, water of Kariqu, water of Yueguzongliequ[2]
And all those filigree lakes strewn like turquoise stones

---

[1] Bayankela is a mountainous area at the source of the Yellow River. In the language of local inhabitants, its name means "opening in rich mountains."

[2] Zhaqu, Kariqu and Yueguzongliequ are the first three source streams of the Yellow River.

This territory of whiteness has no near shore or yonder shore
It has only water's thinking—corolla of a flower that climbed a
    railing
Each birth that takes place is a magnificent nativity
Like a revelation, in which that remote echo is heard
Here there is only stone, volition has not taken form
With an inner core emitting coded suggestions of darkness
By virtue of height alone, each drop of water amazes us
Thousands of veins slurp down its colorless balm as yet unfelt
Soliloquy of antelope, arc of snow leopard, horned bellow
At a storm's apex, shaking awake the drowsy messenger

O Great River, nobody can give you a name
Because your very color gives utterance to your name
On your arms grow fields of golden wheat
Stars poised on high stir winds in herbage-scented air
Yellow mud is molded into dazzling bodies
Dancing men and women disappear at midnight
Yet gain lasting life on swirls of painted pottery
Water allowed their hands to feel the touch of dreams
Enabled a maker of offerings to grasp the fire within ice
By dawn's first light, in children and livestock and smoke
Whenever eyes opened, a mask of god might appear

O Great River, before your words were spoken as words
You never told us of your past lifetimes
Once your words were spoken as words
You never revealed your mirror's obverse
Your confiding murmurs moved spirit-endowed creatures
Yearning lips were dotted with fir trees and bracken
You are the primal mother; once you were an infant
A protective cradle of mountains witnessed your growth
Divinely inspired epic, with ritual implement in hand as key
When your lustrous hair was combed by wind at dawn
Your girlish poise commanded the glances of gods
Such dazzling beams were enough to blind all gazers
That was your blue era, time of overpowering beauty

Declaring that truth is another suppositional quality
If knowledge of your girlhood years were to slip away
We and all others who give you the title Mother
Would be unworthy and unfit to be your progeny
In your motherly image, you have long stood before us
Like a megalith, not to be shaken by anyone

We give you the title Mother, whose dark nipples at dusk
Were broached countless times with sssp-sssp-ing sounds
On the naked body of the good earth, our rhythm
Is the rhythm of waves, the rhythm of flowing water
Along with seeds in springtime we make lucid vows
High skies of autumn in time show scenes of fruition
Before the dark of night comes, a boundless weariness expands
Like returning sheep, as yak chips glow ruddy in a fireplace
This is the lane of freedom, from yurt to mud-brick house
Where dreams like stones climb to lofty vantage points
Children sleep under fur robes, and autumn leaves sway
In windy treetops hung with stars and moon for lamps
On this high plateau dreams extend insurreal directions
A music is made in patterned moves and breaths of creatures

O Great River, deep in the yellow earth along your banks
Are buried many heroes and wise ones, their silent bones
Once raised the banner of justice, stirred storms of wrath
Had all this never been, mortal oaths wouldn't have been cast
Toward latent fire in tones of bold, sorrowful, plaintive songs
Earthen walls of uniform color having fallen, new earthen walls
Were raised by other hands, but enduring spirits of forebears
Abided and passed through a millennial caravan with its livestock
Witnessing ancient death and new births that were surely no novelty
On this stretch of land dwelt people who were silent and voiceless
When the tempest came, raining blows of unheard cruelty
On body and beloved ground, testing every ounce of mettle
They succeeded in holding back the rapacious enemy
In stories thereof, handed down from living memory, the narrators
Are like those who tell of heirlooms with their warm auras

O Great River, your language outdoes gold and precious stones
On the tongue-tip of your poet, the jolt of mysterious force
Accesses secret word-strings, stepping up a naked tension
Behind kindred entities, generating life among substances
Facing those whose intoned words prove to be undying
Whether of the millennium past or the millennium to come
We feel the weight and luminosity of their abundant fruits
And that is you, altering your form of existence in reality
In this world, no other river touched by the god of poetry
Resembles the poetic canon you lent yourself to
The moat of words you have built is still unrivalled

When we bend toward you, to receive salt and hourglass sand
An unseen hand passes through a glinting needle's eye
That is your original water, newly discovered and verified
It takes the mother tongue's indeterminacy to reach that pristine spot
Or this may be the crowning vantage point of Oriental civilization
It is the magnetic red spot at the center of a geomancer's dial
By tolerance of otherness, it widens the creases in iron
In the place closest to you, those diverse ethnic groups
Identify with co-existence, oppose division, guard tradition
In different languages they describe the brilliance of sunset
In that faraway place, nestled high among ranged mountains
When freedom blows hither on a wind from depths of the cosmos
All alone, you eschew your mask of sacred yellow
So freedom's color can weave the future's sky-canopy
So extinguished lamps can be relit by the sun
So a fertile womb can bloom with scent of osmanthus
So a thousand grain mills along with timeworn millstones
Can grind and rumble through piles of grain on plazas
So firewood in stove-bellies can burn more hotly
Casting red light on farm wives' faces for years to come

O Great River! Your two banks, aside from growing crops
Nurtured generations of singers, each worthy of renown
Each in different vocal tones put this world into song
Into songs needing no translation, only a heedful heart

They have power to move listeners time and time again
You make singers forget their lot in life, forget themselves
On this planet, you are the navel of the Orient
Through your vessels trickle different types of blood
Yet all are red, and this color belongs to you alone
You are not a single person's memory, if anyone's—
You can only be found in the memory of millions
Yes, it is collective memory, the memory of a people

When you were still a single drop of water,
Still a tiny portion of life within an embryo
When you were still an unseen entity
Not big enough to be discovered by us
When you were just a word, an opening
Not having assumed the proportions of an epic
O Great River! Did you hear the call from the ocean?
Likewise, Great Sea! Across your unbounded reaches
Freedom is the very element of your esteemed soul
Embodying justice, you defend life and human rights
Only for such causes will poets of various mother tongues
Do their utmost to praise your glory in their verses
Yet at this time, Great Sea, I have to ask a question
Amid your ever-surging swells, when rays of dark-matter
Beam down on you from black holes of the cosmos
When weariness follows your tides and a huge, dark stillness
Occupies the many dimensions of space and time
When whiteness flies like banners from masts, resembling
Thousands of seagulls in a wheeling dance at noon
O Great Sea! At such a time, it is important to know
Have you called out to that original, single drop?
Have you heard the first note of the piping of Heaven?
Do you know the first word spoken by the creator?

All such things are possible, because this watercourse
Has already told us its entire secret history
It is real, just like the land it moistens and nurtures
On its banks we work and sing, life always engenders life

Through generations, welcoming births, dying placidly
It grants us life's gifts, quiet days, joy and acceptance
Now they outweigh by far the sorrow and misery it brings
Without question, this river with its tenacity and earthy goodness
Has imparted to a remarkable but long-suffering Oriental people
A singular wisdom, as well as its moral dignity as part of humanity
It is of the spirit, because the onrush of years has never kept it
From manifesting in our dreams; as hours rush by
It slips into our consciousness; as minutes slip away
It is part of our breath and heartbeat and being alive
O Great River! Allow me once more, with great reverence
And deep sentiment, to tell the world again
Your name of enduring renown: **YELLOW RIVER!**

        Translated by Denis Mair

火焰上的辩词

> 我在火塘的上方
> 另一个我
> 在火塘的下方
> 不是我被火焰分割
> 而是我与另一个我
> 在语言的沙场
> 进行着殊死的搏斗!
>
> ——题记

2019.8

我:
我将返回源头
河流的静脉发出
子宫白色的光 [1]
鹰翅的羽毛 [2] 悬垂于
天宇寂静的门户
将神枝插满大地
星象隐秘循环往复
我不会真的死亡
死亡只是一种仪式
在飞鸟的影子里
在石头脊柱的核心
语言沉没于风的穹顶
而我在火焰上的词语
终于融化成了泪滴。

另一个我:
时间或许是虚拟的存在
万物通过死亡见证一切

---

[1] 在诺苏神话中,人类存在始于白色,终于白色。生前灵魂来自雪乡,死后通过白色道路去往来世。

[2] 诺苏人认为鹰是神圣祖先。

在空旷粗粝的原野
蚁穴的智慧不为人知
那是环形交错的迷宫
国王的威严呼风唤雨
不同的等级列队而行
它们的疆域足够辽阔
积累的财富装满了国库
但是一只巨大的牛蹄
纯属偶然踏碎了蚁穴
我不知道蚂蚁的触觉
是否听到了这死亡的消息
但这并非偶然的结局
却改变了一个王国的命运。

我:
在母语的声音里回去
久违的高地闪现着蓝光
被铁的火镰[1]点燃的蒿草
漂浮着乳汁和生殖的香味
潜入词语最深的根部
吮吸被遗忘的盐的密码
沿着送魂经的方向行进
毕摩告诉我,语言的记忆
比土地的记忆更要久长
回到母语的故乡和疆域
诗人才会成为真的祭司
词语将在风中涌动光芒
神授的力量永不枯竭
创造的火焰再不会熄灭。

1 火镰是诺苏人用来生火的器具,由钢片和火绒及火石组成。钢片撞击火石产生火花,点燃火绒。

2019.8

另一个我:
为所有的生物哭泣
因为每一天每一个时辰
都有兄弟姊妹在死亡
我们看见资本和技术的逻辑
成为了这个世界的主宰
每一个临界死亡的植物
为我们敲响了世纪的丧钟
所有弱势微小的生命
发出的呐喊虽然微弱
但它依然洞穿了铜墙铁壁
这穿越针孔和未来的声音
已经响彻天宇之外
不要阻挡这正义的呼唤
它不会被任何力量消减。

我:
摘下我古老的面具
真实地面对这个世界
我是雄鹰唯一的儿子
父子连名是我们的传统
捍卫荣誉比生命更为重要
当我们的肩上落满鸦群
部落的彩旗迎风飘扬
从先辈那里获取智慧
旋转的酒杯传递着死亡
为了传统而延续生命
这并非是个人的选择
集体的力量在牛的脖颈
生命的存在铸造颅骨
它在最后战胜了虚无。

另一个我：
在这片生我养我的土地
当犁铧翻开它的心脏
我已经再也无法看见
它的血管流出鲜红的汁液
没有一只蚯蚓在眼前蠕动
那些微小无名的生命
早已被无情的技术杀戮
谁能为消失的事物忏悔？
罪过至今未有谁来承担
当我们搬开煮熟的土豆
总会想起大地的恩情
但是当吟诵古老的谚语
我们便会在模糊的泪眼中
看见已经逝去的家园。

我：
赞颂每一种古老的粮食
是诗人最不可剥夺的天职
我们把苦荞称为母亲
那是因为它延续了生命
你能在我们的部落中看见
母亲在用咀嚼过的荞麦
口对口地喂养怀中的婴儿
当那高地上生长的荞麦
在那星光下自由地摇曳
它的故事将被我们诉说
成为一个民族集体的记忆
不知道是从什么时候开始
对它们的赞颂就成为了习惯
多么幸运，这是我们的使命。

另一个我：
在我家中的墙壁上
挂着两副古老的马鞍
一副马鞍是公性的
另一副当然就是母性
我的祖先征战的时候
如果佩戴公性的马鞍
母性的就会守护着家园
谁能解释这其中的缘由？
每一种生命的存在
似乎都被别的生命护佑
一个个体生命的毁灭
将预示出另一个的不测
我们不能为一个弱者的死亡
而像一个旁观者熟视无睹。

我：
穿过了钢铁和资本的峡谷
我听见了口弦的诉说
那声音是如此的微弱
但它是另一种动人的语言
它是最基本古老的词汇
只表达自由和爱情的含义
那纯粹的弹拨来自灵魂
每一个音符都扣人心弦
这样的旋律如泣如诉
像一把匕首刺中了心脏
谁能说出演奏者的名字？
他分明就是神灵的化身
只要能听懂这其中的奥秘
你就是一个真正的彝人。

另一个我：
那是我的荞麦地
生长于时间的回忆
风吹过麦尖窸窣有声
在那白银一般的夜空
布满了黄金切割的影子
那是空中倒挂的摇篮
摇响了手中催眠的铃铛
萤火沉落于季风的海洋
完整的麦地开始飞翔
我已经很难站在山顶
去瞩望落日无形的翅膀
因为那星光下的麦地
已经看不见那个孩子
还在那里听风的声音。

我：
我会秉承我的方式
那是群山的传统
那是火焰的钥匙
那是燃烧的格言
那是从创世纪开始
就在血液里的那些东西
当群山在灵魂中
注定成为了一种影子
当钥匙被火焰一千次地
纯洁和净化
当格言成为了铠甲
那些血液里的东西
总会在返乡的路上
发出羊皮鼓面的声音。

另一个我：
站在碉楼的高处
那里是祖先的疆域
四周是护卫的群山
河流奔腾于幽深的峡谷
我能听懂它们的诉说
野鸡高声地鸣叫
那是一个求偶的季节
松鼠留下秘密的语言
山鹰注视着野兔的轨迹
在那阳光反射的岩石上
斑斓的昆虫拖住了时间
更远的地方，蜿蜒的路上
那个穿小裤脚的男人
开始唱一曲布拖高腔。

我：
那条河流蜿蜒而下
穿越了古老的语言
它在词语的核心
绽放出骨质的光芒
每一滴水都被镀金
如同柔软的金属
我们的诗歌将它赞颂
因为它是家园的屏障
不是每一条大河
都能将灵魂变得沉重
不是每一条河流的名字
都能让词语感到疼痛
有时它并非是一种存在
但它的伤痕却清晰可见。

另一个我：
在通往吉勒布特的山坡上
那一棵树已经站立了好久
没有人知道它经历过的时光
它的存在似乎就是一种隐喻
在黎明点燃群山的时候
风的诉说将它的歌谣吹动
当星光布满透明的穹顶
它的孤独盛满了大地的杯盏
那些茂密的森林曾被大肆砍伐
或许并不仅仅是为了人类的生存
作为一棵树你迎送过无数的路人
在他们的眼里你就是神灵的化身
你的枝叶时常飘浮于另一个空间
潜藏于意识中的树，战胜了死亡。

Disputation Over the Flames

I am over a hearth
My other self
Is down in that hearth
It's not that flames have severed me
But that I and my other self
Are engaged in mortal combat
On the battlefield of language

1. In Nuosu mythology, human existence begins and ends in whiteness. Before birth, souls come from a "land of snow," and after death they travel along a white road to the afterworld.
2. The Nuosu people believe in the eagle as a divine progenitor.

Myself:

I am about to return to the source
Behold the whiteness of womb-light [1]
Gleaming from riverine veins
An eagle suspended by its pinions
Swoops from heaven's silent gate [2]
To insert holy branches across the land
As star signs cycle through hidden courses
I shall not truly die
Death is only a ritual
In the shadow of a flying bird
In the core of a rocky spine
Speech sinks into the lonely sky-vault
And my words above these flames
Transform themselves into tears

My Other Self:

Time is perhaps a virtual dimension
Living things by dying bear witness to all
In a wild place…weed-choked and deserted
An anthill shows intelligence that few understand
Within its maze of interlocking rings
All transpires under a monarch's beck and call
Each caste marches in distinct formation

Their rangeland gives them plenty of room
With stores of wealth to fill their treasury
But purely by chance, a passing ox
Smashed their nest with its giant hoof
I don't know if the antennae of ants
Could sense the imminence of death
But this ending, for whatever reason,
Added a dark chapter to that kingdom's fate

Myself:
In the sounds of my mother tongue I return
Beckoned by half-light to that long-missed highland
Amid tall grass, which gives off a milky fertile scent,
Sparks from a fire-sickle [1] fall and smolder
And crept into the deepest roots
Nursing the forgotten code of salt
Advancing in the direction of the Soul Sending Scripture
The bimo-priest tells me that the memory of language
Is far longer-lasting than the land's memory
Only back on the rangeland of his mother tongue
Can the poet become a true priest
Whose words stir a river of light in the wind
With divine power that never runs dry
Flames of creation inextinguishable

My Other Self:
O weep for all living things
For brothers and sisters are dying
Every hour of every day
We see the logic of capital and machines
Gaining sovereignty over this world
Every plant on the verge of obliteration
Tolls the mourning bell of this century
Though disadvantaged lives, taken together,
Can raise no more than a muted outcry
Yet it pierces fortress walls of iron
Passing through a needle's eye, into the future

---

[1] A "fire-sickle" is a fire starter used by the Nuo-su people. It is a piece of steel carried in a pouch with tinder: when struck against a stone, the "fire-sickle" produces sparks.

To resound beyond heaven's dome
Do not obstruct this call for justice
It will not be abrogated by any force

Myself:
Strip off my ancient mask
To face this world truthfully
I am the eagle's sole begotten son
We bear patronymic names by tradition
Defense of honor outweighs life
As crows flock and land on our shoulders
The wind lifts our colored tribal banners
Wisdom comes down from our forefathers
Vows to die are passed around with a wine cup
For the sake of tradition's extended life
This was not by one person's choice
In a bull's neck lies our collective strength
In a skull forged by travails of existence
To prevail in the end over nothingness

My Other Self:
On this soil that birthed and raised me
As my plow turns over its living heart
I cannot see any longer
The stain of blood runs from its veins
No earthworm wriggles before my eyes
Tiny nameless lives have been slaughtered
By heartless mechanisms
Which person will repent for vanished things?
Up to now, none accept the burden of sin
Each time a boiled potato is peeled
We remember how the land nurtures us
But as we recite sayings of the old days
We see, through eyes swimming in tears,
That our homeland is already gone

Myself:

To praise all ancient food crops
Is the poet's inalienable vocation
We call bitter buckwheat "Mother"
Because it keeps us alive
Among people of our tribe you can see
A mother chews buckwheat, then passes it
Mouth-to-mouth to the child in her lap
As long as buckwheat grows on highland slopes
Tossing freely under starlight
Its story will be told by our people
It has entered our collective memory
No one can say when praise for buckwheat
First became one of our customs
As luck would have it, this is a mission for poets

My Other Self:

On the wall of my house
I've hung two old-fashioned saddles
One of the saddles is male
The other, of course, is female
When my ancestor went on campaigns
With the male saddle,
The female one stayed to watch his household
Who can explain the basis for this?
The existence of every living thing
Apparently was protected by another being
The destruction of an individual life
Portended ill fate for another life
We cannot witness the death of the weak
And treat it as a matter of no concern

Myself:

Having passed through capital's steel canyons
I hear the plaint of a jaw harp
It is such a thin, reedy sound
But it has a moving language of its own

2019.8

O, that is the most primal, ancient tongue
Conveying nothing but freedom and love
Plucked straight from the soul
Each note touches the heartstrings
It strikes up a plaintive melody
Able to pierce the heart like a knife
Who can speak the player's name?
He is clearly a divine force personified
If only you can understand its subtle secret
Then you are truly a member of the Yi people

My Other Self:
That is my field of buckwheat
It is memory growing through time
Wind rustles the nodding tips of buckwheat
And up in silvery reaches of the night sky
Where a shadow is demarcated with glints of metal
That is an inverted cradle, hanging in space
Which shakes the hypnotic bell in my hand
Fireflies are immersed in night's sea
The whole buckwheat field rises in flight
It is not easy now to reach a mountain peak
To watch sunset spread its unseen wings
Because in that starlit buckwheat field
One can no longer see that young boy
Who once stayed listening to rustling wind

Myself:
I will inherit my ways
Which are the tradition of the mountains
Which are the key to the fire
Which are the burning proverbs
And which are those in our blood
Since the beginning of the world.
In our souls those ranged mountains
Are destined to become a shadow

When the key is cleansed and purified
One thousand times by flame
Then proverbs become the armor
That flows within in our blood
Emitting sounds of a sheepskin drum
Along the road to our homeland

My Other Self:
Stand high on a fortified tower
Yonder is the rangeland of ancestors
On all sides protected by linked mountains
Brawling rivers race through deep hidden gorges
I make out the sense of their confessions
The crowing of feral chickens
Can be heard in the mating season
The chatter of squirrels imparts secrets
An eagle fixes its stare on a rabbit's path
And on a boulder catching afternoon sunlight
Spotted beetles tug at threads of time
Farther off, along a winding road
A young man in sky-blue pantaloons
Sings a ballad in the high tones of Butuo

Myself:
The river wends its way down the valley
Passing through an ancient language
From within the core of words
It blooms into corollas of bone
Every droplet is gilded
Like beads of softened metal
To which our poems give praise
For that is a moat around our homeland
Not every major watercourse
Can instill such gravity in men's souls
Not every major river's name
Carries such freight of pain in a word
At times, it is not an entity to be known

Yet its scars are clearly visible

My Other Self:
On the road that leads to Jile Bute
There is a tree that has stood for centuries
No one knows the times it's been through
Its existence seems to hint at something
When dawn comes to ignite mountaintops
Rustling breezes stir it into plaintive song
As stars gleam in heaven's clear reaches
Its solitude fills the good earth's cup
Once-lush forests were willfully laid low
Maybe not even for the sake of survival
O tree, you greeted and sent off countless strangers
In their eyes, you were an avatar of divine force
With branches ever swaying in an alternate space
Deep down in our minds, you overcome death

Translated by Denis Mair

死神与我们的速度谁更快
——献给抗击2020新型冠状病毒的所有人

死神的速度比我们更快，
因为它出其不意，
它在枪响之前已经跑在了前面。
死神！这一次似乎更快，
它莫非是造物主
又一次最新的创造？
还是人类在今天
必须勇敢面对的更严峻的考验？
死神并非都戴着明显的面具，
这一次它同样隐没于空气。
死神的速度比我们更快，
在统计的数字出来之前
它罪恶的手仍然在使用
那该被一千次诅咒的加法！
因为死亡的数字还在增加，
而此刻，我们渴望的只是减法！
死神已经到过许多地方，
杀死了老人、青年，还伤害了
我们柔弱的孩子，
肆虐我们的城市、街道以及花园，
它所到之处，敲击着黑色的铁。

死神的速度比我们更快，
因为它出其不意
它在枪响之前已经跑在了前面。
然而，这一次！就像有过的上一次！
我们与死神的比赛，无疑

已经进入了你死我活的阶段，
谁是最后的强者还在等待答案。
让我们把全部的爱编织成风，
送到每一个角落，以人类的名义。
让我们用成千上万个人的意志，
凝聚成一个强大的生命，在穹顶
散发出比古老的太阳更年轻的光。
让我们打开所有的窗户，将梦剪裁成星星
再一次升起在蓝色幕布一般的天空。

你说死神的速度比我们更快，不！
我不相信！因为我看见这场
与死亡的赛跑正在缩短着距离。
请相信我们将会创造一个新的纪录，
全世界都瞪大着眼睛，在看着我们！
我们的速度正在分秒之间被创造，
这是领袖的速度，就在第一时间，
那坚定、自信、有力的声音传遍了
祖国的大地、森林、天空和海洋，
创造这一速度的领跑者永远站在最前列。
这是人民的速度，无论是城市还是乡村，
每一个公民都投入了没有硝烟的战斗，
任何一个岗位都有临危不惧的人坚守。
这是体制的速度，一声声驰援的号令
让无数支英雄儿女的队伍集结在武汉。
这是集体的速度，个人主义的狭隘和自私
在这里没有生存的空间，因为严峻的现实
告诉我们，任何生命都需要相互依存。
这是奉献的速度，这种奉献绝不是一句豪言，
亲人们时刻都在焦急地等待着他们平安归来，
而每一天他们与死神的搏斗更是异常激烈，

当面部的颧骨呻吟无声，生与死比纸要薄，
那是阵地的抢夺战，每一次冲锋都不能后退，
他们与死神抢夺的是一个个鲜活的生命。
我不相信上帝的存在，但相信天使就在我们中间，
她昨天哭了，当她又拯救了一个生命，
虽然她穿着密不透风的防护服，我还是能看见
一双大大眼睛里滚下的感动的泪水。
是的，在电视机前，我们曾在防护罩前看见过
无数双这样的眼睛，虽然不知道他们的真实姓名
但可以肯定，我们一定会从这一双双眼睛里
看到一个民族所拥有的无限希望和未来。
这是生命的速度，从共和国的病毒专家
到一个普通的护士，从城市的管理者到黎明时
还在为每一座城市刷新面容的环卫工人，
他们对生命的尊重，都体现在每一个岗位上，
由于他们的付出，我们才有了足够的冷静和从容。
这是国家的速度，或者说这就是中国的速度，
火神山医院和雷神山医院的建设，
当然不是火神和雷神的恩赐，它的建设速度
毫无疑问也创造了一个令人为之动容的奇迹。
那些塔吊或许就不是钢铁的面具，而是人的脊柱
它将渴望的钉子牢牢地置入铅色的虚空。
这不是幻想，这是不容置疑的现实，
要知道它的施工，同样是在死亡的刀尖上舞蹈，
从电视上看见一双现场工人的手，虽然转瞬即逝
但对我而言却刻骨铭心，这双手似乎正在变大，
在天空和大地相连的榫头发出胫骨低沉的吹奏，
因此我断言，有了一双双这样勇敢勤劳的手，
我们的幸福、命运、安宁就不会握在别人的手上。
因为那双手，不是造物主的，更不是所谓诸神的，
他是一位中国劳动者粗糙、黝黑但充满了自信的手。

2020.2.1/2

2020.2.1/2

死神正在与我们进行殊死的赛跑,
它是病毒的另一个可怖的代名词。
让我们在未知的空间以勇气杀死它,
不是用鲁莽,而是用超过常规的理性和科学,
让我们隔离对流的空气、看不见的水雾,
但不影响我们心灵之间的温暖和慰藉。
与死神赛跑有前方,可后方有时也是前方,
与死神赛跑,没有观众,我们都是选手。
这不是孩子手中的魔方,在今天的中国
每一条街道都是战壕,每一个家庭都是堡垒。
哦!变异的病毒,看不见的死神!
你是人类的邻居,影子的影子,与生命相随
谁也无法告诉我们你已经存活了多少年?
当你从睡眠中复活,灾难的红矛就会刺向肋骨,
你以无形的匕首偷袭人类最虚弱的地带。
哦!没有面具的死神,这一次你又以隐形的方式
进入了我们没有设防的自由的家园,
我们的战争已经开始,我知道这是一场攻防战,
在实验室我们的精锐部队正在直抵你的心脏,
总有一刻会找到能够杀死你的那件武器。
对于大众,我们打响的防卫战的红色信号弹
也已经无数次照亮过中国的城市、乡镇和学校。
哦!这是阻击战,也是一场将被这个世纪
记载的十四亿人口参加的人民战争。
我们必须坚持,因为死神也开始精疲力尽,
只有忍耐!只有挺住!我们才能耗死进攻的敌人!

世界的部分中国,中国的中心世界,
当你的呼吸急速,地球的另一半
也会面部通红。有一种战争,与古老的
宗教无关,与国家冲突无关,与政治无关,

哦！世界！今天的中国正在全面打响的
是一场捍卫人类的战争，旋转的地球
就是一个家庭，当灾难来临，没有旁观者，
所有的理解、帮助、哪怕道义上的支持
都会给处于困境中的人们巨大的力量。
哦！世界！中国从来就是你的一部分，
她分担你的忧患，从未推卸过自己的责任，
这个东方古老民族以其坚韧、朴实和善良
始终在给人类的文明奉献出智慧和创造。
哦！中国！从不把责任和担当作为标签，
为了维护世界和平，你牺牲的维和战士
蓝色头盔上生长着永远不会消失的鸽子。
当埃博拉病毒的恐惧笼罩着黑非洲，乌木的
神像传递着比羚羊更快的死亡的消息，
在几内亚、利比里亚、塞拉利昂的国土上
就有过数百名中国医疗队战斗的身影，
是他们与当地的人民一起阻止了疫情的蔓延。
无论多么遥远，只要非洲鼓的声音在召唤
中国！就会向非洲兄弟伸出黄色皮肤的援手，
相信吧，在最危难的时刻，我们都会不离不弃。
这就是我们的国际主义，这就是我们的人道主义，
它没有颜色，如果有它就是阳光的颜色，就是
天空的颜色，就是大地的颜色，就是海洋的颜色，
就是血液的颜色，就是眼泪的颜色，就是灵魂的颜色。
哦！世界！请加入到今天中国这场
抗击病毒的战役中来吧，中国的战役就是世界的战役！

数字还在增加，这不是冰冷的数据，
在每一个数字的背后都是一个生命。
也许恐慌的情绪还会在我们中间蔓延，
也许你还会在短暂的无奈中惊慌失措，

哦！朋友们，同志们，要相信整体的力量
但是我们任何时候都不能忘了个体的责任。
哦！死神！它爬上了飞机，它爬上了高铁，
它爬上了不同的交通工具，但是朋友们
你们发现没有啊！死神就常常跟随着我们。
哦！不能给死神可乘之机，戴好一次口罩
其实就是一次单兵出击，一个人的阻击战，
只有当千百万人都成为士兵，这才是
我们最终战胜死神的最最关键的法宝。
阻击它！给它最猛烈的击打！不能让它喘息
不给它反击我们的颅骨和臂部的机会。
死神在寻找着我们，它知道我们看不见它，
它在寻找万分之一防守者可能失控的地方，
哦！朋友们，同志们，假如有一次失控，
我们的损失和代价就真的难以估量，
就会有更多的生命徘徊在死亡的边缘，
还有的亲人也将会永远地离开我们。
直到今天死神的幽灵还在大地上游荡，
它用看不见的头撞击我们的每一扇门窗，
嘴里发出另一个世界才能听见的声音。
它绑架空气、胁迫物质，混迹于人群之中
在任何一个我们可能接触的部位，隐匿着
一把又一把地狱的钥匙，它是不折不扣的
来自冥界的邮递员，毁灭生命的寄生虫。
死亡其实伴随人类的历史已经千百万年
这本身是自然的法则，不可改变的逻辑。
但是，死神！这一次你对人类的侵袭充满了
从未有过的疯狂，你让冒汗的碎片中断了生命
让家庭不再完整，爱情缺失了恋人，本该回家的人
再不能回到家。哦！死神！无论今天你在哪里
我们都要集合起千千万万的生命向你发起反击。

死神与我们的速度谁更快？
虽然它在枪响前已经跑在了前面，
但你看见了吗？我已经清楚地看见
当自由的风吹动着勇士三色的披肩，当太阳的
箭矢穿过黑色的岩石，当光明的液体反射向宇宙
逃离了地球的引力，当人类的子宫再次孕育地球
植物的语言变成比三倍还要多的萤火
当所有动物的眼睛，都能结构多维度的哲学
在每一个人的胸腔中只生长出救赎的苦荞。
当自己成为大家，当众人关注最弱小的生命，
一个人的声音的背后是一个民族的声音，而从一个人
声音的内部却又能听见无数人的不同的声音。
是的，我已经真切地看见了，我们与死神的赛跑
已经到了最后的冲刺，相差的距离越来越近，
这是最艰难的时候，唯有坚持才能成为最后的英雄。
相信吧！我们会胜利！中国会胜利！人类会胜利！
因为这场生与死的竞赛相差的距离已经越来越近……！

Who is Faster, Us or Death
—To all who beat against COVID-19 in 2020

Death is faster than us,
because he took us by surprise
and began to run before the starting gun.
Death! This time he seems faster,
but can he really be the Creator's
most recent creation?
Or is this a severe test
that humankind must bravely face today?
Death doesn't wear an obvious mask,
and this time he can disappear into thin air.
Death is faster than us,
and before the statistics even came out
his evil hand was at work
at his accursed additions!
Death's numbers are still increasing,
as now we hope only for subtractions!
Death has traveled far,
killing the elderly, the young,
injuring our vulnerable children,
ravaging the cities, streets, and parks,
everywhere he goes, he beats black iron.

Death is faster than us,
because he took us by surprise
and began to run before the starting gun.
But this time is just like the last time!
We are competing with Death, and now undoubtedly
it is a life and death competition.
Who will come out victorious has yet to be decided.
Let us knit love into our daily practice,
and send it out to every corner, in the name of humanity.
Let us collect the determination of thousands of people

into a single great life force, and from the dome above
send out a light younger than the ancient sun.
Let us open all the windows and snip our dreams into stars
and again lift up a sky as blue as a waterfall.

You say Death is faster than us, but no!
I don't believe it! Because I can see
that the distance between us and Death is reducing.
Please believe that we will create a new record in this race,
with the eyes of whole world looking on!
Our speed is building by seconds and minutes,
along with the speed of our leaders—and from the first moment
that steadfast, confident, and powerful voice spread
across the nation's land, forests, sky, and oceans,
producing a frontrunner of speed that will always be ahead.
This is the speed of the people, whether in the city or the countryside,
and every citizen will fight in this fight without gun smoke,
while every job is held by someone fearless.
This is the speed of the system, rushing to the rescue with commands
that sent an army of countless heroic men and women to Wuhan.
This is the speed of the collective, and the narrowness and selfishness
    of individualism
has no place here, because the harsh reality
tells us, every single life depends on others for survival.
This is the speed of devotion, a devotion that isn't in declarations,
but in families anxiously waiting for their safe return,
and their daily struggle with Death is fierce.
When the cheekbones groan and fall silent, life and death are thinner
    than paper,
and that becomes the battlefield, where one cannot let up the charge,
as what they and Death vie for is one vibrant life after another.
I do not believe in God, but I believe there are angels among us.
Yesterday one cried as she saved another life,
and even with her airtight protective suit, I could see
the tears streaming from her big eyes.
Yes, in front of the television, we watched countless such eyes
behind face shields, and although we don't know their names,

we can be sure that we will see in each pair of eyes
a people's infinite hope and future.
This is the speed of life, from the country's infectious disease specialists
to regular nurses, from city management to every
sanitation worker who still appears at dawn to scrub the face of the city.
Their respect for life is reflected in every job,
and thanks only to their efforts can we maintain our calm and composure.
This is the nation's speed, or one should say China's speed—
the construction of the Mt. Huoshenshan and Mt. Leishenshan hospitals
wasn't gifted by the mountain gods, and the speed of their construction
undoubtedly aroused admiration and wonder.
Those tower cranes aren't masks of iron, but people's spines,
as they pound nails of hope firmly into the leaden void.
This isn't an illusion, it is the unquestionable reality.
Their construction was like dancing on a knife's edge of death.
On TV I saw the hands of one of the workers and they seemed to be growing bigger,
while the joint where the sky meets the earth let out the low note of a shinbone.
So I can affirm that there are many such brave hardworking hands,
and our happiness, fate, and peace will not be held in anyone else's hands—
those hands, not the hands of Jesus Christ or the Buddha or Allah,
but the hands of a Chinese laborer, coarse and dark, but full of confidence.

We are in a deadly race with Death,
another synonym for the virus.
In a yet unknown time, let us bravely destroy him,
not with crudeness or rashness, but with extraordinary rationality and science.
Let us separate our air currents, the invisible vapors,

but not let it influence the warmth and comfort between us.
In the race with Death, there is a frontrunner, but a pursuer can
 become a frontrunner.
In the race with Death, there are no spectators, we are all partici-
 pants.
It is not a Rubik's cube in a child's hand, in today's China
every street is a wartime trench, every home is a fortress.
Oh, this changing disease, this invisible Death!
You are humanity's neighbor, the shadows' shadow, tailing life.
No one can tell us how long you have existed.
When you revived from your sleep, the red spears of disaster stabbed
 into ribs.
With an invisible dagger you launched your attack on people's weak-
 est area.
Oh, maskless Death, this time you once again use your invisibility
to enter our defenseless, free homes.
Our fight has already begun, and I know it is both a defensive and
 offensive battle.
In our laboratories, our finest soldiers are going straight to your
 heart,
and they will find a weapon that can kill you.
For the rest of us, the red signal flares of our frontline defenses
have already lit up Chinese cities, towns, and schools countless times.
Oh, these are the first parries in a people's war
fought by 1.4 billion people.
We must persist, because Death is already wearying.
Have patience! Be strong! Only then we can defeat our enemy!

China in the world, the world in China,
when you struggle to breathe, the earth's other half
feels its face turn red as well. There is a sort of battle that has nothing
 to do
with ancient religion, nothing to do with international conflicts or
 politics.
Oh, world! Today China is facing a fight
to protect the welfare of humanity; the rotating earth
is one family, and when disaster comes, there are no bystanders.

Every bit of understanding, help, or even moral support
will give those in need a source of great power.
Oh, world! China has always been a part of you,
she shares in your suffering, and has never refused responsibility for you.
The ancient peoples of the East and their tenaciousness, sincerity, and decency
have always given wisdom and creativity to all cultures.
Oh, China! You have never used your responsibility and undertakings as a badge,
but to protect world peace, your sacrificial guards and soldiers,
and on their blue safety helmets are born everlasting doves.
When the terror of Ebola surrounded Africa, ebony
idols transmitted the news of death faster than a gazelle.
In The Republic of Guinea, Liberia, Sierra Leone,
more than a hundred Chinese medical teams joined the fight,
and working alongside of locals, they stopped the spread of the epidemic.
Despite the great distance, Africa's drumbeat called to China!
We extended our yellow helping hands to our African brothers,
and trust that in the worst of times, we will never think less of you.
This is our practice of internationalism, and our humanitarianism.
It has no color, but when it's present, there is the color of sunshine
and the color of the sky, and of the earth and oceans,
the color of blood, the color of tears, the color of the human spirit.
Oh, world! Join China's fight today
to beat back the virus, China's battle is the world's battle!

The numbers are still increasing, and they are not just cold numbers,
as each number has a life behind it.
Perhaps the panic will spread among us,
or perhaps you will find yourself panicked in temporary helplessness.
Oh, friends, comrades, you must believe in our collective power,
but we must also remember our individual responsibility.
Oh, Death! He boards airplanes, boards high speed trains,
boards all kinds of vehicles, but friends—
have you realized?—Death is often following us.

Don't give him an opportunity! Wear your masks,
as a single soldier launching an attack, a personal battle,
and only when everyone has become a soldier
will we finally have the magic weapon to defeat Death.
Block him! Hit him as hard as you can! Don't let him breathe,
don't give him a chance to attack our skulls or arms,
as he looks for tiny openings where we let down our guard.
Oh, friends, comrades, if there is an opening,
our losses will be hard to measure,
and more lives will be pulled into Death's orbit,
and those we love will be taken from us forever.
Today Death's spirit still travels the earth,
using his invisible head to beat against every window,
his mouth making sounds that can only be heard in another world.
He kidnaps the air, manipulates matter, cons his way into the crowd,
and on every part of us that can be touched he conceals
key after key to hell. He is unquestionably
a messenger from the netherworld, a parasite that destroys life.
Death has accompanied humans through thousands of years of history.
It is a natural fact, an unchanging logic.
But, Death! This time your surprise attack on humanity
is more frenzied than ever before, cutting off lives amid the sweat.
You break apart families, rip loved ones apart, keep those who should go home
from ever going back again. Oh, Death! No matter where you are,
we must gather our strength and beat you back together!

Who is faster, us or Death?
Although he began to run before the starting gun—
do you see?—I can clearly see
when the free wind rustles the red cape of heroes, when the sun's
arrows pierce the dark cliffs, when light's liquid reflects back to the universe
and escapes the pull of the earth, when women's wombs conceive the earth again,
the language of plants becomes triple the glow of fireflies,
when all the animals' eyes can compose multi-dimensional philosophies,

in every person's chest a stalk of lifesaving buckwheat will sprout.
When we each become the other, when we all pay attention to the smallest life,
behind every person's voice will be the community's voice, and from one person's voice
we will hear the voices of the countless many.
Yes, I can distinctly see, our race with Death
has reached the final sprint, and we are about to overtake Death.
This is the hardest moment, and the one who persists will be the hero.
Believe this! We will win! China will win! Humanity will win!
We have already begun to overtake Death!

        Translated by Gu Ailing

裂开的星球
——献给全人类和所有的生命

是这个星球创造了我们
还是我们改变了这个星球?

哦,老虎!波浪起伏的铠甲
流淌着数字的光。唯一的意志。

就在此刻,它仍然在另一个维度的空间
以寂灭从容的步态踽踽独行。

那永不疲倦的行走,隐晦的火。
让旋转的能量成为齿轮,时间的
手柄,锤击着金黄皮毛的波浪。

老虎还在那里。从来没有离开我们。
在这星球的四个方位,脚趾踩踏着
即将消失的现在,眼球倒映创世的元素。
它并非只活在那部《查姆》[1]的典籍中,
它的双眼一直在注视着善恶缠身的人类。

不是我们每一个人都有明确的罪行,当天空变低,鹰的
　　飞翔再没有足够的高度。

天空一旦没有了标高,精神和价值注定就会从高处滑
　　落。旁边是受伤的鹰翅。

当智者的语言被金钱和物质的双手弄脏,我在二十年前
　　就看见过一只鸟,在城市耸立的

---

[1]《查姆》:彝族古典创世史诗之一。

2020.4.5/16

黑色烟囱上坠地而亡，这是应该原谅那只
　　鸟还是原谅我们呢？天空的沉默回答
　　了一切。

任何预兆的传递据说都会用不同的方式，
　　我们部族的毕摩[1]就曾经告诉过我。

> 1 毕摩：彝族原始宗教中的祭司、文字传承者。

这场战争终于还是爆发了，以肉眼看不见的方式。

哦！古老的冤家。是谁闯入了你的家园，用冒犯来比喻
似乎能减轻一点罪孽，但的确是人类惊醒了你数万年的
　　睡眠。

从一个城市到另一个城市，从一个国家到另一个国家，
它跨过传统的边界，那里虽然有武装到牙齿的士兵，
它跨过有主权的领空，因为谁也无法阻挡自由的气流，
甚至那些最先进的探测器也没有发现它诡异的行踪。

这是一场特殊的战争，是死亡的另一种隐喻。

它当然不需要护照，可以到任何一个想去的地方，
你看见那随季而飞的候鸟，崖壁上倒挂着的果蝠，
猩红色屁股追逐异性的猩猩，跨物种跳跃的虫族，
它们都会把生或死的骰子投向天堂和地狱的邮箱。

它到访过教堂、清真寺、道观、寺庙和世俗的学校，
还敲开了封闭的养老院以及戒备森严的监狱大门。
如果可能它将惊醒这个世界上所有的政府，死神的面具
将会把黑色的恐慌钉入空间。红色的矛将杀死黑色的盾。

当东方和西方再一次相遇在命运的出口

是走出绝境?还是自我毁灭?左手
　　对右手的责怪,并不能
制造出一艘新的诺亚方舟,逃离这
　　千年的困境。

孤独的星球还在旋转,但雪族十二
　　子总会出现醒来的先知。
那是因为《勒俄》[1]告诉过我,所有的动物和植物都是
　　兄弟。

尽管荷马吟唱过的大海还在涌动着蓝色的液体,海豹的
　　眼睛里落满了宇宙的讯息。
这或许不是最后的审判,但碗状的苍穹还是在独角兽出
　　现之前覆盖了人类的头顶。

这不是传统的战争,更不是一场核战争,因为核战争没
　　有赢家。
居里夫人为一个政权仗义执言,直到今天也无法判断她
　　的对错。
但她对核武器所下的的结论,谢天谢地没有引来任何诽
　　谤和争议。

这是曾经出现过的战争的重现,只是更加的危险可怕。
那是因为今天的地球村,人类手中握的是一把双刃剑。

多么古老而又近在咫尺的战争,没有人能置身于外。
它侵袭过强大的王朝,改写过古代雅典帝国的历史。
在中世纪它轻松地消灭了欧洲三分之一还多的人口。
它还是殖民者的帮凶,杀死过千百万的印第安土著。

[1]《勒俄特依》,彝族古典史诗,流传于大小凉山彝族聚居区。

2020.4.5/16

这是一次属于全人类的抗战。不分地域。
如果让我选择，我会选择保护每一个生命，
而不是用抽象的政治去诠释所谓自由的含义。
我想阿多诺[1]和诗人卡德纳尔[2]都会赞成，
　　　因为哪怕
最卑微的生命在任何时候也都要高于空洞
　　　的说教。

如果公众的安全是由每一个人去构筑，
那我会选择对集体的服从而不是对抗。
从武汉到罗马，从巴黎到伦敦，从马德里
　　　到纽约，
都能从每一家阳台上看见熟悉但并不相识
　　　的目光。

我尊重个人的权利，是基于尊重全部的人权，
如果个人的权利，可以无端地伤害大众的利益，
那我会毫不留情从人权的法典中拿走这些词，
但请相信，我会终其一生去捍卫真正的人权
而个体的权利更是需要保护的最神圣的部分。

在此时，人类只有携手合作
才能跨过这道最黑暗的峡谷。

哦，本雅明[3]的护照坏了，他呵着气在边境那头向我
　　　招手，
其实他不用通过托梦的方式告诉我，茨威格[4]为什么
　　　选择了自杀。

对人类的绝望从根本上讲是他相信邪恶已经占了上风
　　　而不可更改。

---

1 阿多诺：西奥多·阿多诺（1903-1969），德国哲学家、社会学家。

2 卡德纳尔：埃内斯托·卡德纳尔（1925-2020），尼加拉瓜诗人、神甫、革命者。

3 本雅明：瓦尔特·本雅明（1892-1940），德国哲学家、马克思主义文学理论批评家。1940年自杀。

4 茨威格：斯蒂芬·茨威格（1881-1942），奥地利小说家、剧作家。1942年2月自杀。

2020.4.5/16

哦！幼发拉底河、恒河、密西西
　　比河和黄河，
还有那些我没有一一报出名字的
　　河流，
你们见证过人类漫长的生活与历
　　史，能不能
告诉我，当你们咽下厄运的时候，
　　又是如何
从嘴里吐出了生存的智慧和光滑
　　古朴的石头。

当我看见但丁的意大利在地狱的
　　门口掩面哭泣，
塞万提斯的子孙们在经历着又一
　　次身心的伤痛。
人道的援助不管来自哪里，唉，都是一种美德。

打倒法西斯主义和种族主义在这个世纪的进攻。
陶里亚蒂[1]、帕索里尼[2]和葛兰西[3]在墓地挥舞红旗。

就在伊朗人民遭受着双重灾难的时候
那些施暴者，并没有真的想放过他们。
我怎么能在这样时候去阅读苏菲派神秘的诗歌，
我又怎么能不去为叙利亚战火中的孩子们悲戚？

那些在镜头前为选举而表演的人
只有谎言才让他们真的相信自己。
不是不要相信那些宣言具有真理的逻辑，
而要看他们对弱势者犯下了多少罪行。

此时我看见落日的沙漠上有一只山羊，

---

1 陶里亚蒂：帕尔米罗·陶里亚蒂（1893-1964），意大利共产党创始人之一、国际共产主义者。
2 帕索里尼：皮埃尔·保罗·帕索里尼（1922-1975），意大利共产党诗人、电影导演。
3 葛兰西：安东尼奥·葛兰西（1891-1937），意大利共产党创始人、马克思主义理论家。

不知道是犹太人还是阿拉伯人丢失的。

毕阿什拉则[1]的火塘,世界的中心!
让我再回到你记忆中遗失的故乡,以那些
　　最古老的植物的名义。

在遥远的墨西哥干燥缺水的高地
胡安·鲁尔福[2]还在那里为自己守灵,
这个沉默寡言的村长,为了不说话
竟然让鹦鹉变成了能言善辩的骗子。

我精神上真正的兄弟,世界的塞萨尔·巴列霍[3],
你不是为一个人写诗,而是为一个种族在歌唱。
让一只公鸡在你语言的嗓子里吹响脊柱横笛,
让每一个时代的穷人都能在入睡前吃饱,而不是
在梦境中才能看见白色的牛奶和刚刚出炉的面包。
哦,同志!你羊驼一般质朴的温暖来自灵魂,
这里没有诀窍,你的词根是206块发白的骨头。

哦!文明与野蛮。发展或倒退。加法和减法。
——这是一个裂开的星球!

在这里货币和网络连接着所有的种族。巴西热带雨林中
最原始的部落也有人在手机上玩杀人游戏。

贝都因人在城市里构建想象的沙漠,再看不见触手可摘
　　的星星。
乘夜色吉普赛人躺在欧洲黑暗的中心,他们是白天的隐
　　身人。

---

1 毕阿什拉则:彝族古代著名毕摩(祭司)、智者、文字传承者。
2 胡安·鲁尔福:(1917-1986),墨西哥小说家、人类学家。
3 塞萨尔·巴列霍(1892-1938),秘鲁印第安裔诗人、马克思主义者。

在这里人类成了万物的主宰,对蚂
　　蚁的王国也开始了占领。
几内亚狒狒在交配时朝屏息窥视的
　　人类呲牙咧嘴。

在这里智能工程,能让未来返回过
　　去,还能让现在成为将来。
冰雪的火焰能点燃冬季的星空已经不是一个让人惊讶的
　　事情。

在这里全世界的土著妇女不约而同地戴着被改装过的帽
　　子,穿行于互联网的
迷宫。但她们面对陌生人微笑的时候,都还保持着用头
　　巾半掩住嘴的习惯。

在这里一部分英国人为了脱欧开了一个玩笑,而另一部
　　分人为了这个
不是玩笑的玩笑却付出了代价。这就如同啤酒的泡沫变
　　成了微笑的眼泪。

在这里为了保护南极的冰川不被更快地融化,海豚以集
　　体自杀的方式表达了
抗议,拒绝了人类对冰川的访问。凡是人迹罕至的地方,
　　杀戮就还没有开始。

在这里当极地的雪线上移的时候,湖泊的水鸟就会把水
　　位上涨的消息
告诉思维油腻的官员。而此刻,鹰隼的眼泪就是天空的蛋。

在这里粮食的重量迎风而生,饥饿得到了缓解,马尔萨
　　斯[1]在今天或许会

[1] 马尔萨斯:托马斯·罗伯特·马尔萨斯(1766-1834),英国教士、人口学家、经济学家。

修正他的人口学说，不是道德家的人，并
　　不影响他作为一个思想者的存在。

在这里羚羊还会穿过日光流泻的荒原，风
　　的一丝振动就会让它竖起双耳，
死亡的距离有时候比想象要快。野牛无法
　　听见蚊蝇在皮毛上开展的讨论。

在这里纽约的路灯朝右转的时候，玻利维
　　亚的牧羊人却在瞬间
选择了向左的小道，因为右边是千仞绝壁
　　令人胆寒的万丈深渊。

在这里俄罗斯人的白酒消费量依然是世界第一，但叶赛
　　宁[1]诗歌中怀念
乡村的诗句，却会让另一个国度的人在酒后潸然泪下，
　　哀声恸哭。

在这里阿桑奇[2]创建了"维基解密"。他在厄瓜多尔使
　　馆的阳台上向世界挥手，
阿富汗贫民的死亡才在偶然间大白于天下。

在这里加泰罗尼亚人喜欢傍晚吃西班牙火腿，但他们并
　　没有忘记
在吃火腿前去搞所谓的公投。安东尼奥·马查多[3]如果
　　还活着，他会投给谁呢？

在这里他们要求爱尔兰共和军和巴斯克人放下手中武器
却在另外的地方发表支持分裂主义的决议和声明。

在这里大部分美国人都以为他们的财富被装进了中国人

1　叶赛宁：（1895-1925）俄罗斯抒情诗人。1925年12月自杀。
2　阿桑奇：朱利安·阿桑奇（1971- ），"维基解密"创始人。
3　安东尼奥·马查多：（1875-1939）西班牙现代著名诗人、"九八年一代"主将。

的兜里。
摩西从山上带回的清规戒律，
　　在基因分裂链的寓言中系
　　统崩溃。

在这里格瓦拉和甘地被分别请进
　　了各自的殿堂。
全球化这个词在安特卫普埃尔岑瓦德酒店的双人床上被
　　千人重复。

在这里国际货币基金组织和世界银行，他们的脚迹已经
　　走到了基督不到的地方。
但那些背负着十字架行走在世界边缘的穷人，却始终坚
　　信耶稣就是他们的邻居。

在这里社会主义关于劳工福利的部分思想被敌对阵营
　　偷走。
财富穿越了所有的边界，可是苦难却降临在个体的头上。

在这里他们对外颠覆别人的国家，对内让移民充满恐惧。
这牢笼是如此的美妙，里佐斯[1]埋在监狱窗下的诗歌已
　　经长成了树。

在这里电视让人目瞪口呆地直播了双子大楼被撞击坍塌
　　的一幕。
诗歌在哥伦比亚成为了政治对话的一种最为人道的方式。

在这里每天都有边缘的语言和生物被操控的力量悄然
　　移除。
但从个人隐私而言，现在全球 97.7‰ 的人都是被监视
　　的裸体。

[1] 里佐斯：扬尼斯·里佐斯（1909–1990），现代希腊共产党诗人、左翼活动家。

在这里马克思的思想还在变成具体的行
　　动,但华尔街却更愿意与学术精英们
　　合谋,
把这个犹太人仅仅说成是某一个学术领域
　　的领袖。

在这里有人想继续打开门,有人却想把已
　　经打开的门关上。
一旦脚下唯一的土地离开了我们,距离就失去了意义。

在这里开门的人并不完全知道应该放什么进来,又应该
　　把什么挡在门外。
一部分人在虚拟的空间中被剥夺了延伸疆界和赋予同一
　　性的能力。

在这里主张关门的人并不担心自己的家有一天会成为
　　牢笼。
但精神上的背井离乡者注定是被自由永久放逐的对象。

在这里骨骼已经成为了一个整体,切割一只手还可以
　　承受,
但要拦腰斩断就很难存活。上海的耳朵听见佛罗里达的
　　脚趾在呻吟。

在这里南太平洋圣卢西亚的酒吧仍然在吹奏着萨克斯,
　　打开的每一瓶可乐都能听见纽约股市所发出的惊喜
　　或叹息。
网络的绑架和暴力是这个时代的第五纵队。哈贝马斯[1]
　　偶然看到了真相。

在这里有人纵火焚烧 5G 的信号塔,无疑是中世纪愚昧

[1] 哈贝马斯:尤尔根·哈贝马斯(1929-),德国哲学家、当代西方马克思主义主要代表人物之一。

的返祖现象。

澳大利亚的知更鸟虽然最晚才叫，但它的叫声充满了投机者的可疑。

在这里再没有宗教法庭处死伽利略，但有人还在以原教旨的命令杀死异教徒。

不是所谓的民主政治都宽容弱者，杰斐逊[1]就认为灭绝印第安人是文明的一大进步。

在这里穷人和富人的比例并没有根本的改变，但阶级的界限却被新自由主义抹杀。

当他们需要的时候，一个跨国的政府将会把对穷人的剥夺塑造成慈善行为。

在这里不是所有的国家都能生产一颗扣子，那是为了扣子能游到凡是有海水的地方。

所有争夺天下的变革者最初都是平等的，难怪临死的托洛斯基相信继续革命的理论。

在这里推倒了柏林墙，但为了隔离又构筑了更多的墙。墙更厚更高。

全景监狱让不透明的空间再次落入奥威尔[2]《一九八四》无法逃避的圈套。

在这里所谓有关自由和生活方式的争论肯定不是种族的差异。

因疫情带来的隔离、封城和紧急状态并非是为了暧昧的大多数。

---

[1] 杰斐逊：托马斯·杰斐逊（1743-1826），美国第三任总统、美国独立宣言主要起草人。

[2] 奥威尔：乔治·奥威尔（1903-1950），英国小说家、社会评论家，其名著为小说《1984》。

哦！裂开的星球，你是不是看见了那黄金一般的老虎在
　　转动你的身体，
看见了它们隐没于苍穹的黎明和黄昏，每一次呼吸都吹
　　拂着时间之上那液态的光。
这是救赎自己的时候了，不能再有差错，因为失误将意
　　味着最后的毁灭。

当灾难的讯号从地球的四面八方发出
那艘神话中的方舟并没有真的出现
没有海啸覆盖一座又一座城市的情景
没有听见那来自天宇的恐怖声音
没有目睹核原子升起的蘑菇云的梦魇
没有一部分国家向另一部分国家正式宣战
它虽然不是 20 世纪两次世界大战的延续
但它造成的损失和巨大的灾难或许更大
这是一场古老漫长的战争，说它漫长
那是因为你的对手已经埋伏了千万年
在灾难的历史上你们曾经无数次地相遇
戈雅就用画笔记录过比死亡本身更让人
触目惊心的是由死亡所透漫出来的气息
可以肯定这又是人类越入了险恶的区域
把一场本可以避免的灾难带到了全世界
此刻一场近距离的搏杀正在悲壮地展开
不分国度、不分种族、无论是贫穷还是富有
死神刚与我们擦肩而过，死神或许正把
一个强健的男人打倒，可能就在这个瞬间
又摁倒了一个虚弱的妇女，被诅咒的死神
已经用看不见的暴力杀死了成千上万的人
这其中有白人，有黑人，有黄种人，有孩子也有老人
如果要发出一份战争宣战书，哦！正在战斗的人们
我们将签写上这个共同的名字——全人类！

哦！当我们以从未有过的速度
踏入别的生物繁衍生息的禁地
在巴西砍伐亚马孙河两岸的原始
　　森林
让大火的浓烟染黑了地球绿色的
　　肺叶
人类为了所谓生存的每一次进军
都给自己的明天埋下了致命的隐
　　患
在非洲对野生动物的疯狂猎杀
已让濒临灭绝的种类不断增加
当狮群的领地被压缩在一个可怜的区域
作为食物链最顶端的动物已经危机四伏
黄昏时它在原野上一声声地怒吼
表达了对无端入侵者的悲愤和抗议
在地球第三级的可可西里无人区
雪豹自由守望的家园也越来越小
那些曾经从不伤害人类的肉食者
因为食物的短缺开始进入了村庄
在东南亚原住民被城市化赶到了更远的地方
有一天他们的鸡大量神秘地腹泻而死
一个叫卡坦[1]的孩子的死亡吹响了不祥的叶笛
从刚果到马来西亚森林对野生动物的猎杀
无论离得多远，都能听见敲碎颅脑的声响
正是这种狩猎和屠宰的所谓终极亲密行为
并非上苍的旨意把这些微生物连接了起来
其实每一次灾难都告诉我们
任何物种的存在都应充满敬畏
对最弱小的生物的侵扰和破坏
也会付出难以想象的沉重代价。

[1] 卡坦：卡坦·布马鲁，生于泰国西部，2004年1月25日6岁时死于H5N1禽流感，是首批死于这种新型人类病毒的患者之一。

2020.4.5/16

人类！你的创世之神给我们带来过奇迹
盘古开天辟地从泥土里走出了动物和人
在恒河的岸边是法力无边的大梵天[1]
创造了比天空中繁星还要多的万物
在安第斯山上印第安创世主帕查卡马克[2]
带来了第一批人类和无数的飞禽走兽
在众神居住的圣殿英雄辈出的希腊
普罗米修斯赋予人和所见之物以生命
他还将自己鲜红的心脏作为牺牲的祭品
最终把火、智慧、知识和技艺带到了人间
还有神鹰的儿子我们彝人的支呷阿鲁[3]
他让祖先的影子恒久地浮现在群山之上
人类！从那以后你的文明史或许被中断过
但这种中断在时间长河里就是一个瞬间
从青铜时代穿越到蒸汽机在大地上的滚动
从镭的发现到核能为造福人类被广泛利用
从莱特兄弟[4]为自己插上翅膀，再到航天飞机
把人的梦想一次次送到遥远的空间站
计算机和生物工程跨越了世纪的门槛
我们欢呼看见了并非想象的宇宙的黑洞
互联网让我们开始重新认识这个世界
时间与阶级、移动与自由、自我与僭越、速度与分化
恐旷症与单一性、民族国家与全球图景、剥夺与主权
整合与瓜分、面包与圆珠笔、流浪者与乌托邦
预测悖论与风险计算、消除差异与命运的人质
正是因为这一切，我们才望着落日赞叹
只有渴望那旅途的精彩与随之可能置身的危险
才会有足够的理由相信明天的日出更加灿烂
但是人类，你绝不是真正的超人，虽然你已经
足够强大，只要你无法改变你是这个星球的存在
你就会面临所有生物面临灾难的选择

1 大梵天：印度教的创造之神，梵文字母的创制者。
2 帕查卡马克：南美古印加人创世之神，被称作"制作大地者"。
3 支呷阿鲁：彝族神话史诗中的创世英雄。
4 莱特兄弟：指美国飞机发明家威尔伯·莱特和奥维尔·莱特两兄弟，1903年12月17日他们完成了人类历史上第一架飞机的成功试飞。

这是创造之神规定的宿命，谁也无法轻易地更改
那只看不见的手，让生物构成了一个晶体的圆圈
任何贪婪的破坏者，都会陷入恐惧和灭顶之灾
所有的生命都可能携带置自己于死地的杀手
而人类并不是纯粹的金属，也有最脆弱的地方
我们是强大的，强大到成为了这个世界的主宰
我们是虚弱的，肉眼无法看见的微生物
也许就会让我们败于一场输不起的隐形战争
从生物种群的意义而言，人类永远只是其中的一种
我们没有权利无休止地剥夺这个地球，除了基本的
生存需要，任何对别的生命的残杀都可视为犯罪
善待自然吧，善待与我们不同的生命，请记住！
善待它们就是善待我们自己，要么万劫不复。

哦，人类！这是消毒水流动国界的时候
这是旁观邻居下一刻就该轮到自己的时候
这是融化的时间与渴望的箭矢赛跑的时候
这是嘲笑别人而又无法独善其身的时候
这是狂热的冰雕刻那熊熊大火的时候
这是地球与人都同时戴上口罩的时候
这是天空的鹰与荒野的赤狐搏斗的时候
这是所有的大街和广场都默默无语的时候
这是孩子只能在窗户前想象大海的时候
这是白衣天使与死神都临近深渊的时候
这是孤单的老人将绝望一口吞食的时候
这是一个待在家里比外面更安全的时候
这是流浪者喉咙里伸出手最饥饿的时候
这是人道主义主张高于意识形态的时候
这是城市的部落被迫返回乡土的时候
这是大地、海洋和天空致敬生命的时候
这是被切开的血管里飞出鸽子的时候

这是意大利的泪水模糊中国眼睛的时候
这是伦敦的呻吟让西班牙吉他呜咽的时候
这是纽约的护士与上帝一起哭泣的时候
这是谎言和真相一同出没于网络的时候
这是甘地的人民让远方的麋鹿不安的时候
这是人性的光辉和黑暗狭路相逢的时候
这是相信对方或置疑对手最艰难的时候
这是语言给人以希望又挑起仇恨的时候
这是一部分人迷茫另一半也忧虑的时候
这是蓝鲸的呼吸吹动着和平的时候
这是星星代表亲人送别亡人的时候
这是一千个祭司诅咒一个影子的时候
这是陌生人的面部开始清晰的时候
这是同床异梦者梦见彼此的时候
这是貌合神离者开始冷战的时候
这是旧的即将解体新的还没有到来的时候
这是神枝昭示着不祥还是化险为夷的时候
这是黑色的石头隐匿白色意义的时候
这是诸神的羊群在等待摩西渡过红海的时候
这是牛角号被勇士吹得撕心裂肺的时候
这是鹰爪杯又一次被预言的诗人握住的时候
这是巴比塔废墟上人与万物力争和谈的时候
就是在这样一个时候，就是在这样的时候
哦，人类！只有一次机会，抓住马蹄铁。

是这个星球创造了我们
还是我们改变了这个星球?

当裂开的星球在意志的额头旋转轮子
所有的生命都在亘古不变的太阳下奔跑
创世之神的面具闪烁在无限的苍穹

那无处不在的光从天宇的子宫里
　　往返
黑暗的清气如同液态孕育的另一
　　个空间
那是我们的星球,唯一的蓝色
悬浮于想象之外的处女的橄榄
那是我们的星球,一滴不落的水
不可被随意命名的形而上的宝石
是一团创造者幻化的生死不灭的火焰
我们不用通灵,就是直到今天也能
从大地、海洋、森林和河流中找到
它的眼睛、骨头、皮毛和血脉的基因
那是我们的星球,是它孕育了所有的生命
无论是战争、瘟疫、灾难还是权力的更替
都没有停止过对生命的孕育和恩赐
当我们抚摸它的身体,纵然美丽依旧
但它的身上却能看到令人悲痛的伤痕
这是我们的星球,无论你是谁,属于哪个种族
也不论今天你生活在它身体的哪个部位
我们都应该为了它的活力和美丽聚集在一起
拯救这个星球与拯救生命从来就无法分开

哦,女神普嫫列依[1]!请把你缝制头盖的针借给我
还有你手中那团白色的羊毛线,因为我要缝合
我们已经裂开的星球。

裂开的星球!让我们从肋骨下面给你星期一
让他们减少碳排放,用巴黎气候大会的绿叶
遮住那个投反对票的鼻孔,让他的脸变成斗篷
让我们给饥饿者粮食,而不是只给他们数字
如果可能的话,在他们醒来时盗走政客的名字

[1] 普嫫列依:彝族创世神话中的女神之一,是创世英雄支呷阿鲁贞洁受孕的母亲。

2020.4.5/16

不能给撒谎者昨天的时间,因为后天听众
　　最多
让我们弥合分歧,但不是把风马牛都整齐
　　划一
当44隐于亮光之中,徒劳无功的板凳会
　　哭闹
那是陆地上的水手,亚当·密茨凯维奇[1]
　　的密钥
愿睡着的人丢失了一份工作,醒后有三份在等他
那些在街上的人已经知道,谁点燃了左边的房
右边的院子也不能幸免,绝望让路灯长出了驴唇
让昨天的动物猎手,成为今天的素食主义者
每一个童年的许诺,都能在母亲还在世时送到
让耶路撒冷的石头恢复未来的记忆,让同时
埋葬过犹太人和阿拉伯人先知的沙漠开花
愿终结就是开始,愿空档的大海涌动孕期的色韵
让木碗找到干裂的嘴唇,让信仰选择自己的衣服
让听不懂的语言在联合国致辞,让听众欢呼成骆驼
让平等的手帕挂满这个世界的窗户,让稳定与逻辑反目
让一个人成为他们的自我,让自我的他们更喜欢一个人
让趋同让位于个性,让普遍成为平等,石缝填满的是诗
让岩石上的手摁住滑动的鱼,让庄家吐出多边形的规则
让红色覆盖蓝色,让蓝色的嘴巴在红色的脸上唱歌
让即将消亡的变成理性,让尚未出生的与今天和解
让所有的生命因为快乐都能跳到半空,下面是柔软的
　　海绵。
这个星球是我们的星球,尽管它沉重犹如西西弗的石头
假如我们能避开引力站在苍穹之上,它更像儿童手里的
　　气球
不是我们作为现象存在,就证明所有的人都学会了思考
这个时代给我们的疑问,过去的典籍没有,只能自己回答

[1] 亚当·密茨凯维奇:(1798-1855)波兰诗人、革命家、波兰文学最重要的奠基人。

给我们的时间已经不多，那是因为鼠目寸光者还在争吵
这不是一个糟糕的时代，因为此前的时代也并非就最好
因为我们无法想象过去最遥远的地方今天却成了故乡
这是货币的力量，这是市场的力量，这是另一种力量的
　　力量
没有上和下，只有前和后，唯有现实本身能回答它的
　　结果
这是巨大的转折，它比一个世纪要长，只能用千年来算
我们不可能再回到过去，因为过去的老屋已经面目全非
不能选择封闭，任何材料成为高墙，就只有隔离的含义
不能选择对抗，一旦偏见变成仇恨，就有可能你死我亡
不用去问那些古老的河流，它们的源头充满了史前的
　　寂静
或许这就是最初的启示，和而不同的文明都是她的孩子
放弃三的分歧，尽可能在七中找到共识，不是以邻为壑
在方的内部，也许就存在着圆的可能，而不是先入为主
让诸位摒弃丛林法则，这样应该更好，而不是自己为大
让大家争取日照的时间更长，而不是将黑暗奉送给对方
这一切！不是一个简单的方法，而是要让参与者知道
这个星球的未来不仅属于你和我，还属于所有的生命
我不知道明天会发生什么，据说诗人有预言的秉性
但我不会去预言，因为浩瀚的大海没有给天空留下痕迹
曾被我千百次赞颂过的光，此刻也正迈着凯旋的步伐
我不知道明天会发生什么，但我知道这个世界将被改变
是的！无论会发生什么，我都会执着而坚定地相信——
太阳还会在明天升起，黎明的曙光依然如同爱人的眼睛
温暖的风还会吹过大地的腹部，母亲和孩子还在那里
　　嬉戏
大海的蓝色还会随梦一起升起，在子夜成为星辰的爱巢
劳动和创造还是人类获得幸福的主要方式，多数人都会
　　同意

2020.4.5/16

人类还会活着，善和恶都将随行，人与自身的斗争不会停止

时间的入口没有明显的提示，人类你要大胆而又加倍地小心。

是这个星球创造了我们

还是我们改变了这个星球？

哦，老虎！波浪起伏的铠甲

流淌着数字的光。唯一的意志。

Split-Open Planet
—*For all of humankind and all living things*

Did this planet create us
or did we change this planet?

O, tigers, with waves rising and falling on their armor,
flowing with the light of numbers. Their sole determination.

In this moment, they're still in another dimension,
walking alone with the calm gait of Nirvana

That walk which never grows weary, obscure flames.
They make the revolving energy turn into gears, time's
controls hammering the waves of their golden fur.

The tigers are still there. They never left us.
In the four directions of this planet, their toes are treading
on this present about to disappear. Their eyes reflect elements of
    creation.
They don't merely live in the ancient records of the *Chamu*[1].
Their eyes have always been watching a humankind preoccupied
    with good versus evil.

It isn't that every person has committed a specific crime. Once the
    sky begins to hang low, the flight of eagles never again attains
    sufficient height.

As soon as the sky is no longer elevated, consciousness and values are
    destined to slip down from lofty heights. Beside them are injured
    eagle wings.

When the language of sages was sullied by money and materialism,
    twenty years ago, I saw a bird in the city fall to the ground from
    a black chimney and die. Should we forgive the bird or our-

---

[1] *Chama*: Chamma is one of the ancient epics of the Yi People.

selves? The sky's stillness provides the answer to all.

"It's said that every omen will be transmitted in a different way." A bimo[1]-priest from our tribe once stated.

[1] Bimo are the priests who pass on the written language in the original Nuosu religion.

This war has finally arrived in a manner invisible to the naked eye.

O, ancient foe. Who intruded on your homeland, using offend as a metaphor,
as if this could alleviate some of their sins? Yet, without a doubt, it was humankind who roused you from a slumber tens of thousands of years long.

From one city to the next, from one country to the next,
it crosses traditional boundaries even though there are soldiers there armed to their teeth.
It crosses over sovereign territories, because no one can stop the free flow of air.
Even the most advanced probes didn't detect its peculiar whereabouts.

This is a unique war, a different death metaphor.

Of course it doesn't need a passport; it can go wherever it wants.
You see migratory birds that fly in accordance with the seasons, fruit bats hanging upside down from cliffs,
red-bottomed orangutans chasing those of the opposite sex, insects jumping across species;
they all throw the dice of life and death toward the mailboxes of heaven and hell.

It visited churches, mosques, Daoist temples, Buddhist temples, and secular schools;
It struck open nursing homes on lock-down and heavily guarded prisons.

If it can it will rouse every government in the world. The mask of the god of death
will nail black panic into space. The red spear will kill the black shield.

When the East and the West meet again at Fate's exit,
are they leaving dire straits? Or annihilating themselves?
The left hand blaming the right hand can't build
a new Noah's Ark to escape the plight of these thousand years.

The lonely planet is still spinning, but a prophet will always appear among the twelve sons of the snow peoples,
since *Le'e*[1] tells me all animals and plants are brothers.

Although the seas Homer chanted of are still surging liquid blue, the eyes of seals are filled with messages of the universe.
Perhaps this isn't the last judgment, but the bowl-shaped blue heavens covered
the heads of humankind before unicorns appeared.

This isn't a traditional war; it's even less of a nuclear war; a nuclear war has no winners.
Marie Curie spoke out for a just political regime. Even now we have no way to judge if she was right or wrong,
but thank heavens her conclusions concerning nuclear weapons haven't elicited slander or controversy.

This is a reappearance of wars that have appeared before,
but it's even more dangerous and frightening
since the global village of today is a double-edged sword for humanity.

A war is so ancient yet close by, no one can remain beyond it.
It invaded formidable dynasties, and rewrote the history of ancient

---

[1] *Lei'e* is one of the ancient Nuosu epics passed down in the Yi areas of the Greater and Lesser Liangshan Mountains.

imperial Athens.
In the Middle Ages, it effortlessly annihilated over a third of Europe's population.
It was also the colonizers' accomplice, killing hundreds of millions of Indigenous Americans.

This is a war of resistance that belongs to all humankind collectively. It doesn't distinguish between regions.
If I could, I would choose to protect every single life,
not to use abstract politics to interpret the connotations of so-called freedom.
I think Adorno[1] and the poet Ernesto Cardenal[2] would approve, because
even the humblest lives are greater than vacuous preaching.

If public security is constructed by each person,
I'll choose to obey the collective and not to resist.
From Wuhan to Rome, from Paris to London, from Madrid to New York,
we can see gazes on balconies that are familiar to us yet belong to strangers.

My respect for individual rights is based on respect for the rights of the whole.
If individual rights can harm the benefit of the masses without just cause,
I'll ruthlessly remove these words from the code of rights.
But please believe I'll uphold true human rights throughout my life,
and individual rights are the most sacred element we need to protect.

In this moment, humankind can only cross
this darkest canyon by working together.

O, Benjamin's[3] passport failed; he exhaled on the other side of the

---

[1] Theodor Adorno (1903-1969), German philosopher and sociologist.
[2] Ernesto Cardenal (1925-2020), Nicaraguan poet, priest, and revolutionary.
[3] Walter Benjamin (1892-1940), German philosopher, Marxist literary critic who committed suicide in 1940.

border and waved to me.
In reality he didn't need to appear in my dream to tell me why Stefan
    Zweig[1] committed suicide.

Fundamentally speaking, his despair to-
    wards humanity was that he believed
    wickedness had already won and
    couldn't be changed.

O, Euphrates, Ganges, Mississippi, and
    Yellow Rivers,
and all the rivers whose names I haven't
    listed here,
you've witnessed humankind's enduring
    lives and histories; can you
tell me when you swallow adversity, how you
spit back knowledge of survival and shiny,
    unadorned stones?

When I see Dante's Italy inundated with cries at the gates of hell,
Cervantes's descendants are experiencing even more physical and
    spiritual pain;
humanitarian aid is a virtue, no matter where it comes from.

The progress made this century in the fights to overthrow fascism
    and end racism;
Palmiro Togliatti[2], Pier Paolo Pasolini[3], and Antonio Gramsci[4]
    waved Red flags at the cemetery.

In Iran, when people are suffering a double disaster,
those assaulting them have never wanted to let them go.
In times like these, how can I read mystical Sufi poetry,
and how can I not mourn the children suffering in Syria?

Only lies make those who perform before the camera
to get elected truly believe themselves.
It's not that we shouldn't believe their declarations possess true logic,

---

1 Stefan Zweig (1881-1942), Austrian novelist, playwright who committed suicide in 1942.
2 Palmiro Togliatti (1893-1964), one of the founders of the Italian communist party, and international communist.
3 Pier Paolo Pasolini (1922-1975), Italian communist poet, film director.
4 Gramsci Antonio (1891-1937), founder of the Italian communist party, Marxist theorist.

it's that we should look at how many crimes they've committed
against the weak.

Now I see a lone sheep in the desert at sunset;
I don't know if it was lost by a Jew or an Arab.

Biashylazzi's[1] fire pit, center of the world,
let me return to the homeland lost in your memory
through the names of the most ancient plants.

In the distant, arid lands of the Mexican highlands where water is scarce
Juan Rulfo[2] is still there keeping watch over his coffin.
In order not to speak, this habitually silent village leader
even turned a parrot into a capricious swindler who could talk.

My true spiritual brother, the world's César Vallejo[3],
you weren't writing poems for one person, you were singing for a People.
Let a rooster play the backbone flute in the crop of your language,
and let the poor from every era eat enough before they fall asleep; don't let them
only see white milk and freshly baked bread in their dreams.
O, comrade, your alpaca-like simple warmth came from your soul.
It's no secret the origin of your words was 206 pale bones.

O, civilized and uncivilized. Development or retreat. Adding or subtracting.
—This is a split-open planet!

Here, currency and the internet link all peoples together. Even in the most

---

1 Biashylazzi was a famous ancient Nuosu Bimo priest and sage who passed down the written language.
2 Juan Rulfo (1917-1986), Mexican novelist and anthropologist.
3 César Vallejo (1892-1938), Indigenous Peruvian poet and Marxist.

primitive tribes of the Brazilian rainforest, there are people playing killing games on their cell phones.

Bedouins have built an imaginary desert in the city and can no longer see
the stars you can reach out and pluck with your hands.
The gypsies in Europe who ride the night lay in the darkness of Europe's cities; they are invisible during the day.

Here, humankind has become the master of all living things, having begun to occupy the territory of the ant king.
Mating Guinea baboons bare their teeth at the people watching them with baited breath.

Here, smart engineering can make the future return to the past, and can make the present become the future.
Ice flames igniting a winter sky are no longer a surprise.

Here, Indigenous women from all over the world just happen to pass through the maze of the internet wearing refashioned hats.
But when they smile at strangers, they still maintain the custom of covering half their mouths with scarves.

Here, half the British are joking about BREXIT, and the other half are paying the price of this joke's not being a joke.
This is akin to how beer bubbles turn into smiling tears.

Here, in order to protect the glaciers in the South Pole from melting any faster, dolphins protest by committing mass suicide, rejecting humankind's visits to the glaciers.
Wherever people's footprints are rare, the slaughter hasn't yet begun.

Here, when the snow line on the polar region moves upward, the water fowl on the lake send news of the rising water level to officials with slippery thinking.
And now falcon tears are eggs in the sky.

Here, grains grow in headwinds, hunger has been alleviated, perhaps today Malthus[1]
would revise his demographics; his not being a moralist didn't influence his existence as a thinker.

Here, the antelope still passes through wastelands flooded with sunlight. One hint of vibration in the wind will make it raise its ears;
sometimes death comes faster than it imagines. The bison can't hear the discussions unfolding between the mosquitoes and flies on its skin.

Here, when New York's streetlights signal to turn right, Bolivia's shepherds immediately decide to take the small path to the left,
since on the right there are tenacious precipices and a fear-inducing bottomless abyss.

Here, Russia's vodka is still consumed the most, but Sergei Esenin's[2] lines of missing the countryside
make someone in another country cry silently with grief and sorrow after drinking.

Here, Assange[3] created WikiLeaks. As he stood on the balcony of the Ecuadorean Embassy and waved to the world,
the death of the poor in Afghanistan coincidentally became known to the world.

Here, Catalonians like to eat Spanish ham in the evening, but they haven't forgotten
to take care of so-called referendums before eating ham. If Antonio Machado[4] were still alive, who would he vote for?

Here, they request the Irish Republican Army and the Basques to lay down their weapons.

---

[1] Thomas Robert Malthus (1766-1834), English cleric, demographer, and economist.
[2] Sergei Esenin (1895-1925), Russian lyric poet who committed suicide in December, 1925.
[3] Julian Assange (1971-), founder of WikiLeaks.
[4] Antonio Machado (1875-1939), well-known modern Spanish poet, a leading figure in Generation of '98.

but in other places they issue resolutions supporting separatism.

Here, most Americans believe their wealth has been stuffed into the pockets of the Chinese.
The commandments Moses brought back from the mountain systematically collapsed in the fable of the gene-splicing chain.

Here, Guevara and Gandhi were separated and invited into their respective palaces.
The term globalization has been repeated by thousands of people on the double beds at Hotel Elzenveld in Antwerp.

Here, the footsteps of the International Monetary Fund and The World Bank have already walked in places Jesus never went to.
But the poor bearing crosses and walking on the margins of the earth hold steadfast to their belief that Jesus is their neighbor.

Here, some Socialist thinking about labor benefits has been stolen by enemy groups.
Wealth has transcended all borders, but hardship has fallen on the individual.

Here, they overthrow regimes in other countries and create fear among immigrants in their own country.
These cages are so splendid, the poems Ritsos[1] wrote under the prison window have already grown into trees.

Here, television stupefied people into broadcasting live the collapse of the Twin Towers.
In Colombia, poetry has become the most humanitarian means of political dialogue.

Here, each day marginalized languages and lives are quietly removed by controlling powers.
But in terms of personal privacy, 97.7‰ of the people in the world

---

[1] Yiannis Ritsos (1909-1990), modern Greek communist poet, left-wing activist.

are naked under surveillance.

Here, Karl Marx's ideologies are still becoming concrete movements, but Wall Street is more willing to conspire with elite academics,
saying this Jew is only a leader in one academic sphere.

Here, some people want to continue opening doors, but others close the doors that are already open.
As soon as the ground beneath our feet leaves us, distance loses its meaning.

Here, those opening doors don't entirely know what to let in and what to block out.
Some people are in virtual space being deprived of the ability to expand boundaries and receive the same identities.

Here, those who advocate closing doors aren't worried their own houses will one day become cages,
but those who are spiritually exiled from their homelands are eternal targets to be banished from freedom.

Here, the skeleton has already become a whole body. If you cut away one hand it can bear it,
but if you cut the skeleton in half, it will be hard to survive. Shanghai's ears can hear Florida's toes moaning.

Here, the bars in St. Lucia in the South Pacific are still playing saxophones, each soda bottle that's opened can hear the pleasant surprises or sighs of the NY stock market.
Online bullying is the fifth column of the current era. Habermas[1] randomly saw the truth.

Here, people burn down 5G cell towers; this is undoubtedly a foolish medieval reversion.

---

[1] Jürgen Habermas(1929-), German philosopher, one of the main representatives of contemporary Western Marxism.

Even though Australia's red-breasted robin is the last to chirp, its chirping is full of speculators' suspicions.

Here, we no longer have the Inquisition executing Galileo, but there are still people following fundamentalist orders to kill infidels.
It isn't that all so-called democracies indulge the weak; Jefferson[1] thought that eliminating Indigenous peoples was great cultural progress.

Here, the ratio of rich to poor hasn't actually changed, but class boundaries have been erased by new liberalism.
When they need to, a translational government will reconfigure depriving the poor into a benevolent act.

Here, not all countries can manufacture a button; of course the purpose of this is to enable the button to swim to all places that have an ocean.
All those fighting over transforming the world were equal at the beginning. No wonder on his deathbed, Trotsky believed in arguments for continuing the revolution.

Here, they knocked down the Berlin Wall, but built more walls in order to separate. The walls are thicker and taller.
The panoramic prison made opaque space once again descend into the inescapable trap in Orwell's[2] *1984*.

Here, debates about freedom and lifestyle definitely aren't about racial differences,
since the lockdown brought about by the pandemic isn't for a vague majority.

O, split-open planet, did you see the golden tigers spinning your body?

---

[1] Thomas Jefferson (1743-1826), the third president of the United States, primary author of The Declaration of Independence.

[2] George Orwell (1903-1950), original name, Eric Arthur Blair, English novelist and social critic. His masterpiece was the novel *1984*.

Did you see them disappear into the sunrises and sunsets of the vast sky? Each breath they take caresses the liquid light above time.
This is the time to save ourselves. We can't make any more mistakes; missteps will mean ultimate destruction.

When the signs of catastrophe were sent from all directions
the legendary ark didn't actually appear.
There were no scenes of tsunamis covering one city after the next.
We didn't hear that terrifying sound coming from the heavens.
We didn't witness the mushroom cloud's atomic nightmare rising.
There wasn't one group of countries declaring war on another.
Even though it's not the continuation of the two wars of the twentieth century,
the losses and immense damage it creates might be even greater.
This is an ancient, endless war. I say it's endless
because your enemy has been lying in wait for thousands of years.
In the history of catastrophes, you've encountered it countless times.
Goya used his paintbrush to record that the odor of death
was even more shocking than death itself.
It can be ascertained that humankind has entered another dangerous arena
and brought a disaster that could have been avoided to the entire world.
Now, close-range killing is tragically being carried out.
It doesn't distinguish between countries or races, whether we're rich or poor.
When the god of death has just brushed past us, perhaps death is
knocking down a strong man or, in the same instant, pushing over a feeble woman.
The god of death, being cursed, has already used intangible violence to kill countless people;
among these are whites, blacks, and yellow-skinned peoples, including children and seniors.
If we wanted to issue a declaration of war, O, people fighting now,
we would sign this joint name—Humankind!

O, when we step into the habitats where other living beings reproduce

at a speed never seen before,
cutting down primitive forests on both sides of the Amazon River in Brazil,
causing a great fire to blacken the green lungs of the earth,
every advancement for the so-called survival of humankind
conceals a mortal danger for the future.
In Africa the popularity of killing wild animals
has caused a constant increase in the number of endangered species.
When the territory of lion-packs is compressed into a pitiful area
the animal at the top of the food chain faces danger everywhere.
Its continuous roars at dusk on the plains
express its indignation toward and protest against the senseless intruders.
In the Third Pole, in the uninhabited region of Hoh Xil,
the homeland the snow leopard watches over is also shrinking.
The carnivores who previously never hurt humans
have started entering villages due to food shortages.
In Southeast Asia, Indigenous peoples have been forced further away by urbanization.
One day a great number of their chickens mysteriously got diarrhea and died.
The death of a child named Kaptan[1] blew an inauspicious mouth harp.
From the Congo to Malaysia when the forest animals are killed
no matter how faraway you are, you can hear the sound of their skulls cracking open.
It's precisely this so-called intimate behavior—hunting and slaughter—
that goes against the mandate of heaven and links these micro-organisms.
In reality, each disaster tells us
we should feel deep reverence for all species.

---

1 Kaptan Boonmanuch, born in western Thailand, and died of H5N1 Aviary Flu on January 25, 2004 at the age of six, was among the earliest to die from this new type of human virus. -not quite accurate according to info I found.

We'll pay a price that's hard to imagine
for encroaching upon and destroying even the weakest organisms.

O, humankind, your creation gods have brought us miracles.
When Pangu split heaven and earth, animals and people walked out from the mud.
On the banks of the Ganges, the limitless magical power of Lord Brahma[1]
created living things more numerous than the stars in the sky.
In the Andes Mountains, the Indigenous deity Pacha Kamaq[2]
brought the first peoples and countless birds and beasts.
In Greece, where numerous gods resided in the temples and heroes came forth in large numbers,
Prometheus bestowed humans and visible objects with life.
He also offered his own crimson heart as a sacrifice
and finally brought fire, wisdom, knowledge and the arts to the human world.
And the son of eagles, our Nuosu Zhyge Alu[3]
made our ancestors' shadows eternally float above the present mountains.
Humankind, perhaps your civilization's history may have been cut off from that time forward,
but that type of interruption is a mere instant in the long river of time.
From the Bronze Age to the age when steam machines rolled across the earth;
from the discovery of radium to nuclear energy's benefits to humankind being vastly exploited;
from when the Wright Brothers[4] put wings on themselves until spacecraft carried people's dreams, one after the next, to the distant

---

1 Lord Brahma, the creator god in Hinduism, creator of written Sanskrit checking this with Biplab
2 PachaKamaq, ancient Incan deity said to have created the world.--not quite accurate according to info I found
3 Zhyge Alu, creator hero in the Nuosu epics.
4 Wright Brothers, American brothers Wilbur Wright and Orville Wright, inventors of airplanes. On Dec.7th, 1903, they made the first successful test flight of an airplane in human history.

space station,
computer and bioengineering stepped across the threshold of a century.
We cheered when we saw the black holes in the universe that weren't actually imagined.
The internet allowed us to understand the world anew.
Time and social class, migration and freedom, self and overstepping one's authority, speed and separation,
agoraphobia and one-sidedness, ethnic nations and global views, expropriation and sovereignty,
integration and dividing, bread and ballpoint pens, vagabonds and utopias,
predicted paradoxes and risk calculations, eliminating differences and hostages to fate—
it's precisely because of all these that we gasp in admiration at the setting sun.
Only the thirst for the wonder of the journey and the subsequent probable danger
give us sufficient reason to believe that tomorrow's sunrise will be even more splendid.
But, humankind, without a doubt you are not real supermen; even though you're already formidable enough,
as long as you can't change the fact that you are the existence of this planet,
you will face the same choices all living things face during catastrophes.
This is the fate the gods of creation set forth, no one can easily change this.
That invisible hand made all living things form a crystal circle;
any avaricious destroyer will sink into fear and drown.
All living beings might be carrying their own murderer in their bodies.
Moreover, humankind isn't made of metal, and it has the weakest parts.
We're powerful, so powerful we become the world's dictators.
We're so weak perhaps a micro-organism invisible to the naked eye
can defeat us in an invisible battle.

Humans will always be just one among the biological groups;
we don't have the right to ceaselessly expropriate this earth.
Aside from the most basic survival needs, any slaughter of other living things can be viewed as a crime.
Treat nature well, treat lives other than our own well, please remember this!
Treating them well is treating ourselves well. The alternative is eternal doom.

O, humankind, this is the time disinfectants flow along national borders.
It's the time when you'll be next if the person beside you gets it.
It's the time when dissolving time and thirsty arrows are in a race.
It's the time when we mock others and can't do good by ourselves.
It's the time when that zealous ice is carving the raging inferno.
It's the time when the earth and people simultaneously don facemasks.
It's the time when eagles in the sky fight with red foxes in the wilderness.
It's the time when all the boulevards and public squares fall silent.
It's the time when children can only imagine the ocean from beside the window.
It's the time when angels in white and the god of death approach the abyss.
It's the time when lonely seniors will devour despair in one gulp.
It's a time when it's safer to stay home than it is to go out.
It's the time when the outstretched hand in the throat of vagabonds is the hungriest.
It's the time when advocates for humanitarian aid are greater than ideology.
It's the time when urban tribal peoples are forced to return to the countryside.
It's the time when the earth, sea and sky pay their respects to living beings.
It's the time when doves fly out from cut-open veins.
It's the time when Italian tears blur Chinese eyes.
It's the time when moans in London make Spanish guitars whimper.

It's the time when New York nurses cry with God.
It's the time when lies and the truth appear and disappear on the
    internet.
It's the time when Gandhi's people disturb the faraway elaphure.
It's the time when humankind's glory and evil come face to face.
It's the time when it's hardest to believe the other side or doubt one's
    enemies.
It's the time when language gives people hope yet provokes hatred.
It's the time when half the people are perplexed and the other half
    are worried.
It's the time when the breath of blue whales stirs peace.
It's the time when the stars send off the dead on behalf of relatives.
It's the time when a thousand priests curse a shadow.
It's the time when the faces of strangers start to become distinct.
It's the time when people in the same bed with different dreams now
    dream of each other.
It's the time when people seemingly together but actually divergent
    start a cold war.
It's the time when the old is on the verge of collapse and the new
    hasn't yet arrived.
It's the time when the divine branches declare misfortune or disaster
    will be averted.
It's the time when black stones conceal white meanings.
It's the time when the sheep of all gods are waiting for Moses to cross
    the Red Sea.
It's the time when the bull-horn blown by warriors tears you up with
    grief.
It's the time when the eagle goblet is grasped once again by the poet
    prophet.
It's the time when the people and living things on the Tower of Babel
    earnestly engage in peace talks.
It's precisely a time like this. It's precisely a time like this.
O, humankind. There's only one chance to end this war.

Did the planet creat us
or we changed the planet?

When the split-open planet spins the wheel on volition's forehead,
all lives will run under the ever-unchanging sun.
The masks on the gods of creation will
 glimmer in the boundless dome of the
 heavens.
That omnipresent light will return from the
 sky's womb into
the dark, pure air of another space, like the
 liquid womb.
That's our planet's, the only blue,
a virgin olive floating beyond the imagination.
That's our planet, a single water droplet that doesn't fall,
the metaphysical gemstone that can't be casually named.
It's a flame not extinguished by life or death, transformed by the
 creator.
We don't need to be mediums, even up to the present,
we can find its genes of its eyes, bones, fur, and blood vessels in the
 earth, oceans, forests and rivers.
That's our planet, it nurtures all lives.
In spite of wars, plagues, disasters or regime changes,
it's never ceased to nourish and be charitable towards life.
When we caress its body, even though it's beautiful as before,
we can see scars on it that break our hearts.
This is our planet, no matter who you are, what race you belong to,
no matter which place on its body you're living in,
we should all gather together for its vitality and beauty.
Saving the planet can never be separated from saving ourselves.

O, goddess Pumolieyi[1], please let me borrow your needle that sews
 skulls,
and that ball of white-wool yarn in your hands, because I want to
 sew together
this planet we've already split open.

Split-open planet. Let us give you Monday from beneath our ribs.
Let them decrease carbon emissions, let the green leaves from the
 Paris Agreement

---

[1] Pumolieyi, a goddess in the Nuosu creation myths, the virgin mother of the hero Zhyga Alu.

block the nostril casting the dissenting vote, turn his face into a cloak.
Let us give the hungry sustenance, and not just give them numbers.
If it's possible, when they awaken, steal away
    the names of politicians,
don't give liars yesterday's time, because
    the audience will be the largest the day
    after tomorrow.
Let us heal divisions, but this doesn't mean
    making things that are irrelevant uniform.
When 44 are hidden in beams of light, the wooden stool that works
    to no avail will cry out.
That's the sailor on dry land. Adam Mickiewicz's[1] secret key
hopes that those who sleep, having lost one job, will wake up to three
    jobs waiting for them.
The people on the streets already know whoever lights the left house
    on fire,
the yard of the house on the right can't narrowly escape. Despair
    makes the streetlamps grow donkey lips.
Let the hunters of yesterday become today's vegetarians.
Every childhood pledge can be fulfilled when their mothers are still alive.
Let the stones of Jerusalem recover future memories.
Let the desert of the Jewish and Arab prophets who've been simulta-
    neously buried bloom.
I hope the end is the beginning, and that the empty sea surges with
    pregnant colors.
Let the wood bowl find parched lips, let faith choose its own clothes.
Let languages that can't understand each other address one another
    at the United Nations.
Let the listeners cheer until they become camels.
Let flags of equality hang in windows all over the world.
Let stability and logic have a falling out.
Let every person become themselves, let themselves like that person
    more.
Let convergence abdicate authority to individuality, let the universal
    become equal.
The cracks in stones are brimming with poems.
Let the hands on rocks grab hold of slippery fish.

---

[1] Adam Mickiewicz (1798-1855), Polish poet, revolutionary, main founder of Polish literature.

Let bankers spew out a polygon of regulations.
Let red cover blue, let the blue mouth sing on the red face.
Let that which is about to die out become rational, let the unborn reconcile with the present.
Let all living things jump with joy into the air; there are soft sponges below them.
This planet is our planet, even though it's as heavy as Sisyphus' boulder.
If we can defy gravity and stand in the sky, it seems more like a child's balloon.
Just because we exist as phenomena doesn't mean all humans have learned to think.
The questions this age has given us weren't in the ancient records, we must answer them ourselves.
We don't have much time remaining, since short-sighted people are still quarreling.
This isn't a disastrous era; we don't know for sure that past eras were superior,
since we're unable to imagine the most remote places from the past have become our homelands in the present.
This is the power of currency, this is the power of the market, this is another power's power.
It has no above or below, it only has what's behind and in front of us; only reality itself can reply to its outcome.
This is an enormous shift, it's longer than a century, it can only be calculated in terms of a millennium.
We can't return to the past, because the old houses have all disappeared.
We can't choose to close ourselves off; no matter what material becomes a high wall, it only implies separation.
We can't choose to resist; as soon as prejudice turns to hate, you or I could die.
We don't need to ask those ancient rivers; their sources are full of prehistory's silence.
Perhaps this was the original enlightenment, diverse civilizations in harmony were all her children.
Give up the difference of three and try hard to find consensus among seven; this isn't putting the problem off on others.

Within a square might be a round possibility; it's not being prejudiced by first impressions.
Let everyone abandon the laws of the forest; this should be better, not viewing oneself as most important.
Let people try to make bright times last longer rather than bestowing darkness on each other.
None of this is a simple method; it's making all participants aware
the future of this planet doesn't just belong to you and me, it belongs to all lives.
I don't know what will happen tomorrow; it's said poets have the ability to foretell the future,
but I won't predict the future, since the boundless oceans didn't leave any traces in the sky.
The light I've praised countless times is now on a triumphant march.
I don't know what will happen tomorrow, but I know the world will be changed.
Yes! No matter what happens, I firmly and steadfastly believe
the sun will still rise tomorrow, dawn's light will be as before, like a lover's eyes.
The warm wind will still blow over the earth's abdomen, mothers and children will still be playing there.
The blue of the sea will still rise with dreams and, at midnight, become the lovenest of stars.
Most people agree labor and creation will still be the main means through which people attain fulfillment.
People will keep living, good and evil will keep accompanying them; the struggle between humankind and itself won't cease.
The entrance to time doesn't have an obvious marker.
Humankind, you must be courageously and exponentially careful.

Did this planet create us
or did we change this planet?

O, tigers, with waves rising and falling on their armor,
flowing with the light of numbers. Their sole determination.

Translated by Jami Proctor Xu

迟到的挽歌
——献给我的父亲吉狄·佐卓·伍合略且

2020.4.22/26

当摇篮的幻影从天空坠落
一片鹰的羽毛覆盖了时间,此刻你的思想
渐渐地变白,以从未体验过的抽空蜉蝣于
群山和河流之上。

你的身体已经朝左曲腿而睡
与你的祖先一样,古老的死亡吹响了返程
那是万物的牛角号,仍然是重复过的
成千上万次,只是这一次更像是晨曲。

光是唯一的使者,那些道路再不通往
异地,只引导你的山羊爬上那些悲戚的陡坡
那些守卫恒久的刺猬,没有喊你的名字
但另一半丢失的自由却被惊恐洗劫
这是最后的接受,诸神与人将完成最后的仪式。

不要走错了地方,不是所有的路都可以走
必须要提醒你,那是因为打开的偶像不会被星星照亮,
只有属于你的路,才能看见天空上时隐时现的
马鞍留下的印记。听不见的词语命令虚假的影子
在黄昏前吓唬宣示九个古彝文字母的睡眠。

那是你的铠甲,除了你还有谁
敢来认领,荣誉和呐喊曾让猛兽陷落
所有的耳朵都知道你回来了,不是黎明的风
送来的消息,那是祖屋里挂在墙上的铠甲
发出了异常的响动

唯有死亡的秘密会持续。

那是你白银的冠冕，
镌刻在太阳瀑布的核心，
翅翼聆听定居的山峦
星座的沙漏被羊骨的炉膛遣返，
让你的陪伴者将烧红的卵石奉为
　　神明
这是赤裸的疆域
所有的眼睛都看见了
那只鹰在苍穹的消失，不是名狗
克玛阿果[1]咬住了不祥的兽骨，而是
占卜者的鹰爪杯在山脊上落入谷底。

是你挣脱了肉体的锁链？
还是以勇士的名义报出了自己的族谱？

死亡的通知常常要比胜利的
捷报传得更快，也要更远。

这片彝语称为吉勒布特[2]的土地
群山就是你唯一的摇篮和基座
当山里的布谷反复地鸣叫
那裂口的时辰并非只发生在春天
当黑色变成岩石，公鸡在正午打鸣
日都列萨[3]的天空落下了可怕的红雪
那是死神已经把独有的旗帜举过了头顶
据说哪怕世代的冤家在今天也不能发兵。

这是千百年来男人的死亡方式，并没有改变
渴望不要死于苟且。山神巡视的阿布则洛[4]雪山

---

1 克玛阿果：彝族历史传说中一只名狗的名字。
2 吉勒布特：凉山彝族聚居区一地名，彝语意为刺猬出没的土地。
3 日都列萨：凉山彝族聚居区一地名，传说是彝族火把节的发源地。
4 阿布则洛：凉山彝族聚居区布拖县境内的一座神山。

亲眼见过黑色乌鸦落满族人肩头如梦的场景
可以死于疾风中铁的较量，可以死于对荣
　　誉的捍卫
可以死于命运多舛的无常，可以死于七曜
　　日的玩笑
但不能死于耻辱的挑衅，唾沫会抹掉你的
　　名誉。

死亡的方式有千百种，但光荣和羞耻只有
　　两种
直到今天赫比施祖[1]的经文都还保留着智
　　者和
贤人的名字，他的目光充盈并点亮了那条道路
尽管遗失的颂词将从褶皱中苏醒，那些闪光的牛颈
仍然会被耕作者询问，但脱粒之后的苦荞一定会在
最严酷的季节——养活一个民族的婴儿。

哦，归来者！当亡灵进入白色的国度
那空中的峭壁滑行于群山哀伤的胯骨
祖先的斧子掘出了人魂与鬼神的边界
吃一口赞词中的燕麦吧，它是虚无的秘笈
石姆木哈[2]的巨石已被一匹哭泣的神马撬动。

那是你匆促踏着神界和人界的脚步
左耳的蜜蜡聚合光晕，胸带缀满贝壳
普嫫列依[3]的羊群宁静如黄昏的一堆圆石
那是神赐予我们的果实，对还在分娩的人类
唯有对祖先的崇拜，才能让逝去的魂灵安息
虽然你穿着出行的盛装，但当你开始迅跑
那双赤脚仍然充满了野性强大的力量。

---

[1] 赫比施祖：凉山彝族历史上最著名的毕摩（祭司）之一。

[2] 石姆木哈：凉山彝族传说中亡灵的归属地，传说它的位置在天空和大地之间。

[3] 普嫫列依：彝族创世神话中的女神之一。

众神走过天庭和群山的时候，拒绝踏入
欲望与暴戾的疆域，只有三岁的孩子能
短暂地看见，他们粗糙的双脚也
　　没有鞋。

哦，英雄！我把你的名字隐匿于
　　光中
你的一生将在垂直的晦暗里重现
　　消失
那是遥远的迟缓，被打开的门的
　　吉尔[1]。

那是你婴儿的嘴里衔着母亲的乳房
女人的雏形，她的美重合了触及的
记忆，一根小手指拨动耳环的轮毂
美人中的美人，阿呷嫞嫫[2]真正的嫡亲
她来自抓住神牛之尾涉过江水的家族。

那是你的箭头，奔跑于伊姆则木[3]神山上的
羚羊的化身，你看见落叶松在冬日里嬉戏
追逐的猎物刻骨铭心，吞下了赭红的饥馑
回到幻想虫蛹的内部，童年咬噬着光的羽翼。

那是你攀爬上空无的天梯，在悬崖上取下蜂巢
每一个小伙伴都张大着嘴，闭合着满足的眼睛
唉，多么幸福！迎接那从天而降的金色的蜂蜜。

那是你在达基沙洛[4]的后山倾听风的诉说
听见了那遥远之地一只绵羊坠崖的声音
这是马嚼子的暗示，牧羊的孩子为了分享
一顿美餐，合谋把一只羊推下悬崖的木盘

1 吉尔：彝语中的护身符，在凉山彝族不同的家族中都有自己的吉尔。
2 阿呷嫞嫫：彝族传说中一种鸟的名字，此鸟以脖颈细长灵动美丽而著称。
3 伊姆则木：凉山彝族聚居区布拖县境内的一座神山。
4 达基沙洛：凉山彝族聚居区布拖县一地名，此地为诗人父亲出生的地方。

谁能解释童年的秘密,人类总在故伎重演。

那是谁第一次偷窥了爱情给肉体的馈赠
知晓了月琴和竖笛宁愿死也要纯粹的可能
火把节是小裤脚[1]们重启星辰诺言的头巾
　　和糖果
是眼睛与自由的节日,大地潮湿璀璨泛滥
　　的床。
你在勇士的谱系中告诉他们,我是谁!在
　　人性的
终结之地,你抗拒肉体的胆怯,渴望精神
　　的永生。

在这儿父子联名指引你,长矛和盾牌给你
　　嘴巴
不用发现真相,死亡树皮上的神祇被刻在
　　右侧
如果不是地球的灰烬,那就该拥抱自由的
　　意志
为赤可波西[2]喝彩!只有口弦才是诗人自己的语言
因为它的存在爱情维护了高贵、含蓄和羞涩。

那是你与语言邂逅拥抱火的传统的第一次
从德古[3]那里学到了格言和观察日月的知识
当马布霍克[4]的獐子传递着缠绵的求偶之声
这古老的声音远远超过人类所熟知的历史
你总会赶在黎明之光推开木门的那个片刻
将尔比[5]和克哲[6]溶于水,让一群黑羊和一群
白羊舔舐两片山坡之间充满了睡意的星团。

你在梦里接受了双舌羊约格哈加[7]的馈赠

---

1 小裤脚:特指凉山彝族聚居地阿都方言区的彝人,因男人着裤上大下小而被形象地称为小裤脚。

2 赤可波西:彝族历史上最著名的口弦(一种古老的以口腔进行共鸣的乐器)出产地。

3 德古:彝族传统社会中的智者和贤达。

4 马布霍克:凉山彝族聚居区布拖县境内的一座神山。

5 尔比:彝语的谚语和箴言。

6 克哲:彝族中一种古老的说唱诗歌形式。

7 约格哈加:彝族历史上一只著名的绵羊,以双舌著称,其鸣叫声能传到很远的地方。

2020.4.22/26

那执念的叫声让一碗水重现了天象的外形。

你是闪电铜铃的兄弟,是神鹰琥珀的儿子
你是星座虎豹字母选择的世世代代的首领。

母性的针孔能目睹痛苦的构造
哦,众神!没有人不是孤儿
不是你亲眼看见过的,未必都是假的
但真的确实更少。每一个民族都有
自己的英雄时代,这只是时间上的差别
你的胆识和勇敢穿越了瞄准的地带
祖先的护佑一直钟情眷顾于你。

那是浩大的喧嚣,据说在神界错杀了山神
也要所为者抵命,更何况人世血亲相连的手指
杀牛给他!将他围成星座的
肚脐,为即将消失的生命哀嚎
为最后的抵押救赎
那是习惯的法典,被继承的长柄镰刀
在鸦片的迷惑下,收割了兄长的白昼与夜晚
此刻唯有你知道,你能存活下来
是人和魔鬼都判定你的年龄还太小。

那是你爬在一株杨树,以愤怒的名义
射杀了一只威胁孕妇的花豹,它皮上留下
的空洞如同压缩的命运,为你预备了亡灵
的床单,或许就是灭焰者横陈大地的姿态
只要群山亦复如是,鹰隼滑动光明的翅膀
勇士的马鞍还在等待,你就会成为不朽。

并不是在繁星之夜你才意识到什么是死亡

而拒绝陈腐的恐惧,是因为对生的意义的
　　渴望
你知道为此要猛烈地击打那隐蔽的,无名
　　的暗夜
不是他者教会了我们在这片土地上游离的
　　方式
是因为我们创造了自我的节日,唯有在失
　　重时
我们才会发现生命之花的存在,也才可能
在短暂借用的时针上,一次次拒绝死亡。

如果不是哲克姆土[1]神山给了你神奇的力量
就不可能让一只牛角发出风暴一般的怒吼
你注视过星星和燕麦上犹如梦境一样的露珠
与生俱来的敏感,让你察觉到将要发生的一切
那是崇尚自由的天性总能深谙太阳与季节变化
最终选择了坚硬的石头,而不是轻飘飘的羽毛。

那是一个千年的秩序和伦理被改变的时候
每一个人都要经历生活与命运双重的磨砺
这不是局部在过往发生的一切,革命和战争
让兄弟姐妹立于疾风暴雨,见证了希望
也看见了眼泪,肉体和心灵承担天石的重负
你的赤脚熟悉荆棘,但火焰的伤痛谁又知晓
无论混乱的星座怎样移动于不可解的词语之间
对事物的解释和弃绝,都证明你从来就是彝人。

你靠着那土墙沉睡,抵抗了并非人的需要
重新焊接了现实,把爱给了女人和孩子
你是一颗自由的种子,你的马始终立于寂静
当夜色改动天空的轮廓,你的思绪自成一体

[1] 哲克姆土:凉山彝族聚居区布拖县境内的一座神山。

就是按照雄鹰和骏马的标准，你
　　也是英雄
你用牙齿咬住了太阳，没有辜负
　　灿烂的光明
你与酒神纠缠了一生，通过它倾
　　诉另一个自己
不是你才这样，它创造过奇迹也
　　毁灭过人生。

你在活着的时候就选择了自己火葬的地点
从那里可以遥遥看到通往兹兹普乌[1]的方向
你告诉长子，酒杯总会递到缺席者的手中
有多少先辈也没有活到你现在这样的年龄
存在之物将收回一切，只有火焰会履行承诺
加速的天体没有改变铁砧的位置，你的葬礼
就在明天，那天边隐约的雷声已经告诉我们
你的族人和兄弟姐妹将为你的亡魂哭喊送别。

哦，英雄！当黎明的曙光伸出鸟儿的翅膀
光明的使者伫立于群山之上，肃穆的神色
犹如太阳的处子，他们在等待那个凝望时刻
祭祀的牛头反射出斧头的幻影，牛皮遮盖着
哀伤的面具，这或许是另一种生的入口
再一次回到大地的胎盘，死亡也需要赞颂
给每一个参加葬礼的人都能分到应有的食物
死者在生前曾反复叮嘱，这是最后的遗愿
颂扬你的美德，那些穿着黑色服饰的女性
轮流说唱了你光辉的一生，词语的肋骨被
置入了诗歌，那是骨髓里才有的万般情愫
在这里你会相信部族的伟大，亡灵的忧伤
会变得幸福，你躺在亲情和爱编织的怀抱

---

[1] 兹兹普乌：地点位于云南省昭通境内，是传说中彝族六个部落会盟迁徙出发的地方。

每当哭诉的声音被划出伤口,看不见的血液
就会淌入空气的心脏,哦,琴弦又被折断!
不是死者再听不见大家的声音,相信
　　你还在!
当那个远嫁异乡的姐姐说:"以后还
　　有谁能
代替你听我哭泣",泪水就挂在了你
　　的眼角
主方和客人在这里用"克哲"的舌头
　　决定胜负
将回答永恒的死亡是从什么时候来到人间
逝去的亲人们又如何在那白色的世界相聚
万物众生在时间的居所是何其的渺小卑微
只有精神的勇士和哲人方才可能万古流芳
送行的旗帜列成了长队,犹如古侯[1]和曲涅[2]又
回到迁徙的历史,哦,精神的流亡还在继续
屠宰的牛羊将慰藉生者,昨天的死亡与未来
的死亡没有什么两样,但被死亡创造的奇迹
却会让讲述者打破常规悄然放进生与死的罗盘
那里红色的胜利正在返回,天空布满了羊骨
的纹路,今天是让魂灵满意的日子,我相信。

哦,英雄!古老的太阳涌动着神秘的光芒
那群山和大地的阶梯正在虚幻中渐渐升高
领路的毕摩[3]又一次抓住了光线铸造的权杖
为最后的步伐找到了维系延伸可能的活水
亡者在木架上被抬着,摇晃就像最初的摇篮
朝左侧睡弯曲的身体,仿佛还在母亲的子宫
这是最后的凯旋,你将进入那神谕者的殿堂
你看那透明的斜坡已经打开了多维度的台阶
远处的河流上飘落着宇宙间无法定位的种子

[1] 古侯:凉山彝族著名的古老部落之一。
[2] 曲涅:凉山彝族著名的古老部落之一。
[3] 毕摩:彝族原始宗教中的祭司和文化传承人。

送魂经的声音忽高忽低,仿佛是
　　从天外飘来
由远而近的回应似乎又像是来自
　　脚下的空无
送别的人们无法透视,但毕摩和
　　你都能看见
黑色的那条路你不能走,那是魔鬼走的路。

沿着白色的路走吧,祖先的赤脚在上面走过
此时,你看见乌有之事在真理中复活,那身披
银光颂词里的虎群占据了中心,时间变成了花朵
树木在透明中微笑,岩石上有第七空间的代数
隐形的鱼类在河流上飞翔,玻璃吹奏山羊的胡子
白色与黑色再不是两种敌对的颜色,蓝色统治的
时间也刚被改变,紫色和黄色并不在指定的岗位
你看见了一道裂缝正在天际边被乘法渐渐地打开
那里卷轴铺开了反射的页面,光的楼层还在升高
柱子预告了你的到来,已逝的景象淹没了膝盖
不用法律捆绑,这分明就是白色,为新的仪式。

这不是未来的城堡,它的结构看不到缝合的痕迹
那里没有战争,只有千万条通往和平之梦的动物园
那里找不到锋利的铁器,只有能变形的柔软的马勺
那里没有等级也没有族长,只有为北斗七星准备的梯子
透明的思想不再为了表达,语言的珍珠滚动于裸体的空白
没有人嘲笑你拿错了碗,这里的星辰不屈服于伪装的炮弹
这里只有白色,任何无意义的存在都会在白色里荡然无存
白色的骨架已经打开,从远处看它就像宇宙间的一片叶子。

哦,英雄!你已经被抬上了火葬地九层的松柴之上
最接近天堂的神山姆且勒赫[1]是祖灵永久供奉的地方

[1] 姆且勒赫:凉山彝族聚居区布拖县境内的一座神山。

这是即将跨入不朽的广场，只有火焰和太阳能为你咆哮
全身覆盖纯色洁净的披毡，这是人与死亡最后的契约
你听见了吧，众人的呼喊从山谷一直传到了湛蓝的高处
这是人类和万物的合唱，所有的蜂巢都倾泻出水晶的音符
那是母语的力量和秘密，唯有它的声音能让一个种族哭泣
那是人类父亲的传统，它应该穿过了黑暗简朴的空间
刚刚来到了这里，是你给我耳语说永生的计时已经开始
哦，我们的父亲！你是我们所能命名的全部意义的英雄
你呼吸过，你存在过，你悲伤过，你战斗过，你热爱过
你看见了吧，在那光明涌入的门口，是你穿着盛装的先辈
而我们给你的这场盛典已接近尾声，从此你在另一个世界。

哦，英雄！不是别人，是你的儿子为你点燃了最后的火焰。

Late Elegy
—For my father, Jidi Zuozhuo Wuhelüeqie

When the phantasmal cradle falls from the sky
a hawk's feather covers time, and your thoughts
slowly turn clear, to an unknown mayfly of stolen time
over the mountains and rivers.

Your body sleeps curled on its left side
like your ancestors, and an ancient death trumpets the return
it is the ox horn of all living beings, and repeats
and repeats, but this time sounds more like an aubade.

Light is the only messenger, and those roads no longer lead
to strange places, instead guiding your goats up those steep slopes of grief
those hedgehogs who always stand guard do not call your name
though the other lost half of freedom has been looted in terror
this is the last acceptance, and all the spirits and people will complete
the final rites.

Don't lose your way, not every road can be traveled
a reminder that these are images that when opened won't be lit by
stars
and only on your own road you can catch glimpses
of the traces left by the saddle. Inaudible speech commands the false
shadows
troubling the sleep of the proclaimed nine ancient Yi words before
dusk.

This is your armor, and who aside from you
would dare come claim it, honor and shouting once made the beasts
subside
every ear knows of your return, and it isn't the dawn wind
that brings the news, but the armor hung on the walls of the ances-

tral room
emitting the strange sounds of stirring
only the secrets of death will continue.

This is your silver crown,
engraved on the center of the sun's waterfall
the wings listen closely to the long-settled
    mountains
and the constellations' hourglass is repatriated
    by a stove of goat bones,
let those who accompany you receive the burn-
    ing red pebbles for the gods
this is a naked territory
and all the eyes can see
the hawk disappear into the firmament, it isn't
    the famous hound of legend
Kemaaguo[1] biting an unlucky animal bone, but rather
the diviner's hawk-talon goblet tumbling from the mountain ridge to
    the valley.

Is it you escaping the fetters of the body?
Or are you declaiming your clan genealogy as a warrior?

The announcement of death often spreads faster
than news of success, and travels farther.

In this place called Jilebute[2] in the Yi language
these mountains were your one cradle and foundation
when the cuckoos call and call in the mountains
those breached hours do not happen only in spring
when the blackness becomes crags, and the roosters crow at noon
terrible red snow falls over Riduliesa[3]
signifying that Death has raised his flag all the way to the top
some say that on this day even if the enemy comes, soldiers cannot be
    dispatched.

This is how centuries of men have died, without change

---

1 A famous dog in the legends of Yi people.
2 A place in Liangshan, the biggest area of China where Yi people live in compact communities. "Jilebute" means "the haunt of hedgehogs" in Yi language.
3 A place in Liangshan. According to legend, it is the cradle of Torch Festival of Yi ethnic group.

but desire must not die as well. Mountain dei-
    ties inspect the holy Mt. Abuzeluo[1]
those who have seen black crows fall on the
    shoulders of their clansmen like in a
    dream
can die in a trial of iron gales, or die guarding
    their honor
or die from ever-changing fate, or die in a
    celestial joke
but they cannot die from humiliating provoca-
    tion, with spit effacing their reputation.

There are many ways to die, but there are only
    two kinds of honor and shame
even today, the classics of the highest Yi priest
    Hebishizu[2] keep the names of sages
and virtuous people, and his vision amplified and illuminated that
    road
although the lost eulogy will be unfolded anew and those who still
    farm
inquire about flashing oxen necks, yet after threshing, the bitter
    buckwheat
will feed a people's children in the harshest seasons.

Oh, returning one! When souls of the departed enter the white
    country
a precipice in the sky slides over the distressed hipbones of the
    mountains
the hatchets of the ancestors unburied the boundary between human
    souls and spirits
come eat some oats in tribute, it is the secret book of the firmament
and Shimumuha[3], the boulder where souls gather, is pried away by a
    weeping spirit-horse.

Those are your hurried footsteps crossing over the human and spirit
    realms
the beeswax in your left ear collects dizzying light, your shoulders

---

1 A holy mountain located at Butuo County, Liangshan.
2 A famous bimo (priest) in the history of Yi people in Liangshan.
3 According to the legends of Yi people, as the place where the souls of the departed belong, it is located somewhere between heaven and earth.

stitched with clamshells
Goddess Pumolieyi's[1] flock are as peaceful as a pile of stones at dusk
these are the gifts bestowed by the spirits, given to fertile humanity
only worship of the ancestors can put those who have passed to rest
you may wear the fine clothes of a long journey, but when you begin to race
your bare feet are still filled with the wilderness's enormous power.

As the spirits cross the heavens and mountain ranges, they refuse to step into
the domain of desire and violence, and only three-year-old children
can catch a glimpse of them, with their rough unshod feet.

Oh, hero! I hide your name in light
your life will appear and disappear in the hanging gloom
it is a distant slowness, a Jier[2] for an opened door.

This is your infant suckling at the mother's breast
an embryo of a woman, her beauty coinciding
with memory, a tiny finger setting an earring trembling
beauty among beauties, genuine kin to the Agachamo[3]
and descendent of the clan that crossed the river grasping the spirit-ox's tail.

This is your arrow, running across sacred Mt. Yimuzemu[4]
the incarnation of an antelope, you see larch trees playing in the winter sun
grateful to the prey you hunt, swallowing ochre famine
you returned to an imaginary pupa, the light-biting wings of childhood.

This is your ladder to the heavens, a wasp nest plucked from a cliff

---

[1] One of the goddesses in the creation myth of Yi people.
[2] An amulet in Yi language. Each clan in Yi ethnic group of Liangshan has their own *Jier*.
[3] According to Yi legends, it is a kind of beautiful bird famous for its long neck and being quick-witted.
[4] A holy mountain located at Butuo County, Liangshan.

and every little friend opens his mouth and
    closes his satisfied eyes,
happy, and welcoming the golden honey fall-
    ing from heaven.

This is you in the back hill of Dajishaluo[1],
    listening to the wind's story
and hearing the sounds of a sheep slipping
    over cliffs in that distance place
it is the hint of the bridle, where to enjoy a nice
    meal
a shepherd boy conspired to push a sheep over
    the cliff's tray
who can explain the secrets of youth, humans
    are always up to the same old tricks.

This is the first glimpse of love's gifts to the body
discovering the guitar and recorder and the possibility of purity in
    death
the Torch Festival is the scarves and candy of small-trouser-bottoms[2]
    who rekindle the stars' promises
a festival of the eyes and the freedom, the damp resplendent bed of
    the earth.
With your hero's genealogy, you tell them who you are! In the place
    where human nature
ends, you resist the timidity of the body, longing for the immortality
    of the spirit.

Here, the names of fathers and sons guide you, spears and shields
    give you a mouth
no need to discover the truth, the gods are engraved on the right side
    of the dead bark
if it isn't the earth's ashes, then we must embrace the will of freedom
and cheer for Chikeboxi[3]! Mouth harp is the language of poets
and because it exists, love can safeguard nobility, subtlety, and modesty.

This is the first time you and language came to embrace the legend of fire

---

1. A place in Butuo County, Liangshan. This is the birthplace of the poet's father.
2. The Yi people of the Adu dialect region in Liangshan, since the waist of local men's trousers is wide while the bottom is narrow.
3. The most famous home of the mouth harp, an ancient musical instrument resonating in oral cavity, in the history of Yi ethnic group.

from Degu[1] you learned aphorisms and how to
    observe the sun and moon
when the river deer on Mabuhuoke[2] deliver
    their tender mating calls
the ancient sound far surpasses the history that
    humans know
at dawn you would always hurry to push open
    the wooden door
and dissolve Erbi[3] and Kezhe[4] in water, letting
    the black goats
and white goats lick the drowsy stars hanging
    between the mountain slopes.

In a dream you accepted the gift from the two-
    tongued sheep Yuegehajia[5]
and its far call made the celestial sphere ap-
    pear in a bowl of water.

[1] A sage of ancient Yi society.
[2] A holy mountain located at Butuo County, Liangshan.
[3] The ancient sayings and maxims in Yi language.
[4] In the oral literature of Yi people, it is an ancient style of poem composed of singing and talking.
[5] A famous sheep in the history of Yi people renowned for its two tongues. Its bleating can be heard from afar.

You are lightning and copper bell's brother, are the son of condors
    and amber
you are the chieftan chosen by generations of celestial tiger and leop-
    ard letters.

Maternal pinholes can see the structure of pain
oh, spirits! Everyone is an orphan,
if you haven't seen it yourself, it must be false,
but true certainty is even rarer. Every people has its own
time of heroes, it's just a question of when.
Your courage and insight cut across an entire region
and the ancestors' protection has always lovingly enveloped you.

This is a great clamor, some say when a mountain deity is wrongly
    killed
it must be paid for with a life, or better yet, the hands of blood
    relatives
should sacrifice an ox for him! Encircle him in the constellations'
navel, and wail at the life about to end

redeem the final payment
this is the familiar scripture, and the inherited long-handled sickle,
it reaped the nights and days of our elders as
 they lay stunned by opium,
now only you know, if you can still survive
people and demons have judged you too
 young.

This is you climbing a poplar, and with righteous cause
shooting a leopard that threatened a pregnant woman, on its skin
was left a hole like its shortened fate, and for you it laid out
a funereal bed, or perhaps it is the pose of a flame-killer across the
 earth
so long as the mountains remain, the hawks and falcons will glide on
 lit wings
the saddles of warriors will wait, and you will become immortal.

It wasn't in the canopy of stars that you discovered what death is
and rejected fear of decay, it was because of your desire about meaning
that you knew why one must fiercely fight that hidden, nameless
 darkness
others did not teach us a way to drift above this land
it is because we created our own festivals, the only weightless time
when we can see the flower of existence, and can,
for the briefest of moments, refuse death.

If holy Mt. Zhekemutu[1] had not given you a mystical power
then the ox horn could not have howled like a storm
you once watched the stars and oats as though they were dewdrops in
 a dreamscape
and the body's sensitivity gave you an awareness of all that will happen
that instinct to uphold freedom was well versed in the shifts of the
 sun and seasons
and finally chose solid stone instead of floating wings.

[1] A holy mountain located at Butuo County, Liangshan.

This is a time of changing orders and principles
everyone must undergo the double trials from
 life and fate
not just a part of what has happened, revolution and war
let our brothers and sisters stand firm in rain
 storms and tempests, witnesses to hope
and see their tears, bodys and spirits undertaking the heavy burden of heavenly stones
your bare feet were accustomed to thorns, but
 who knows now of the pain of flames
no matter how the chaotic constellations shift between unknown
 words
your understanding and casting aside of things prove you have always been Yi.

You sleep deep against the earthen wall, resisting needs not entirely
 human
welding a new reality, giving love to woman and children
you are a free seed, your horse is ever tranquil
when night changes the contours of the sky, your thoughts come into
 their own
matching the eagle and the steed, you are a hero
you grip the sun with your teeth, not disappointing the resplendent light
you and the god of wine were always entangled, you used it to pour
 out your heart
it isn't only you—It has created miracles and destroyed lives as well.

While alive, you chose the place for your own cremation
from there you can see far off toward Zizipuwu[1]
you told your eldest son, the drinking cup will always be passed to
 one who is absent
so many of our elders did not live to your age
all living things will be taken back in, only fire will fulfill its promises
the accelerating stars have not changed the anvil's position, your
 funeral rites
are tomorrow, the faint thunder at the edges of the horizon tells us

---

[1] A place located in Zhaotong, Yunnan Province. According to Yi legends, it is the place where six Yi tribes formed an alliance and started their migration.

your clansmen and relatives will weep and
    mourn and see your spirit off.

Oh, hero! When the dawn glimmers off the
    birds' outstretched wings
the light's messengers will stand among the
    mountains, solemn and respectful
like the sun's scholars, they will wait until that
    certain time
when the sacrificial ox's head reflects the hatchet's image, and the
    ox's hide covers
the masks of grief, this is perhaps the entrance to another life
another return to the placenta of the earth, and death must also offer
    a eulogy
let every person at the rites share the meal
while alive, the deceased often said that this was his final request
to extol your virtue, the women wearing black
speak in turns of your glory, and the ribs of the words
are imbedded into poems, the kinds of emotion found only in the
    marrow
here you will trust in the greatness of the tribes, and the sorrow of
    the departed spirit
will transform into joy, you lie in the embrace of love and affection
and each time the sound of crying marks the wound, hidden blood
will trickle out into the heart of the air, and oh, the instrument's
    string snaps again!
The dead can go on hearing the voices of the living, I trust you are
    still here!
When my married sister says, "Now who will
listen to my weeping?" tears gather in the corners of your eyes
the host and guests use tongues of Yi poetry to determine success or
    failure
addressing when eternal death will arrive in the human world
how do our departed relatives gather in that white world
all living things residing in time are so paltry, so trite
only spiritual warriors and sages will leave names that live on forever
the farewell banners form a line, like the Guhou[1] and Qunie[2]

---

1 One of the most famous ancient Yi tribes in Liangshan.
2 One of the most famous ancient Yi tribes in Liangshan.

returning to our migratory history, and oh, the spiritual exile continues
the butchering of oxen and goats comforts the living, the dead of yesterday and the dead
of tomorrow are not different, but the traces left by death
allow the storytellers to surpass us and quietly enter the compass of life and death
there red success is returning, the sky fills with the lines
of goat bones, and today is the day we satisfy the spirits, I trust in this.

Oh, hero! The ancient sun gushes with mysterious rays
the ladder from the mountains and earth lifts in a mirage
Bimo[1] again grabs hold of the staff cast from light
and in the final step, he finds the running water that maintains all possibility
the dead is lifted on his wooden bed, swaying as though in the first cradle
a body cuddle up to the left, as though still in his mother's womb
this is the last triumphant return, you will enter the oracle's palace
you look at that transparent slope opening into many multi-dimensional steps
and on the distant river floats a seed whose position in the universe hasn't been fixed
the voices sending off the spirit rise and fall, as though falling from heaven
and spiraling echoes seem to come from the unreality under our feet
those seeing you off have no perspective, but Bimo and you can see
that dark road you cannot walk, the road is for the devil.

Walk along the white road, where the ancestors walked barefoot
you will see unreal things be revived in the truth, and the body splits
a pride of tigers stands in the center of a silver eulogy, and time becomes a flower
the trees smile in the open, and the algebra of the seventh space spreads on the rocks

---

[1] In the primitive religion of Yi people, a bimo is the high priest who is also responsible for cultural inheritance.

invisible fish fly over the river, glass plays music
    on the mountain goats' beards
white and black are no longer opposite colors,
    blue rules
over time, which has just been changed, purple
    and yellow are not at their stations
you see a crevice in the horizon gradually mul-
    tiplying open,
and there a scroll reveals a reflective page, the floor of the light is still
    rising
pillars announce your arrival, a faded image covers the knees
no need for the law to bind, the whiteness demarcates a new rite.

This isn't the castle from the future, the sutures leave no traces in its
    structure
here there is no war, only millions of zoological gardens that have
    passed through dreams
here there is no sharp silverware, only malleable ladles
here there are no ranks or leaders, only ladders prepared for the Big
    Dipper
clear ideas are no longer for expressed, pearls of language roll on
    naked clarity
no one laughs if you take the wrong bowl, the stars do not yield to
    false artillery shells
here there is only white, any meaningless existence will be destroyed
    in the whiteness
the skeleton of the whiteness has opened, and from afar it looks like a
    leaf in the universe.

Oh, hero! You have been lifted onto nine layers of pinewood, the
    cremation fire
Muqielehe[1], the holy mountain closest to heaven, is the consecrated
    place of our ancestors
on the border of the eternal arena, where only sun and fire can roar
    for you
your body is covered by a spotless cloak, the final bond between the
    living and the dead

---

[1] A holy mountain located at Butuo County, Liangshan.

you can hear it, our shouts in the valley lifting up to the blue heights
humans and the universe singing in a chorus, and the crystal notes pour from all the hives
that is the power and mystery of our language, the one thing that can make a people cry
it is the tradition of humanity's father, it should pierce through dark unadorned space
it has just arrived here, it is you whispering to me, saying that your immortality has begun
oh, our father! You are the hero of everything meaningful
you breathed, you lived, you suffered, you struggled, you loved
you can see it, in the gleaming door, your ancestors dressed in the finest garments
and the grand ceremony for you comes to the end, and now you are in another world.

Oh, hero! It is none other than your son who lit the final flames for you.

Translated by Gu Ailing

LITERARY LECTURES AND INTERVIEWS

文学演讲和访谈

鹰的诞生和死亡

诗影光芒中的茅屋

——在2017年第一届"国际诗酒文化大会"开幕式演讲

无论是在中国还是在外国,总有一些伟大诗人生活过的地方,被后人视为尊崇的圣地,但像杜甫草堂这样的地方,却在中国文人和民众的心里更具有一种特殊的地位。

所谓草堂,其实就是一间茅屋,但在这一千多年被时光所雕刻的中国精神史上,这间曾是现实中的茅屋,却毫无悬念地成为了有关中国诗歌黄金时代最重要的符号之一,这一符号既承载着中国诗歌传统中的一条重要脉流,同时它还寄托了此后无数诗家对先贤的致敬和怀念。

毫无疑问,伟大的杜甫代表了一种传统,因其崇高的儒家仁爱思想和强烈的忧患意识,他的诗见证了他所置身的那个非凡而动荡的现实,其诗作内容的深刻性和技艺的精湛,都是那个时代无人能与之比肩的。

这位被誉为"诗圣"的诗歌巨人,不仅在当时的中国诗歌史上,就是把他放在那个时期的世界诗歌史上,他同样也是一座巍峨的高峰。

杜甫一生都在游历之中,历时长达几十年,他的重要作品都是在客居他乡时写下的,尤其他在蜀地的生活在他的诗歌中留下了许多经典,其中《春夜喜雨》《茅屋为秋风所破歌》《蜀相》等都已成为被千古传颂的名篇。而作为一个一生都伴随着苦难和不幸的现实主义诗人,其创造力的丰沛也是他的同代人不可企及的,尽管一直处在颠沛流离的境遇中,他还是为我们留下了一千五百多首光辉的诗章。

　　这间茅屋既是现实又是想象，它在一代又一代中国诗人的追寻中，成为被共同视为珍宝的集体记忆，杜甫曾写下过这样的名句："江山有巴蜀，栋宇自齐梁"，这难道是偶然的吗？当然不是。巴蜀之地的自然灵气，对人及万物的孕育滋养，曾创造过无数的奇迹以及足以让后人赞叹的辉煌，而诗歌在这片广袤的土地上，就如同千里沃野种植的粮食，以它似乎并不引人注意的姿态和谦恭，为我们这个朴实敦厚的民族提供了如此丰富的精神营养，这在世界民族发展史上也是不多见的。

　　如果我们去翻阅一下中国文学史，就会发现在中国历史上许多伟大的诗人都与巴蜀之地有不解之缘，而这片土地从某种意义而言，也成了这些诗人精神上的又一个摇篮。说我们是一个诗歌浸润的民族，那是因为诗歌在很多时候代表了这个民族精神的高度，而对此没有人表示过任何怀疑。

　　今天的"国际诗酒文化大会"就是一个最好的证明，来自四面八方的诗人将汇聚到这里，共同来捍卫和守护人类诗歌的理想，而在此时此刻，我以为那间现实和想象中的茅屋，就是由我们的诗歌和精神所构建而成的神圣殿堂，我想任何狂风和暴雨都不可能将它撼动，没有别的原因，那是因为这间茅屋的根基已经深深地扎入了人类自由、正义而永不向任何邪恶势力低头的灵魂，也正因为这个原因，我们才将诗歌的火炬一次又一次高高地举起，并始终对就要来临的明天抱有信心，人类美好的未来必将时刻会有诗歌伴随。精神不灭，诗歌不朽！

Du Fu's Thatched Cottage—Both a Reality and a Legend

—Address at the Opening Ceremony of 2017 International Festival of Poetry & Liquor

Be it in China or any other country in the world, there are certain haunts of the great writers and poets who have worked and lived being immortalized and sanctified to posterity. No other place like the present hamlet (expanded now into a huge park) holds such a special place in the hearts of the Chinese nation and Chinese poets.

This cottage has been so extensively commemorated and celebrated by posterity, in so many novels, poems, anecdotes, and legends in the past millennium that it has become an abstraction instead of a reality, an arch icon of the golden age of the Chinese Tang poetry, the apogee of one of the most important poetic schools of the Classic Chinese poetry in general.

It should be emphasized that our Poet Saint, after whose name this cottage has been named, represents a great tradition, the tradition of Confucianism, which is the state religion and state ideology for the Chinese mind since the Han dynasty, is one of the three greatest spiritual pillars of the medieval and contemporary civilized world. As Jesus speaks of love, Buddha, of compassion, Confucius makes the core mental paraphernalia of the elite, the scholar, mandarin, poet, the twin preoccupation with the wellbeing of the common people who struggle and crave for happiness and the political fate of the nation. Because of this, Du Fu's poems have been epic-class testament to the turbulence and violence of the Mid Tang and immensity of the sufferings sustained by the civil society in depth and artistry unrivalled by any of his contemporaries.

Du Fu is not only Poet Saint for China, but also compares supremely with any other great poet in his time and of all time. Kenneth Rexroth says he has saturated himself with Du Fu's poetry for forty-five years and confesses Du Fu has made him "a better man, as a moral agent and a perceiving organism."

Du Fu's prime years overlapped with the worst years of the Tang. Yet the personal misfortune proved to be the fortune of the Chinese poetry in its classic phase. Due to the collapse of central authority and the subsequent famine, devastations, Du Fu spent his mature years in wandering, retreat or exile. As the most famous tenant of Chengdu and Shu of all time, he wrote a number of poems now being masterpieces chanted by primary school goers and established poets alike. For depth of observation of the political chaos of his time, and craftsmanship, for praise of love, magnanimity, calm and compassion, his recipe to redeem the nightbound world, Du Fu is unsurpassed and unprecedented.

Both a legend and a reality, this cottage has been the Mecca of Chinese poets over centuries. Du Fu sang up unabashedly Shu land's landscape and natural bounty, not without a reason. The agricultural potential and the strategic position elevated it to a major Chinese granary, commercial and cultural center since the Han and Tang which spawned an aura, imperceptibly and unobtrusively, to nurture the growth of Chinese poetry rarely seen anywhere in China or in the world.

An overview of Chinese history of literature will lead us to a discovery that Shu land (contemporary Sichuan) has always been associated with many a great poet and artist in ancient China. It has been argued that the finest flower of Chinese culture is poetry and poetry has certainly embodied the spiritual dimension of the Chinese people supposedly without a religion as center of spirit.

The successful inauguration of this poetry festival affords us solace and assurance that so many great poets from all corners of the globe are gathered in this cottage, consecrated and dedicated to Du Fu, in defense of the sanctity of poetry and the hallowing of one of the greatest poet saints China has to offer to the world. Momentarily we all revert to another time, another place and we are all Du Fu's contemporaries. This cottage, unfazed by any storm, unshaken by any wind, has been deeply enshrined in the inner recesses of the human psyche in their quest for justice and freedom in defiance of all the evil and dark forces, as malicious and sinister in Du Fu's time as in ours.

Because of this, I am fully convinced, hoisting the torch of poetry in our hands, as long as human eyes can see, men can breathe, poetry will outlast and human songs will forever prevail upon the face of our troubled planet.

Translated by Huang Shaozheng

个人身份·群体声音·人类意识
——在剑桥大学国王学院"徐志摩诗歌艺术节论坛"上的演讲

2017.7.29

十分高兴能来到这里与诸位交流,这对于我来说是一件十分荣幸的事。虽然当下这个世界被称为全球化的世界,网络基本上覆盖了整个地球,资本的流动也到了几乎每一个国家,就是今天看来十分偏僻的地方,也很难不受到外界最直接的影响。尽管这样,我们就能简单地下一个结论,认为人类之间的沟通和交流就比历史上的其他时候都更好吗?很显然在这里我说的是一种更为整体的和谐与境况,而沟通和交流的实质是要让不同种族、不同宗教、不同阶层、不同价值观的群体以及个人,能通过某种方式来解决共同面临的问题,但目前的情况却与我们的愿望和期待形成了令人不安的差距。进入21世纪后的人类社会,科技和技术革命取得了一个又一个重大的胜利,但与此同时出现的就是极端宗教势力的形成,以及在全世界许多地方都能看见的民族主义的盛行,各种带有很强排他性的狭隘思想和主张被传播,恐怖事件发生的频率也越来越高。就是英国这样一个倡导尊重不同信仰多元文化的国家,也不能幸免遭到恐怖袭击,2017年以来,已经发生了四起袭击,虽然这一年还没有过去,但已经是遭到恐怖袭击最多的一年。正因为这些新情况的出现,我才认为必须就人类不同种族、不同宗教、不同阶层、不同价值观群体的对话与磋商建立更为有效的渠道和机制,毫无疑问这是一项艰巨而十分棘手的工作,这不仅仅是政治家们的任务,它同样也是当下人类社会任何一个有良知和有责任的人应该去做的。是的,你们一定会问,我们作为诗人在今天的现实面前应当发挥什么作用呢，这也正是我想告诉诸位的。很长一段时间有人怀疑过诗歌这一人类最古老的艺术形式，是否还能存在并延续下去，事实已经证明这种怀疑完全是多余的，因为持这种观点的人大都是技术逻辑的思维，他们只相信凡是新的东西就必然替代老的东西，而从根本上忽视了人类心灵世界对那些具有恒久性质并能带来精神需求的艺术的依赖，不容置疑诗歌就在其中。无须讳言，今天的资本世界和技术逻辑对人类精神空间的占领可以说无孔不入，诗歌很多时候处于社会生活的边缘地带，可是任何事物的发展总有其两面性，所谓物极必反讲的就是这个道理。令人欣慰的是，正当人类在许多方面出现对抗，或者说出现潜在对抗的时候，诗歌却奇迹般地成为人类精神和心灵间进行沟通的最隐秘的方式，诗歌不负无数美好善良心灵的众望，跨越不同的语言和国度，进入了另一个本不属于自己的空间，在那个空间里，无论是东方的诗人还是西方的诗人，无论是犹太教诗人还是穆斯林诗人，总能在诗歌所构建的人类精神和理想的世界中找到知音和共鸣。

　　创办于2007年的中国"青海湖国际诗歌节"，在近十年的过程中给我们提供了许多弥足珍贵的经验和启示，有近千名的各国诗人到过那里，大家就许多共同关心的话题展开了自由的讨论，在那样一种祥和真诚的氛围中，我们深切体会到了诗歌本身所具有的强大力量。特别是我有幸应邀出席过哥伦比亚"麦德林国际诗歌节"，我在那里看到了诗歌在公众生活和严重对立的社会中所起到的重要作用，在长达半个多世纪的哥伦比亚内战中，有几十万人死于战火，无数的村镇生灵涂炭，只有诗歌寸步也没有离弃过他们。如果你看见数千人不畏惧暴力和恐怖，在广场上静静地聆听诗人们的朗诵，尤其是当你知道他们中的一些人，徒步几十公里来到这里就是因为热爱诗歌，难道作为一个诗人在这样的时刻，你不会为诗歌依然在为人类迈向明天提供信心和勇气而自豪吗？回答当然是肯定的。诸位，我这样说绝没有试图想去拔高诗歌的作用，从世俗和功利的角度来看，诗歌的作用更是极为有限的。它不能直接去解决人类面临的饥饿和物质匮缺，比如肯尼亚现在就面临着这样的问题，同样它也不能立竿见影让交战的双方停止战争，今天叙利亚悲惨的境地就是一个例证。但是无论我们怎样看待诗歌，它并不是在今天才成为了我们生命中的不可分割的部分，它已经伴随我们走过了人类有精神创造以来全部的历史。

  诗歌虽然具有其自身的特点和属性，但写作者不可能离开滋养他的文化对他的影响，特别是在这样一个全球化的背景下，同质化成为一种不可抗拒的趋势，诚然诗歌本身所包含的因素并不单一，甚至诗歌在形而上的哲学层面上，它更被看重的还应该是诗歌最终抵达的核心以及语言创造给我们所提供的无限可能，为此，诗歌的价值就在于它所达到的精神高度，就在于它在象征和隐喻的背后传递给我们的最为神秘气息，真正的诗歌要在内容和修辞诸方面都成为无懈可击的典范。撇开这些前提和要素，诗人的文化身份以及对于身份本身的认同，就许多诗人而言，似乎已经成了外部世界对他们的认证，因为没有一个诗人是抽象意义上的诗人，哪怕就是保罗·策兰那样的诗人，尽管他的一生都主要在用德语写作，但他在精神归属上还是把自己划入了犹太文化传统的范畴。当然，任何一个卓越诗人的在场写作，都不可能将这一切图解成概念进入诗中。作为一个有着古老文化传统彝民族的诗人，从我开始认识这个世界，我的民族独特的生活方式以及精神文化就无处不在地深刻影响着我。彝族不仅在中国是最古老的民族之一，就是放在世界民族之林中，可以肯定也是一个极为古老的民族，我们有明确记载的两千多年的文字史，彝文的稳定性同样在世界文字史上令人瞩目，直到今天，这一古老的文字还在被传承使用。我们的先人曾创造过光辉灿烂的历法"十月太阳历"，对火和太阳神的崇拜，让我们这个生活在中国西南部群山之中的民族，除了具有火一般的热情之外，其内心的深沉也如同山中静默的岩石。我们还是这个人类大家庭中保留创世史诗最多的民族之一，《勒俄特依》《阿细的先基》《梅葛》《查姆》等等，抒情长诗《我的幺表妹》《呷玛阿妞》等等，可以说就是放在世界诗歌史上也堪称艺术经典，浩如烟海的民间诗歌，将我们每一个族人都养育成了与生俱来的说唱人。毫无疑问，一个诗人能承接如此丰厚的思想和艺术遗产，其幸运是可想而知的。彝族是一个相信万物有灵的民族，对祖先和英雄的崇拜，让知道他的历史和原有社会结构的人能不由自主地联想到荷马时代的古希腊，或者说斯巴达时代的生活情形，近一二百年彝族社会的特殊形态，一直奇迹般地保存着希腊贵族社会的遗风，这一情形直到上个世纪50年代才发生了改变。诗人的写作是否背靠着一种强大的文化传统，在他的背后是否耸立着一种更为广阔的精神背景，我以为对他的写作将起到至关重要的作用，正因为此，所有真正从事写作的人都明白一个道理，诗人不是普通的匠人，他们所继承的并不是一般意义上的技艺，而是一种只能从精神源头才能获取的更为神奇的东西。在彝族的传统社会中并不存在对单一神的崇拜，而是执着地坚信万物都有灵魂，彝族的毕摩是连接人和神灵世界的媒介，毕摩也就是所谓萨满教中的萨满，就是直到今天，他们也依然承担着祭祀驱鬼的任务。需要说明的是，当下的彝族社会已经发生了很大的变化，在其社会意识以及精神领域中，许多外来的东西和固有的东西都一并存在着，彝族也像这个世界上许多古老民族一样，正在经历一个前所未有的现代化的过程，这其中所隐含的博弈和冲突，特别是如何坚守自身的文化传统以及生活方式，已经成了一个十分紧迫而必须要面对的问题。我说这些你们就会知道，为什么文化身份对一些诗人是如此的重要，如果说不同的诗人承担着不同的任务和使命，有时候并非是他们自身的选择。我并不是一个文化决定论者，但文化和传统对有的诗人的影响的确是具有决定意义的。在中外诗歌史上这样的诗人不胜枚举，20世纪爱尔兰伟大诗人威廉·巴特勒·叶芝，被誉为巴勒斯坦骄子的伟大诗人马哈茂德·达尔维什等人，他们的全部写作以及作为诗人的形象，很大程度上已经成为一个民族的精神标识和符号。如果从更深远的文化意义上来看，他们的存在和写作，整体呈现的更是一个民族幽深厚重的心灵史。诚然，这样一些杰出的天才诗人，最为可贵的是他们从来就不是为某种事先预设的所谓社会意义而写作，他们的作品所彰显的现实性完全是作品自身诗性品质的自然流露。作为一个正在经历急剧变革的民族的诗人，我一直把威廉·巴特勒·叶芝、巴勃罗·聂鲁达、塞萨尔·巴列霍、马哈茂德·达尔维什等人视为我的楷模和榜样。在诗人这样一个特殊的家族中,每一个诗人都是独立的个体存在,但这些诗人中间总有几个是比较接近的,当然这仅仅是从类型的角度而言,因为从本质上讲每一个诗人个体就是他自己,谁也无法代替他人,每一个诗人的写作,其实都是他个人生命体验和精神历程的结晶。

  在中国,彝族是一个有近900万人口的世居民族,我们的先人数千年来就迁徙游牧在中国西南部广袤的群山之中,那里山峦绵延,江河纵横密布,这片土地上的自然遗产和文化精神遗产,是构筑这个民族独特价值体系的基础,我承认我诗歌写作的精神坐标,都建立在我所熟悉的这个文化之上。成为这个民族的诗人也许是某种宿命的选择,但我更把它视为一种崇高的责任和使命,作为诗人个体发出的声音,应该永远是个人性的,它必须始终保持独立鲜明的立场,但是一个置身于时代并敢于搏击生活激流的诗人,不能不关注人类的命运和大多数人的生存状况,从他发出的个体声音的背后,我们应该听到的是群体和声的回响,我以为只有这样,诗人个体的声音,才会更富有魅力,才会更有让他者所认同的价值。远的不用说,与20世纪中叶许多伟大的诗人相比较,今天的诗人无论是在精神格局,还是在见证时代生活方面,都显得日渐式微,这其中有诗人自身的原因,也有社会生存环境被解构得更加碎片化的因素,当下的诗人最缺少的还是荷尔德林式的,对形而上的精神星空的叩问和烛照。是否具有深刻的人类意识,一直是评价一个诗人是否具有道德高度的重要尺码。

  朋友们,我是第一次踏上英国的土地,也是第一次来到闻名于世的剑桥大学,但是从我能开始阅读到今天,珀西·比希·雪莱、乔治·戈登·拜伦、威廉·莎士比亚、伊丽莎白·芭蕾特·布朗宁、弗吉尼亚·伍尔芙、狄兰·托马斯、威斯坦·休·奥登、谢默斯·希尼等等,都成了我阅读精神史上不可分割并永远感怀的部分。最后请允许我借此机会向伟大的英语世界的文学源头致敬,因为这一语言所形成的悠久的文学传统,毫无疑问已经成为这个世界文学格局中最让人着迷的一个部分。

Personal Identity · Group Voice · Human Awareness
—Speech given at the Xu Zhimo Poetry and Art Festival, University of Cambridge

I feel honored to gather here for an exchange of ideas with all of you. We are told that our current world is a globalized world, that internet coverage basically extends over the whole planet, and that the flow of capital crosses boundaries of almost every nation. Even in apparently remote places, it is hard to escape direct influence from the outside world. Even so, can we conclude from this that human communication and exchange are better now than in any past era? Clearly we are talking here about something that facilitates overall harmony. In substance, communication and exchange are supposedly means to solve problems faced in common by people of different religions, different classes, and different value systems. Yet the present situation is unsettling because it falls so far short of our wishes and expectations. As the twenty-first century unfolding, the technological revolution has proceeded from victory to victory, but for humanity, this has been accompanied by the emergence of extremist religious forces and a resurgence of nationalism in many areas of the globe. We have seen the dissemination of narrow-minded, exclusionist views and positions, and terrorist incidents are happening with increasing frequency. Even a country like England that upholds respect for different beliefs has not managed to elude terrorist attacks. Four attacks have happened already in 2017. The year is not over, but this is already the highest number of attacks in one year. Precisely because of such developments, I think there is a need to establish more effective channels and mechanisms for dialogue and consultation between different races, different classes and different value systems. This is doubtless an arduous and thorny job. This is not just a task for politicians; it is something that any person of conscience should take upon himself or herself. You may ask what functions we as poets can fulfill in facing current reality. This is what I want to talk with you all about.

For quite some time some people have been questioning whether poetry—the most ancient of arts—can go on existing. Well, facts have demonstrated that such doubts are completely superfluous. Why? Because those who raise such questions are thinking in terms of technology and logic. They believe that all old things will inevitably be replaced by new things. They fundamentally ignore the reliance of human inner life on art that possesses enduring qualities and meets a spiritual need. Poetry is unquestionably one of such art form. There is no denying that, in today's world, human spiritual space is pervasively occupied by capital and technical logic. There are many times when poetry is situated at the margins of social life. Yet there are two sides to the development of any entity, which is the basis for the saying—"extreme things tend to swing the other way." I take solace in one thing: when many aspects of human affairs stand in overt or latent opposition, poetry miraculously becomes a hidden means for bridging the inner worlds and spiritual realities of human beings. Poetry does not let down the collective hopes of kind-hearted, beauty-loving people. Spanning different languages and nationalities, it takes one into a space that was not originally one's own. Within that space, it makes no difference whether you are Oriental or Western, Muslim or Jewish: you can still find a receptive heart that resonates with yours in mankind's realm of spiritual ideals.

The Qinghai Lake International Poetry Festival, founded in 2007, has provided precious experience and insights over the ten-year courses of its operation. Nearly 1000 poets from various countries have made the journey there, where they engaged in free discussions on topics of mutual concern. In that ambience of felicity and earnestness, we could deeply sense the inherent power in poetry. What is more, it was my good fortune to be invited to attend the Medellin Poetry Festival in Colombia. There I saw the important effect of poetry on public life in a strife-torn society. Hundreds of thousands of people have died in violent deaths in Colombia's civil conflicts lasting over half a century, and thousands of villages have been reduced to rubble. Only poetry has stood up for the sufferers and never spurned them. So thousands of people braved the risk of violence and terror to listen raptly to readings by poets in Medellin; many of them had walked dozens of kilometers to reach that Square. If you had seen how they made their way there, out of enthusiasm for poetry, wouldn't you as a poet be proud that our art still helps to provide faith and courage for human beings as they stride toward tomorrow? The answer will surely be affirmative. My friends, in saying this I am not trying artificially elevate the effects of poetry. From a mundane, utilitarian angle, the effects of poetry are inherently limited. It cannot directly solve the hunger and material shortages that humans face. Right now, for instance, Kenya is facing such problems. Likewise, poetry does not automatically take effect to defuse the kind of civil war that Syria is mired in. Yet however we figure things, poetry became an integral part of our inner being long before yesterday. It has kept company with humans for as long as we have been producing creations of the spirit.

Although poetry has its own qualities and attributes, the one who writes it cannot separate himself from the culture that nurtured him, especially against a backdrop of globalism as its trend toward uniformity becomes overwhelming. In all honesty, we must admit that the ingredients of poetry are by no means uniform: this is all the more true on a metaphysical, philosophical level, where poetry's ultimate telos and creative resources of language offer limitless possibilities. Thus the value of poetry lies in the spiritual height it attains, and in the breath of mystery imparted by its symbols and metaphors. Genuine poetry can serve as a model in terms of both content and rhetoric. Putting aside such assumptions and inherent qualities, seeing the cultural identity of "poet" affirmed seems to offer confirmation from the outside world to many poets. That is, there is no such thing as a poet in an abstract sense. Even for a poet like Paul Celan, despite his lifetime of writing was in German, his sense of spiritual allegiance belonged to paradigms of the Jewish cultural tradition. Of course no outstanding poet, when actually sitting down to write, would diagrammatically reduce all this to concepts to be included in his poems. As a poet from the Yi people, which possesses an ancient cultural tradition, I was pervasively and deeply influenced by our unique way of life and our spiritual culture, right from the time I was aware of the world. Yi people are Not only one of China's most ancient ethnic groups, we hold a place in the grove of the world's most ancient peoples. We have records in writing that clearly date back 2000 years. The stability of the Yi writing system is noteworthy even in the context of the world's writing systems, and our ancient writing system is still being used and handed down today. Our forebears created the illustrious "Ten Month Calendar." Worship of fire and sun has instilled fiery passions in my people, but aside from that our mountainous dwelling place has given us gravitas like a silent boulder on a slope. Within the extended family of humankind, we are one of the few ethnicities that has preserved an impressive number of creation epics: *Hnewo Teyy, Asei-po Seiji, Meige, Chamu*. We also have long lyrical poems like *My Youngest Cousin* and *Gamo Anyo*— when placed in the history of world poetry, they deserve to be called classics. An ocean of folk poems has instilled the knack for verse storytelling in minds of all my compatriots. Without a doubt, it is a blessing for a poet to inherit such a rich intellectual, artistic heritage. The Yi people embrace pantheistic beliefs and worship ancestral heroes, causing those who know the history and previous social structure of the Yi to associate them with ancient Greeks of the Homeric era, or perhaps with ways of life in Sparta. Our Nuosu society of the past two centuries miraculously preserved features that harken back to the ancient Greek aristocracy; this phase persisted right down to the 1950s. I think that the question of whether there is a powerful cultural tradition behind one's writing has essential importance: that is, is there an intangible background of great breadth looming behind a poet? For this reason, those who are genuinely engaged in writing poetry all understand one truth, namely that we are not ordinary artisans, and what we inherit is not a craft in the general sense. Rather, it is something marvelous that can only be obtained at a spiritual fountainhead. In traditional society of the Yi people, there was no worship of a monotheistic god. Instead, we firmly believed that all things in Nature have souls. The bimo-priest of the Yi people was the medium between people and the world of divine beings. The bimo is like a shaman in Shamanism. Even today there are Bimos who undertake the duty of making offerings and exorcising ghosts. What needs to be explained here is that our Yi society has undergone huge changes. In our social consciousness and in a spiritual context, many things from outside coexist with what was handed down. Like many ancient ethic groups in the world, the Yi ethnic group is undergoing an unprecedented process of modernization. As we face an interplay of clashing forces, how to maintain our cultural tradition and way of life is a question that we urgently need to face. When I speak of these things, you will realize why cultural identity is so important for a poet. If we say that different poets undertake different duties and missions, then there are times when this may not be by their own choice. I am not a cultural determinist, but the influence of cultural tradition on some poets may be decisive. The history of poetry in China and elsewhere holds numerous examples of such poets. Two examples from the 20th century come to mind: William Butler Yeats and Mahmoud Darwish, who has been called the pride of Palestine. In both cases, poetic oeuvre plus public persona can be taken as spiritual emblems of their people. In terms of deeper cultural significance, through their existence and their writing, they manifest the deep-seated, long-accumulated inner history of their people. In truth, these highly talented poets deserve esteem because they did not write to convey a certain predetermined social message. The reality manifested through their works flowed naturally from the inherent poetic qualities of the poems. As a poet of an ethnic group that is going through intense transformation, I have taken these figures as exemplars and models: William Butler Yeats, Pablo Neruda, César Vallejo, and Mahmoud Darwish. In our special family made up of poets, each of us is an independent being, but one is drawn more closely to a certain few. Of course, this is a matter of affinity by types, because in essence each poet can only be himself, and no one can replace anyone else. Each poet's writing is a crystallization of his life encounters and his spiritual journey.

The Yi people in China are a long-standing, stationary ethnic groug with a population of over nine million. Our forebears came in waves of nomadic migrants, over thousands of years, to the vast mountain ranges of southwest China. That is a land of far-stretching successive ridges, densely interlaced with rivers. This natural patrimony and our intangible cultural heritage underlie the unique value system of my group. I admit that the intangible coordinates of my writing are established based on the culture I am familiar with. To become a poet of this people was perhaps my predestined choice, but more than that I view it as an exalted responsibility and calling. One's voice as a person who writes poetry should forever be that of an individual, and it should reflect one's independent, distinct stance. Yet a poet who finds himself in this particular era and who dares to launch his life into its turbulent currents cannot help but concern himself with human fate and with living conditions of the majority of people. Behind his voice we should be able to hear reverberations of a choir of voices. I feel that only in this way can an individual voice be rich with charisma; only then will it carry value with which the other can identify. We need not speak of distant eras. In comparison with many great poets of the mid-20th century, today's poets seem to be declining in terms of spiritual scope and of witnessing life. Part of the reason for this lies with the poets themselves, and another cause is the fragmentation of our social environment. Among poets today there is a lack of what Holderlin could do at a metaphysical level, which is to interrogate and illuminate the starry reaches of the spirit. Whether or not a poet is deeply conscious of humanity has always been an important measure of his or her moral dimension.

My friends, this is the first time I've set foot on English soil, and it is my first visit to University of Cambridge. Even so, from my early efforts at reading until today, I have been grateful to British writers and poets for being an essential part of my growth through reading. The ones who come to mind are Percy Bysshe Shelley, George Gordon Lord Byron, William Shakespeare, Elizabeth Barrett Browning, Virginia Woolf, Dylan Thomas, Wystan Hugh Auden and Seamus Heaney. Finally, let me seize this chance to give thanks to the literary fountainhead of the English speaking world, from which a time-honored tradition has emerged, because no other portion of the world literary edifice has been quite so captivating.

Translated by Denis Mair

诗歌与光明涌现的城池
——在2017年"成都国际诗歌周"开幕式上的演讲

我在这里说的成都,既是现实世界中的成都,同时也是幻想世界中的成都,尤其是当我们把一座城市与诗歌联系在一起的时候,这座城市便在瞬间成为了一种精神和感性的集合体,也可以说,正是我们从诗歌的纬度去关照成都时,这座古老的城市便像梦一样浮动起来。我去过这个世界上许多的国家,也有幸地到过不少富有魅力的城市,如果你要问我在这个世界上,有哪些城市与诗歌的关系最为紧密,或者说这些城市其本身就是诗歌的一部分,那么我会毫不犹豫地告诉你,那就是法国的巴黎和中国的成都,当然我的这种看法和观点,一定会有人不同意,甚至持相反的意见。

需要说明的是,我说巴黎和成都的内在精神更具有神秘的诗性,并不仅仅是说在历史上有许多重要的诗人曾经生活在这里,有许多无论是在中国诗歌史上,还是在世界诗歌史上的重要事件在此发生,毋庸讳言,这些当然是这两个城市所拥有的诗歌记忆的重要组成部分。

巴黎不用我在这里去赘述,最让人捉摸不透的是,在漫长的中国历史上,成都都是一个在诗的繁荣上从未有过长时间衰竭的城市,当然我说的这种衰竭是从更大的时间段落来进行比较的,就唐朝而言,可以说它是中国诗歌的黄金时代,如果我们做粗略统计,那个时期的伟大诗人李白、杜甫、白居易、岑参、刘禹锡、高适、元稹、贾岛、李商隐、温庭筠、初唐四杰等都来到过蜀地,许多人还长期在成都滞留居住,诗圣杜甫就两次逗留成都,时间长达三年零九个月,留下了200多首描写成都的诗歌。

从某种意义来讲,蜀地成了不同历史时期许多诗人在诗歌和精神上的栖居地,以及停止流亡避难的另一个故乡。难怪诗仙李白在《上皇西巡南京歌》(其二)中写出了如此经典的诗句:"九天开出一成都,万户千门入画图。草树云山如锦绣,秦川得及此间无。"李白本身就出生于蜀地,我以为他对成都的赞叹和热爱,并不仅仅完全来源于对这片山水之地的乡情,而是作为一个诗人对这座汇聚着深厚人文历史的城市的理解和洞悉。

同样我们还知道,中国历史上最早的一部词总集《花间集》就出现在成都,时间是后蜀广政三年(940年),由赵崇祚所编集,其时间跨度大约有一个世纪,作品的数量达到五百首。虽然这些诗词作者并不限于后蜀一地,但这一影响后来中国诗词形成更大繁荣的前奏,就发生在公元后10世纪30年代到11世纪40年代的一百多年中,最为重要的是中国抒情诗词伟大传统的形成,也正是在那个时期达到了从未有过的高度。

在历史上,蜀地也曾经遭遇过多次的战乱和政权的无端更替,正如古人常说的那样一句话"天下未乱蜀先乱,天下已治蜀未治"。但与整个中国别的地域相比,蜀地更多的时候还是丰衣足食,自然灾害也少有发生,政治权力和平民百姓的生活都趋于稳定,特别是千里沃野以成都为中心的平原地带,可以说是中国农耕文明最精细发达,同时也是持续得最长的地方。

正因为此,古代的许多中国诗人都以把游历寻访蜀地作为自己的一个夙愿和向往,这其中还有一个重要的原因,就是千百年来蜀地似乎孕育了一种诗性的气场,它特殊的地理环境和能把时间放慢的市井与乡村生活,毫无疑问是无数诗人颠沛流离之后灵魂和肉体所能获得庇护的最佳选择。我不是在这里想象和美化蜀地不同历史阶段的生活,而是想告诉大家四川的确是一个神奇的地方,尤其是在漫长的封建农耕文明的时代,中国没有一个省能像四川那样完全做到自给自足,粮食、棉帛、铜铁、石材、食盐、毛皮、茶叶、美酒等等,可以说应有尽有。

当然任何事物都有它的两面性，我们也可以看到许多出生于蜀地的文化巨人，他们最终成为巨人也大都是走出了夔门才被世人所知晓的，但不能不说这方土地的确是人杰地灵，唐代的李白，宋代的苏轼三父子是其中最有代表性的。就是到了近现代，在中国文化史上产生过重要影响的作家、诗人和画家就有郭沫若、巴金、李劼人、张大千、沙汀、艾芜等等，如果要排下去，这个名单还会很长，而在中国近现代历史上蜀地出生的政治家和军事家更是比比皆是，他们其中的一些人深刻地改变了中国和人类历史的进程，中国改革开放的总设计师邓小平就是最重要的代表人物。最有意味的是，这些伟大的人物大都在成都读过书，有的就出生在成都，有的在成都度过了人生中一段或长或短的美好岁月。

中国新诗的开拓者和旗手郭沫若，1910年2月就来到了成都，后来入读于四川高等学堂。当时也在成都就读的，后来名闻遐迩的小说大师李劼人，也因为这片地域所给予他的丰厚滋养，其一生的创作都把蜀地作为自己永恒的主题。伟大的人道主义者巴金，这位出生于成都正通顺街李公馆里的作家，他的名作《家》《春》《秋》，所记录的是成都一段令人悲伤而又对明天充满向往的梦一样的生活。

画家张大千1938年为躲避战乱生活在成都，他创作的《蜀山图》《蜀江图》等佳作，其作品所透出的品质和韵味，完全是一个蜀中画家才可能具有的通灵和大气象，他的大写意和汪洋肆意的泼墨，直接催生了中国画的又一次巨大变革。

我说成都和巴黎是东方和西方两个在气质上最为接近的城市，还因为这两座城市在延续传统的同时，还对异质文化有着强大的包容和吸收能力，他们都有一种让诗人和艺术家能完全融入其中的特殊氛围以及状态，有不少文化学者和社会学家并非固执地认为，有些城市从一开始就是为诗人、艺术家以及思想者而构筑的。

不用再去回顾历史，就发生在上个世纪70年代末80年代初的中国现代诗歌运动来讲，蜀地诗群就是唯一一个能与北京现代诗群难分伯仲的诗人群体，当然，这一影响深远的现代诗歌运动，其中心就在成都。对外面的人而言，这一切就如同一个诗歌所铸造的神话，当时写诗的诗人数量之多，出现的诗歌流派更是目不暇接。毫不夸张地说，现在在中国诗坛最活跃、最具有影响力的诗人中，起码有数十位就是从蜀地走出来的。从他们的一些回忆文章以及中国现代诗歌运动研究专家的论述中，我们都能发现一个有趣的现象，这些诗人毫无例外几乎都在成都居住生活过，事实上这一切都变成了一种现实，就是成都毫无争议地被公认为中国现代诗歌运动最重要的两个城市之一，成都又一次穿越了历史和时间，成为中国诗歌史上始终保持了诗歌地标的重镇。

你说这一切难道都是偶然的吗？我的回答，那当然不是。如果说一个人的身上会携带有某种独特气质的传承，一个族群的集体意识中有无法被抹去的符号记忆，那一座城市、一座古老的城市，难道就没有一种隐秘的精神文化密码被传递到今天？我们的回答同样是肯定的，否则我们就不会也不可能去解析一个并非谜一般的问题，那就是为什么从古代到今天，成都这座光辉的城池与中国诗人结下的生命之缘是如此深厚。尤其是本届"成都国际诗歌周"的如期成功举办，再一次证明了我对这座光荣的诗的城市的认识和判断是正确的，我相信来自世界不同国家的诗人们，最终也会得出这样一个同样的结论。朋友们，在我们的眼前你所看见的这座诗歌与光明涌现的城池——就是成都！

A City Hemmed in with Radiant Beams of Poetry
—Address at the Opening Ceremony of 2017 Chengdu International Poetry Week

This ancient city, Chengdu, under discussion, with no aesthetic appeal in its modern contours notwithstanding, is very special in the sense of being both sublunary and fairy, locus of sensibility and spirit, taking wings to the skies instantly by alchemies of imagination, when we attempt to associate things urban with the poetic side of human beings, especially to probe into the fortuitous converging of its physical topography and metaphoric coordinates. A widely travelled man, I have roamed among the many charming cities of many countries on the planet; if I am approached with similar questions like "which city do you believe is mostly akin in ethos, in aura of enchantment to poetry?" my answer out of hand would be Chengdu in China and Paris of France. Some, I am aware, might not agree to my pride and prejudice, as there is no accounting for taste.

It is greatly to be debated on my part that both Chengdu and Paris seem to be possessed with some inner ethos or mystery of sensibility qualified to be called capitals of poetry, not only because Chengdu has, over centuries, produced, and been home to a dozen of great poets, also because many major artistic movements that have impinged substantially upon literary histories of both China and the world. The near-cult status accorded to poetry has justifiably lulled Chinese into believing Chengdu is a city famed for the depth and sophistication of its poetic heritage.

Paris, of course, has its own share of laureates. What has perennially intrigued me is that Chengdu has continually and continuously radiated a nationwide image of inexhaustible poetic creativity, flaunting an envious continuity of tradition even since the city was born 4th century BC. While Tang dynasty, the golden of the most golden ages for Chinese poetry, saw an extraordinary efflorescence of poetic blossoms, Chengdu has unbelievably never been short of good poets who have chronicled the China experience, the mutations of the human condition, joie de vivre or the human idiocies of this world. Indeed Chengdu has beckoned to an awesome array of genius. Li Bai, Du Fu, Bai Juyi, Cen Shen, Liu Yuxi, Gao Shi, Yuan Zhen, Jia Dao, Li Shangyin, Wen Tingyun, and not to mention the four talents of the early Tang, many of whom had sojourned here. Du Fu, our Poet Saint, loyal repeat visitor, made Chengdu as his home and lingered in retreat for three years and nine months, leaving a legacy of 200 poems extolling the virtues of common folks here and around.

In a sense, Chengdu has been the spiritual home of poets wandering or in exile. *Hark to the Poet Immortal* when Li Bai sang up:

From nine celestial vaunts emerges Chengdu
Where towns and villages loom like scrolls
Grass, trees, clouds and mountains all as chic as brocade
Whose beauty beyond compare anything China proper offers.

What Li Bai so evocatively sums up does not strike only a personal note, as he is, among others, more appreciative of the subtleties and richness of culture and nature of Chengdu both as resident and poet.

Equally worthy of note is the first anthology of *Ci Poems* ever to be published in Chengdu which dates at 941, compiled by scholar official Zhao Chongzuo, inclusive of five hundred Ci poems, authored by poets, many being non-natives, spanning over one century long, foretelling the dawn of a larger renaissance in days to come. We are talking about another peak performance of Chinese lyrical poets in the Song dynasty in the brewing. The anthology turns out to be a major cataclysm in triggering the greatest outpourings of lyricism sweeping Song times.

In a way, Chengdu has been historically turbulent, surviving devastations of many a renegade independent state and runaway kingdom skirmishing with another or defying central authority. "Order and peace breaks down first in Shu and restores the last in the country", so the ancients aptly put it. Yet, in all fairness, for much of its eventful history, Chengdu reveled in its prosperity, grateful for the strategic geography and cultural splendor which had elevated it to one of the commercial and cultural centers in medieval and contemporary China alike. Agricultural innovations, the installation of the Dujiang Yan Irrigation System, in particular, opened up Chengdu Plain to intensive farming, which quickly transformed the area into an economic base, a cornerstone of Chinese society. Thanks to this and others, Chengdu leapt to periodic prominence at several major national crises.

Where nowadays tourists predominate, Chengdu has always been rendevousing with artists and poets as it has been celebrated in so many poems, stories, anecdotes, paintings for one important reason: remoteness from the whirlwinds of Chinese politics in Central Plains and the famed nonchalance of local population who are nicely laid back, reclining on bamboo couches, idling away all day long, indulgent in their staid teahouse culture and gentle pace of living. Such perfect location and slowing down of life provide the best sanctuary for many wandering and troubled souls looking for a temporary relief. I am not idealizing the lives of struggling poor artists and nobility of peasantry. I am merely reminding you at certain historical moments, Sichuan was the place for some poets fleeing wars and other disasters, and indeed, for centuries past, feudal, agrarian, Sichuan has been much sustained and contained within a considerable measure of self sufficiency in terms of produce and supply of food, cotton, cloth, copper, iron, salt, fur, tea and wine–all being prerequisites for bare subsistence of lower caste and the elite in their attempt to create the good life.

Of course, such self-sufficiency bred naturally a bias of outlook and petty-minded Philistinism. For one thing, local budding talents, as a rule, don't get scouted and recognized unless they move on beyond the secluded territory. This is, of course, not to deny Sichuan is a source for great men. Li Bai in the Tang dynasty, the Three Sus of the Song dynasty, are four of the most illustrious poets on hand. In contemporary China, lots of giants, such as poet Guo Moruo, novelists Ba Jin and Li Jieren, master painter Zhang Daqian, short story writers Sha Ting and Ai Wu have illuminated the night of Chinese culture and the list of artists and poets can go on without end. Reaffirming the global weight of Sichuan, one must mention the name of Deng Xiaoping, who having initiated the late 1970s' reform and opening up to the world, the classic way to guarantee distinction and eminence if followed assiduously, has once for all put China on the map of one of the foremost places among the relatively well to do, advanced civilizations of the world, say, in a brief space of three decades. The rise of these great minds and the vital roles they have played all take us back to the beginnings of greatness, that is, they were all born here, got educated or spent a certain portion of their memorable adolescence or youth in this beloved city of ours.

We are rightly proud of Chengdu as our native Guo Moruo's launching pad to blaze the path of New Poetry a hundred years ago. In 1910, Guo first landed in Chengdu, Study in Sichuan Higher Learning Institute and groomed himself as the future standard bearer of New Poetry. Novelist Li Jieren's lifelong passions and theme are this land that has endowed him with a pathos and lyricism that earns him the renown of master of regionalism, on a par with Lao She. Great humanitarian writer Ba Jin came from a family of officials and scholars, residing in the grand Li Mansion in Zhengtongshun Street and rose to fame by his trilogy of *Family, Spring* and *Autumn*, half autobiography, half revelation, all being classic tales of social oppression despairing of a past beyond redemption and dreaming of a tantalizing future out of reach. For a blistering look at the decadent society, Ba Jin offers the remedy of compassion, love and magnanimity.

Master Painter Zhang Daqian, fleeing war torn interior China, settled down in Chengdu in 1938 to complete his masterpieces *Mountains in Shu* and *Rivers of Shu*. In reaffirmation of traditional landscape techniques, Zhang expanded and finally exploded into dynamic fury, ink, movement, color, line—that are ingeniously patterned but in such cluttered abundance as to appear unprecedented—almost, by hindsight, tantamount to a revolution in spearheading Chinese painting in sync with post-impressionist trends in France. Zhang's artistic activity in Chengdu attests ultimately to his genius in pacesetting Chinese expression of artistic styles in modern times.

When I speak of Chengdu and Paris have same breath, they both to me demonstrate a continuity of tradition while evincing an ability to learn and absorb things foreign and new to a preeminent degree, an aura enticing and luring poets and artists with alien cultural background to make Chengdu their comfort zone. Some cultural critics and sociologists postulate, not without good reasons, that some city was conceived and built for poets, thinkers and artists.

For those familiar with Chinese poetry, an overview of what happened culturally in the late 1970s and the early 1980s when Chinese poetry, deriving inspiration from French or Anglophone or Spanish models, began to free itself from the orthodox rigidity of Soviet realism, whose far-reaching and profound repercussions are still felt today, will lead one to one bold claim Chengdu has staked out: as an alternate center of stylistic innovation together with Beijing perhaps in complementary pairs, like Li Bai and Du Fu, a phenomenon deserving pondering as it must represent some historic need to keep human faculties in balance. Hence the legend due to two essential facts, (i.e., Chengdu's poets population growing ever beyond count and the poetic schools mushrooming to such unfettered scale), as to concretize and corroborate this city's power and status, if not greater than that of Beijing. It is not boastful at all to say over two dozen of established contemporary Chinese poets, still clinging to the honored career with gusto and vitality, are Chengdunese, former residents or still natives. Claim is here equal to boast: Chengdu, besides Beijing, defines Chinese poetry and possesses an ingrained lineage, without peer by any other city in China. It is the country's artistic bank together with Beijing.

So to speak, the city of Chengdu retains pockets of Tang and Song's elegant spiritual past, an inheritance of certain traits atypical, some marks very stubborn to be erased in the inner layers of the collective psyche of a race, a group, carried over from generation to generation. And in the last analysis, is there any city under the sun that does not have cultural genes of its own to be inherited in a linear progression? My answers are of course, in the affirmative definitely. Although Chengdu is a city in flux culturally and socially, it still lures poets from all directions for the same compelling reason: the visiting of so many haunts of so many native great poets and artists who have lived, worked and played here. The idea alone will send a vicarious thrill down your literary spine as you will discover the city's genuine splendor and firm link with budding and maturing years of so many wonderful artists and poets, especially the presence of mementos of Li Bai and Du Fu, two minds conterminous in their depth and scope with the poetic limits of man. The fact that 2017 Chengdu International Poetry Week is inaugurated today in honor of Chengdu's glorious past, as reflected in its rich legacy of art and poetry, evidenced by the attendance of so many distinguished poets home and abroad, has proved the fullness of the truth value of my point.

Fellow poets and friends, don't you see, right in front of you, under your very noses, a city hemmed in with radiant beams of poetry?

Translated by Huang Shaozheng

光明与鹰翅的天石
——在2017年第二届中国凉山"西昌邛'丝绸之路'国际诗歌周"开幕式上的致辞

在这个美好而充满诗意的季节,我们如期迎来了第二届中国凉山"西昌邛海'丝绸之路'国际诗歌周"的召开,在这里,请允许我代表中国作家协会并以本届诗歌周组委会主席的名义,热忱地欢迎来自不同国家和地区的诗人光临这一诗歌的盛会,并预祝本届诗歌周获得圆满的成功。同时,还要借此机会向为本届诗歌周的筹备安排付出了辛勤努力的各相关机构和个人表示最衷心的感谢。

朋友们,今天的世界仍然是一个动荡而充满了不确定的世界,人类如何选择自己的未来同样是生活在这个地球上不同地域的人们共同面临的问题,为了构建一个更加合理、更有利于和平与发展的国际新秩序,需要今天的人类在国际政治的层面之外,还应该从更多的方面贡献出智慧以及更富有建设性的意见,只有这样,我们才可能在面对重重危机来临的时候,去有效做到求同存异、共谋发展。

中国国家主席习近平所提出的"一带一路"宏伟构想,正是站在人类社会发展全局的高度,为真正构建起人类命运共同体而绘制的一幅面向未来的蓝图。也正因为此,由不同的文化作为深厚基础所进行的对话和互动才更显示出强大的力量,而诗歌作为不同民族精神文化的精髓,它并没有远离我们的现实和生活,毫无疑问,在今天,它已经再一次成为了不同国家、不同民族、不同文化背景、不同价值取向的人们进行沟通和交流最有效的方式之一，诗歌依然在发挥着介入生活和现实的作用。

朋友们，就在此时此刻，我想到了"光明与鹰翅的天石"这样一句充满了象征和隐喻的诗句，因为在这片天空与群山静默如初的疆域里，亘古不变的太阳依然在巡视着大地上的万物和生命，时间的光影同样在周而复始地行走过黑暗与光明所构筑的世界，如果你相信所有的存在都不是孤立的个体，而同时你还相信所有的存在都有其隐秘的来源，那么你的心灵和思想才可能与你眼前的这个并非虚拟的现实融为一体。

从这个意义上而言，我从根本上是肯定和坚信哪怕一粒微尘，它的运行毫无疑问也是宏大宇宙的一个部分，而一粒微尘本身其实就是一个宇宙，无论它多么微小，但它所承载的信息和能量，都是我们无法用简单的数据去衡定的。

当我们伫立在苍茫的大地心无旁骛地去聆听，我们就能从时间的深处听见风的呓语和光的赞词，由此，我们也才有可能在瞬间目睹并接近真理的化身，难怪伟大的德语诗人荷尔德林，在自己的诗歌中始终把形而上的力量和具有灵性的语言紧密地融为一体，从而使他的每一句诗都如同神授的箴言。

在浩如烟海的彝族历史典籍中，探索生命和宇宙的形成一直是最为核心的主题，这其中既包含了事物之间的相互关系，同时也揭示了生命的无常以及死亡作为规律的存在。作为诗人我想告诉大家，当我们今天承接下来的是如此丰富、厚重的伟大传统时，我们除了感到无比幸福和骄傲之外，更重要的是，我们还必须树立在当下创造新的壮丽史诗的雄心，否则我们将有愧于这片土地上世代英雄谱系中的勇士们所创造的业绩。

我无法想象但这一切都是现实，当然这也给我们这个崇拜祖先和英雄的民族，找到了继续坚守自己的信仰和传统最直接的理由，不用在这里去一一陈述，我们的先人给我们留下了这个世界上最多的创世史诗，它们的名字已经深深地镌刻在了我们民族的集体记忆中，《查姆》《勒俄特依》《宇宙人文论》《彝族源流》《洪水泛滥》《阿细的先基》《阿黑西尼摩》《俫罗巫经》《梅葛》，也已经成为当今人类共同的精神财富，尤其是当我们面对这些伟大的传统和遗产时，任何溢美之词都会显得苍白无力，我以为我们只能勇敢地承担起我们这一代人的责任和使命，才可能创造出无愧于这一伟大诗歌传统的经典作品。

  当然，生活在这个世界不同地域的诗人们，也同样肩负着传承和弘扬各自民族诗歌传统的使命和责任，能真正写出划时代的具有人类整体高度的诗歌精品，都是我们作为诗人共同追求的目标。

  诗人朋友们，我们只能把诗歌的火炬烧得更亮，当正义战胜邪恶成为不可抗拒的法则，而每一个人真的都拥有神圣的自由和尊严，那么，请相信光明与鹰翅的天石就会在我们的前方。也正因为此，我们迈向明天和未来的脚步才不会停止，永远不会停止！谢谢大家！

Heavenly Stones Made of Eagle Wings and Light
—Remarks at the Opening Ceremony of the 2nd Liangshan, Xichang Silk Road International Poetry Week

It is my pleasure to welcome you, on behalf of the organizing committee, in my capacity as both deputy chairman of China Writers Association and chairman of the organizing committee, to the 2nd Liangshan, Xichang Silk Road International Poetry Week on the occasion of this grand opening ceremony. I, for one, wish for a most successful operation of the week. My heartfelt gratitude must be also registered here for the wonderful myriad preparatory work put in by all individuals, institutions and the organizing staff to make this event a reality.

Friends, our world is a world characterized by turmoil and uncertainty. How we humans, inhabiting different quarters of this world, choose the life we lead in the forthcoming future is the common challenge before us all. Other than on the political planes whereupon politicians wrack their brains to come out with schemes and programs as how to construct a new world order amenable to justice, peace and sustainable development, we need also draw in the wisdom and insight from other sectors of the society to better cope with the crisis lurking ahead and co-develop while seeking common ground on major issues and reserving differences on minor ones.

The One Belt, One Road Initiative, proposed by Chinese President Xi Jinping is a most visionary blueprint to maneuver, hitch and move our world towards the direction with a shared future, woe or joy, rain or sunshine. Because of this, dialogues and interactions involving various cultures, races and religions have the potential to iron out the differences and oil the wheels of history. Poetry, as the best flower of each culture, more than any other social or political parameters, stands to create a status quo out of a plethora of problems, either racial or religious or cultural in origin. Poetry has the unique power to alleviate mistrust and generate a feeling of brotherhood and fraternity where only hate and injustice existed before.

Friends, the above lapse conjures up a sophisticated metaphor of "heavenly stones upon eagle wings and light" in my mind. Look, the ageless sun has never failed, on its chariot across the immense vaults of the sky to perform its daily patrol over this Yi region of ranged mountains, silent and speechless from the primordial times, flora and fauna, life forms bustling and hustling making their homely rounds. Likewise, light and shadow of time have never ceased flickering upon the sublunary world of light and darkness. Only if you are convinced of the ultimate fact of all living things being not isolated atomic substances and issuing from one common hidden source, your heart and soul can merge with the reality before your eyes that is in no way virtual and fairy.

What do we make of this occultist revelation? Well, personally I am unswervingly of the opinion that even a grain of dust acts and is acted upon as part of the overarching cosmos. The idea is, tiny and infinitesimal a grain of dust might be, it is nevertheless, self-sufficient, a cosmos carrying its own share of energy and information, defying any reductionist attempt in the positivistic vein.

Left alone to a quiet corner of this vast domain of ours, I sometimes pause and take stock, my eyes shut and my ears open, to hear a distinct, though somewhat obliterated, soliloquy of wind in praise of light coming from the depths of time, the incarnation of truth we are on the threshold of witnessing. No wonder the great German poet Holderlin, in his poems, always identifies the supernatural as heralding the creation of a sacred spiritual language worthy of poetry. He is best read as a poet divinely inspired.

Yi is such a people of history, culture and tradition that as one of the 9 million descendants, I am rightly proud of the oceanic repository of historic texts, mostly epics, left to us by our ancestors and I fully embrace our forefathers recalcitrant and relentless cosmological penchant, among other things, our deeply felt interrelatedness of humans with all creatures as well as our due respect for the law of impermanence of life and death as a precondition of mortal existence. As a poet inheriting such grand intangible matrimony, a sense of pride and being fully blessed swells up that I feel entitled to enhance my Yi heritage by initiating a process of renaissance, revitalization and regeneration worthy of the Yi spirituality.

Legacies do not just happen and persist. To be meaningful, we must keep negotiating between them and our contemporary life and carry on with the great task our ancestors have so nobly pioneered and advanced. For a people famed for hero worship, we draw inexhaustible inspiration from our animistic faith and tradition made up of an unrivalled wealth of creation epics such as: *Hnewo Teyy, Asei-po Seiji, Amo Xinimo, Chamu, Meige, Shamanic Scripture of the Lolos, On the Cosmos and Human Learning, Origins of the Yi People, The All-Engulfing Flood,* all being now common assets of mankind, commending themselves despite adulators or debunkers. Yet, this is no time for wistful thinking or nostalgic retreat. Culture changes, shifts and perishes if it does not adapt with time. This is the moment to recharge ourselves and set off on a new mission to be undertaken by our generation, that is, to actually quarry new sky stones, worthy of Yi legend, fit for the vaults of heaven.

Of course, poets from across the world are all born with the mandate to create their own heavenly stones upon eagle wings and light. Under our pens should flow poems that reach into the hearts of our people and make them laugh, cry, feel and think. Our voices should be raised anew in celebration of human glory and toil, our passionate search for justice, our tender loves and profoundest longings.

Dear friends, let's ignite our torches to light our way, convinced of the invincible justice prevailing upon a globe "with limping sway disabled" eventually, loyal perennially to the dual principles of sanctity and freedom of each individual simply because the heavenly stones so much treasured are out there for us to be hit upon and quarried. Let this be realized among men that our footsteps forward will not be halted and reversed on our way towards a promising tomorrow. Thank you.

Translated by Huang Shaozheng

诗人仍然是今天社会的道德引领者
——答英国诗人格林厄姆·莫特

格林厄姆·莫特： 诗歌是为着什么而存在的？你怎么看待历史上和未来诗歌同人类文化之间的关系？

吉狄马加： 诗歌的存在就如同人类的历史存在那样悠久，诗歌是人类精神生活中最古老的方式之一，在原始宗教中，诗人的身份就是部族酋长和祭司的合一，在古代社会，诗歌很多时候都是连接人与天地的桥梁，人与鬼神沟通的媒介，诗歌是人类精神创造最为极致也最为纯粹的一种方式，它不仅仅就是一种语言魔力神秘的升华，更重要的是，它是人类精神创造中不可缺少的致幻剂，也就是说，只要有人类的精神需求和创造存在，那么诗歌就会存在下去，也不可能有消亡的那一天，这是我坚信无疑的。无论从现实和未来来看，基于诗歌的这种特殊性，诗歌都是人类文化中令人瞩目的一部分，文化当然在不同的历史阶段会出现新的变化，但文化在传统中总有一部分是相对固定的，这就如同对诗歌需求的稳定性一样，不会有更大的改变。当然，诗歌与不同时代的文化所构成的关系，却会经常发生着变化，而诗歌的处境也会因为这种变化而出现不同的情况，比如，在今天这样一个物质和消费主义的时代，诗歌的边缘化是不言而喻的，但尽管这样，也没有从根本上改变人类精神生活和文化延续中诗歌不可能被替代的作用，如果相信人类的精神生活和创造还会延续下去，那么诗人和诗歌就将会存在下去，尽管他们的处境有一天还会更糟。

格林厄姆·莫特：你如何看待诗歌的书写文本形式和诗歌的声调、韵律之间的关系？

吉狄马加：之所以诗歌是形式和语言的一种创造，书写文本本身的重要性就自不待言，在很多时候，文本的创新和语言的创新都同等重要，这与绘画和音乐的创新均有很多相同的地方，绘画永远不能停留在古典主义的美学主张上，有了后来印象派、野兽派、立体主义、未来主义以及各类现代艺术的出现和创新，才自然地肯定了绘画形式和绘画语言创新的极端重要性，诗歌的情况也一样。在这里不同的是，诗歌的创造任何时候都不能离开语言，我以为离开了诗歌的声调和韵律，诗歌内在的生命也就停止了呼吸，声调和韵律是诗歌的心脏的律动，也可以说是诗歌血管中血液的呼啸，为什么有人说诗歌是最难翻译的，我想在这里指的不是一般意义上的内容，而指的就是这种声调和韵律里发出的声音，真正伟大的诗人都是这个声音的捕捉者，同样他也是这个声音的最神秘的传递者，很多时候他可以说就是这种声调和韵律的喉舌。

格林厄姆·莫特：诗歌的神话维度同当代科学知识之间如何才能协调一致？

吉狄马加：诗人的写作并非是与传统的割裂，而许多诗人哪怕就是置身于当代复杂多变的现实中，他们也不可能忘记自己的传统和民族的历史，而对神话的重新书写也会在不同的诗人中出现。希腊现代诗人塞弗里斯的名篇《神话与历史》以及他的同胞埃里蒂斯的史诗《理所当然》，都是对希腊神话与现实转化的成功书写，他们都是希腊诗歌在现代意义上的精神传承人，同样，他们也是两位获得过诺贝尔文学奖的诗人，他们从神话的维度写出了现实的人如何从精神遗产中去获得慰藉，从而让人类再一次找到走出迷途的方向。另一位伟大的希腊诗人卡赞扎斯基通过他上万行的史诗《新奥德赛》，同样寓言般地写出了20世纪人类的苦难、救赎、悲剧和新的重生。诗歌的神话维度同当代科学知识之间的关系，并非是一种对立的不可调和的关系，特别是在精神世界中，我以为，唯有诗人及其精神创造者，才能在这两者之间找到平衡点。因为诗歌神奇的创造，最终毕竟是对生命的热爱和呈现，而对神话和人类原始精神母体的敬畏绝不是迷信，科学的理性知识，也会被诗人和诗歌有机地融入到每一次的创造中去。

格林厄姆·莫特：新的通讯交流技术将会如何影响诗歌形式和出版？

吉狄马加：今天的全球化和互联网时代，实际上已经为诗歌的传播提供了新的可能，甚至还有机器人每天都在制造出诗歌，我并不担心诗歌可以用新的形式进行传播和出版，我更担心的是如果诗人都成了机器人，那诗歌还有存在下去的必要吗？有一点不用我们担心，机器人或许不可能在修辞上成为技艺的败将，但是它们却一定不会在感情和灵魂上成为胜者，因为只要人类的诗歌还发乎于情感和心灵，那么没有灵魂的机器人就不可能战胜我们。现在每天在网络上都有成千上万的诗歌被推送出来，而网络的传播同样在花样翻新，这是一个从未有过的情况，我们必须理性地正视它的存在。

格林厄姆·莫特：在全球化的世界，政治结构和经济结构环环相扣，诗人作为社会评论家和道德引领者的角色是什么样的？

吉狄马加：并不是因为全球化的存在，也不是因为社会政治和经济发展的原因，诗人就理应放弃自己对社会政治和经济生活的介入度，正因为在这样一个政治多维和崇尚物质主义的现实中，诗人更应该成为社会的良心，他当然不是高高在上的道德裁判者，而是在人民的前行中手捧烛光的那一位，在时代和现实面前，他是参与者，也是见证者，更是秉持真理的批判者。从这个角度而言，诗人仍然是今天和未来社会的道德引领者。

格林厄姆·莫特：诗歌如何在社会内部的少数民族群体和主体族群之间居中调解？

吉狄马加：诗人和外部世界的关系可以说是单纯的，也可以说是复杂的，诗歌当然应该居中发挥调解各种族群和社会阶层的关系，爱尔兰诗人叶芝和希尼都持有这样的观点，特别是希尼的作品，从精神上实际上是弥合了英格兰人和爱尔兰人的看不见的分歧和不和。虽然叶芝和希尼都是爱尔兰文化和传统的捍卫者，但他们同样也是人类自由精神的捍卫者，伟大的诗歌必然超越一切狭隘，并使其具有普遍的人类意义而最终成为大家共同的财富，真正的诗人也必须高举起友爱、和平和人道的旗帜，去真正促进不同族群之间的和睦共处、友好往来。

格林厄姆·莫特：诗人的国际交流是否重要？这样的交流纽带会如何令诗歌向跨文化现象的方向发展？

吉狄马加：不同国度和文化背景之间的诗歌的交流，当然是一项非常有益的工作，德国诗人歌德在他生活的那个年代就梦想着有一天，能形成真正的并能进行沟通的世界文学，现在看起来在今天也已经逐步变成了现实，我想这一切主要还是来自于人类科学技术的发展，为人类提供了大大要好于过去的交流渠道，人类之间在时间和空间的距离也变得越来越短。在文学和诗歌交流中，过去更多的是在文本的翻译上，而在当下，除了文本的翻译，诗人与诗人直接地相互来往也要远远比过去更多，特别是在近三十年，因为冷战的结束，不同社会制度国家诗人之间的交流来往，也变成了一种常态，应该说，这种交流已经在全方位展开，其深度和广度都是过去无法比肩的，最重要的是，世界性的诗歌运动和诗歌创作思潮，也会在很短的时间内被彼此了解和熟悉。当然也因为有了这样的交流，诗歌与自身语言隐秘的关系、与内在传统的关系、与形式重构内容的关系以及无意识与修辞的关系，又都在更广阔的空间里成为了话题，今天的诗歌交流能让我们更能看清别人，同时也能让我们更能看清自己。这种跨文化的交流给我们提供了很好的借鉴，但每一种语言诗歌的写作仍然会按照它自身所选择的方向往前走，这就是交流的成果之所在，而绝不会是其他。

格林厄姆·莫特：我们正进入日益全球化的世界，你怎样看待译者和翻译所扮演的角色？

吉狄马加：世界上还有这么多诗人在用不同的语言在进行写作，当然诗歌的翻译仍然是重要的，翻译扮演的角色不仅起到了桥梁的作用，更重要的是，翻译都是新的诗歌的创造者，或者说，每一首诗最终变成一首好的翻译诗歌，它都是两个人的成果，有时还是三个人的成果，没有好的原作，没有好的翻译，我们就不可能看到卓越的翻译作品。我不想说翻译从事的工作是一项遗憾的工作，而我认为，他们做的完全是一项创造性的工作，我在阅读一部翻译作品的时候，我的眼前浮现的是原作者和译者交叉的身影。尤其是诗歌，旋律和声音是多么的重要啊，但我力求听到的是译者试图告诉我们的原来最初的声音，或许这就是遗憾，这是任何一种翻译都无法做到的，但是我仍然愿意去倾听和阅读，那是因为译者在另外一个语言中对这个声音的接近，让我们听到了他试图表达的那种创造的声音。这个世界不能没有翻译，他们的使命和任务仍然是光荣的，请向他们致敬。

格林厄姆·莫特：越来越多的人似乎更倾向于写诗而非读诗，那么写作文化的民主化影响到了阅读文化吗？

吉狄马加：你说越来越多的人似乎更倾向于写诗而非读诗，我想这是每个人的一种权利，尤其是现在网络写作的门槛很低，你只要写出你自己认为是诗的东西，你都可以放到网上去发表，就是过去没有网络的时候，你只要有写诗的爱好，你还可以写出来放在抽屉里自己欣赏。但我仍然认为，所谓写作文化的民主化与真正的有精神品质的诗歌仍然是有差别的，否则，对人类构建的经典精神文化的标准就会毁灭，而那些已经进入人类正典的不朽作品，也会失去它们存在下去的价值和前提，并不是因为科学和技术的发展就会改变，人类精神创造的成果永远是有高低优劣之分的，所谓写作文化的民主化就是一个泛民主化的虚拟概念。

格林厄姆·莫特：你有一个漫长而辉煌的写作生涯——是什么驱使你动笔写出你的下一首诗？

吉狄马加：我曾经在别的访谈上说过这个问题，可能是某一种冲动让我写出了第一首诗，但是对于一个选择了以诗歌为一生写作追求的人，完全是因为对经典诗歌的阅读，让我发现了自己,是那些诗人唤醒了我的心灵,开始去思考生命的意义和存在的价值。还是在童年时代,我就意识到死亡的存在,并在那个时候有了奇怪的幻想。我还能想起也一定不会忘记,当我第一次阅读俄罗斯诗人普希金的作品时给我带来的震撼,是他让我知道了诗歌表达的东西不仅仅是个人的东西,它还是人类对爱情、自由、平等和一切美好理想的追求,可以说,我的诗歌写作生涯就是在这样的心境和选择中开始的。

2017.8.9

格林厄姆·莫特,英国著名诗人、作家,兰开斯特大学(Lancaster University)创意写作教授,同时也是该大学跨文化写作与研究中心主任。已出版了九本诗集。他的第一本书《着火的国家》(1986年出版)获得了美国作家协会(Society of Authors)颁发的埃里克·格雷戈里(Eric Gregory)大奖。在《可见性:新诗与诗选》(赛轮出版社,2007年)出版之后,《卫报》的一篇评论将他描述为"当代诗歌最有成就的实践者之一"。这本书完美地展示了格式严谨、富于感性和智性三者的融合,正是这些造就了他的声誉。格林厄姆的作品还赢得过许多其他重要的诗歌奖项,包括切尔滕纳姆诗歌奖。另外,他还凭借个人小说获得了2007年的布里波特奖(Bridport Prize)和2014年的国际短篇小说奖(Short Fiction International Prize),他的第一本全集《触摸》(赛轮出版社,2010年)获得了Edge Hill奖,他的作品被翻译成了世界十余种文字在多国出版。

Poets Are Still the Moral Leaders of the Civic Society Today
—Written replies to Graham Mort

Graham Mort: What is a poem for? How do you see its function in relation to human culture historically and in the future?

Jidi Majia: Poetry is as old as human history, the primary mode of human spiritual life as the identity of a poet in primitive religions strides the offices of tribal chiefs and shamans, and in most ancient societies poetry bridges man and heaven & earth and communions man with super natural beings. In essence, poetry is the purest human creation, not only linguistically a magical sublimation but also indispensable in the human spirit to create hallucinogens, that is to say, as long as human spiritual needs dictate, poetry will survive. And it's not going to die, that's what I believe. Either from the perspective of reality and the future based on the particularity of poetry, poetry is a remarkable part of human culture. Of course, as culture varies from time to time, there will be changed, but there will always be portions of it stabilized and fixed, becoming what we call by the name of tradition or canon. Such is the interaction of reality and poetry and the constancy of which explains the marginality of poetry in this present era of consumerism and rampant materialism. But it also tells us poetry does have an irreplaceable role in the spiritual life and cultural continuity of mankind. If it is believed that the spiritual life is an absolute necessity for mankind, then poets and poetry will continue to be with us, although that does not preclude the further worsening of the fate of poets.

Graham Mort: How do you see the relationship between the forms of written text and the sounds and music of poetry?

Jidi Majia: In a way poetry is a kind of form, a form of linguistic construct. Since the importance of writing and textuality is self-evident, in many cases textual innovation and even poetic innovation are equally important, so much so forth they do have much in common with innovation that have occurred to painting and music, either in synchronic or diachronic terms. We all agree what holds true, I mean, the tenets of painting of Pericles' Greece does not for Renaissance painters and the successive emergence of practitioners of impressionism, fauvism, cubism, futurism commonly dubbed modern art falsify those of Classical Greece or 18th century French tradition. The same is true with poetry, I mean the absolute need for innovation for both visual art and poetry. As poetry is written, it means one thing for sure that poetic innovation is essentially linguistic reshaping of the status of poetry, and for poetry its inner form like tone and rhythm, or prosody is thrust into eternal alteration to the extent we might say this constitutes the life of poetry. If the prosodic side of poetry stagnates, then the inner life of poetry ceases. Indeed, tone and rhythm are the hearts of poetry, or metaphorically the roar of blood vessels of poetry. That partially accounts for the notorious complaint of the impossibility of poetic translation. I reckon the content, or the sense to be made, the message to be imparted is only partial trouble. The sound, the prosodic aspect of poetry, the tone and rhythm proves more troublesome. Great poets are great because they are good at identifying and catching the poetic voice of each nation. Invariably they are also deemed the voice of their own people.

Graham Mort: How can the mythological dimensions of poetry be reconciled with contemporary scientific knowledge?

Jidi Majia: No poet's writing is breaking away with tradition, and many poets even if they are stranded and caught in the rather complex realities and intricacies of history of each nation, they are not quarantined from their own tradition and history. One obvious evidence is the rewriting myth repeatedly among poets in different eras. modern Greek poet George Seferis's masterpiece *Myth-History*, his compatriot Odysseas Elytis's epic *The Axion Esti* are both written to treat Greek myth with a modern sensibility, both being finest specimen of building up the mythology and institutions of today's Hellenism since both poets won the Nobel Prize in Literature. They compose poems to rid their countrymen's conscience from remorses unjustifiable, to achieve the highest degree of lucidity in expression, to find true solace in their cultural heritage and to finally succeed in approaching the mystery of light. Another great Greek poet, Nikos Kazantzakis, published his monumental poem *The Odyssey: A Modern Sequel* in 1960, an epic of 33,000 verses in which he praises in behalf of modern man in the prototype of Odyssey the passionate though tragic search for freedom as well as paints an image of ordinary people engaged in the incessant strife between spirit and flesh, their redemption and resurrection. In all these giants mentioned above, we can see the mythical element reconciled with modern scientific knowledge and their relationship is by no means an antagonistic one. On the contrary, they all succeed in merging a modern sensibility with a historical perspective which is a fundamental problem bedeviling all ancient civilizations in modern times.

Graham Mort: How might new information and communications technology affect poetic form and publication in the future?

Jidi Majia: We are living in an era of globalization and the internet which in fact offers new possibilities for the spread of poetry, and even robots are said of being capable of composing poems, isn't it? I'm not worried about poetry being written and spread in new channels and tools. What I am really worried about is the possible scenario of all poets becoming robot-like, parroting and copying one another, with no individuality or personality, then what is the rason d'etre for poets to go on writing and living in the name of poetry? For sure one thing we need not worry about is that robots may one day overrun us technically and rhetorically, but they certainly will not be able to win the hearts and souls, for as long as human poetry exists in the hearts and minds, robots without souls cannot defeat us. Now, thousands of poems are being churned out every day on the internet, and their spread may take some of the most exotic forms and speed. Unprecedented? Yes. But still, this is not the end of the world. We simply must muster up courage and intellect enough to take the measure of it and make the true sense of it.

Graham Mort: In a globalized world with interlocking political and economic structures what is the poet's role as social commentator and moral leader?

Jidi Majia: The reality of globalization, as well as the attendant transformations so triggered and caused, should predispose poets to be engaged, aesthetically and socially since the fact of so many people consumed by rampant consumerism and crass materialism should serve a clarion call to all poets to action. To say poets should be the conscience of our age does not mean we should sit in judgment on the world but in that he should uphold a torch, a candle as illuminator, he is a participant, a witness, a critic of the age he is living in. I am aware I am echoing Shelley's central faith in poets being the ultimate upholder and preserver of great virtues that distinguish man from all other species on earth.

Graham Mort: How can poetry mediate between minority ethnic groups and more dominant groupings within societies?

Jidi Majia: A poet's relationship with the outside world is both simple and complex. It depends. Ideally, poetry should be at the center of various ethnic and social class relations, binding them and mediating in case there is dispute, a view held by Irish poets Yeats and Heaney, especially the latter one whose writings the poet as healer of ancient wounds and feuds that divide British–Irish peoples. They also deem themselves as custodians and defenders of Irish culture and tradition, more important, as those of the spirit of human freedom. Indeed, great poetry must transcend all insularity of ideology and partisanship of ism and act as repository of common property of universal human significance. A true poet must also hold high the banner of friendship, peace and humanity to truly promote harmonious coexistence and friendly exchanges among different races and nations.

Graham Mort: How important is it that poets communicate internationally and how might such links develop the poem as an inter-cultural phenomenon?

Jidi Majia: Poetic communication between different countries and across different cultural background barriers is always a bonus, a blessing. German poet Johann Wolfgang von Goethe in the 19th century harbored a dream that one day national literatures will phase out into world literature and by hindsight we can say his dream has come true due to largely new tools and channels conferred by the strides of science and technology, which has increasingly globalized our world into a village where human contact is made easy like instant Nestle. In the past, exchange of literature and poetry relied heavily on literary translation, and in the present day, in addition to translation, poets and writers meet and talk on a very short notice, especially in the past 30 years, the end of the cold war has brought about en masse face-to-face communications and encounters involving poets and writers operating under different social systems. A good word should be put in for such literary exchanges as they develop and evolve unprecedented in substance, depth and breadth to the extent that new trends in poetic writing quickly get spread, known benefiting practitioners and professionals from quarters unimagined. This fact explains why some of the knottiest issues confronting the first class literary critics and theorists as well as major poets and writers across the world make topics and themes for seminars, conferences, poetic festivals, etc., such as the mysterious relationship between language and poetry, the notorious intrinsic duality between content and form, consciousness and rhetoric. Such cross-cultural communications prove to be both revelatory as well as soul-searching, self-discovery. We all become better artists, if not better men and women.

Graham Mort: How do you see the role of translators and translation as we move into an increasingly globalized world?

Jidi Majia: This world is filled with poets writing in different languages but poetic translation is still important as it has played an essential role in bridging various cultures and poetic traditions, the catalyst in boosting the emergence of new poetry. Indeed, many good translations are good poetry in their own right, some being solo, others, collaboration of two or three translators. This is another way of saying that translation is at times the nursery of good poetry. Admittedly poetic translation is an attempt never from regrets, but being human spiritual adventures, poetic translation is essentially creative of the highest order and as such, deserves our respect and heart-felt gratitude. Each time I pick up a poetic translated work, a mental picture of original poet and translator arises before me struggling to row a boat across the other shore. The only trouble is that tone and sound, being such important building blocks of a poetic structure, gets lost in the process of translation. How I envy the original author who creates a thing of beauty with message, sense, tone and prosody all locked up within, yet off limits to a poet or reader who strains to peep into it or to open his ear-drums to catch the slightest shred of it. The world cannot go around without translators. Their mission is daunting but still honorable. Please pay tribute to them.

Graham Mort: Has the democratisation of writing culture affected reading culture, with more people perhaps wanting to write poetry than to read it?

Jidi Majia: You characterize our age with more poets than readers and you seem to have scored a point considering that the internet has drastically lowered the threshold of the vocation of being a poet. All you have to do is sit down at your computer, move the mouse and follow your whims wherever they go before submitting them online. Even in the past without Internet, one could always poetize and put them into his desk drawers and be the sole reader of his own work bothering not a whit about finding a publisher. That being the case, I still think there are poems and poems. Certain mechanism or criteria seem to have been at work all the time separating dross from gold. There is a way of calling it—the process of canonization which explains we all agree there is a common cultural heritage composed of Homer's *Iliad,* Pushkin's *The Bronze Horseman* and Li Bai's immortal lines. No matter how advanced science and technology has evolved, it seems those criteria or standards by which great literary qualities are measured remain eternal and changeless. All this makes the concept of the democratization of writing culture more virtual than real.

Graham Mort: You've had a long and distinguished career—what motivates you to write the next poem?

Jidi Majia: I have answered this inquiry on various occasions. I will try to repeat. I guess for any serious poets, his stumbling upon a good poem could be what drives him to compose his first poem on the paper in the first place. Such a random encounter with classical and canonical poets in particular proves to be fortuitous and decisive as it has awakened me deep down to find meaning and purpose in my life. I have come into my own, as they say, that is, I discover my true self, my lifelong passion and mission. Now, earlier in my childhood, I was haunted by the stubborn issue of death, and fancy struck me one day I must learn the aptitude of reading; lucky enough, I did lay my hand at a book of selected poems of Pushkin. Eureka! I was shocked. I was pounded. I was woke up. From that moment, I was no more what I used to be. I was reborn in a sense. From Pushkin I had the revelation that poetry is not something purely private and personal. In it one can transcend one's own little ego to be used by a bigger purpose in the scheme of things. Pushkin is a model poet as he writes to be the conscience of his own nation, to be the pioneer of his own mother tongue and indeed, to be the mouth piece of humanity in their heroic pursuit of love, freedom, equality and all beautiful ideals. That is how I track down the genesis of my poetic career.

Translated by Huang Shaozheng

Graham Mort (1955—) is a British poet who lives in the northwest of England. He is professor of Creative Writing and Transcultural Literature at Lancaster University, where he co-directs the Centre for Transcultural Writing and Research. He has worked extensively in sub-Saharan Africa, developing creative writing projects for emergent writers, also visiting Vietnam for the Asia Pacific Poetry Festival and developing a new narrative project in Kurdistan–'*Many Women, Many Words*'–with the University of Soran. Graham has published nine collections of poetry. His first book, '*A Country on Fire*' (Littlewood Press, 1986), won a major Eric Gregory award from the Society of Authors. '*Circular Breathing*' (Dangaroo Press, 1997) was a Poetry Book Society Recommendation and following the publication of '*Visibility: new and selected poems*' (Seren, 2007) a review in *The Guardian* newspaper described him as, "One of contemporary verse's most accomplished practitioners. This book perfectly exhibits the blend of formal scrupulousness, sensory evocation and intellectual rigour that has shaped his reputation." Graham also writes short fiction, winning the Bridport Prize (2007) and Short Fiction International Prize (2014) for individual stories and the Edge Hill Prize for his first full collection '*Touch*' (Seren, 2010). His second collection of stories '*Terroir*' appeared from Seren in 2015. Graham's writing has been translated into more than ten kinds of languages, such as Turkish, Vietnamese and Greek.

另一种创造：从胡安·鲁尔福到奥克塔维奥·帕斯
——在北大"中墨建交45周年文学研讨会"上的演讲

当我在这里说到胡安·鲁尔福、奥克塔维奥·帕斯的时候，我便想到一个关键的词：创造，或者用一句更妥帖的话来说那就是：另一种创造。我想，无论是在墨西哥文学史上，还是在拉丁美洲文学史上，甚至扩大到整个20世纪的世界文学史，胡安·鲁尔福和奥克塔维奥·帕斯都是两个极具传奇色彩并充满了神秘的人物。

最有意思的是，与这样充满了传奇又极为神秘的人物在精神上相遇，不能不说从一开始就具有某种宿命的味道，首先，让我先说说我是如何认识胡安·鲁尔福这个人和他的作品的。我没有亲眼见过胡安·鲁尔福，这似乎是一个遗憾，这个世界有这么多神奇的人，当然不乏你十分心仪的对象，但都要见面或要认识，的确是一件十分困难的事。

但对胡安·鲁尔福这个人和他的作品，从我第一次与之相遇，我就充满了好奇和疑问，好奇是因为我读了他的短篇小说集《平原烈火》和中篇小说《佩德罗·帕拉莫》之后，我对他作为一个异域作家所具有的神奇想象力惊叹不已。记得那是在20世纪80年代初，这样的阅读给我带来的愉悦和精神上的冲击毫无疑问是巨大的。

可以说就在短短几个月的时间内，我把一本不足二十万字的《胡安·鲁尔福中短篇小说集》反复阅读了若干遍，可以说有一年多时间这本书都被我随身携带着，以便随时翻阅抽看。因为阅读胡安·鲁尔福的作品，我开始明白一个道理，此前在世界许多地方的"地域主义"写作，在语言和形式上都进行了新的开拓和探索，不少作品具有深刻的土著思想意识，对人物的刻画和描写充满着真实的力量，尤其是对地域文化和自然环境的呈现更是淋漓尽致。

在这些作品中包括厄瓜多尔作家霍尔赫·伊卡萨的《瓦西蓬戈》、委内瑞拉作家罗慕洛·加列戈斯的《堂娜芭芭拉》、秘鲁作家阿格达斯的《深沉的河流》、秘鲁作家西罗·阿莱格里亚的《广漠的世界》等等，如果把它的范围扩大得更远，在非洲地区还包括尼日利亚作家阿契贝小说四部曲《瓦解》《动荡》《神箭》《人民公仆》，肯尼亚作家恩古吉的《一粒麦种》《孩子，你别哭》和《大河两岸》等等。

当然还有许多置身于这个世界不同地域的众多"地域主义"写作的作家，这对于20世纪而言已经是一个令人瞩目的文学现象，对他们的创作背景和作品进行解读，不管从政治层面，还是从社会和现实的层面，都会让我们对不同族群的人类生活有一个更全面、更独到的认识。因为这些作家的作品都是对自己所属族群生活的独立书写，而不是用他者的眼光所进行的记录。这些作品的一次次书写过程，其实就是对自身文化身份的一次次确认。这些杰出的作家在后现代和后殖民的语境中，从追寻自身的文化传统和精神源头开始，对重新认识自己确立了自信并获得了无可辩驳的理由。

可以说对于第三世界作家来说，这一切都是伴随着民族解放、国家独立而蓬勃展开的。但是，对于胡安·鲁尔福来说，虽然他的作品和生活毫无争议地属于那个充满了混乱、贫困、战争、动荡而又急剧变革的时代，但他用近似于灌注了魔力的笔为我们构建了一个人鬼共处的真实世界，这种真实的穿透力更能复现时间和生命的本质。胡安·鲁尔福最大的本领是他给我们提供了新的时间观念，他让生和死的意识渗透在他所营造的空间和氛围里，他用文字所构筑的世界，就如同阿兹特克人对宇宙、对生命、对时间、对存在所进行的神秘而奇妙的描述，这种描述既是过去，又是现在，更是未来。

在20世纪众多的"地域主义"写作中，请允许我武断地这样说，是胡安·鲁尔福第一个也是第一次真正打开了时间的入口，正是那种神秘的、非理性的、拥有多种时间、跨越生死、打破逻辑的观念，才让他着魔似的将"地域主义"的写作推到了一个梦幻般的神性的极致。

难怪加西亚·马尔克斯在回忆录中深情地回忆，他很早就能将《佩德罗·帕拉莫》从最后一个字进行倒背，这显然不是一句玩笑话，我们今天可以并非毫无根据地下这样一个结论，是胡安·鲁尔福最早开始了魔幻现实主义写作的实验，而其经典作品《佩德罗·帕拉莫》是一个奇迹，是一座再也无法被撼动的真正的里程碑。

一个兴起于拉丁美洲的伟大的文学时代，其序幕被真正打开，胡安·鲁尔福就是其中最重要的人物之一。《佩德罗·帕拉莫》开创了现代小说的另一种形式，它将时空和循环、生命和死亡天衣无缝地融合在了一起，它是梦和神话穿越真实现实的魔幻写照，在此之后，不仅仅在拉丁美洲，就是在世界范围内，许多后来者都继承、遵循了这样的理念，成长于中国20世纪80年代的许多先锋作家，他们都把胡安·鲁尔福视为自己的导师和光辉的典范。

胡安·鲁尔福之所以能得到不同地域、不同民族的作家高度评价，并成为一个永远的话题，那是因为他从印第安原住民的宇宙观以及哲学观出发，将象征、隐喻、虚拟融入了一个人与鬼、生与死的想象的世界，并给这个世界赋予了新的意义。据我们所知，在古代墨西哥人的原始思维中，空间与时间是相互交融的，时间与空间在不同方向的联系，构成了他们宇宙观中最让我们着迷的那个部分。

最让人称道的是，胡安·鲁尔福的写作并不是简单地将原始神话和土著民族的认知观念植入他所构建的文学世界中，他的高明之处，是将环形的不断变化着的时间与空间联系在了一起，这种生命、死亡与生命的再生所形成的永恒循环，最终构成了他所颠倒与重建的三个不同的世界，这三个世界既包括了天堂，也包括了地狱，当然也还有胡安·鲁尔福所说的地下世界。

胡安·鲁尔福的伟大之处还在于他把他所了解的现实世界，出神入化地与这些神奇的、荒诞的、超自然的因素形成了一个完美的整体，也让他的书写永远具有一种当代性和现场感，他笔下的芸芸众生毫无疑问就是墨西哥现实世界中的不同人物，他们真实地生活在被边缘化的社会的最底层，但他们发出的呐喊和其他声音通过胡安·鲁尔福已经传到了世界不同的角落。

我对胡安·鲁尔福充满了好奇，那是因为我在阅读他的作品的时候，他给我带来从未有过的启示以及对自身的思考。从比较文化的角度来看，墨西哥原住民和我们彝族人民有许多相同的地方。

墨西哥人不畏惧死神，诞生和死亡是一个节日的两个部分，他们相信人死后会前往一个名叫"米特兰"的地方，那里既不是天堂也不是地狱。我们彝族人把死亡看成是另一种生命的开始，人死后会前往一个名叫"石姆姆哈"的地方，这个地方在天空和大地之间，那里是一片白色的世界。彝族人认为人死后会留下三魂，一魂会留在火葬地，一魂会跟随祖先回到最后的长眠地，还有一魂会留给后人供奉。

是因为胡安·鲁尔福，我才开始了一次漫长的追寻和回归，那就是让自己的写作与我们民族的精神源头真正续接在一起，也就是从那个时候开始直到今天，我都把自身的写作依托于一个民族广阔深厚的精神背景成为一种自觉。记得我访问墨西哥城的时候，就专门去墨西哥人类学博物馆进行参观，我把这种近似于膜拜的参观从内心看成是对胡安·鲁尔福的敬意，因为我知道，从1962年开始他就在土著研究院工作，他的行为和沉默低调的作风，完全是墨西哥山地人的化身。

那次我从墨西哥带回的礼物中最让我珍爱的就是一本胡安·鲁尔福对墨西哥山地和原住民的摄影集，这部充满了悲悯和忧伤的摄影集可以说是他的另一种述说，当我一遍遍凝视墨西哥山地和天空的颜色时，心中不免会涌动着一种隐隐的不可名状的伤感。

胡安·鲁尔福这个人以及他的全部写作对于我来说，都是一部记忆中清晰而又飘忽不定的影像，就像一部植入了流动时间的黑白电影。因为胡安·鲁尔福所具有的这种超常的对事物和历史的抽象能力，他恐怕是世界文学史上用如此少的文字，写出了一个国家或者说一个民族隐秘精神史最伟大的人物之一，也许是因为我的孤陋寡闻，在我的阅读经历和范围中，还没有发现有哪一位作家在抽象力、想象力以及能与之相适应的语言能力方面能与其比肩。

而奥克塔维奥·帕斯对于我来说就是一个现实存在，这个存在不会因为他肉体的消失而离开我，他教会我的不是一首诗的写法，而是对所有生命和这个世界的态度。他说过这样一段话："我不认为诗歌可以改变世界。诗歌可以给我们启示，向我们揭示关于我们人的秘密，可以为我们带来愉悦。特别是，它可以展示另一个世界，展示现实的另一副面孔。我不能生活在没有诗的世界里，因为诗歌拯救了时间、拯救了瞬间：时间没有把诗歌杀死，没剥夺它的活力。"

作为诗人，奥克塔维奥·帕斯虽然不是第一个，但确实是最好的将拉美古老史前文化、西班牙征服者的文化和现代政治社会文化融为一体写出经典作品的划时代的诗人。他的不朽长诗《太阳石》，既是对美洲原住民阿兹特克太阳历的礼赞，同时也是对生命、自我、非我、死亡、虚无、存在、意义、异化以及性爱的诗性呈现。他同样是20世纪为数不多的能将政治、革命、批判性融为一体，对现实的干预、对自己诗的写作把握得最为适度的大师之一，难怪他曾说过近似于这样的话，"政治是同另一些人共处的艺术，而我的一切作品都与另一种东西有关。"

我们知道20世纪是一个社会革命和艺术革命都风起云涌的时代，在很长一个阶段不同的意识形态所形成的两大阵营，无论是在社会理想方面，还是在价值观念方面，以及对重大历史事件的判断看法，都是水火不相容的。而在那样一个时期，大多数拉美重要诗人和作家都是不容置疑的左翼人士，当然这也包括奥克塔维奥·帕斯。

但是，也是从那个时候开始，奥克塔维奥·帕斯就表现出了思想家、哲人、知识分子的道德风骨和独立思考的智慧能力，他对任何一个重大政治事件的看法和判断，都不是从所谓的集体政治文化的概念出发，而是从人道和真实出发去揭示出真相和本质。1968年10月2日在特拉特洛尔科广场发生的屠杀学生的事件，就遭到了他的强烈谴责，他也因为这个众所周知的原因辞去了驻印度大使的职务。

可以说，是奥克塔维奥·帕斯在墨西哥开创并确立了一种独立思想的批评文化，打破了"不左即右"二元对立的局面，他的这种表达政治异见的鲜明态度，甚至延伸到了他对许多国际重大事件的判断，比如引起整个西方和拉美左派阵营分裂的托洛茨基被暗杀事件，就是他首先提出了对另一种极权以及反对精神自由的质疑，也因此他与巴勃罗·聂鲁达等朋友分道扬镳，他们的友谊直到晚年才得以恢复。

他创办的杂志《多元》《转折》，是拉丁美洲西班牙语世界不同思想进行对话和交锋的窗口，他一直高举着自由表达思想和反对一切强权的人道主义旗帜，他主办过一个又一个有关这个世界未来发展，并且带有某种预言性的主题讨论，这些被聚集在一起的闪耀着思想光芒的精神遗产，对今天不同国度的知识分子同样有着宝贵的参照和借鉴作用。

奥克塔维奥·帕斯是最早发现并醒悟到美洲左翼革命以及这一革命开始将矛头对准自己的人之一，他的此类言论甚至涉及古巴革命后的政治现实、南美军人政权的独裁统治、各种形式游击组织的活动、东欧社会主义在全球范围内的境况，以及对美国所倡导的极端物质主义和实用主义外交政策精准批判。他发表于1985年的《国家制度党，其临终时分》一文，对该党在奇瓦瓦州操纵选举的舞弊行为进行了揭露，这一勇敢的举动使墨西哥大众的民主意识被进一步唤醒。

在这里我必须说到他的不朽之作，当然也是人类的不朽之作《孤独的迷宫》，是因为它的存在我们才能在任何一个时候，瞬间进入墨西哥的灵魂。《孤独的迷宫》是墨西哥民族的心灵史、精神史和社会史，它不是一般意义上的墨西哥民族心理和文化现象的罗列展示，而是打开了一个古老民族的孤独面具，将这一复杂精神现象的内在结构和本质呈现给了我们。

在一次演讲中帕斯这样告诉听众："作家就是要说那些说不出的话，没说过的话，没人愿意或者没人能说的话。因此所有伟大的文学作品并非电力高压线而是道德、审美和批评的高压线。它的作用在于破坏和创造。文学作品与可怖的人类现实和解的强大能力并不低于文学的颠覆力。伟大的文学是仁慈的，使一切伤口愈合，疗治所有精神上的苦痛，在情绪最低落的时刻照样对生活说是。"

我要说，伟大的奥克塔维奥·帕斯是这样说的，同样他也是这样做的，他用波澜壮阔的一生和无所畏惧的独立精神，为人类做出了巨大的贡献，并为我们所有的后来者树立了光辉的典范。

从胡安·鲁尔福到奥克塔维奥·帕斯，这是属于墨西哥，同样也属于全人类的必须被共同敬畏和记忆的精神遗产，他们是一种现实，是一种象征，更重要的是他们还是一种创造。也正因为这种充满了梦幻的创造，在太阳之国的墨西哥谷地，每天升起的太阳才照亮了生命和死亡的面具，而胡安·鲁尔福和奥克塔维奥·帕斯灵魂的影子，也将在那里年复一年地飘浮，永远不会从人类的视线中消失。

To Create Differently: From Juan Rulfo to Octavio Paz
—A speech given at a seminar held in Peking University marking the 45th Anniversary of Sino-Mexico Diplomatic Relations

At the mere mention of the two Mexican names, Juan Rulfo and Octavio Paz, one overworked buzzword, not necessarily drained of its clear meaning, comes up instantly in my mind: creativity, or to be more precise in the present context, alternative creativity, as I trust these two Mexicans remain a legend and even something of a mystery for contemporary Mexican literature, for the Hispanic world and even beyond.

Therefore, it is utter coincidence why I chanced upon getting to know and grow eventually intimate familiarity with their work and personality, cast in such unconventional tone and artistically innovative mould. To begin with, I might say a few words about Juan Rulfo. Sure enough, I never met with him in person, a seemingly pitiable thing, although I wish that. Yet on second thoughts, one will be much consoled given this is a world populated by over 7.5 billion souls. We are not meant to meet with each of them in the average short lifespan of ours.

Yet an accidental acquaintance with Juan Rulfo turns out to be a lifelong obsession, well rewarded by a quick understanding of the various subtleties in his writing before reinforced into an informed appreciation of his greatness fed upon initial thirst and curiosity for the exotic and foreign. His two literary works, *The Burning Plain El Llano en llamas*(1953), a collection of short stories, and *Pedro Páramo*, a 1955 tale of a man discovering a ghost town, have never ceased teasing my imagination. For a literary novice of ethnic origin from China just opening up to the world in the early 1980s, Juan Rulfo was absolutely a knock-out and eye-opener experience.

Thus the first reading of his *El Llano en llamas* made me his perennial fan. In the months that followed, that slim collection of stories less than 200,000 Chinese characters became my compulsory reading and for over one year I kept the book in my pocket or in my baggage for repeated perusal. It dawned upon me there were different varieties of regionalist writings the world over and much remained to be explored and aped in the way of fellow regionalists' experimentation with technique and language. Rulfo, for one, gives his work an air of historical authenticity in his employment of a unique prose style and his seemingly bizarre characterization, and above all, in his ability to present a thoroughly Hispanic world in thoroughly Hispanic terms forerunning the Boom of the Latin American Novel that was to sweep the literary world, eastem and westem countries soon.

Although critics and writers debate which authors or works fall within the regionalist genre, the following authors represent without dispute the narrative mode. Within the Latin American world, the most iconic of magical realist writers are the Ecuadorian novelist Jorge Icaza (*Huasipungo*), the Venezuelan Rómulo Gallegos (*Doña Bárbara*), the Peruvian Indigenous writers José María Arguedas (*Deep Rivers*) and Ciro Alegría (*Broad and Alien is the World*). This literary trend also includes in the African tradition eminent writers such as Chinua Achebe (*Things Fall Apart; No Lonfer at Ease; Arrow of God; A Man of the People*) and Ngũgĩ Wa Thiong'o (*Weep Not, Child; A Grain of Wheat; The River Between*).

The popularity of regionalist literature is enduring and great and the production and proliferation throughout the developing countries is extensive in the 20th century, not at all restricted to names given above who supply some of the most prototypical specimen. One thing in common is that these writers not only chronicle the contemporary social and political histories of each's country but also reflect the dominant economic plight and intellectual concerns of their own people, attaining a high artistic dimension that makes it possible for them to comment on the natural and human landscape as well as the welter of forces and causes that lead to such situations in the third world.

Regionalist writing, by its logic, will yield a group of writers who have at heart an anthropological mission: to probe into the culture of each's people by studying their folklore, linguistic peculiarities, beliefs, mores and customs and provide an insider's synthesis and interpretation other than the version supplied by outsiders. It is, in essence, an exercise at rediscovering and reaffirming one's cultural identity in a post-colonial and even post-modernist context under the implication that one can only renew one's confidence indisputably by identifying the uniqueness of individual nation's spirituality owing to their peculiar natural features.

For the third world writers, the novels were the fictional counterpart of discovering and affirming the cultural identity of individual countries in the wake of de-colonialisation waves engulfing former colonial powers in the 1950s. Yet, for Juan Rulfo, there is a stark mingling of aestheticism and social protest. Of course, he reacted in horror to the times he was living in characterized by political chaos, deprivation, incessant internecine wars, turbulence and senseless violence, but he is also one of the first to break with the lingering traces of realism-naturalism to adapt avant-garde, post-Joycean tricks to his subject matter with amazing results. His *Pedro Páramo*, a tale of a man named Juan Preciado who travels to his recently deceased mother's hometown, Comala, to find his father, only to come across a literal ghost town–populated, that is, by spectral figures. Rulfo, the subjective and anguished artist, by destroying the line of demarcation that separates what seems real from what seems fantastic, what is today, tomorrow and future, fuses both realistic and surrealistic approaches into one that is more universal in outlook and more sophisticated in style, language and temporal-spatial development. There are obvious mythical overtones in the story reminiscent of non-European views, drawn from Aztec lore, of the earth, life, individual existence, all being consonant with the ambience of the fictional town and the starkness of the narrative.

Up to this point I make bold to say, among the principal and powerful regionalist trends, Juan Rulfo might count the veritable pioneer who pushes the native theme genre to its logical extreme by breaking loose the floodgate of time, logic and concretizing the magic realism to magical heights.

No wonder Gabriel García Márquez has said that it was only his life-changing discovery that opened the way to the composition of his masterpiece, *One Hundred Years of Solitude*. He even boasted he could recite every word of the short novel by heart. Arguably mentor of the magical realism genre, Rulfo has written two books, of a high quality as good as most of those of his disciples, if not better, truly fictional milestones, winning him a place among the most prestigious practitioners of the new Latin American novel.

Pedro Páramo signals the coming-of-age of South American literature. Juan Rulfo enchants us by blazing trails in modern novel writing as he marries myth with narrative modeled on and further expanding Joycean formulas (dislocation of linear time, shifts in the narrator and his viewpoint, the probing of the psyche). He does not try to recapture the actual world with realist conventions but creates a new one endowed with magical coherence projecting onto the chaos of reality. There are scenes and situations that blur the line of life and death. There are beams of light that shoot through the unfathomable veils of the fantastic and unreal. As revolutionary as the technique, *Pedro Páramo* is not only remarkable for pacesetting the exposition through a non-linear structure, but also for its insights into the essence of what a modern novel is, affording both example for much older and more sophisticated western writers and the bulk of non-Western literary practitioners, the emerging avant garde Chinese writers in the late 1980s in particular, to follow and emulate.

How Juan Rulfo came by his magic art, of unquestioned literary merits and of universally critical appraisal remains an inexhaustible topic. Some suggest he has drawn heavily from the Indigenous Indian cosmology and philosophy in depth and great value and that he has created a fictional world so much embedded in the Aztecan symbolism, metaphor and allegory inhabited by spectral beings. To the best of my knowledge, ancient Aztecs see a unity of temporal and spatial relationship in all directions, an idea both enigmatic and revelatory.

What makes Juan Rulfo truly impressive is this: apart from being one of the first to have adopted the latest literary theories in vogue in the western country, he has blended the native belief systems and cognitive models in his fictional Comala town. He envisages an eternal loop into which time and space being linked in parallel, life, death and rebirth are cast in a process of circular motion which ushers in three different worlds, i.e., the hell, the paradise and of course the subterranean realm in Rulfo's mind.

Juan Rulfo's mythical and fantastical perspectives, as commentators aptly put it, project a sense of the complex realities by portraying "fantastical events in an otherwise realistic tone." He brings fables, folk tales, and myths into contemporary social relevance in favor of the socially and economically marginalized strata in the then Mexico, even though he seldom preaches against social abuses.

I am really interested in Juan Rulfo has been an obsession with me, a perennial source of inspiration and enlightenment has impact on me a lot. From comparative anthropological perspectives, both Yi in southwestern China and aborigines in Mexico share enough traits in common to permit a few generalizations. All display a profound faith in supernatural forces which they believe shape, influence and guide their lives.

Death is not to be feared as birth and death are actually celebrated as two integral parts of a local festivity. The communal stability and sanctity of living rest on a firm conception of an afterworld called Mitran, neither hell nor paradise. Similarly, we Yi people regard death as the beginning of another life. When a Yi ceases to breathe, he sets off to a certain destination called "Symmuha", situated between the sky and the earth, an imaginary white world. To the Yi who cling to ancient mores and values, they have three souls to leave behind upon dying. One soul will remain in the cremation ground. The second will follow a special soul trail to return to the final ancestral resting place, and the last one, to be worshipped by posterity.

I owe Juan Rulfo a word of gratitude as he prompted me to embark on a long, arduous quest for identity, one to seek my tribal root and reconnect myself with my own cultural beginnings out of which I have come into my own, a truly Yi poet, aspiring to identify with and to translate faithfully the realities of Yi's life. I still remember during a visit to Mexico City, I went to the Museum of Anthropology as a token of homage to Juan Rulfo, my own cult of personality as he was known to be on the staff of the institution since 1962, or more specifically, he was in charge of the editorial department of the National Institute for Indigenous Studies, a government agency devoted to the protection and economic improvement of the primitive Indian communities. The meek, unobtrusive and low-key manner in which he conducts himself is widely deemed as epitomizing the distinctive character and temperament of the Mexican mountain people.

Among the souvenirs brought back home is a photo album, much treasured and valued, by Juan Rulfo who shot the rare photos of native Mexicans by himself. To me he is simply composing a book of fiction in the visual mode. At times lost in the reveries of the melancholic Mexican mountains and sky over and over again, my heart contracts for condolence. Sadness overwhelms me unrestrainedly.

The man and his oeuvre are for me an image, clear and erratic, like a black-and-white movie embedded in time in constant motion as he possesses the extraordinary skills and intellectual equipment much needed to symbolize and objectify his people's dilemmas, thoughts and actions whose deeper meanings remain hitherto hidden even to themselves. The combination of historiographical rigor, stylistic precision, verbal economy, and psychological insight into the generalized human misery, the plight of his country per se, has been rarely, if ever, surpassed in Latin American fiction. Apology for my possible ignorance, due to a limited reading purview on my part, I have yet to find a single writer who can match him in intellect, imagination, and succinct mode of expression in world literature.

And Octavio Paz is a ubiquitous presence, a master of modern narrative techniques in an era that sees a general boom of poetic art. He is held high in my esteem not only because he has taught me much as a poet but also because he reaffirms powerfully his faith in sanctity of life and poetry as ultimately redemptive. In fact, as he himself pointed out in an interview, he was basically an optimist: "I don't think poetry can change the world. Poetry gives us inspiration, reveals to us the secrets of heart, fragility of life, the dilemmas of intimacy. It both entertains and educates. In particular, it creates another supra-sensible world. Show us the other face of reality. I can't live in a world without poetry because poetry salvages time and the moment: it doesn't kill it, it doesn't deprive it of its vitality."

As a poet, Octavio Paz is not the first, but he is certainly the best writer who, by presenting an epoch-making, all-embracing picture of the social, economic and political reality, achieves heightened insights and providing important perspective on the fatal collision of the experiences of Pre-historic Latin America, Spanish colonialism and modern Hispanic world at the mercy of recurrent violence, civil strife, economic stagnation, moral and intellectual backwardness. Epic in scope, his immortal poem, "*Sun Stone*," is a hymn of praise to the Aztec Solar Calendar of Native Americans, including sophisticated discussions of philosophical and theological as well as cultural and sociological subjects on life, self, non-self, death, nothingness, existence, meaning, alienation, and sexual love. He is also one of the few masters in the 20th century who can offer sad yet affirmative views of life in all its complexity, to be admired for neither sacrificing political engagement nor compromising his artistic integrity. No wonder he once commented on politics as an art of co-existing with others and he further added that his work pointed to the side of others.

We know that the 20th century is an age swollen with social revolutions and artistic fashions at one swoop. At a time, nay, for an extended span of time, the monstrous absurdity and division of our world was such that even half of the peopling was pitted against the other half based upon a set of artifices and man-made ideologies. It was a global situation that destroyed man's spirit, his spontaneous impulses towards life, admitting no doubt, hesitation, even half measures. The name of the game was unquestioning political commitment to either one cause or another without even blinking one's eyes to the extent that most of the important poets and writers in Latin America were standing up to be counted in the leftist camping. Of course, Octavio Paz was no exception.

But our Octavio Paz, the philosopher, moralist and thinker in him, affords a detachment that made it possible to control his passionate reactions to the brutality of events in contrast to most other engaged Latin American writers. He obviously avoids taking his stand upon the insecure foundations of political or cultural collectivism. He does not easily quarrel with those who cause his anguished antagonism for antagonism's sake. With him, things and events are humanized and individualized. In a world submerged by madness, he still deems truth a greater friend above any ideological fidelity. And for truth's sake, he was strongly equivocal in condemning the massacre of students at the Tlatelolco Square on October 2, 1968 and for which he resigned his post as ambassador to India, a price paid for a noble gesture of civil disobedience.

The shift to a more rational and objective plane of vision becomes increasingly evident as Octavio Paz has been credited with singlehandedly initiating a non-partisan cultural status quo in which polemically leftist or rightist arguments were frowned upon in favor of measured, critical thinking and independent dissent in major international events. Take one example, the assassination of Trotsky that polarized the entire Western and Latin American leftists, he was the first to voice his query about the questionable character of the triumphant marches of totalitarianism at the expense of freedom of conscience even that meant being alienated from friends like Pablo Neruda and we are told that their intimate affinity was not restored until his later years.

The two journals *Taller* and *El Hijo Pródigo* he founded, by hoisting the haughty standard of freedom of expression and humanitarianism to defy any brand of authoritarianism, have proven to be an ideal venue where different and even hostile opinions were subjected to the rational Socratic inquiry among intellectuals in the Latin American world. Adding to these vital discursive attempts are a series of seminars he hosted as to the possible scenarios of our world in a quarry and disarray, and the opinions he put forth, the prophetic accuracy and all the virtues of intellectual honesty typical of him, a knowledgeable reader will discern and detect, forms part of his more endurable legacy, radiating with metaphysical light, leaving a rich burning, enlightening flavor behind.

Octavio Paz was one of the earliest clairvoyants who realized the stupidity of unabashedly romancing with leftist approaches to all the social and political ills plaguing Latin America. Deliberate misunderstanding, if not outright ignorance, characterized the leftist perceptions of the fatal continent. To do the job, he bothered himself to pull back the veils of myth to glimpse reality and even pointed fingers at himself. His harsh remarks did not spare the then supposedly salutary Cuban revolution and the popular military dictatorship because of their physical strength, of larger, more intricate political maneuvering, the various forms of guerrilla organizations who have had their opportunities to effect change, the reformers, theirs, yet all failing to institute development, to solve the major continental problems. He also called into question of the so-called progressiveness of the Eastern European socialist bloc. His indictment of the cynicism of the materialistic and pragmatic foreign policy advocated by the United States proved unanswerable and convincing, and perhaps, because of abundant examples of USA misbehaviors lingering longer in the public mind than its acts of benevolence. His article entitled *"The State Institution Party in 1985, at the end of its life"* was a debilitating exposé of the party's fraud at manipulating election in Chihuahua, a courageous move which further purified the Mexican public's awareness of democracy.

Here I must reserve my greatest laudation to his monumental work, not only in my estimation, of course, the immortal work of mankind, *The Labyrinth of Solitude*, personally the open sesame to enter into the Mexican soul in an instant. *The Labyrinth of Solitude* presents a vast synthesis of social, economic and political evils bedeviling his home country, remarkable for its insights into the workings of the Mexican mind. We understand Mexico better for having read this book as he imparts not only the grisly stark reality, the tormented mentality of a strife-torn nation whose intense wrestling with a hostile natural and social milieu leave them frustrated and alienated, but also unmasks an ancient people condemned to solitude through the humanistic elements of aesthetic perception and empathy, the essence of Mexican culture graphically conveyed.

In a speech, Paz reiterates the tenet fundamental to his work: "A writer is supposed to say something nobody has said before, or cares to say, or is unable to or even dare not say it. Therefore all great literary works are not electric power lines literally but so literarily in terms of their moral and aesthetic values, designed both to destroy and create. The power of a work of art to resolve and reconcile human feuds and hostility equals that of subverting reality. Great literature is merciful, healing all wounds and embalming all spiritual agonies, affirming life at its lowest ebb and flow."

I make bold to declare our great Octavio Paz means every word of what he says. His avid interest in improving human affairs, his strength of character and devotion, his daunting and incorruptible judgment are of a kind rarely joined in an ordinary being of blood and flesh, a leading and towering personality vital and significant for the course of history, greater than his purely artistic achievements.

Juan Rulfo and Octavio Paz belong to Mexico, to all the world, looked up to in universal awe and cherished in popular memory. Both iconic figures, they tell us more of humanity, credited justifiably as an alternative source of artistic creativity, dedicated to reflecting the dominant intellectual concerns and explaining to their people how and why their world came to be the way it is today. We also know more of Mexico which has little to do with change of the seasons or the return of the stars. Because of the grandness of their literary achievements as well as the seminal and revolutionary influence upon contemporary poetry and fiction the world over, the sun rising every day in the solar valley of the country called Mexico illuminates the mask of life and death, while the souls of Juan Rulfo and Octavio Paz will hover over the human scene without fail, forever on the horizon of our earth.

Translated by Huang Shaozheng

词语的盐·光所构筑的另一个人类的殿堂——诗歌语言的透明与微暗

——在2018年中国自贡"一带一路"诗歌之灯点亮世界国际诗歌周开幕式上的演讲

与日常的语言相比较,毫无疑问,诗歌的语言属于另一个语言的范畴,当然需要声明的是,我并不是说日常的语言与诗歌的语言存在着泾渭分明的不同,而是指诗歌的语言具有某种抽象性、象征性、暗示性以及模糊性。诗歌的语言是通过一个一个的词所构成的,从某种意义而言,诗歌语言所构成的多维度的语言世界,就如同那些古老的石头建筑,它们是用一块一块的石头构建而成的,这些石头每一块似乎都有着特殊的记忆,哪怕就是有一天这个建筑倒塌了,那些散落在地上的石头,当你用手抚摸它的时候,你也会发现它会给你一种强烈的暗示,那就是它仍然在用一种特殊的密码和方式告诉你它生命中的一切,很多时候如果把一首诗拆散,其实它的每一个词就像这些石头。

在我们古老的彝族典籍和史诗中,诗歌的语言就如同一条隐秘的河流,当然,这条河流从一开始就有着一个伟大的源头,它是所有民族哺育精神的最纯洁的乳汁,也可以说它是这个世界上一切具有创造力的生物的肚脐,无一例外,诗歌都是这个世界上生活在不同地域族群的最古老的艺术形式之一。

在古代史诗的吟唱过程中,吟唱者往往具有双重的身份,他们既是现实生活中的智者,又是人类社会与天地冥界联系的通灵人。也可以说人类有语言以来,诗歌就成为我们赞颂祖先、歌唱自然、哭诉亡灵、抚慰生命、倾诉爱情的一种特殊的方式。如果从世界诗歌史的角度来看,口头的诗歌一定要比人类有文字以来的诗歌久远得多,在今天一些非常边远的地方,那些没有原生文字的民族,他们的口头诗歌的传统仍然还在延续,最为可贵的是,他们的诗歌语言也是对日常生活用语的精炼和提升,在我们彝族古老的谚语中就把诗歌称为"语言中的盐巴",直到今天在婚丧嫁娶集会的场所,能即兴吟诵诗歌的人还要进行一问一答的博弈对唱。

而从有文字以来留存下来的人类诗歌文本来看,在任何一个民族文字书写的诗歌中,语言都是构建诗歌最重要的要素和神奇的材料,也可以说在任何一个民族的文字创造中诗歌都是最精华的那个部分,难怪在许多民族和国度都有这样的比喻"诗歌是人类艺术皇冠上最亮的明珠",而诗歌语言所富有的创造力和神秘性就越发显得珍贵和重要。诗歌通过语言创造了一个属于自己的世界,而这个世界的丰富性、象征性、抽象性、多义性、复杂性都是语言带来的,也就是说,语言通过诗人或者说诗人通过语言给我们所有的倾听者、阅读者提供了无限的可能。

正因为语言在诗歌中的特殊作用,它就像魔术师手中的一个道具,它可能在一个瞬间变成一只会飞的鸽子,同样,它还会在另一个不同的时空里变成了鱼缸中一条红色的鱼。在任何一个语言世界中,我以为只有诗人通过诗的语言能给我们创造一个完全不同的世界,甚至在不同的诗人之间,他们各自通过语言所创造的世界也将是完全不同的,这就像伟大的作曲家勋伯格的无调音乐,它是即兴的、感性的、直觉的、毫无规律的,但它又是整体的和不可分割的。

很多时候诗歌也是这样,特别是当诗人把不同的词置放在不同的地方,这个词就将会在不同的语境中呈现出新的无法预知的意义。为什么说有一部分诗歌在阅读时会产生障碍,有的作品甚至是世界诗歌史上具有经典意义的作品,比如伟大的德语诗人策兰,比如说伟大的西班牙语诗人塞萨尔·巴列霍,比如说伟大的俄语诗人赫列勃尼科夫等等,他们的诗歌通过语言都构建了一个需要破译的密码系统,他们很多时候还在自己的写作中即兴创造一些只有他们才知道的词,许多诗人都认为从本质意义上来讲诗歌的确是无法翻译的,而我们翻译的仅仅是一首诗所要告诉我们的最基本的需要传达的内容。

诗歌的语言或者说诗歌中的词语,它们就像黑色的夜空中闪烁的星光,就像大海的深处漂浮不定的鲸的影子,当然,它们很多时候更像光滑坚硬的卵石,更像雨后晶莹透明的水珠,这就是我们阅读诗歌时,每一首诗歌都会用不同的声音和节奏告诉我们的原因。对于每一位真正的诗人来讲,一生都将与语言和词语捉迷藏,这样的迷藏当然有赢家也会有输家,当胜利属于诗人时,也就是一首好诗诞生的时候。

语言和词语在诗歌中有时候是清晰的,同样,很多时候它们又是模糊的。语言和词语的神秘性,不是今天在我们的文本中才有,就是在原始人类的童年期,我们的祭司面对永恒的群山和太阳吟诵赞词的时候,那些通过火焰和光明抵达神界的声音,就释放着一种足以让人肃穆的力量。毫无疑问,这种力量包含的神秘性就是今天也很难让我们破译。

在我的故乡四川大凉山彝族腹心地带,就是在现在我们的原始宗教掌握者毕摩,他们诵读的任何一段经文,可以说都是百分之百的最好的诗歌,这些诗歌由大量的排比句构成,而每一句都具有神灵附体的力量,作为诗歌的语言此刻已经成为现实与虚无的媒介,而语言和词语在它的吟诵中也成为这个世界不可分割的部分。我以为,这个世界最伟大的诗篇都是清晰的、模糊的、透明的、复杂的、具象的、形而上的、一目了然的、不可解的、先念的、超现实的、伸手可及的、飘忽不定的等等一切的总和。

Word as Salt · an Alternative Human Paradise Made of Light–Transparence and Dimness of Poetic Diction
—*Address at the Opening Ceremony of 2018 Zigong "Belt and Road" International Poetry Week*

Compared to natural language, poetic diction belongs to a distinct category, discernibly removed to a considerable degree from daily usage in the real world. However, it is not to be inferred, in this connection, there is a clearcut and ingrained borderline between both. Rather I mean poetic language, of necessity, is at times abstract, suggestive, symbolic and cryptic. To be sure, the edifice of poetry is erected of words, one by one, one atop another, as Roman aqueducts and Egyptian pyramids, one piece laid upon or across another adroitly and seamlessly. The similitude of this poet-as-verbal-mason analogy ends where words seem to be culturally loaded to the extent, once such a poetic monument falls to pieces, the stones scattered about will respond lovingly to the human touch. Here is an occasion called forth to reflect on the primary, and indeed, primal origin and function of poetic language. A poet is, by definition, a word-conscious person committed to, even obsessed with words, so as to be empowered to give expressive, suggestive and precise shape to what he wishes to say, a shape that could do the trick of suggestion, evocation, while the poet need avoid as much as possible rhetoric and moralizing and hardly ever move into explicit generalization.

In the ultimate pooling of the Yi canonical works passed down, the pride of place goes to epics, composed without exception in parallelism or stanzas which bring with it the coming-of-age of Yi language on par with the respectable Chinese, mores, idiosyncrasies which would in good time affect every aspect of Yi culture characterized by diversity, instability and strife. Indeed, epics, not necessarily a jewel in the literal sense, but each one, verbal emerald and verbal opal, of intrinsic quality and character, collectively mark and forge a cultural heritage which nourishes Yi spirituality and give vent to local bards who vocalize and tap the rhythmical sources of their culture. It is not coincidence that linguists all surmise in some hypothetical beginning of things poetry is the only way of using language. And anthropologists basically sign up to the same notion of poetry operating both as opener of language and preserver of identity for ethnic people inhabiting the remotest corners of our globe.

As epics anchor the riddles of life amid the mundane realities of chores and toils, traditionally, epic bards within a typical Yi community perform a dual function, i.e., singers who entertain and delight by "boiling elsewhere with such a lyric yeast" as well as sages making sensible statements about the immediate world while negotiating between the secular and the divine. Thus language and poetry are believed to be linked with ritual in most of the agricultural, gathering and herding societies. Poetry, so they claim, arose at the outset in the form of magic spells invoked to fend off a famine or ensure a good harvest before being later expanded to honor forebears, explain the alteration of the seasons, life and death, and register the pathos of love forlorn lass and lad, pray away evil, comfort those who submit to bereavement. Historically, writing is subsequent to speech in that man poeticizes orally long before he writes it down. In places still inaccessible, extremely remote, where no writing system, either character or alphabet, has been evolved, oral tradition still survives for tribesmen and tribeswomen who persist in concentrating, compressing and intensifying their speech in order to render a particular experience, crystallizing it into a channel of "the spontaneous overflow of powerful feelings", centering around subjects from nature and rustic life to show their dignity and artistic validity. One of our Yi proverbs likens poems to linguistic salt. Even into today, on important occasions such as weddings and funerals, village wits still sing songs or recite poems that have call and response patterns as Negro spirituals, with lead singers setting out a line or phrase and his rival or the group responding by repeating or playing variations on it.

From the extant poetic fragments left by people of classic antiquity, we take our cues that language accounts for the making of all exemplars for poetry, of sufficient import and weight, and we must add timely such linguistic resources that go into the production of a national treasure should be deemed the cream of a national language. No wonder many a country prides itself on possessing such blessings divinely bestowed in line with the grain of their life. Indeed, the exalted views about a poet's proper place in society have been a consensus among nations "with veins full of poetic stuff" that "most needs poets and will doubtless have the greatest and use them the greatest." For the simple reason the imposing works of language by poets, executed expressively, suggestively, opaquely or evocatively, employ language as a window on experience, so varied, complex and heterogeneous, and supply an infinity of aesthetic possibilities for audience and readership.

Poets are sometimes called magicians of words, and words to poets are like wands to magicians. Flying carpets at a time and a pigeon to take wings in a wink of eye or a red fish in a tank at a spatial and temporary nodal point. For all their variety, whimsicality and creativity, poets fashion a world of their own, in its own right, which might be a far cry from what we all know and light-years removed from what we inhabit. Just like Schoenberg's innovations in atonality, sensual, spontaneous, instinctive, "sonic orgies" (as someone calls it who detests it) sound they might, they form an integral and indivisible whole, multum in parvo, and his approach, both in terms of harmony and development, has been one of the most pioneering and influential of 20th-century musical thought.

Allow me here to cite a wise passage, to the credit of a certain American poet: "A poet must be drenched in words, literally soaked in them, to have the right ones form themselves into the proper patterns at the right moment." I totally agree with him that we poets, on top of three desiderata, i.e., the conventional concern with formal properties (rhythmical or riming schemes, inner cadence), typographical arrangement (the balance and shift of the line, couplet, stanza) and ultra-modern propensity to view poetry as a linguistic construct in these toppling times, we must never toy with the ultimate problem of the diction of poetry in the whole process. It is a diction, as it were, as always, "very conscious of its power of choosing terms with an affect of precision and of combining the terms into phrases with the same affect of peculiar precision." This time-honored Homeric sensitivity and striving for lexical precision is the ultimate test of good poetry vs bad which partially accounts for the emotive obscurity and riddling intellectual opacity exemplified in the poetry of German Paul Celan, Hispanic César Vallejo, Russian Boris Khlebnikov. Veritably the poetic artifice they have labored at and constructed is forbidding for many, a poetic Morse code, hermetically closed, to be attacked and deciphered even by professional critics, notoriously inhospitable to translators. Imaginative creations in this vein serve to indicate the complexity of the modernist temper, for a poem in essence, is not so much a sentiment, volition, passion as it is a mind, a mode of thought, perception, in short, a way of both seeing and saying. All said, they have infused their artistic complexity with a profound sense of human worth, offering occasional but important lessons, moments of illumination, however dim and obscure, brimming with the quality of affirmation that we expect from great poets.

Poetic language, or rather, verbal strands woven into a poetic fabric, to the initiated, conjures up a majestic view of a starry sky, elusive sharks in the unfathomable depths, shiny pebbles on a dry riverbed and rain drops on a flower pedal after a downpour. All of these instances provide clues as to why we delight in poetry, the sounds of words, their rhythms and rimes, as it appeals to our intellects and stimulates our imaginations by demanding that we visualize and conceptualize events, place and character outside the realm of everyday experience. For a poet of any worth, the whole span of his life is too short for wrestling with language, a hide and seek game. Sometimes he tumbles along upon it—a token of genuine blessing. Sometimes he loses any track of it. When at last he comes around to the right word, his trophy: a good poem is born. The perennial squabble remains: the limits to perception, the accessibility of truth, the nature and scope of knowing and naming.

Word are both opaque and crystal, ambiguous and mysterious. This is nothing new as our Bimos would stand testimony, dating from the infancy of mankind: chanting grandiloquently a hymn, gazing and gasping at the sprawling ranges of mountains, the sun arising and setting, and his voice being carried through fire and light to the Celestial Vaults, reverberating high and low, thither and hither. What a way of contemplating the mystery and power of the divinities and releasing cosmic energy in syn with motions of heavenly bodies! Here is another case of untranslatability, equally notoriously baffling and inscrutable as the most arcane poetic texts.

In my native place, in the Daliangshan, heartland of Yi culture, our priest figures—Bimos, still revered to ply their trade and do their business upon the human spirit, habitually say a prayer in form of poems, the best ones the Yi people can boast, "happily by the coincidence of forms that locks in the poem", the bulk of Yi poetry comprise parallelism, each divinely charged with a haunting ethos, energy, mythical might that escalates upward further and further, the ideal medium negotiating between reality and nothingness, an integral and indivisible part of our world. Our Bimos, like all great poets, enrapture us by raising their voices always, at the end, of transcendence, because they have both seen clearly and tasted poignantly the glory and misery of the miserables. The sum total of our poetic legacy, tradition and experiment, an amazing and dazzling garnering of the transparent, the cryptic, the ambiguous, the concrete, the abstract, the metaphysical, the symbolic, the surreal, the elusive, the accessible, the pat, discloses to us this vital truth intimately and distinctly.

Translated by Huang Shaozheng

诗歌的责任并非仅仅是自我的发现
——在2018年塔德乌什·米钦斯基表现主义凤凰奖颁奖仪式上的致答词

2018.9.18

非常高兴能获得本年度的塔德乌什·米钦斯基表现主义凤凰奖，毫无疑问，这是我又一次获得了来自一个让我在精神上最为亲近的国度的褒奖。我必须在这里说对这份褒奖，我的感激之情是难以用语言来表达的，我这样说并不是怀疑语言的功能和作用，而是有的感情是用语言无法在更短的时间内极为准确地表达出来，如果真的要去表达，它必须用更长的篇幅去表述。但我相信，在此时此刻，我的这种对波兰的亲近之情和感激，在座的诸位是完全能理解的。

我现在还清楚地记得在一篇文章中看到，20世纪波兰最伟大的诗人之一切斯瓦夫·米沃什在雅盖隆大学做过一篇题为《以波兰诗歌对抗世界》的演讲，他在这次演讲中集中表达了这样一种思想，就是波兰作家永远不可能逃避对他人以及"对前人和后代的责任感"。这或许就是多少年以来，我对波兰文学最敬重的原因之一。

如果我们放眼20世纪以来的世界文学，东中欧作家和诗人给我们带来的精神冲击和震撼，从某种意义而言，要完全超过其他区域的文学，当然，俄罗斯白银时代的文学是另外一个特例。从道德和精神的角度来看，近一百年来，一批天才的波兰作家和诗人始终置身于一个足以让我们仰望的高度，他们背负着沉重而隐形的十字架，一直站在风暴和雷电交汇的最高处，其精神和肉体都经受了难以想象的磨难，熟悉波兰历史的人都不难理解，为什么波兰诗歌中那些含着眼泪微笑的反讽，是能让那些纯粹为修辞而修辞的诗歌汗颜的原因。

不用怀疑，如果诗歌仅仅是一种对自我的发现，那诗歌就不可能真正承担起，对"他人"和更广义的人类命运的关注，诚然，在这里我并没有否认诗歌发现自我的重要。这个奖是用波兰表现主义的领军人物之一，也是超现实主义的先驱塔德乌什·米钦斯基的名字命名的，作为一位富有创新精神的思想者，塔德乌什·米钦斯基也十分强调创作者，必须在精神和道德领域为我们树立光辉的榜样。

当下的世界和人类在精神方面所出现的问题，已经让许多关注人类前景的人充满着忧虑，精神的堕落和以物质以及技术逻辑为支配原则的现实状况，无论在东方还是在西方都成为被追捧的时尚和标准，看样子这种状况还会持续下去。

以往社会发展史的经验已经告诉我们，并不是人类在物质上的每一次进步，都会带来精神和思想上的上升。这一个多世纪以来，人类又拥有了原子能，计算机，纳米，超材料，机器人，基因工程，克隆技术，云计算，互联网，数字货币，但是，同样就在今天，在此时此刻，叙利亚儿童在炮火和废墟上的哭声，并没有让屠杀者放下手中的武器。在今天的人类手中，仍然掌握着足以毁灭所有的生物几千遍的武器。

在这样一个时代，作为一个有责任和良知的诗人，如果我们不把捍卫人类创造美好生活的权利当成义务和责任，那对美好的诗歌而言都将是一种可耻的行为。谢谢大家。

Narcissistic Self —Seeking Is Not the Sole Responsibility of a Decent Poet
—*Acceptance speech at the Awarding Ceremony of Tadeusza Micińskiego Prize*

I am, indeed, overwhelmed with the award given to me today, veritably a true literary distinction which leaves a good excuse for revisiting the realm of belle lettres mostly akin to my personal slant in the affairs of the world and in matters of the heart. Forget any mistrust on my part of the normal function of language when I fumble for words of gratitude as a proper act of response at this moment. I surmise a narrative of a certain length might do the trick. All said, all the audience today should be fully acquainted with my special affection for Polish letters.

My mind returns to an oration delivered by one of the greatest Polish poets the 20th century can offer, i.e., Czeslaw Milosz, the moralist, at Jagiellonian University entitled "Counter the World with Polish Poetry", a speech of enormous ethical and artistic importance, both as an incentive to his counterparts and as fair warning to world poets, wherein he set forth his unequivocal position to the effect that "Polish writers shall never extenuate themselves to their predecessors and posterity in matters of the mind, the cross of their trade." With this self-inflicted obligation and shout of call to responsibility emitted, he demystifies any claim of a literature free of commitment and he speaks for us all that poetry must always serve a cause and for this alone I bow to no one in my admiration for his poetry and his personality, and indeed, the Polish poetry in general.

A cursory glance at the 20th century world literature onward will lead us to the fact, no matter how grudgingly allowed by some, that Poland, together with East Europe and Middle Europe, has startled and fascinated the world by the quality of imagination and language that was called upon and brought to bear upon both national and human experience as well as by the wealth of exemplary Polish men and women of letters arising out of their sufferings and out of the lessons they derive for us. Equally or more deserving of credit, it could be argued, is the exceptional accomplishments of Russian geniuses of Silver Age, as ever, standing on the high ground of artistic integrity and moral duty. For in the past 100 years or so, the great panoply of Polish poets, in particular, taking up the yoke upon them unflinchingly, trapped in circumstances which would easily crush and destroy any other human group but adduce superhuman virtues, have emerged from the morass of "moronic apathy, drunken torpor and morbid, wounded nationalism" as a result of national misfortunes, to come out with works of art, of refined taste, tender irony and mingled pathos, sometimes marked by apocalyptic or humorously macabre visions. Anybody familiar with the terrible fate of Polska, again and again, partitioned by both strong and even weaker neighbors, the Teutons, Turkey, Muscovy, Prussia, erased from the map of the world for over 120 years, will knowingly reckon with, arguably the more or less permanent trait of Polish letters, i.e., "a strong emotional moralism" fed obviously by Christian ethic. What is offered is nothing short of a triumph of distillation of crushing experiences of Poles in particular or of the existential depths visited practically by all of us nowadays. In comparison, any rhetoric's-for-rhetoric's-sake poetry, stripped of such human caring would still look pale and lack weight and substance.

Beyond dispute, the universal recognition of Polish poetry lends itself, in the flux of literary history, to the cardinal thesis that poetry has no meaning if contained within the bounds of narcissistic indulgences and exaggerations and this is not to deny the importance of a poet to legitimately wrestle with falsifying emotions by "concern with form" and due effort at "unsentimental purity of things". But Milosz's treatment of the basic theme of Polish poetry remains valid: "the tension between a poetic dedication to form and compassion for human suffering." This award, named after Tadeusz Miciński, who earns our respect for his expressionist fascination with originality and innovation, has never disavowed, indeed, he has fulfilled preeminently the wishes of all Polish poets for a balance between an all-out social protest and faith in man as well as pursuit of artistic excellence.

We confront a world still chaotic and full of incongruities. Complaints of its spiritual poverty as well as paucity of good poetry are as old as the art itself. This heart-rending state of affairs, buttressed by a logic of material and technology holding sway the spirit, the fad of the 21st century, constitutes the biggest reason to call forth our most vigorous efforts to keep pace with the age as poets.

Carried away, as we are, by waves of technological breakthroughs, past experience sometimes surprises the pessimists who foresee the durable effects of modernization. With an awesome array of new gadgets at our disposal, robots, genes engineering, cloning, cloud computing, internet, superconductivity material, digital currency, there seems to be a place for euphoria, triumphant mankind and exuberant poets enveloped within the intricacy of syntax and deconstructed lexicon, who could "perform a spontaneous dance without recourse to compulsive justifications". Yet the images of Syrian imps screaming audibly over the loss of their mothers on the debris of their former cozy homes inundate our TV screens, which compels our unkempt attention, a timely reminder we are still situated between the holocaust of the last war and the atomic devastation, a danger not exactly imminent, but still lurking ominously somewhere ahead of us, for the existing arsenal of atomic bombs, we are told, can still decimate humans and all the sentient beings thousands of times.

Milosz rightly admonishes us that the act of writing poetry is an act of faith. Our activity is certainly tantamount to an offense if we juggle with poetry and fail to produce poems that rival the immortal pieces of the old in defense of human civilization and exemplify the attempt to resist the growing disparity in the cultural and economic life in the world.

Translated by Huang Shaozheng

附体的精灵：诗歌中的神秘、隐蔽和燃烧的声音
——在2019年第四届"西昌邛海·丝绸之路"国际诗歌周上的演讲

> 据说，歌德谈及帕格尼尼的天才时，他对后者的赞叹接近洛尔伽对"杜恩德"的理解：这是一种神秘的力量，人人都有意会，而从未有过哲学家解释过。
> ——题记

当我们回到这片土地的时候，我们便会与这片土地上所有神奇的事物融为一体，无论是肉体还是精神，我们都会从最初的源头再一次获得神秘的力量，这似乎是一次末端和开始的必然对接。人类精神创造的经验告诉我们，那些基本的定义和规律从未有过改变，尤其是在语言和词语所构筑的世界中，当创造者在舌尖与笔端将语言和文字燃烧成宝石的时候，这一过程给我们的惊叹和震撼其实并不是我们所能看见的宝石本身，而是我们无法捕捉的那种光一般幽暗的隐秘，当然也包括宝石所闪现出的难以定义的隐喻。

在我们生活的这片群山中，所谓神秘主义并非是我们的一种发现，数千年来，我们的祖先就相信万物有灵，我们的毕摩（祭司）一直是联系天和地的使者，同样，他们也承担着人鬼之间的沟通和联系，在他们的身上始终留存着一种力量，那就是超越肉体能够与另一个精神世界进行对话的禀赋。毫无疑问，这一能力是一般人所不具备的，就是在21世纪的人类已经步入更现代的社会生活中，他们仍然顽强地在我们彝人的现实世界里存在着，我们还能看到他们在为死去的魂灵超度，还能听到他们浑厚悠远的声音诵读的经文，也能遇到他们在做法事的现场插下的神枝，这些神枝对应着天象的图案。

在今天这个急速变化着的现实面前，虽然我们置身于多种文化的交织中，现代的生活方式正在被更多的人所接受，但是那

种来自于意识深处的观念和信仰却如影随形。多少年来，作为诗人我一直在思考一个问题，就是如何去理解诗歌。就其本质而言，所能给我们提供的那些更多的未知的东西是什么？因为每当我听到毕摩（祭司）在诵读经文的时候，特别是当他进入一种特殊的状态时，他的语言和词语就在瞬间如同飘浮的火焰，这种语言和词语传达给我们的不仅仅是内容，而更多的是一种神秘的召唤，这种召唤要高于语言和词语，当然它始终还是语言和词语的一个部分，就我的理解和特殊的感受，我必须相信一切伟大的创造，其实都需要来自于一种所谓超越理性的强大的源动力。

在这一点，伟大的西班牙诗人加西亚·洛尔加印证了我的看法，他始终认为，通过有生命的媒介和联系传达诗的信息，最能发挥诗歌中"杜恩德"（duende）的作用，如果直接翻译成中文就是"灵性的力量"。

同样，伟大的俄罗斯女诗人马琳娜·茨维塔耶娃在其文章《现代俄罗斯的史诗与抒情诗——弗拉基米尔·马雅可夫斯基与鲍里斯·帕斯捷尔纳克》这样说道："马雅可夫斯基是会被穷尽的，不能被穷尽的是他的力量，他用这力量使事物穷尽，那准备就绪的力量，就像土地每一次都卷土重来，每一次都一劳永逸。……帕斯捷尔纳克的行动相当于梦的行动，我们不理解他，我们陷入他之中，落到他的下面，进入他的里面，对于帕斯捷尔纳克，我们理解他的时候，也即是抛开他、抛开了意义进行理解。"

英国诗人特德·休斯也一直认为巫师和诗人有许多共同的地方，那就是他们都强调个体所具有的先知意识，在他们的身上均被赋予了通神的能力，而这种能力往往是常人所不具备的，巫师的特殊身份和诗人的特殊身份都是被那种神秘的力量选择的，特德·休斯曾这样评价他的前辈诗人、伟大的爱尔兰人叶芝，"爱尔兰民族精神和超自然的力量充满了叶芝的内心，爱尔兰神话、民间传说充满了他的诗歌。他披上了神秘主义的精神护甲，在很短的时间里，建立起了自己壮观的人生目标：重建爱尔兰的能量，挑战英雄祖先、失落的神，以及爱尔兰屈服的灵魂。"

这一切都充分说明，通过语言和词语所进行的创造，其内在的神秘的源动力一直围绕着我们,而语言和词语所延伸出的一切未知和空白,从来就是诗歌最富有魅力最耐人寻味的部分,也因此,我才将这次诗歌圆桌会议的主题确定为——附体的精灵:诗歌中的神秘、隐蔽和燃烧的声音。

2019.6.6

Poets Empowered by a Mysterious, Dark and Burning Sound

—*Address at 2019 4th Xichang Qinghai Silk Road International Poetry Week*

> *Goethe, who in speaking of Paganini hit on a definition of the Duende: "A mysterious force that everyone feels and no philosopher has explained."*

To speak personally for a moment, one place, in this troubled world, calls me home; one place recharges my spirit and fires my imagination each time I find my way back. I mean Greater Liangshan, "the most favored spot on earth", my native place and ancestral home. In that holy place, as if I drink there from a well, I am repossessed by that mysterious power, a dark electricity, the Duende, as Lorca termed it, "from which," he said, "comes the very substance of art." Duende is the edge original art is made on; it is the darkness in the art that fashions enduring poems; it is the artistic iconoclasm fresh performance embodies. It is the newness that poetry sometimes makes. Most of us poets have now and then neared that source—have found ourselves turning out miraculous lines or poems that surprise even us who make them. Duende is the source good poems issue from; we know it "when they hit us hard, teach us, reach home". There comes sometimes a moment like a flaring of truth, when words, no longer merely ours, are burned into gems—a chemistry performed, an alchemy conjured, in the poet's throat and in her writing hand. In such rare moments, Lorca's Duende attends, walks us behind her into the promise of "something newly created, like a miracle", which it is our task to form. The miracle is not so much the poem we sometimes pull off; it is how the Duende feels—elusive, mysterious, murky, oracular.

I love this esoteric concept of the Duende; it accords with the animism at the heart of Yi culture. We Yi people have inhabited the hard and stubborn mountain ranges called the Greater Liangshan for many thousands of years, and our contributions to the Chinese civilization—to world civilization—are countless and varied. Anomalous among the big family of China, we are an animistic people: our places are legended, animate; our culture's ethos is Occultist; our priests—Bimos or shamans—still perform the eternal task of interceding between the people and the spirits of the earth, of the heavens, making peace between the present and the past.

Bimos are our spiritual and ceremonial leaders; they are still charged with mediating between the secular and the divine; they are esteemed as the bearers of spiritual wisdom essential and inherent to our people. All ancient spiritual practices are rooted in nature, and the chief work of the Bimos is naturally to waken and conserve the people's connection with the natural world. Greater Liangshan—the place and its people—is as dynamic as it is enduring. Although modernization and globalization menace and encroach, although modernity makes deafening inroads, in no other place is spiritual practice so entwined with everyday civil life. Even while urban Yi folk stride into the 21st century, still you'll find our Bimos doing what they've done since the Bronze Age—performing rites that ensure the safe passage of the deceased to heaven; chanting prayers in deep voices. In more sequestered places, villages one only reaches by foot, you might still witness a village funeral, you might take note of sacrificial branches and twigs placed carefully on the ground, although they seem scattered at random—laid out below to mirror the constellations above.

What appears to be a reshuffling of attitudes and lifestyles in many Yi communities is mostly surface. Deeper, although change is taking place on massive scale, with smart phones, laptops and an awesome array of gadgets woven into the fabric of Yi life, the ageless verities and loyalties remain; they run in the veins of the Yi. The Muse or some Angel above is the usual suspect poets turn to explain what drives them to the page. But we would do well to heed Lorca's Duende exhortation that to deserve and perhaps endure the Duende, one must never cease from the struggle to inhabit one's self—our real selves that slumber to be awakened, the ones we barely recognize—because we are so often far alienated from our racial roots. At times when I am in the reverent presence of Bimos chanting a prayer, perhaps in a trance, I see before me, the shaman's words floating like flames, and this vision leads me to a door that opens on the real rationale for being a poet—or continuing to be one. To make a poem is a call from beyond, made of words, but encapsulating something powerful, but given only to one who's made a leap of imagination—one might almost say of faith. It is a power that will lead you outside or push you inside yourself; it will wake you wider; it will infuse you—intoxicate, perhaps—with an urge to create, to seek "answers for unformed questions, to stop time, to understand the undecipherable, to reach out for a kind of magic". It is Lorca's "miracle".

The genesis of Lorca's concept of Duende was the Gypsy tradition of the "Deep Song", a predecessor to Flamenco in Lorca's native Andalusia. During his sojourn in New York in the years of 1929-1930, Lorca involved himself in American folk traditions of jazz, blues, and spirituals, which brought him to the proposition: the "dark sounds"—canto jondo—and their relationship to life and art. For me, a Chinese equivalent of the Duende, a better translation of it, maybe, might be soul force, which we Yi people identify as the essence of our culture.

Marina Ivanovna Tsvetaeva, the great Russian poet, once labored to expound a similar theme in her article dedicated to Vladimir Mayakovsky and Boris Pasternak: "Yes, Mayakovsky will be exhausted thematically some day, but his power will survive and stay as earth will survive and stay, once and for all. As for Pasternak, his action resembles that of a dreamer. He plunges us into him, underneath him, in him. We understand him by shunting him aside and we are drawn to him irresistibly by not attempting to understand him."

One of the giants of 20th century British poetry, Ted Hughes pinpoints things in common between a poet and a witch—a prophet's vision, psychic power, guardianship of the racial memory, divine rights and a status assigned by tradition or chosen by supernatural beings, and he extols the various virtues of his brilliant predecessor Irish Yeats in superlatives: "Yeats is suffused with Irish national spirit and supernatural ethos and folklore and legends populate his poems. By donning the mysterious mantle, he builds a spectacular aim in life and in poetry: revive the Irish energy, rehabilitate the deposed pantheon of Irish divinities and reforge the unconquerable Irish soul."

Countless encounters with it, hard facts I can't account for otherwise, convince me the arch-reason that hovers like a haze of wisdom around poetic writing is that elusive pitch of being Lorca calls the Duende, which others might name the soul, the psyche, the subconscious or the unconscious. We know it's there; we feel it working in our hearts and days as surely as Galileo Galilei felt the earth moving underfoot 400 years ago against prevailing orthodoxies. One is as powerless to know when, or how, or even why it strikes as one is to predict a mood or call up a dream. But this rare pitch of being, this way of the spirit, is what sustains a poet and lends him a voice to say the unsayable, to name the unnamable, to discern the undiscernible. This dark and burning sound, that the otherness the Shaman divines, is the exhilarating mystery that surrounds and enables the profoundly human activity of making poems.

Translated by Huang Shaozheng

诗歌中未知的力量：传统与前沿的又一次对接
——第六届"青海湖国际诗歌节"主题演讲

　　传统可能是一种更隐秘的历史，而诗歌的传统是什么呢？如果从精神的传承而言，它就如同一条河流，已经穿过了数千年的时间，或许说它是一个神话的开始，也可以说，它是我们的祭司在舌尖上最初的词语。无论这个源头是多么的遥远，但当我们屏息静听的时候，它空阔浩渺的声音依然能被我们听见，这个能被我们感知的真实告诉我们——传统是不会死亡的。

　　传统一直活在我们的语言中，正因为它是一种特殊的记忆，这种记忆甚至超过人类在土地上留下的痕迹，在这个世界上没有一种力量能比语言的力量更强大，那些无数迁徙的部落和族群，我们可能已经无法找到他们数万年前的历史，但从语言这条幽深的河流里，我们仍然能感知到词语的密码给我们传递的信息。当土地上的遗产和埋在地下的尸骨都变成了灰尘，你背负的行囊再不是第一个行囊，由于路途的遥远，也可能是岁月的漫长，真实的记忆变成了传说，你再不可能用任何一种实证的方式，明确地告诉我们你生命的源头在哪里，而在这样的时候唯有灵性的语言，才能用更隐秘的方式暗示我们你生命的故乡在哪里。从远古的人类到现在，人类从本质上而言，都在经受着两种特殊的远游，一种是肉体的远游，另一种当然就是精神的远游，所有人类有记载的历史都告诉我们，这两种远游从来就没有停止过，不过我需要声明的是，我所说的肉体的远游并非是一种线性的时间概念，而我所说的精神的远游，似乎更接近于是一种绝对意义上的远游，它是形而上的，甚至是更为观念性的一种存在。也正因为此，我只相信语言中隐藏的一切，它给我们提供的不完全是能诠释的某种神秘的符号，而更像是被火焰穿越时间的彼岸，所照亮的永恒的隐喻。

传统是一种意识的方式，如果用更清晰的哲学语言来表达，它就是人类世界不同的思维方式，而这一切都不仅仅只体现在某个族群的观念形态里，就是在现实世俗的生活中，它也会显现在集体无意识的日常经验里。很多时候，我们的生活方式或许在发生着不知不觉的变化，也可能被某种强大的力量所改变，但那种基因般顽强的思维方式还会伴随着我们，让我们看见别人看不见的星空，让我们说出不为他人所理解的神授的赞词，也因为这种无处不在的力量的庇护，我们也才能在群山上迎接每一个属于自己的黎明。诚然，这种意识的传统已经成为整个人类精神的某个部分，而我必须承认这个部分是属于我们的。我无法告诉你什么是诗的更形而上的传统，但我想，当我们一旦真的握住诗歌伟大传统的时候，就必将让我们在一种新的创造中成为前沿。

我们经常思考所谓的现代性，而诗歌的真正前沿是什么呢？如果我们把自己置身的这个时代，都看成是一个从未有过的现实，那我们就必须去见证这个时代，因为任何当下只能属于生活在当下的诗人，固然古希腊的荷马给我们留下了经典的史诗，而天才的唐朝诗人们更是创造了一个诗的黄金时代，但是任何一个伟大的活在时间深处的诗人，其肉体都不可能又一次得到复活，诚然他们的诗歌已经成为了不朽，或许这就是命运的选择，今天的诗歌还必须由我们来完成。有一位并非是哲人的人说过这样的话，在半个世纪前，人类的生活并没有发生过真正意义上的质的变化，但这五十年，人类的历史却经历了数千年来最剧烈的嬗变，难道我们不应该用诗的方式来记录这样一种惊心动魄的变化吗？如果说诗歌从来就没有离开过人类的灵魂，我不相信这种人类从未有过的境遇，就没有给我们的诗歌提供另一种无限的可能吗？我认为，诗歌的前沿在今天并非是一种虚拟的想象，它就在我们的面前，只是时间已经在今天让我们感受到了它的速度，我认为诗歌的前沿绝不是一种时间的概念，而是这一时间中，我们所能看见的活生生的现实。

我们必须创造我们诗歌的形式，同样，我们也要创造我们诗歌的语言。如果没有形式的创新，同样如果没有语言的创新，我们就不可能真正理解，什么是诗歌中未知的力量，也就不可能真正抵达那个"诗歌构筑的前沿"。在很多时候，诗歌的形式变化和词语的玄妙都具有某种神秘主义的色彩，这也是诗歌不同于别的艺术形式最珍贵的东西，诗歌通过形式和语言魔幻般告诉我们的一切，不仅具有象征和隐喻的意义，更重要的是，它呈现给我们的并不完全是内容本身，它是黑暗中的微光，同样也是光明和黄金折射的黑暗。它不是哲学，因为它把思辨的座椅放在了飞鸟的翅膀之上，那只飞鸟一直翱翔于未知的领域；它不是数学，但它把抽象的眼睛植入了宇宙的天体，当我们瞩望它的时候，它只是一些我们永远无法统计的数字。诗歌并没有前沿，要寻找它的前沿，我们只有一个办法，那就是将它与自己的传统再一次进行对接。

正因为我始终相信，诗歌中存在着未知的力量，我才如此地迷恋它给我们带来的这些奇迹。

Forces Hidden in Poetry: Let's Make a Rendezvous with Tradition!
—*Address at the 6th Qinghai Lake International Poetry Festival*

Tradition is arguably one of the most important human institutions astride both good poetry and history. Then in what way does our poetic tradition let us into the secret of great poets? Our poetic tradition, as it stands, can be likened to a river, driblets at their glacial source, gathering many a streamlet before forming into a mighty current, rushing passionately over rapids and past gorges, down through a staggeringly long time. Or they can still be seen as the first note of the symphony score of a myth, prayer at the tongue tip of our Bimos (Yi priests or shamans). The idea is that no matter how much shrouded in antiquity of which the beginning of tradition, so far as our ears give due audience, we will be much reassured of the message, words of nature, speaking to us out of the dense darkness that it is still pretty much around, dying really hard.

Tradition, if anything, lives in our language all the time, which, being a special human memory, is as indestructible as the most stubborn trace left by humans on earth. Indeed, no other power can boast of equal omnipotence. Historians, by fathoming the depth of this undercurrent of language, by piecing together innumerable evidences unearthed, countless artifacts and cultural relics scattered around the globe, conjure up the Neolithic sociological patterns of various migrating tribes and herds. While mountains and oceans have risen and drained away, human remains buried deep have turned into mulberry fields or fossilized, the baggage upon your back is no more a pack, millions and millions of years have elapsed during which your clear remembrance becomes a legend, and no amount of positivistic research and archeological reconstruction will tell the truth for sure: the truth about where we in the first place launch forth in life and wander widely asunder in the world. Only at this moment, halting at the crossfire of reasoned speculation, all the elements of which the science is sure and frankly mysticism, we content ourselves with the reassuring oracle made of words that suggest some clues so as to appease our inquisitive turn of mind.

Ever since the beginning of things, human travels fall into two categories: mental and physical. I must observe, of course, even physical wandering that I am talking here does not merely carry the Darwinian sense of linear progression. Human travels, mentally speaking, have utter metaphysical undertones, and because of this, I trust what is encrypted in language is far more a metaphor of eternity illumined by the torch through time.

Tradition is both a state of mind and a mode of thinking and if it is set forth more distinctly with ontological implication, as to encompass mankind at large, it is the universal mental processes prevalent in all civilized lands, functioning in all aspects of social life, from philosophizing in the ivory tower to daily intercourse of ordinary folk, indeed, so deeply embedded in the unconscious of most of us (We are such unconscious people!). Our world has certainly become more worldly. Some mighty invisible forces are at work making havoc on manners, mores and customs of honest days of yore—when as yet I only believed them to be all that poets had painted them;—"being gradually worn away by time, but still more obliterated by modern fashion." But in this season of irreversible change, tradition, with a pleasing vengeance, asserts its immortality most vigorously, as tenacious as our gene chromosomes, empowering us to see the starry sky rarely seen by others, to sing the hymns which are Greek to everybody not of our paternal home, and more important, tradition-conscious, we have been able to keep watch on the returning dawn of another tomorrow. Tradition as human spirituality, I claim proudly as core ICH (intangible cultural heritage) of our Yi people above all else. I plead ignorant when asked whether there is a poetic tradition of higher antiquity than ours, but this much I can tell you for sure: once we have come to grips with the essence of our glorious poetic tradition, we will become the vanguard to usher in a new phase of artistic innovation.

We often speak of modernity as approbative or synonymous of the frontier of modern poetry but we might remind ourselves that modernity is as inevitable as breathing, since we are all literally living in this modern age and that we should be none the worse for failing to record what happens under our very noses as chronicler and eyewitness, simply because we cannot live elsewhere, say the Tang or the Pericles' time, fully aware of the immortal pieces left to us by a Li Bai or Homer, all super beings "radiant with the emanations of their genius", secure in the quiet recesses of the bosom of time in perennial renown. For good or bad, "it is still a turn-up of a die, in the gambling freaks of fate", whether we do our part or fail in our ultimate capacity as poets of our age. One of the Chinese poets, not necessarily a prophet, whose name escapes my memory at the moment, is remembered as saying something to the effect: "The past five decades could well be termed the most amazing period in this country's history as it sees nothing short of a revolution being materialized." Shame on us if we only sit idle decrying economic growth, deploring galumphing consumerism or fretting about urbanization. It simply does behoove us, aside from the excitement of creation and the feeling of achievement, to translate the sensory impressions of such unprecedented mind-boggling, striking events, external and internal, into beauty on a verbal plane.

Granted poetry has always kept company of us, I must confess my firm faith in poetic possibilities in galore for each generation born into every period in history. The world of poetry is wide and rich, there is enough room in it for every person who wants to poeticize. Barriers of temperament, talent, artistry and bottleneck in ambition are natural and should be expected. But a whole-hearted zest to take risk to be frontrunners is not flimsy daydreaming. It is a goal, nay, a reality, all of a sudden, sprung unto us and we feel it palpably as the world is spinning under our feet with all its motion and velocity. Hence, poetic innovation in this era of dazzling alterations is no more a subject that invites discussion and hypothesis, it is a reality confronting us, each of us who will willingly renounce the relative security of the present niche we have earned and deserved in society for the unpredictable life of dare-to-shine-or-perish innovator.

I have given my speech the title of "Forces Hidden in Poetry", because, shorn of innovation in new style and diction, we are leading to nowhere in our attempt to have the faintest inkling of where the hidden forces lie and by which way we will get to the forefront. Innovation is the ordeal of good poetry. New trends or even reversal in style and diction sometimes don the garb of bewildering mysticism to the point of something like a mumbo jumbo, but it is an effort worth making, should be deemed norm rather than abnormity, and indeed, the yardstick by which one can tell good art from something like a fad to be soon lost in the sand, or a much exalted school totally saturated, on the verge of being repudiated en masse, "victim of a new unforeseen reversal in stylistic innovation". The ideal for poetic innovation is to create new forms and come out with new style and new diction, which stand both for a new set of symbols and metaphors in an age calling forth drastic stylistic experiment much in arrear of material progress.

I have dwelt upon possible ways of identifying these UFO in poetry, because, as it is one of the most sacred duties of each good poet, so is it the overarching office of poetry. All those refusing to be weak, limited artistic personalities must necessarily make the leap into the unknown, eternally unattainable of poetic writing. Such bouts might prove futile for a gigantic enterprise, a faint glimmer in a murky room, or even darkness as reflection of light and gold. Poetry sets no front-line or limitation on the still mysterious nature of human creativity. To truly discover such a one, we might as well turn ourselves into logs, bricks, barbwire, cement, ammunition and forge our forward position. Good or bad lot, a poet innovates ultimately by dating and romancing with tradition again, which will, like a holy flame, illumine the road ahead of him.

A good poet invariably comes to reckon with these unforeseen forces and his growth, paradoxically, is measured by the extent to which he retreats into the tradition of his own people, which will goad and sustain him to awareness, understanding and eminence.

Translated by Huang Shaozheng

诗歌：不仅是对爱的吟诵，也是反对一切暴力的武器
——在中捷文化交流 70 周年暨捷克独立日"中捷文学圆桌会议"上的主题演讲

正值中华人民共和国成立 70 周年，中捷文化交流 70 周年暨捷克独立日之际，非常高兴能以一个中国诗人的身份，来参加今天这个具有特殊意义的"中捷文学圆桌会议"，在此，首先要向今天莅临这个圆桌会议的诸位朋友，致以最美好的祝愿。

我曾经两次访问过捷克，一次是 2016 年春天应捷克维区出版社的邀请，出席我的捷文版诗集《火焰与词语》在布拉格的首发和朗诵活动，这本诗集是由捷克汉学家李素和诗人泰博特合作翻译的，当然此前，我已经有一本诗集《时间》在捷克出版，那是一本从英文转译的诗集。2018 年秋天，我又有幸应邀参加了第 28 届"布拉格作家节"，与瑞典诗人恩瓦迪凯、伊朗诗人伊斯梅尔普尔（他也是我诗集波斯文版的译者）等共同参与了由布拉格作家节主办者迈克尔·马奇主持的主题为"活着的邪恶"的圆桌对话，并回答了听众的提问。这两次对捷克，特别是对布拉格这座闻名遐迩的城市的访问，的确给我留下极为深刻和美好的印象。

在这里我想告诉大家的是，我了解并向往布拉格当然是在更早的时候，德国哲学家弗里德里希·威廉·尼采说："当我想以一个词来表达音乐时，我找到了维也纳，而当我想以一个词来表达神秘时，我只想到了布拉格。"德国诗人约翰·沃尔夫冈·冯·歌德还说过："在那许许多多城市像宝石般镶成的王冠上，布拉格是其中最珍贵的一颗。"但是布拉格对于我的感召力或许还要更多，对于一个热爱古典建筑的人，布拉格无疑是一座建筑的博物馆，

它拥有这个世界上为数众多的、不同历史时期、不同风格的建筑，特别是巴洛克风格和哥特式建筑，可以说占据着欧洲建筑史上无法被撼动的最重要的位置。作为一个音乐爱好者，这里诞生了我热爱并直到今天还令我着迷的作曲家安东尼·德沃夏克、贝德里赫·斯美塔那和莱奥什·雅纳切克。德沃夏克的《致新大陆》曾给我带来无穷的想象，并从此相信音乐能在另外一个空间复活一个民族的灵魂；斯美塔那的交响诗《我的祖国》让我从音乐中看见了被旋律和音符所命名的一切不朽的事物，都将永远存活在时间的深处；雅纳切克的狂想曲《塔拉斯·布尔巴》以及《小交响曲》，给我带来的启示和震撼要远远超过一部概念化的哲学著作，因为它让我明白了动人心魄的旋律，很多时候都是从母语和民歌中提炼出来的，也因为这个可以上升到道德层面的认知，我对这个世界上所有弱小民族使用的语言都充满了深情和敬畏。

  作为一个歌德所说的那样一种"世界文学"的赞同者，特别是在歌德逝世一百多年之后的今天，我们虽然看到在不同的文化之间，抹平差异性的进程还在以加速度的方式进行着，但对多元文化存在的认同和保护，却被更多的人认识到其重要性，文化的多样性与人文主义的传统仍然是"世界文学"这个概念的基石，就是在今天面对当代现实中的复杂性和社会变革，我们所说的"民族文学"实际上已经与"世界文学"深度地融合或者说叠加在了一起，这是一个普遍主义的概念，它会让我们在全球化的背景下重新去理解并定义歌德所说的"世界文学"，在这一点上捷克就是一个示例。现代派文学的鼻祖、划时代的表现主义作家弗兰兹·卡夫卡一辈子就生活在布拉格，可以说早已是这座城市的一个文化符号，不用从更早的时候说起，就是从20世纪以来捷克就涌现出了一大批杰出的作家，他们既提升了捷克文学在欧洲的高度，同时也让世界感受到了捷克文学的伟大存在，我们熟知的就有雅洛斯拉夫·哈谢克、弗拉迪斯拉夫·万楚拉、卡·恰佩克、瓦茨拉夫·哈维尔、米兰·昆德拉、伊凡·克里玛。另外，还有我最钟情的赫拉巴尔，也因为我对他心怀由衷的热爱和尊敬，我在访问时间很紧张的状态下，还专门驱车去了他在布拉格郊区用于隐居写作的森林小屋和如同他生前生活一样朴素的墓地,这块墓地是赫拉巴尔生前就为自己选好的,可以看见来自世界不同国家的崇拜者,在他的墓地上摆放着许多千里迢迢带来的玩具猫,他们都知道猫是赫拉巴尔的朋友,在他活着的时候他就在森林小屋喂养了许多他最亲近的猫。

作为对语言学、结构语言人类学、符号学有着特殊兴趣的探秘者,布拉格对我的吸引力更是无可比拟的,因为在这里天才的罗曼·雅各布森创立了布拉格学派,毋庸置疑他是真正的结构主义思潮和运动的先驱,是他首先将结构主义语言学与诗学批评联系在了一起,揭开了隐喻与转喻在诗歌中的神秘作用,这一开创性的研究和发现,让后来所有诗歌作为自在的词,在语言中的探险和实验都成为能被阐释的可能。雅各布森就曾经从诗歌语言和词语的创新上,对俄罗斯未来主义诗人赫列勃尼科夫的诗歌从语言和修辞的角度进行了深度解析。

作为诗人,我对捷克诗歌的热情是超乎寻常的,还在我大学时期,我就阅读过捷克新时代诗歌奠基人卡雷尔·希内克·马哈的长诗《五月》,他的作品以爱情为主题,不仅仅抒发了一个民族渴望复兴的愿望,更重要的是他从人性出发,将个体的情感提升到了人类道德的精神高度。如果姑且从当代中国诗歌史对诗人写作时段的划分,我属于上个世纪80年代开始成名的诗人,也就是说在我的诗歌写作过程中,外来诗歌对我的影响是一个重要的方面,这其中就包括现当代捷克诗人的作品,在这些诗人中间就包括了维杰斯拉夫·奈兹瓦尔。这位超现实主义大师,不仅影响了无数的捷克诗人,其以消除禁欲主义和理性主义的诗歌主义主张,还给后期超现实主义注入了一些新的观念。雅罗斯拉夫·塞弗尔特,一生都在赞颂美的诗人,他的诗句:"天堂也许只是/我们久久期待的一个笑颜/轻轻呼唤着我们名字的芳唇两片/然后那短暂的片刻令人眩晕/令人忘却了/地狱的存在",阅读后给我带来的感动,就是现在回想起来,仍然有最初诵读时的那种心颤的感觉。在捷克访问时,为了去他的故乡瞻仰他的墓地,我们匆忙赶到他安息的墓园时已经是傍晚,墓园的管理者刚要锁上沉重的铁门,我下车后便第一个向他疾呼:"塞弗尔特!塞弗尔特!"我不懂捷克语,但我想这位管理员完全听懂了我的意思,他迅速打开了门,把我们一行远道而来的人带到了塞弗尔特的墓地。弗拉迪米尔·霍朗,这位离群索居,一直居住在布拉格康巴岛上的隐士诗人,他精粹的短诗充满了玄妙的哲理和隐喻,其诗歌中的神秘感笼罩着生与死、存在与虚无的冥想,他的诗句:"哦,是的/我爱生活/因此我才经常歌唱死亡/没有死亡/生活就会冷酷/有了它/生活才可以想象/也因此才那么荒唐……"霍朗告诉了我什么是生命的意义,当然也包括了它隐含的荒唐。诗人米罗斯拉夫·霍卢布,我以为他在诗歌上的成就要远远高于他在医学领域的成就,因为精神的创造从更广阔的时间而言,他的不朽性和延伸性都将是无可限量的,他的著名诗篇《加利列·伽利略》中有这样的诗句:"我/加利列·伽利略/置身在米内维纳教堂/只穿一件衬衣/靠一双细腿/承受着世界的压力/我/加利列·伽利略/低声/低声地说/为了孩子们/为了搬运工/为了太阳——/我低声地/终于说……/地球/确实/在转动",是他让我懂得了诗歌在当下一旦失去了思想和勇于承担人类的苦难,诗歌也将会失去它更重要的价值。我在捷克访问时,专门向好友泰博特索要了一个光盘,里面储存有现当代捷克重要诗人朗诵的诗歌,在这些年繁忙喧嚣的日子里,我总会抽时间去聆听奈兹瓦尔、弗·哈拉斯、霍朗、塞弗尔特等人的声音,他们的诗歌和声音始终陪伴着我,给我的心灵和精神所带来的抚慰、感动和激励,是他人永远无法真正能体会得到的,从这个角度而言,任何一个已经逝去的伟大诗人,他都不会真的被死亡带走。

  捷克民族是一个达观幽默的民族,在欧洲历史上曾多次被周边的强权和国家所侵扰,作为中欧一个具有深厚文化传统的国家,它的特殊性远远超出了其地缘的概念,被世人所知晓的波西米亚的精神历史,经过了饱经沧桑的沉淀,实际上已经成为今天捷克精神文化传统的一个重要组成部分,从捷克现当代诗人的丰厚创作中,我们能看到他们用诗歌为自己也为他们身边的生活,构建了一个用词语来对抗暴力的世界。他们从对人的爱和对这个世界一切美好事物的赞颂出发，以惊人的内在忍耐力，去面对他们曾经经历过的那些最悲惨的日子，就是在被纳粹严酷统治的时期，他们的诗歌也没有失去反讽的力量，对生命、个性和人的尊严的彰显，也从未在捷克诗人的写作中失去传承。在许多具有悲悯情怀的诗歌中，我们能真切地感受到诗歌在维护人类道德和崇高理想上所应承担的使命，研究和观察近现代的捷克历史你会发现，诗歌一直和它的人民站在一起，它的每一个词都如同闪亮的金属般的子弹，以其坚硬的真理的力量，洞穿了现实中的谎言和虚伪。上个世纪30年代开始登上捷克诗坛的这个诗人群体，他们中一些杰出的天才代表，以其独特的富有个性的诗性表达，让我们真实地看到了半个多世纪以来，诗歌在人类为争取幸福生活、见证时代历史，以及恢复道德尊严等方面所发挥的巨大作用。历史的经验和今天的现实告诉我们，诗歌永远不仅仅是对爱的吟诵，也是反对一切暴力的最宝贵的武器。

Poetry, a Tribute to Love, an Arsenal Against All Violence

—A keynote address delivered at the Sino-Czech Roundtable on Literature on the Commemoration of the 70th Anniversary of Sino-Czech Republic Cultural Exchange and the Independent Czechoslovak State Day

Today marks the 70th anniversary of the founding of the People's Republic of China, the 70th anniversary of Sino-Czech Republic Cultural Exchange, and the Independence Day of Czech. Upon this important occasion, I am very happy to join with you, as a poet from China, at the Sino-Czech Roundtable on Literature. Please therefore allow me to convey my best and most sincere wishes to each of you.

I visited the Czech Republic twice, the first time upon invitation of my Czech publisher in spring 2016 for the launch and first public reading of my poetry anthology *Flames and Words*, in fact a co-translation by Czech sinologist Zuzana Li and poet Jaromír Typlt. Therefore I believe I am not a stranger to your country. Of course, prior to this I had already had another anthology published in the Czech Republic, entitled *Time*, a rendition from its English version. And shortly in autumn 2018, I had the privilege to be invited to the 28th annual Prague Writers' Festival (PWF), an occasion upon which I participated along with a Swedish poet Cletus Nwadike and Iranian poet Abolghasem Esmailpour—the latter of whom also happened to be translator of my anthology in Persian—in a roundtable themed "The Evils of Living" hosted by Michael March, founder of the PWF, where I had the opportunity to field some questions from the audience. My Czech visit, especially that to the world-renowned city of Prague, left indelibly good impressions upon me.

At this moment there is something which I hope to say to all of you, that it was in fact at a much earlier time when a fascination with Prague as an enchanting city began to burgeon in me, along with an irresistible longing to visit it someday. That was when I chanced upon a passage by Friedrick Wilhelm Nietzsche, the legendary German philosopher who put it beautifully in parallelism: "When I seek for a word to express my love of music, I find Vienna; when I seek for a word to express my idea of mystery, Prague comes to my mind." And if my memory serves me right, it is the German literary giant Johann Wolfgang von Goethe who famously defines the city as, "the most beautiful jewel in the crown of the globe."

Prague fascinates me yet in more ways than one. For one thing, to me, a passionate amateur of classical architecture, Prague is nothing short of a de facto museum of architecture in every sense of the term, home to architectural legacies of an endless long list of historical periods and feathering a large variety of fashions and tastes, most noticeably the Baroque and the Gothic, earning the city an unshakable and most prominent place in the architectural history of the Continent. To me, an inveterate aficionado of classical music, the city was birthplace to Antonín Dvořák, Bedřich Smetana, and Leoš Janáček, all of whom great composers, whose masterpieces, after repeated listenings, still hold me captive even to this day, casting me spellbound whenever the melodies spring up. Among their masterpieces, the most thought-provoking is perhaps Dvořák's Symphony *No.9*, more famously known as New World Symphony, which for a time would render me pensive and lost in imagination, leaving me with a belief that music can revitalize a people's soul on a separate place of existence from ours; a symphonic poem by Smetana, *Má vlast*, or *My Country*, revealed to my sight every immortal thing possibly found in music, brought to life by notes and melodies, which did not simply fade away, but rather continued their vital existence in the depths of time; the revelation and shock incited and triggered by Janáček's orchestral rhapsody *Taras Bulba* and his *Sinfonietta* far exceeded any abstract tome of philosophy I had ever chanced upon, for they had instilled in me a knowledge that oftentimes it was from the elements of native languages and folk songs that soul-stirring melodies were best distilled, a fact which must have also hold true from such moral sentiments as caring for the underdogs to make their voices heard, a sentiment striking me in sympathetic awe of the tongues spoken by every downtrodden peoples worldwide, including the Yi tribe to which I belong.

Myself being a fan of Goethe's concept of "world literature", especially more than a full century after his passing, and despite the ongoing wipeout of cultural differences resulting from cultural immersions happening at an ever-increasing pace, more and more are awakening to the goodness of multicultural preservation, cultural diversity, and the great humanist traditions, which remain the unshakable cornerstones of this "world literature". The concept of "national literatures" has already collided, and now overlaps with "world literature", a universalized concept, prompting us to redefine the latter, of which Czech literature is just an epitome. The epoch-making expressionist writer Franz Kafka, primogenitor of modernist literature, who lived in Prague all his life, could be said to have already become a cultural symbol of the city. This is to say nothing of an earlier time period, when the emergence of a big batch of eminent writers on the literary scene of the country as early as the 20th century, whose coming-of-age both elevated the status of Czech literature among European intelligentsia, and made palpable to the world the looming Czech literary presence. Among these writers, we are most familiar with Jaroslav Hašek, Vladislav Vančura, Karel Čapek, Václav Havel, Milan Kundera, Ivan Klíma, and in addition to them, Bohumil Hrabal, out of heartfelt admiration for whom I took some time out of my hectic schedule here to drive over for a special visit to his forest bungalow, to which he had retired from the world for the sole purpose of writing; and then to his graveyard, shrouded with a like air of simple austerity in which he had led his life, a graveyard which he chose for himself, now scattered with doll cats brought halfway across the world by admirers of all nationalities, for we know cats had been his best friends—in fact, he had even kept food in his forest bungalow for these close confidants of his!

As an intellectual explorer fascinated with linguistics, linguistic anthropology, and semiotics, Prague charms me, for it was here that the genius Roman Jakobson, undoubtedly a trailblazer in structuralist thought and movements, who founded the Prague School, became the very first thinker to establish linkages between structural linguistics and poetic criticism, revealing a mysterious effect of metaphor and metonymy in poetry, a pioneering intellectual achievement making possible all the subsequent explorations in and experimentations with language. It was also Jakobson who, capitalizing on linguistic and rhetorical discoveries in poetry, ventured to undertake in-depth analyses of the works of Velimir Khlebnikov, the Russian futurist poet.

As a poet myself, I cannot deny the extraordinary zeal I have for Czech poetry, many of which I have read while still in college, including the long poem *May* by Karel Hynek Mácha, pioneer of poetry of a new era, whose works themed around romantic love, expressing the earnest wishes of a people yearning for national rebirth. Most importantly, proceeding from human nature, he hoisted individual sentiments up to the majestic heights of human morality. In a periodizing poets in contemporary Chinese poetry, I can be loosely pigeonholed as one who came of age in the 1980s, the heyday of China's open door policy; which is to say, foreign influences including Czech poets constitute a sizable part of my poetic and intellectual pedigree. They include, but are not limited to, contemporary poets such as Vítězslav Nezval, the master surrealist, under whose influence countless Czech poets adopted the novel poetical assertions against asceticism and rationalism, not to mention his infusing late-surrealism with the latest values and attitudes.

The poet Jaroslav Seifert extolled beauty all his life, such as in the following verse: "Heaven may be just / A smile we've been waiting for so long / Two lips softly calling our name / And then for a brief moment it was dizzying / The existence of hell is forgotten". These lines moved me so much after one reading that, whenever upon retrospection, I still feel a thrill through me as the first time I stumbled upon them. During my Czech visit, at one time we rushed to his graveyard, arriving there no sooner than the dusk had befallen his hometown, when the graveyard warden was just about to lock up the heavy iron gates. In no time did I dart out from the car, screaming "Jaroslav Seifert! Jaroslav Seifert!" at him desperately. No, I did not know a single word of Czech, yet he must have understood what I meant, for he unlocked the gates, and let in our group of visitors who came all the way from the other end of the globe. Oh, Vladimír Holan, the hermetic poet who had stayed on Kampa Island in Prague, whose terse and witty epigrams abounded with esoteric philosophy and metaphors, whose poetry was shrouded in mysticism of meditations over life and death, existence and non-existence, such as this: "Oh yes / I love life / that's why I sing so much about death / without death / life would be so cold / with it / life could be imagined / and that's why it's so absurd..." It was Holan who opened my eyes to the true meaning of life which, of course, was at the same time not without an twinge of the absurd. O, master poet Miroslav Holub., arguably more accomplished in poetry than medicine which he also practiced—since viewed within the grander scope of time, any spiritual creation is unfathomably unperishable and malleably extendible—who in the famous masterpiece of the verse *Galileo Galilei* had uttered this: "I / Galileo Galilei / in the church of Mineweina / in a shirt / on thin legs / under the pressure of the world / Me / Galileo Galilei / in a low voice / for the children / for the movers / for the sun— / In a low voice / at last... / The earth / indeed/is spinning around under my feet" and who has made me understand that, should poetry at any moment cease to be thought-provoking and to sustain human suffering, it would at that very moment be stripped of all its raison d'etre. During my Czech visit, I had my friend Jaromír Typlt prepare for me a disk containing poems for recitations by the most important contemporary Czech poets. All these hectic years, I would often take some time off to listen to Vítězslav Nezval, František Halas, Holan, Serfeit, whose works and voices were always there with me, and for me, bestowing me some touching moments of solace and of encouragement, and upon my bedraggled heart, mind, and soul feelings which could never have really been shared with and felt by anybody else. In a sense, no great poet who has passed away would "wander in Death's shade", but instead they live on forever and ever.

The Czechs are known for their magnanimous outlook, and for

their good sense of humour, due to the fact that Central European people had been repeatedly harassed and oppressed by surrounding powers and such historical fate goes beyond the geopolitical into the cultural sphere, as the Bohemian spirit which throughout history has braved the vicissitudes of time, now an inseparable part of the Czech cultural tradition as seen in the voluminous creations by contemporary Czech poets who have, as we can see, created a safe haven of words, a shelter from the violence so palpably felt in their own lives and those of others around them. Out of love for mankind and for everything beautiful in this world, with stunning forbearance and stamina they have confronted the abject misery and the most intolerable hardships, that is to say, under the draconian rule of the Nazis, when nevertheless their poetry retained its power of irony, appreciation of life, individual character, and human dignity, which despite the ups and downs have nevertheless been passed down in their works. From many compassionate poems on human suffering, we can see the power of poetry at work and at its best, carrying out its mandate as the guardian keeper of human morals and lofty ideals. Anyone studying closely the Czech history of modernization will find that for this nation, poetry has always been with the common people, each and every word like a shining metal bullet, penetrating lies and hypocrisies with its all-conquering power of truth. With their unique and richly individualistic poetical expression, this variety of poetic genius who began to make the Czech poetic stage in the 1930s made visible to us the enormous role which poetry played over more than half a century in helping humanity strive for happiness, testifying for us to the zeitgeist, restoring us to moral dignity, and more. Our history and reality have told us that poetry is not merely a tribute to love, but also a most treasurable arsenal against all violence.

Translated by Huang Shaozheng

诗歌本身的意义、传播以及其内在的隐秘性
——在第三届泸州国际诗歌大会诗歌论坛上的演讲

诗人切斯瓦夫·米沃什曾在上个世纪的1990年写过一篇《反对不能理解的诗歌》的文章，在其中表达了他对诗歌如何能被理解以及得到应有传播的关注，他认为诗歌和每一件艺术品一样，都被视为是一种神圣的创造，但是对那些"不能理解的诗歌"的所谓形式和语言试验，特别是对"诗歌愈是不能理解就愈好"的观点却不予苟同，因为它使诗人与读者形成了无法沟通的隔绝。

另外，有关诗歌在语言和形式上所进行的所谓"最纯粹"的探险却也从未有过停止，从后期象征主义、超现实主义、未来主义以及现代主义诗歌诸流派所付诸的实践中，对诗歌其神秘性、隐喻性、象征性，以及由词语本身所构建的在意义上的多种可能，这些探险和试验实际上已经告诉我们，从接受美学的角度来看，诗人个体所完成的一首诗，最终会被无数个他者来共同参与完成。这一现象并不是今天才存在，早在上个世纪20年代俄罗斯未来主义诗歌的主将之一——赫列勃尼科夫就通过对语言和词语的重新熔铸，甚至通过创造新的词语所形成的节奏和声音，将诗歌语言本身的意义与所谓被创造的意义加入到新的形式中，可以说，他给读者提供了两套语言系统，一套是所谓的公共语言符号，另一套就是诗人传递给我们的语言密码。

也因此20世纪最伟大的语言学家之一、布拉格学派的创始人雅各布森就根据他的诗歌，将语言学与诗歌之间的生成对比放在一起研究，从而在理论上深刻地解析了诗歌语言的独特性和复

杂性，并对"诗歌是自在的词"从学理上也进行了富有说服力的阐释，揭示了"诗歌语言之所以成为诗歌语言"的内在本质特征。毫无疑问，因为雅各布森在这一领域开创性的发现，使他成为真正意义上的形式主义诗学理论最重要的奠基人。

从诗歌创作的实践本身而言，任何一个伟大的诗人其实都永远徘徊在对其诗歌内容的直接呈现，与所谓语言和形式的不断创造中，这两者的关系始终是相辅相成的。切斯瓦夫·米沃什强调并反对在诗歌中使用大量的艺术隐喻，对那些所谓的"纯诗"始终持怀疑的态度。

我以为从诗歌价值本身的选择来看，我是赞成他的主张的，因为我们应该从我们自身的创作实践中去力争和解决，诗歌不可避免的就一定会晦涩和难懂这样一种认识。同样，我们也要反对那样一种对形式和语言的创新持保守的观点，因为很多时候，诗人的创造都不完全是与他的读者在进行直接的沟通，很多时候是通过主观所创造的客观对应物来完成的。而在形式和语言上的创造，还会给接受者提供再创造的无限的可能，这也许正是诗歌语言不同于别的语言最重要的地方。真正伟大的诗人，必须在这两者之间找到最合适的方式和平衡点，他就如同一个在高空中走平衡木的人，只有保持了应有的平衡，他才有可能永远立于不败之地。

20世纪拉丁美洲诗歌的雄狮巴勃罗·聂鲁达就曾经用一段最朴素、最简明的语言说明了这一切，他这样智慧地告诉我们："如果一首诗，能被所有的人看懂，肯定不会是一首好诗；同样，如果一首诗，不能被所有的人看懂，它同样不会是一首好诗。"

有关诗歌本身的意义、传播以及其内在的隐秘性这样一个话题，还会长久地被持续议论下去，或许这正是诗歌具有永恒的魅力之所在。也因为诗歌将与人类共存，我们在其内容、形式和语言上的创新也永远不会停止。

The Meaning, Dissemination and Inner Secrecy of Poetry
—Address at the seminar of 3rd International Poetry & Liquor Conference

Czeslaw Milosz, back in 1990 wrote an article entitled *Against Incomprehensible Poetry*, in which he made explicit some of the tacit implications in his view of poetry to the effect that he should be deemed on the side of those who hanged on to virtues of poetic accessibility and traditional poetic ambition about spiritual consolation or social effectiveness or duty. Basically he believes a poem, like any artistic creation, is of supreme human import while eschewing largely the obscurantist and elitist stance, in vogue among some quarters, prioritizing opacity that characterizes some extreme poetic experiment of forms to the extent the more incomprehensible, the better the poem, as if non-communicability is an absolute good.

True, from our retrospective position, it makes most sense to see innovation and tradition as existing in a symbiotic relationship. Experiments in the name of a diminished aesthetic or "purest forms" and forays into the secrecy, metaphoricity and symbolicity of poetry have pullulated and sustained generations of poets that enable them to emerge into notoriety, in a spate of poetic postures available as the legacy of post-symbolism, surrealism, futurism and modernism. These ventures have importantly reshaped the contours of contemporary poetry and colored our discourse in poetic discussions. I do see eye to eye with one key aesthetic assumption of reader criticism as to how thousands of readers, historical or implied, join with a poet "to help the text mean". Such aesthetic principles hearken to Velimir Khlebnikov, a poets' poet lauded by Mayakovski, both iconic figures of the Russian Futurist movement. In his work, Khlebnikov experimented with the Russian language, drawing upon its roots to invent huge numbers of neologisms, and finding significance in the shapes and sounds of individual letters of Cyrillic. He even developed "an incoherent and anarchic blend of words stripped of their meaning and used for their sound alone" known as Zaum. The result was that he supplied the readers two linguistic systems, one for public reading, the other, sheer encrypted code to be broken by poets only.

As a pioneer of the structural analysis of language, which became the dominant trend in linguistics during the first half of the 20th century, Roman Jakobson was among the most influential linguists from the Prague School and he also became a pivotal figure in investigating poetry by adapting insights from semiotics etc. Jakobson, fascinated with the idea of poetry as autonomous, theorized convincingly about what intrinsically undergirded poetic art by positing binary opposites, i.e., poetic diction vs ordinary diction before unraveling the uniqueness and complexity of poetic idiom. To sum, Jakobson meant to "purify poetry of all that is not poetry," ensuring us to assess the aesthetic unity of the poem with a tool by which we could separate chaff from the wheat with ease.

It is hardly surprising that literary history is littered with unpredictable trajectories of poets oscillating between a commonsense faith in the autonomous, coherent self to represent both self and world in transparent language and a corresponding skepticism concerning metaphysical claims and openly rhetoric and opaque use of language. Contemporary poetry is more meaningfully seen in many ways as a larger continuum, at once linked and segregated by this set of seemingly contradictory dualities. A master like Czeslaw Milosz is highly various and subtle in his rhetorical kit and despite a progressive stylistic thinning out, he remains a staunch skeptic of the so-called "pure poetry" shunning any "metaphysical claims" or "epic imperative".

By temperament, in the face of a world that has so tragically gone wrong, I feel quite comfortable to subscribe to Milosz's concern with "the impact of history upon moral being, the search for ways to survive spiritual ruin in a ruined world", deeply aware of the viability of the claims made by modernists' scrupulous devotion to the craft of poetry. Yet, this does not mean that a poet, in his effort to register the world beside and beyond the self and to be constantly at the cutting edge in technique and thought, has to make virtue of obscurity, bad organization, neglect of logic, intent on "his own world and his own forms" at the expense of increasingly limiting poetry's terrain. Easy legibility, caused by mass literary and mass journalism, should always be guarded against as a baneful influence in poetry. We as poets do need some external or inner reality to refer to or even self-refer to, yet we should also transcend the triviality of material reality if not to submit our work to the astringency of "pure poetry", since poetry has its genuine value primarily in "the sphere of the intangible and the imaginary" as well as of the social and the ethical—a sphere different from other arts where a high-minded practitioner is expected to create beauty by reinvigorating language, both chaste and creative, to discard conventions outmoded and invent new ones instead, and last but not least, to affirm the value of human life, no matter how hard. A truly great poet looks to me like a magician teetering on the high tension wire, assured of all the hazards, still safe and secured.

To conclude, I feel tempted again to quote Pablo Neruda, one of the Latin American poetic giants of the 20th century, when he discloses to us most intimately the ultimate recipe for his crowning achievement: "If a poem is intelligible to everybody, it won't be a good one for sure; likewise, if a poem remains enigmatic to all, it is a bad one without fail."

The subject of the meaning of poetry, its dissemination, and its inherent secrecy will continue to engage and challenge the community of poets—arguably the eternal charm of the craft of poetry for decades, perhaps, centuries, to come. That means we must content ourselves wrestling relentlessly with this perennial tension embedded in the fundamental aesthetic premises upon which both modern poetry and poets' vocation rest.

Translated by Huang Shaozheng

让诗歌为我们迈向明天和未来注入强大的力量
——在 2020 年印度克里提亚国际诗歌节上的致辞

在这里我首先要向印度克里提亚国际诗歌节的举办表示祝贺，向通过网络视频参加这一活动的所有朋友们致以最美好的祝愿！当下，全人类都面临着一个特殊的时刻，那就是我们正在全力以赴地抗击病毒这一人类共同的敌人，我们欣慰地看到，诗歌在这样一个艰难的时候仍然发挥着鼓舞人类迈向明天的重要作用，而我们的诗人同样在这一场战役中没有缺席。更让我们自豪的是，为了促进人类的和平和这个星球的美好未来，我们的诗人在不同的国度和地域都发出了自己正义的声音，对一切有碍于人类不同文明和民族间构建理解、和谐以及美好关系的邪恶势力都开展了坚决的斗争，特别是对还在甚嚣尘上的种族主义、新法西斯主义和恐怖主义也予以了强烈的谴责，我相信，只要有全世界诗人们的团结和合作，我们的诗歌就一定会产生强大的精神力量，从而也能使全人类在迈向明天和未来的征途上充满信心和勇气。当下病毒还在世界肆虐，人类还在极度的艰难和迈向希望的明天之间徘徊，在此，请允许我朗诵一段我的长诗《裂开的星球》来表达对人类永不屈服于任何灾难崇高精神的致敬。

哦，人类！这是消毒水流动国界的时候
这是旁观邻居下一刻就该轮到自己的时候
这是融化的时间与渴望的箭矢赛跑的时候
这是嘲笑别人而又无法独善其身的时候

这是狂热的冰雕刻那熊熊大火的时候
这是地球与人都同时戴上口罩的时候
这是天空的鹰与荒野的赤狐搏斗的时候
这是所有的大街和广场都默默无语的时候
这是孩子只能在窗户前想象大海的时候
这是白衣天使与死神都临近深渊的时候
这是孤单的老人将绝望一口吞食的时候
这是一个待在家里比外面更安全的时候
这是流浪者喉咙里伸出手最饥饿的时候
这是人道主义主张高于意识形态的时候
这是城市的部落被迫返回乡土的时候
这是大地、海洋和天空致敬生命的时候
这是被切开的血管里飞出鸽子的时候
这是意大利的泪水模糊中国眼睛的时候
这是伦敦的呻吟让西班牙吉他呜咽的时候
这是纽约的护士与上帝一起哭泣的时候
这是谎言和真相一同出没于网络的时候
这是甘地的人民让远方的麋鹿不安的时候
这是人性的光辉和黑暗狭路相逢的时候
这是相信对方或置疑对手最艰难的时候
这是语言给人以希望又挑起仇恨的时候
这是一部分人迷茫另一半也忧虑的时候
这是蓝鲸的呼吸吹动着和平的时候
这是星星代表亲人送别亡人的时候
这是一千个祭司诅咒一个影子的时候
这是陌生人的面部开始清晰的时候
这是同床异梦者梦见彼此的时候
这是貌合神离者开始冷战的时候
这是旧的即将解体新的还没有到来的时候
这是神枝昭示着不祥还是化险为夷的时候
这是黑色的石头隐匿白色意义的时候

这是诸神的羊群在等待摩西渡过红海的时候
这是牛角号被勇士吹得撕心裂肺的时候
这是鹰爪杯又一次被预言的诗人握住的时候
这是巴比塔废墟上人与万物力争和谈的时候
就是在这样一个时候,就是在这样的时候
哦,人类!只有一次机会,抓住马蹄铁。

Let Poetry Empower Us Strongly for Marching Toward Tomorrow and Future
—An Address on 2020 Kritya Poetry Festival, India

First of all, I would like to extend congratulations for the inauguration of Kritya Poetry Festival and best regards toward all dear friends attending this Festival through internet videos! At present, all human beings face a special moment that we are devoting every effort to fight against COVID-19 virus, the common enemy of humankind. It is a pleasure to see that in such a difficult time, poetry still plays a role of encouraging people to march toward tomorrow, that we poets are also not absent in this battle. We are especially proud that in order to promote human peace and a better future of this planet, we poets speak up for justice in various countries and areas, fighting resolutely against all evil forces impeding the establishment of understanding, harmony and better relationship among different civilizations and nationalities, particularly condemning the arising clamour of racism, Neo-Nazism and terrorism. I believe that as long as the poets of the whole world unite and cooperate with each other, our poetry must produce the mighty spiritual power, so that all human beings will be full of confidence and courage on the journey to tomorrow and future. Currently, the virus wreaks havoc on the world, and humankind is hovering between exceptional arduousness and advancing to tomorrow of hope. Please allow me to recite a part of my long poem, *Split-Open Planet*, to express my tribute to the lofty spirit of human beings who have never yielded to any disaster.

O, humankind, this is the time disinfectants flow along national borders.

It's the time when you'll be next if the person beside you gets it.
It's the time when dissolving time and thirsty arrows are in a race.
It's the time when we mock others and can't do good by ourselves.
It's the time when that zealous ice is carving the raging inferno.
It's the time when the earth and people simultaneously don face-masks.
It's the time when eagles in the sky fight with red foxes in the wilderness.
It's the time when all the boulevards and public squares fall silent.
It's the time when children can only imagine the ocean from beside the window.
It's the time when angels in white and the god of death approach the abyss.
It's the time when lonely seniors will devour despair in one gulp.
It's a time when it's safer to stay home than it is to go out.
It's the time when the outstretched hand in the throat of vagabonds is the hungriest.
It's the time when advocates for humanitarian aid are greater than ideology.
It's the time when urban tribal peoples are forced to return to the countryside.
It's the time when the earth, sea and sky pay their respects to living beings.
It's the time when doves fly out from cut-open veins.
It's the time when Italian tears blur Chinese eyes.
It's the time when moans in London make Spanish guitars whimper.
It's the time when New York nurses cry with God.
It's the time when lies and the truth appear and disappear on the internet.
It's the time when Gandhi's people disturb the faraway elaphure.
It's the time when humankind's glory and evil come face to face.
It's the time when it's hardest to believe the other side or doubt one's enemies.
It's the time when language gives people hope yet provokes hatred.
It's the time when half the people are perplexed and the other half are worried.
It's the time when the breath of blue whales stirs peace.

It's the time when the stars send off the dead on behalf of relatives.
It's the time when a thousand priests curse a shadow.
It's the time when the faces of strangers start to become distinct.
It's the time when people in the same bed with different dreams now dream of each other.
It's the time when people seemingly together but actually divergent start a cold war.
It's the time when the old is on the verge of collapse and the new hasn't yet arrived.
It's the time when the divine branches declare misfortune or disaster will be averted.
It's the time when black stones conceal white meanings.
It's the time when the sheep of all gods are waiting for Moses to cross the Red Sea.
It's the time when the bull-horn blown by warriors tears you up with grief.
It's the time when the eagle goblet is grasped once again by the poet prophet.
It's the time when the people and living things on the Tower of Babel earnestly engage in peace talks.
It's precisely a time like this. It's precisely a time like this.
O, humankind. There's only one chance to end this war.

Translated by Hu Wei

太阳还会在明天升起
——在第三十届麦德林国际诗歌节开幕式上的致辞

2020.8

各位诗人朋友们:

在这样一个特殊的时刻,我们迎来了第三十届麦德林国际诗歌节的召开,这无疑是一件令全世界所有的诗人和热爱诗歌的人们值得祝贺的盛举,因为我们知道,当下这一场肆虐全球并还在蔓延的病毒已经从整体上改变了这个世界,病毒是全人类共同的敌人,生活在这个地球不同地域的人们都真切地感受到了这种巨大的变化,从某种意义而言,这种变化所带来的冲击和影响并不亚于上一个世纪至今所爆发过的两次世界大战,由于这场疫情所带来的国家间的关系、地缘政治的关系、不同族群的关系、不同价值体系的关系、不同经济体的关系,实际上都已经被深刻地重塑。我以为,这个全球化和逆全球化激烈博弈之后的世界,或许将会进入一个完全不同于今天的亚全球化时代。正是在这样一个人类正在经历最艰难的时刻,诗人和诗歌更应该承担起引领人类精神的崇高使命,要把捍卫自由、公平和正义作为我们共同的责任,对一切以排他为目的的法西斯主义、种族主义以及不同类型的恐怖主义,我们都要发出强烈的抗议之声,为了促进全人类的和平、进步与发展,我们要用诗歌去打破任何形式的壁垒和隔离,要为构建一个更加公平、合理和人道的世界做出我们的贡献。也正因为此,不同凡响、令人瞩目的第三十届麦德林国际诗歌节才在这里拉开了序幕,最后请允许我引用我的长诗《裂开的星球》中的诗句来结束我的致辞。

这是巨大的转折，它比一个世纪要长，只能用千年来算
我们不可能再回到过去，因为过去的老屋已经面目全非
不能选择封闭，任何材料成为高墙，就只有隔离的含义
不能选择对抗，一旦偏见变成仇恨，就有可能你死我亡
不用去问那些古老的河流，它们的源头充满了史前的寂静
或许这就是最初的启示，和而不同的文明都是她的孩子
放弃三的分歧，尽可能在七中找到共识，不是以邻为壑
在方的内部，也许就存在着圆的可能，而不是先入为主
让诸位摒弃森林法则，这样应该更好，而不是自己为大
让大家争取日照的时间更长，而不是将黑暗奉送给对方
这一切！不是一个简单的方法，而是要让参与者知道
这个星球的未来不仅属于你和我，还属于所有的生命
我不知道明天会发生什么，据说诗人有预言的秉性
但我不会去预言，因为浩瀚的大海没有给天空留下痕迹
曾被我千百次赞颂过的光，此刻也正迈着凯旋的步伐
我不知道明天会发生什么，但我知道这个世界将被改变
是的！无论会发生什么，我都会执着而坚定地相信——
太阳还会在明天升起，黎明的曙光依然如同爱人的眼睛
温暖的风还会吹过大地的腹部，母亲和孩子还在那里嬉戏
大海的蓝色还会随梦一起升起，在子夜成为星辰的爱巢
劳动和创造还是人类获得幸福的主要方式，多数人都会同意
人类还会活着，善和恶都将随行，人与自身的斗争不会停止
时间的入口没有明显的提示，人类你要大胆而又加倍小心。

祝本届麦德林国际诗歌节取得圆满的成功，诗歌万岁！和平万岁！

2020.8

The Sun Will Still Rise Tomorrow
—*Speech for the Opening Ceremony of the Thirtieth Medellin International Poetry Festival*

My Dear Poet Friends:

In these unusual times, we're coming together to convene the Thirtieth Medellin International Poetry Festival. This is a grand undertaking deserving congratulations from poets and lovers of poetry from all over the world, because we all know that in this moment, a virus that's devastated the entire world, and that's still spreading, has already changed the world as a whole. The virus is the shared enemy of all humankind. People living in different regions of the world have vividly experienced this immense change. In some sense, the shock and impact of this change is no less than that of the two world wars during the previous century.

In reality, this pandemic has already profoundly reconstructed relations between nations, geopolitical relations, relations between different ethnic communities, and between systems with different values, as well as different economic systems. I think this world after the contest between globalization and anti-globalization will enter a second kind of global era that's completely different from the present one. It's precisely in the most difficult times like these that poets and poetry should undertake the majestic mission of leading humanity's spirit. We need to consider defending freedom, fairness, and justice as our shared responsibility. We must speak out in strong voices of protest against all sorts of exclusionism, including fascism, racism, and different forms of terrorism to promote the peace, progress and development of all humankind. We must use poetry to smash barriers and separation in all forms; we must do our part to construct an even more equitable, fair, humane world. And it's precisely because of this that the outstanding Thirtieth Medellin International Poetry Festival is opening here. In closing, please allow me to quote from my long poem, *Split-Open Planet*.

This is an enormous shift, it's longer than a century, it can only be calculated in terms of a millennium.
We can't return to the past, because the old houses have all disappeared.
We can't choose to close ourselves off; no matter what material becomes a high wall, it only implies separation.
We can't choose to resist; as soon as prejudice turns to hate, you or I could die.
We don't need to ask those ancient rivers; their sources are full of prehistory's silence.
Perhaps this was the original enlightenment, diverse civilizations in harmony were all her children.
Give up the difference of three and try hard to find consensus among seven; this isn't putting the problem off on others.
Within a square might be a round possibility; it's not being prejudiced by first impressions.
Let everyone abandon the laws of the forest; this should be better, not viewing oneself as most important.
Let people try to make bright times last longer rather than bestowing darkness on each other.
None of this is a simple method; it's making all participants aware
the future of this planet doesn't just belong to you and me, it belongs to all lives.
I don't know what will happen tomorrow; it's said poets have the ability to foretell the future,
but I won't predict the future, since the boundless oceans didn't leave any traces in the sky.
The light I've praised countless times is now on a triumphant march.
I don't know what will happen tomorrow, but I know the world will be changed.

Yes! No matter what happens, I firmly and steadfastly believe the sun will still rise tomorrow, dawn's light will be as before, like a lover's eyes.
The warm wind will still blow over the earth's abdomen, mothers and children will still be playing there.
The blue of the sea will still rise with dreams and, at midnight, become the lovenest of stars.
Most people agree labor and creation will still be the main means through which people attain fulfillment.
People will keep living, good and evil will keep accompanying them; the struggle between humankind and itself won't cease.
The entrance to time doesn't have an obvious marker.
Humankind, you must be courageously and exponentially careful.

I wish Medellin International Poetry Festival complete successfully
Long live poetry! Long live peace!

Translated by Jami Proctor Xu

向河流、高山和大海的致敬
——2020年瓜亚基尔国际诗歌奖致答词

毫无疑问，今天对全世界而言是一个艰难的时刻，肆虐全球的病毒还在许多国家蔓延扩散，置身于这个星球，生活在不同地域的人们都在为人类当下面临的困境以及明天的不确定性而满怀痛苦和忧虑。是的，这不是一个轻松的话题，是一个令所有的人都感到无比沉重但还必须要去面对的现实，从每天大众媒体的报道我们会很快知道，感染和死亡的人数仍然在快速地增加，正如我们所知道的那样，这并不是一场传统意义上的世界性的战争，但它却在多方面从根本上改变了我们的生活以及这个世界原有的风貌。这不是发生在局部的某种变化，而是从整体上动摇了原有的国家间、地缘政治间、不同经济体间的最为基础性的关系，旧的规则正在失去其效力，新的规则尚待取得共识和确立，不管你是否能接受和承认这个局面，当下的这种特殊境遇，无疑是人类正在经历的一场风险巨大的考验，绝非是我在这里危言耸听，这一考验的最终结果，将直接关系到人类世界的命运及其前景，从根本上讲，这个结果将深刻地影响人类的未来和发展方向。纵然人类历史的发展从来不是一帆风顺的，花样翻新的战争，形形色色的灾难，如影随形一直伴随着我们，最让我们不安的是在这个人类陷入困境，绝望和希望共存的时候，在一些国家和地区，排他主义、新法西斯主义、种族主义、恐怖主义等反人类反理性的行为频繁出现，一些政治利益集团为了一己私利，不惜动用国家力量操弄政治，编造虚伪的谎言图谋挑起人类之间的仇恨和对立。

当然，同样也在这样的时候，在这个地球不同的地方，我们看到有千千万万的人仍然坚守团结、公正、平等、合作的原则，捍卫和尊重联合国宪章及国际法，保护我们赖以生存的环境和生态，致力于消除贫困和维护人的基本权利，把推动和平反对战争，进一步促进不同文明的沟通和对话作为神圣的责任，或许正是因为我们真切地看到了这个世界不可抗拒的共同意愿，我们才对人类的明天抱有足够的信心和期待。

无须赘言，打破障碍和壁垒，跨越海洋和大陆，把美好的礼物奉献给他人，我以为在任何国度和民族中都是慷慨的善举。为此，我要由衷地感谢地球另一端的赤道之国厄瓜多尔，感谢我诗歌精神上的另一个隐秘的源头——伟大的诗人生长的拉丁美洲，感谢你们把本年度如此珍贵的这个奖项颁发给我，我非常高兴能成为胡安·赫尔曼、查尔斯·西密克、杰克·赫希曼、豪尔赫·爱德华兹等这个队列中的一员，这是我的荣幸，谢谢你们。作为一个诗人，为了表达感激之情，还有什么比致敬的语言更真挚和合适呢，厄瓜多尔，请接受我的致敬。

向你致敬不是你丰富的单一，而是你整体的有机的多元，是你在精神上的单数和复数的统一，然而最让人惊奇的是，在一千倍的复数中也能找到第一个单数。祝愿你的花园除了有彩色的气球，还有糖果，老人和孩子，永远听不见枪声。

向你致敬不仅是因为你有浩瀚的大海、雄伟的高山和广袤的腹地，更是因为在钦博拉索山的最高峰，那玛雅人五月的太阳，以黄金和巨石在第四维空间的裂变，让每一个还存活在今天的部落，都能感受到那亘古不变的火焰的温暖。但愿这一切，不只属于当下，更重要的是还属于遥远的未来。

向你致敬不仅是因为你有波澜壮阔的亚马孙河，而是因为河流以唯一的方式，从古至今成为你的人民反抗一切暴力的象征，让消失的时间像一只狂暴的美洲豹，从喉咙里发出红色的声音，让自由和正义在你未来的每一天都成为如期而至的晨曦。但愿在灵魂的深处，对自由和正义的尊崇，永远不会改变。

向你致敬不仅是你能用西班牙语告诉这个世界，你的国家有一句闻名于世的格言:"上帝,祖国和自由"。还因为在克丘亚语的疆域,你能通过一个词的核心进入另一个精神的世界,再一次唤醒睡眠中的星星,以及那些早已灭绝的鸟儿。但愿这个古老的语言,比地球要活得更久。

向你致敬不仅是你天空的神鹰二十四小时昼夜都在守护着母亲的身躯,让加拉帕戈斯群岛黎明的曙光如同每一个正在热恋之人的眼睛,更重要的是你还有比生命和死亡本身更刻骨铭心的诗歌,有奥斯瓦尔多·瓜亚萨明那些悲天悯地的绘画,这位人之子从生到死,都站在了穷人和他的种族印第安人一边。但愿他的悲悯和爱能千百次地复活,其实我知道这个人从未离开过我们。

厄瓜多尔,我祝愿你的一切比历史更新,比现实更远,比未来更近,祝愿你的人民伸出的双手已经握住了希望和明天。谢谢!

Paying Tribute to the Rivers, Mountains, and Oceans
—*Acceptance speech for the 2020 Guayaquil International Poetry Award*

This is without question a very difficult time for the world, with a terrible disease continuing to spread through many countries. Anyone living on earth right now is faced with this predicament, along with the uncertainty of what will come tomorrow and the anxiety and pain that entails. This is not a pleasant topic. It weighs heavily upon the mind, yet we all must face the reality. From the day's news, we will quickly learn that the numbers of those infected and dying are still rising. To my understanding, this is not a kind of world war in the traditional sense; but in many ways it has fundamentally altered our way of life and how the world functions. These changes have not been piecemeal, but instead have completely shaken the basic relationships between countries, regional politics, and different economic systems. The old rules are losing their efficacy, and new rules have yet to be established or gain public consensus. Whether or not one is willing to accept or acknowledge this situation, the present circumstances undeniably present a dangerous trial in the history of humankind. I do not mean to sensationalize the situation, but the final outcome of this trial will have a direct effect on the fate of the human world, and will fundamentally influence our future and the direction of our development. Although human history has never progressed smoothly and has involved constant struggle and all conceivable misfortunes that dog us like shadows, what is most worrisome is that during a time when we are facing terrible difficulties, in a time when despair and hope coexist, in some parts of the world xenophobia, fascism, racism, terrorism, and other antisocial and irrational beliefs and behaviors have appeared. For their own benefit, some political interest groups have worked endlessly to use a nation's power to manipulate politics and to fabricate ridiculous lies in order to provoke hatred and opposition between peoples. Of course, at the same time, in different parts of the world, we can see thousands of people working to maintain and uphold the principles of unity, justice, peace and cooperation. They guard and honor the U.N. Charter and international law, and protect the environment and ecology we all depend upon for survival. They devote themselves to relieving poverty and defending basic human rights, consider it a sacred responsibility to promote peace and oppose war and further encourage communication and dialogue between different cultures. Perhaps only when we clearly see our common aspirations will we be able to have faith and confidence in the future of humankind.

In short, I am inclined to think that for many people of different nationalities and ethnic identities, it is a heartfelt goal to break through obstacles and barriers, traverse oceans and continents, and offer tribute to others. Accordingly, I would like to sincerely thank Ecuador, this equatorial country across the world from my own. I would also like to thank one secret source of poetic inspiration for me, namely Latin America, which has given birth to many great poets. I am deeply honored to be the recipient of this year's precious award, and to join the list of such illustrious poets as Juan Gelman, Charles Simic, and Jack Hirschman. Thank you. As a poet, I can find no better way to express my deep thanks than to pay tribute to Ecuador, and hope you all will accept my highest respects.

In paying tribute, I mean to include more than just one rich aspect of your country; I offer tribute to your organic multiplicities, to both the singleness and the complexities of your psyche. Indeed, most astounding is that among the thousands of multiplicities, a singularity can be found. I hope that your gardens burst with colorful balloons, candy, the aged and the young, and gunshots are never heard again.

I pay tribute to you not only because of your vast ocean, magnificent mountains, and fertile land, but also because on the tallest peak of Mt. Chimborazo, all the world's existing tribes today can warm themselves with the eternal fire of the Mayan sun and the fission of gold and boulders in the fourth dimension. I hope that all this does not belong merely to the present, but more importantly, still belongs to the distant future as well.

I pay tribute to you not only because you have the magnificent Amazon River, but also because the river has become a symbol of your people's resistance to violence, from antiquity to the present. It makes vanished time like a wild South American cougar, roaring a red roar from its throat, and makes freedom and justice as timely as the morning sun of your future days. I hope that in the depths of your spirit, the reverence for freedom and justice never changes.

I pay tribute to you not only because you can use Spanish to announce to the world your country's famous saying—*Dios, patria y libertad* (God, homeland, and freedom)—but also because in the Quechua-speaking areas, you can use the kernel of a word to enter into a spiritual realm, reawakening the sleeping stars and long-extinct birds. I hope that this ancient language exists even longer than this earth.

I pay tribute to you not only because in your skies condors unceasingly protect the bodies of mothers, making the dawn over the Galápagos Islands glimmer like the eyes of lovers. I pay tribute because, more importantly, you still have poetry that is even more deeply felt than life and death, and you have the moving and compassionate artworks of Oswaldo Guayasamín, who stood on the side of the poor and his Native American brethren throughout his life. I hope that his compassion and love will live on a thousandfold, though indeed I know that the man himself has never really left us.

Ecuador, I wish you all that is newer than history, more distant than reality, and closer than the future. May your people's hands grasp hold of hope and the days of tomorrow. Thank you!

Translated by Gu Ailng

一只羊,一位农夫与诗人直视的眼睛

——2020年度"1573国际诗歌奖"颁奖词暨诗集《月照静夜》序言

我知道艾利安·尼·朱利安奈这样一位诗人的名字,首先是从爱尔兰诗人帕特里克·科特那里知道的,这并不意味着在全球化的今天作为诗人的艾利安·尼·朱利安奈已经闻名于世,而恰恰相反,在这样一个网络造就红人的时代,诗人往往是社会人群中最寂寞的一种存在,或许正是这种精神上的执着坚守,诗人的珍贵和伟大才显得超凡脱俗。毋庸置疑,艾利安·尼·朱利安奈是一位真正的诗人,她的作品深深植根于爱尔兰诗歌的伟大传统,并将这一深厚的传统在新的语境下进行了无与伦比的创造,这不是一般意义上的简单续接,而是将个人的生命经验与这片古老土地在精神上一次又一次地重构,她的每一首诗都是一次生命的经历,并在永恒的时间和空间中留下了属于自己的痕迹。她的诗与所谓时尚的风花雪月无关,它就像河床里的石头,或者说就如同刚刚从土地中挖出的土豆,没有繁复叠加的修辞,但语言的精准与简洁的形式却高度地统一在了一起,隐喻、象征和意象在其诗中浑然一体、贴切自然,这种接近于原始的朴实,是对生命和自然的无可挑剔地通向本质的抵达,这是诗歌依然保持着其价值不可被替代的又一证明,因为我们始终相信,在曾经盛行并一直有人坚信万物有灵的爱尔兰民族中,虽然在大多数情况下多神教已经演化成了单一的宗教信仰,但无论是从历史还是现实的角度来看,威廉·巴特勒·叶芝都不可能只是单峰独立,而他的存在也不仅仅是爱尔兰现代诗歌史上的一个偶然,当然不是,因为自此以后足以让世界所瞩目的爱尔兰诗歌就证明了这一点,他的同胞谢默斯·希尼等后来者就将这一殊荣延续到了今天,这其中就包括了杰出的艾利安·尼·朱利安奈。越过广袤的陆地和浩瀚的海洋去寻找今天的爱尔兰诗歌,也并不是一个突发奇想,真正的诗歌的交流从来不是平面化的,甚至它并不体现在一种集体的行为,而往往是通过个体去完成的,这个被我们所构建的对话与沟通的方式,实际上更像是一条通往彼此心灵的隐秘通道,让我们感到庆幸的是,在爱尔兰我们幸运地找到了通往这个通道的金色钥匙,这也应验了中国人一句充满了哲理的话,那就是"念念不忘,必有回响",为此,我要为中国诗歌以及中国诗人与爱尔兰诗人艾利安·尼·朱利安奈的必然相遇而由衷地欢欣鼓舞,我说过这一相遇绝不是偶然,那是因为这种相遇的必然总会在时间的过往中实现,也许我们可以把这种相遇称为所有生命中的奇迹。

　　对于今天的世界而言,艾利安·尼·朱利安奈首先是一位爱尔兰民族诗人,当然,同时她也是一位世界公民,如果从文化身份和诗人所使用的语言来讲,她的盖尔语诗歌传统无疑是她诗歌文本的最重要的基础,当然无可讳言,她的诗歌毫无疑问也与英文形成了一种特殊的关系,在这里我不想简单地对这种过渡性关系所产生的作用做出价值性的判断,但可以肯定,游离于两种语言之间的诗人,总会给我们带来一些意想不到的可能。阅读艾利安·尼·朱利安奈的诗歌,会让我犹如听见了"尤利安风笛"的演奏,特别是当这种诗歌从英语进入汉语的时候,我仍然能感受到她最初的母语穿过神秘的疆界在我耳边产生的回响,我以为,任何一种翻译从某种意义而言都是一种桥梁,但在桥梁与桥梁的转化中所承载之物总有一些最基本的东西是不可改变的,这就是那些难以言传的内在精神和神秘的气息。布拉格语言学派的开创性人物雅各布森就有这样一种观点,那就是语言的内部结构与初始语言的呈现方式,就如同人类的基因,尽管若隐若现,但它的存在却是牢固而不可改变的。作为一个卓越的盖尔语诗人,毫无疑问我们的艾利安·尼·朱利安奈是当下跨语言写作中的一位具有典范意义的诗人,正是她的作品在不同语言的翻译过程中证明了这些诗歌的价值和独特性。当然，需要说明的是，这种价值和独特性同样蕴含于人类最根本也最普遍的意义中，也正因为此，它才可能跨越千山万水被不同族群的人们所喜爱和认同。

  她的诗歌世界是广阔而深远的，其背景依然是古老而又年轻的爱尔兰，她的作品为我们提供了古老神话的新的诠释，同时也为我们展现了人在现实生活中最神奇的心灵感受，因为她那些宁静拙朴而又充满了质感的诗歌，让我们深怀敬意地相信，她不仅仅是一个伟大诗歌传统的继承者，同样也是一个能给我们带来想象的古老语言的传人，有鉴于此，我们将2020年度"1573国际诗歌奖"颁发给当代爱尔兰诗歌的杰出代表之一艾利安·尼·朱利安奈。

艾利安·尼·朱利安奈（Eiléan Ní Chuilleanáin），女，爱尔兰诗人、翻译家。1942年生。2020年度中国"1573国际诗歌奖"获得者。

A Sheep, a Farmer and a Poet's Steady Gaze

—*Presentation of the 2020 "1573 International Poetry Prize" and Preface of Lucina Schynning in Silence of the Nicht: A Selection of Poems by Eiléan Ní Chuilleanáin*

I first heard of Eiléan Ní Chuilleanáin through the Irish poet Patrick Cotter. This is not to say that in this age of globalization, Ní Chuilleanáin can be called a global superstar. It is rather the reverse: in a time of internet sensations, poets hold the loneliest place in the crowd. But perhaps it is this stubborn persistence itself that allows the greatness and importance of poets to transcend conventions and the commonplace. There is no doubt that Eiléan Ní Chuilleanáin is a true poet. Her work is deeply rooted in the grand tradition of Irish poetry, and she brings this tradition into a contemporary linguistic context with incomparable creativity. This is not a straightforward continuation, but rather a continuous spiritual reconstruction of an individual's life experience and of an ancient land. Each poem is a life event, and leaves marks of the individual self on eternal time and space. Her poems bear no relationship to popular sentimental works, but instead are like the stones on the bottom of a riverbed. Or one might say they are like newly dug potatoes, unconcerned with complicated rhetorical flourishes, and instead tightly fusing together exacting language and precise shapes. In her work, metaphors and symbols combine into an appropriate and organic whole. Such impeccable purity and simplicity arrives at the essence of life and nature, and is further proof of poetry's enduring value and irreplaceability. Moreover, we believe absolutely that for the Irish— who have historically held animist beliefs that some maintain despite the fact that polytheism has in many cases evolved into monotheistic religions—the existence of William Butler Yeats, whether viewed from a historical or a contemporary angle, was not simply an isolated incident of significance only to the modern Irish poetry scene. The subsequent generations of Irish poets whom the world has embraced demonstrate that he was much more, from his compatriot Seamus Heaney to the others who have carried his torch into the present day, including the outstanding poet Eiléan Ní Chuilleanáin herself. It is not on mere whim that we cross the wide continents and vast oceans to seek out contemporary Irish poetry. The exchange of true poetry does not exist on a single plane; in fact, this exchange does not always happen as part of a collective effort, but is often achieved through the acts of individuals. The dialogues and lines of communication we have developed are more like hidden passageways between souls, and we rejoice at the good fortune of finding the golden key to those passageways in Ireland. This brings to bear the deeply philosophical Chinese expression, "All that is held in the mind will later come to fruition in life." I would like to express my elation at this inevitable meeting between Chinese poets and poetry and the Irish poet Eiléan Ní Chuilleanáin. As I have said, such meetings are far from isolated incidents, since they will inexorably occur over the passage of time, though perhaps we can still consider it one of life's wonders.

Eiléan Ní Chuilleanáin is first and foremost an Irish poet, but at the same time, she is of course a citizen of the world as well. In terms of cultural identity and language, the Gaelic poetic tradition indisputably forms the primary foundation for her poetry. It is self-evident that her poetry also has a special connection to the English language. Here I would like to avoid making a kind of value judgment based on a simplistic idea of a transitional relationship, but I can be certain that those poets who drift between two languages open up previously unimaginable possibilities. Reading Ní Chuilleanáin's work makes me feel as though I am listening to a performance of "uilleann pipes". Even when her poetry is translated from English into a Chinese linguist context, I am still able to perceive echoes of her native tongue, which have mysteriously traversed all boundaries to arrive at my ears. I have thought of translation in a certain sense as a bridge, but even in switching from one bridge to another, something immutable remains, namely some ineffable, inherent, mysterious essence. Roman Jakobson, a founding member of the Prague School of linguistics, was of the opinion that patterns from the internal structure of language and the earliest original language are, like human genes, always faintly perceptible in the background, and their existence is fixed and unchanging. More than a brilliant Gaelic poet, Eiléan Ní Chuilleanáin is also a highly significant poet in multilingual writing circles. The translation of her work into many different languages demonstrates the value and uniqueness of her voice. This particular value and uniqueness implies a more fundamental and broad significance, and it is for this reason that her work can cross continents and oceans to be lauded by people of diverse ethnicities and backgrounds.

The poetic world she creates is vast and far-reaching, set against the backdrop of an ancient yet youthful Ireland. Her work offers us a new interpretation of ancient myths and fairy tales, while at the same time revealing the deepest spiritual experiences people can have in the midst of ordinary life. Her quiet, austere, and highly tactile poetry leads us to the highest respect and admiration, and to the conviction that she is a successor to a great poetic tradition and an expert practitioner who can teach us the ancient language of the imagination. Therefore, we are delighted to present the 2020 "1573 International Poetry Prize" to the outstanding contemporary Irish poet Eiléan Ní Chuilleanáin.

Translated by Gu Ailng

Eiléan Ní Chuilleanáin born in 1942, an Irish poet and translator. She is the laureate of the 2020 "1573 International Poetry Prize" of China.